The Fires of Waterland

Raymond Alexander Kukkee

Raymond Alexander Kukkee

The Fires of Waterland

Author's Notes on Characters and Places

All characters portrayed in *The Fires of Waterland* are complex, composite individuals, but are entirely *fictitious*. Any similarity to the names or lives of individuals in real life is purely coincidental.

The Fires of Waterland **is set in a fictional geographical location in Canada.** The imaginary village of Waterland was inspired by the typically fast-fading fortunes of small, isolated post-war rural villages across North America in the early 1950's. As with the idyllic village of *Waterland* itself, names, locations and events are fictitious, with the noted exception of the names of larger Canadian cities mentioned in dialogue.

Whitewood Forge Publishing   Thunder Bay, Ontario

Raymond Alexander Kukkee

~A Whitewood Forge Book~

DEDICATION

The Fires of Waterland is dedicated with love to Wendy Lee, my wonderful lifetime companion, wife and friend, who has lovingly provided endless years of gentle inspiration. Wendy Lee selflessly continues to aid and encourage the muse patiently as we advance ever further into the world of writing fiction — and exploring creativity itself, which is so essential for the well-being of the soul…

From the bottom of my heart, I thank you.

Raymond Alexander Kukkee

December 2016

~A Whitewood Forge Book~

One

It seems right to me now that no one remembers enough details correctly to speculate or criticize Livvy Manlin, and if they ever did know the *truth* and the *real* Livvy, they also knew that what was done she was *compelled* to do. The rest does not matter. In retrospect, I have to admit that the pain she caused was far more than a bad dream; it was a genuine and immediate commitment to hell for some, *that's where they were going anyway*, that's what Floyd said; and for observers and others lucky to be far enough away, it changed them forever, perhaps more of the mind than the body. I don't know which is worse. It was a long time ago.

Livvy hasn't been seen in this town for over thirty years now, and maybe it is just as well. Nobody asks when she left, or where Livvy Elizabeth Manlin is today. Wherever she is in spirit, I hope she is happy. I choose my words carefully; I have good reason. *I loved her. I always did and always will.*

For years, rumors of Livvy's whereabouts came and went; they were never accurate, you understand, idle gossip, suggestive of the truth, but without merit; titillation for self-entertainment, whispers of needless vitriol that disappeared into the shadows by nightfall.

At one time it enraged me. It was my desire to scold those busybodies, the toothless old hags with wrinkled, distorted and evil minds. In retrospect, I really should have tried to be more respectful in my mind; I mean because Floyd would have killed me if I was blatantly rude, ignorant or acted like *I was grown and raised under a stump*, as he always described people with the condition of perpetual

1

and intractable ignorance. I should, even now, call them *ladies* instead. Floyd said I should also be true to myself, so to be as polite as possible and still be able to tell you that *it is the truth*, at least some of those thoughtless people were mean old prune-faced hags that gossiped about my Livvy Manlin.

To be completely honest, most were just ordinary neighbors, churchgoers and townsfolk, and in spite of what I may have thought at the time, they were not frightening spell-uttering hags, *or* toothless for that matter; in recalling them I know that they did have teeth and some of them were not even *old*. A few observers considered them more or less fine people and blameless for their tendency to idle gossip because they considered gossip to be a *woman* thing which it most admittedly is not; but it always seemed to me they should have been minding their own business and baking pies, or perhaps quilting, doing something really good like joining the Salvation Army and playing the trumpet for God, and making soup, sandwiches, and cabbage rolls for feeding the poor down at the Whiting Road shelter — or *somewhere*.

Perhaps being put to work at jobs disdained by most would have been more appropriate for some. If they were especially nasty, they could have been sent to do something that builds real character instead, something difficult to do; occupations that tax the minds of the proud, something like helping out the nursing staff at Queens Hospital, feeding helpless patients, those impoverished, hungry faces: old, wrinkled, and sometimes, seemingly mindless and inhuman. I really do not know; perhaps some of them in their unrequited guilt tried that remedy for self-improvement, but couldn't stand filling the gummy, salivating mouths of the sheet-white, unresponsive faces with baby food mush.

Floyd laughed when I told him that emptying bed pans in the Queens would have been substantially more suitable as *penance* for the worst of them, but he reminded me that doing anything constructive and useful may have enriched their miserable lives, even stooping to hard, hot labor, like weeding Mrs. Dormally's garden for her; her having become a paraplegic with a tragic fall from her skittish black Morgan *Royal Thraxian*, and that's what I wanted to tell them, every one of those nasty gossips. I was hotheaded in those days. But I didn't, and Floyd said that it took a better man to stay quiet when provoked, so that's what I did. I restrained myself, kept my mouth shut about it, and did hard, hot labor *myself* instead. I weeded Mrs. Dormally's garden on Saturdays before I went to the movie matinee and hauled her firewood in, too, when the weather was cool.

Floyd *ordered* me to do it the first time, not for penance, you understand. He must have had some kind of a reason, but I got to like it and went all by myself after that, and he said it showed that I had *character*. I have to smile about that, even now, because it was not that simple.

Mrs. Dormally always gave me a shiny quarter in the early days. *Here's a quarter for a good day's work, young man* — and a dollar when I got older. That's how I got popcorn. She even made sure that I got finished on time.

> *Good thing you're all done, young man. It's time for you to get moving. It's almost two. It's a nice afternoon. You don't want to miss the cartoons at the Waterland, do you, young man? Well, then, young man, if you don't want to keep that pretty girl of yours waiting, you'd best get going, then!*

That's what she said. *Every* Saturday.

Remembering Livvy makes me think about things. When I think about things, it seems that time and change just happened. Most of the young people *disappeared*, driven from this town; compelled to drift away to unspoken and imagined greater glories far afield. Perhaps, it was the great lure of ambition, greed, or simply their own madness. Those remaining, commute.

Other than a few individuals, aging and glued forever to the surrounding family farms, with their marigolds, crabapple trees and nodding sunflowers, there are only three real families left now; the Whartons, the Bibbs, and the McDalties. I heard the McDalties are going to be the next to move away, which doesn't surprise me at all.

The place is grown in now, with shadows and cool air everywhere. There is very little surrounding me that is not resting quietly in its own shadows. The summer air speaks of drooping wisteria and twisted, ancient lilac; and tiger lilies bravely press their blazing orange against the crooked silvered houses eagerly, as if to hold them up for inspection by God. Even the pavement on the

3

roadways is painted with the dusty camouflage gray of old age. Small plants domesticate undisciplined cracks in the delicate lacework of broken curbstones, and mosses and meticulous ivies advance in their timeless, precise fashion to recapture the precious tiny spaces next to dewdrops that once belonged to them.

In retrospect, I know now that I didn't pay enough attention to see exactly *when* it happened, but the little park over there, and the yards, got filled up with shaggy, uncut grass, decorated season after season with a thick variety of tall weeds and wildflowers, not distasteful in full bloom. And the red mud is gone, out of sight, unless you are foolish enough to dig for it. The neat lawns disappeared beyond control of any human hand long ago with the exception of Jason McDalties'. He's been cutting his lawn diligently since last year, when he decided to sell out. He keeps it pretty well, at least when he remembers. There are only a few yellow dandelions and a lot of knotweed in it, and his cornflowers are six feet high. They fall over after every heavy rainfall. He ties them back up with hemp binder twine. He got to be a grandfather last July, too.

Things are changing. I know it didn't happen this morning, or last week, or even last year, but at the same time my senses tell me that it might have happened only yesterday, which contradicts *everything*. It confuses me. Perhaps, that could be politely construed as a form of madness; therefore, it is probably more prudent to tell you that those changes were gradual and unobserved: something like magic when you close your eyes. *Go ahead, try it.* Everything you see with your eyes closed must be more real, more substantial than the curious mystery I am confused about.

I rock and listen to the crickets and those strange, impossible echoes of long-since moved mothers wearing flowered aprons calling children no longer there; laughing children that were riding shiny, red bicycles with dinger-bells and playing hopscotch on new, damp cement sidewalks with hand prints and familiar names scratched into them in spite of loud scolding from happy, diligent workmen. Or perhaps they are calling out hide-and-seek games among the burr oak trees, *ready or not, you must be caught, first one's it!* My memory tries to persuade me that I am still watching them, seeing them, and, foolishly, I *want to*, but I know I do not see them; I only *hear* them. I don't know how that can be.

The Fires of Waterland

Sometimes, like the dogs that soak up sunlight on the sidewalks, and if Sharon leaves me be, I sleep in the seductive quiet of the afternoon. My rocking chair creaks while crickets sing lazily in the shimmering heat and then hesitate, and start again. Finally, embraced in silence, the shadows grow long into cool moonlight or darkness. The dogs bark at night, but mostly there is little or nothing to bark about.

It wasn't always like this here; but it is a good time, and I am old. When my time comes, I will probably drag my feet and resist passing, but shall undoubtedly take my place tucked in one of those green see-through cookie jars or gleaming oak boxes. Maybe only the brass handles will last for all of eternity or until God digs me out and dusts the red mud off, but it doesn't bother me a bit. I know I will dream forever of Livvy Manlin and savour the sweet wisteria. I know that soon, only the wise, gnarled lilac trees and silvered houses will listen to those rising children's voices that pretend to echo for me.

Two

The village of Waterland, approaching unplanned obsolescence, had to eventually face more than *one* truth. Some of them were uncomfortable and ugly. In reality, the old church steeple fell off during a raging windstorm, and faded sheets of silver-gray spruce plywood were nailed over the hole in the roof, and the doors and windows too. The school was closed since there were not enough children around to bother keeping it open. The old movie-house shut down, and the unused swimming pool at the community center was filled in, for safety reasons.

It wasn't long after Bramson's Black Angus bull smashed a hole in the rotted board fence around the pool that a black-and-white Holstein cow belonging to Archie McKinley eventually grazed her way across the field and through that hole. Annabelle tumbled into the pool trying to get a drink on a hot summer day, or so the gossips deduced. She was found about five days later, bloated and floating upside down in the green slime, hooves and udder accessories pointing right at the sky, and stinking horribly. The rotting carcass had to be lifted out with Mr. Wilson's old Chevy boom truck right away for a suitable burial, according to the local health officer, to prevent flies from congregating and diseases being spread, along with other similarly unfortunate probabilities.

Everyone remembered that occasion, mostly because Archie McKinley upchucked his lunch, complete with blueberry pie while watching the hoisting process. It was generously acknowledged that the upchucking ceremony might have happened to anyone, since it *was* his thousand-dollar red ribbon-winning cow Annabelle that went for a swim. He had raised her from a suckling 4-H Dairy Club calf, and she was a prime producer. It was a sad occasion for him, no doubt, but not quite as sad as some things that managed to change his life later, but we'll get to that...

That's not *all* that happened. Over at the broomstick factory the machinery was switched off in the middle of the afternoon on a hot day, and the place was closed. The busy factory was reduced to eerie, muffled silence. It is too long ago to complain much about now, but thick gray dust, mold and rotted willow leaves smothered and hid the sweet smelling, yellow sawdust that came from the sanding machines. *Nothing* was the same after that.

I was in there more than a few years ago for a look, just inside the big door a bit, you understand. I made sure nobody was watching. No one was supposed to go inside, I know, and for good reason, because I put the sign on it myself; the building was posted as unsafe. 'CONDEMNED—NO ENTRY'—That's what the faded white notice said on the door, but even then it was already yellowed and faded and covered with dust like everything else.

I could still see inside when I squeaked the hinges and opened the door. I could see thick grey cobwebs draped in every doorway and hanging from every shelf, covering up the rusting tools, the now useless machinery; the old fashioned and rotting gray canvas drive belts, the dusty desks and the faded, penciled account books and doodle drawings and unfilled order sheets and dog-eared copies of yellowed, brittle newspaper pages stuck onto cork notice boards with rusty tacks, and old coffee-mugs with pencils still standing up in them with a few sharpened points remaining indignantly intact, pointing accusingly up through the holes at God Himself.

In fact, much to my dismay, I saw that nearly everything I used to work with back in those days was either badly rusted, or faded grey and moldy from the leaky, wind-damaged roof. I could hear the wind whistling through the gaping holes in the tin sheeting, and there were other noises too. Maybe I did not feel well that day, or maybe I was wishing things could be the way they used to be, but it sounded like a moaning, a cold lonesome banshee. Maybe it was Murvie Klinder calling me from Texas, from the dry prairies somewhere, out with the coyotes; it was a sickening sound, an omen of illness, and a sign of death to come.

It did.

The old factory roof fell in the very next day. The huge steel beams carrying the rusty, perforated tin groaned tiredly, and it seemed like the whole building let itself down slowly, like a tired old lady sinking into a forgotten, creaking rocking chair in a dusty attic, with a torn, water-stained and yellowed picture album in her lap, and tears in her eyes, finally yielding and resigning and gasping and meeting her Maker in a choking, rising pillar of dust.

It happened like a pronouncement from God on a warm Sunday afternoon just before church service, and most notably, it was only one day after I had squeaked the door open and looked in there, which surprised me very much, almost as if it was saying *goodbye* to me *personally*. I have to admit it was more likely just coincidence. The cave-in would have remained mostly unobserved, for the factory was shut down for reasons ill-defined. The huge building was ignored and neglected by necessity and the need to get on with our lives. Perhaps, the closing really was by choice, and unhappy investors that despised anything less than a ten per cent return. Maybe it was the continual inconvenience of having to run a dead business here, when other exciting possibilities beckoned from afar.

Gossips preferred to blame the war or a wedding or the price of fuel; but most likely the truth was just a little taste of merriment mixed with a bottle or two of Catcher's Rye and an observant building inspector on a Saturday afternoon.

No matter. I was the foreman and got elected to put the **Closed Until Further Notice** sign on the door whether I liked it or not. *Get used to it, Jack.* I had to tell everyone to go home. It was a bad time.

The truth shall set you free. At least that's what our old preacher, Mr. T. Parker Drummond said like clockwork at the beginning of the service every Sunday, and he said it without fail from behind his rimless, thick half-glasses, adjusting his white collar and nervously thumbing his way through the Good Book like a nervous sixth-grader that forgot to do his homework.

Invariably, by the time he found exactly the right place to start, and as if conditioned to do so, his wife, Harriet, preferring to have a congregation clapping and singing instead of bored and snoring, would immediately take advantage of his hesitation. Harriet would sit bolt upright like a powdered, smiling marionette wearing a prim blue pillbox hat with daisies on it, and coax booming chords of approval from the aged, somewhat ivory-free and detuned congregational piano, commencing the shrieking of *Nearer my God to Thee* or *Amazing Grace* much to the feigned concern of Parker. He would stare at her over his half-glasses and shake his red jowls like a hound shaking off swamp water and say, "Ahem, not yet, Harriet, my dear," in a deep, kind voice, – to which she would blushingly reply, over the rising strains of the ensuing hymn, "Oh, hush, Tommie, don't be so stuffy, can't you see we are singing here first?!"

The color of frustration would seldom rise from his collar into his face as he happily joined the congregation in song, relieved to a modest degree that he had, by the grace of God, been blessed with more time to think about his, at least *to this point*, unplanned sermon: a situation which, strangely, *was* the truth that set him free for the moment.

Sermons being commandeered or unplanned never bothered me a bit. I always liked singing better anyway. Ultimately, Mr. T. Parker Drummond was always allowed to fire up his last-minute flaming Baptist oratory after Harriet finished shrieking out four or five hymns much to the dismay of persons *qualified* to sing. He knew it, too. It happened every week, regular as the opening of a grandfather clock store, in spite of his scolding and apparent admonishments. *Jesus will save. So will Harriet.*

In the end, T. Parker Drummond and Harriet got saved, all right, but it was by an offer to lead a congregation over in Egansville; they moved on, like everyone else did. They had to.

The dirty dust plume from the factory collapse hung in the hot still air over the village of Waterland for an awfully long time. It took

9

its time drifting away on the dead, still air, much the same way that the factory closing itself did back then: creating bad feelings, spreading a sickly pallor across the village, and affecting *everyone*.

"The dust plume was a valuable lesson," T. Parker Drummond the preacher said, speaking wide-eyed and hushed that day. "We should always pay attention to warning signs that are generously offered by God to all, but heeded by few. The beams were old and rotten, and that roof was rusty," he said. "Pieces of iron sheeting were missing here and there, letting the weather in, much like the souls and hearts of each of us," he explained. "Pieces of our very souls missing and letting rot and the devil and his deceivers into our hearts, and we should have known there would be a catastrophic failure sooner than later."

"You see, the roof did fall in, did it not?" he asked, and answering himself almost immediately, forgetting about Harriet tinkling the keys of the piano, and suddenly becoming immensely pleased with himself for thinking up the analogy, and clearly not attributing anything to God at that moment, he excitedly bellowed, "*Hallelujah!*"

The piano chords washed over the congregation, swelling the excitement like the coming of the main feature in a silent movie-house. T. Parker Drummond held up his fist to God. A gasp was heard, as if the man had swallowed the *grapefruit of truth* whole.

"Of *course* the roof collapsed! *The foundation was rotten. The beams were rotten. How could it not collapse?* And how can *our lives* not collapse also? How can our very souls *not* collapse if the foundation and beams are not prepared properly, and maintained and protected by a solid, shiny roof?" He roared, then paused for effect. "*By the armor of God!*" he added, eyes glazed. He fell silent, staring at the ceiling. After a moment, he almost smiled, as if a vision of God Himself had appeared and descended upon him and shouted at him, or perhaps the subject for his sermon finally crystallized before his very eyes. Perhaps both. There was silence.

Pink-scrubbed eager children in the front row playing *x's and o's* in the dust under the pews with their toes suddenly stopped fidgeting, and stared, open-mouthed, as though in agreement and amazement. Their proud mothers nervously and blushingly nodded approval, some apparently even making a connection between the truth and the *intent* of the great, sanctified mysteries of the world.

"*Amen!* You tell 'em, Tommie!" suddenly shouted Mrs. Julie Fillingsworth from the back pew.

"*Amen!*" The preacher yelled, raising his arms to the congregation suddenly, as if he had been stung by an angry yellow hornet.

"*Amen!*" Answered the whole congregation back to the much-pleased preacher, as Harriet and the piano burst into an energetic refrain of *Rescue the Perishing, care for the dying, Jesus is merciful, Jesus will save…*

The preacher resumed his unrequited admiration of old prophets and how they *always* observed the warnings offered to them daily by God. The congregation paid more attention than usual for the rest of the service and nodded in approval, enthusiastically clapped, and interrupted often, shouting *Amen!*

Especially the little old ladies following Mrs. Fillingworth's fine, southern example. Clucking their loudest *Amen!* and *Hallelujah!* and their approval of all of the Sabbath's Godly warnings soon became a congregational *duty* during T. Parker Drummond's church services, much like scrabbling chickens endorsing new offerings of carrot peelings and browned apple cores carelessly thrown in the dust of the chicken coops along the rickety shacks and garages down back lanes.

The preacher's offerings on any *ordinary* Sunday were primly if somewhat reluctantly accepted as appropriate and timely warnings to the flocks; however, on *that* day they must have been deemed inadequate for the magnitude of the occasion and the resultant discovery of the Unholy Plight of the Truly Damned. After the service the ladies collectively offered much finger wagging, stern advice, dire warnings, and prophecies of further doom to anyone who foolishly tarried long enough. The excitement of the factory cave-in pinked up their collective congregational cheeks and cleared the usual Sunday cobwebs, at least those inappropriate and unbiblical ones, from their minds.

The incident had clearly inspired the preacher's flock to declare their faith and revelation by substantially increasing their donations to the collection plate, and justifiably so, for the congregation was admittedly much more interested than it had ever been, and curiously, some were even stricken to animation with exhilaration of the Holy Ghost. After all, the preacher had a revelation in the Light, and right in front of them, too. At the very least he sounded *more right* than usual that day, for the ladies, primly decked out with wagging tongues, pointing fingers, spring lace and lavender with tiny flowers on their hats, were more than excitable, and the dallying congregation was harried from the coatroom all the way out into the parking lot.

That day, the normally giggling collection of pretty, wide-eyed, innocent young girls stood on the sidewalk, pointing at suddenly important revelations like the never-before seen, a menacingly huge dead branch on an ancient, silvered willow tree hanging over the sidewalk, a tree that was very large when I was a boy. Suddenly and inexplicably, it stood genuinely ready to kill anyone foolish enough to stand under it, especially smiling, Sunday-dressed, *unrepentant* Baptists.

Someone pointed out the liver-slick smooth front tires on Jimmy Hodges' old Ford, too. Admittedly, the rusted heap was used primarily as a rain shelter for the dearly enamored at the Moonlight Drive-in show over on Highway 16. Jimmy did leave the parking lot with observably loose '51 Ford kingpins every Sunday, but everyone respected the fact that kingpins were $3.00 each plus installation, which was quite a bit for a struggling student. He never drove over a fly, far as I know.

The excited chatter after that service finished was incessant and the topics far ranging. *What a miracle it is that nobody gets killed every Saturday night at the drags on Highway 14.* Admittedly, that *was* a miracle. There was that *one* racer (*unnamed, not a local, thank God*) that could do the quarter mile in 22 seconds, but considered drinking to be no less than a *Prime Directive*. He was stopped by the cops on his way out to the drive-in show; with four or more wild girls from Egansville riding in the back, too, hair blowing in the hot summer breeze. On the way to the drags, they were collectively and alternately mooning and indecently waving beer bottles at gawky drivers of oncoming cars.

The Fires of Waterland

Another hot topic was Bramson's Black Angus bull that pushed over fences for amusement and easily drove holes right through anything at will to get at the ladies of his choosing, and that bull was obviously a considerable threat to man and beast alike; *to wit*, one of those holes in the fence was the reason McKinley's cow got out and fell into the swimming pool, and *that's why it got filled in, wasn't it; see what happens?*

Other topics were undoubtedly discussed, but after the excitement died down, the stragglers and the trapped mostly satisfied themselves with debating the collapse of the rusty building: its prior condition and most recent demise paralleled to our current society, to many unspecified and hereto mostly *unseen-to-date*, but *now-identified* signs from God, and even to the impending and blatant destruction of the very core of humanity itself at the Coming.

The message of the year was not lost upon murmuring and somewhat distracted baby-carrying mothers wearing flowered summer dresses, or eager young girl-watching bucks wishing to take advantage of a few fence holes themselves. The elders, charcoal-gray-suited, serious and pipe-puffing men folk, were convinced: even the most *skeptical* souls of that ilk, solid men like A.A. McKinley senior, Charlie R.T. Bibbs or even Edgar J. Wharton, just another of the old six-day tractor drivers and seven-day cow milkers.

"Told you that building was a health hazard," he said to Charlie, as he puffed on his pipe. "Should've taken it down a long time ago." Charlie scratched his nose and blinked. He nodded.

"Don't have to bother now, seems to me," Mr. Wharton said, lighting his pipe. *"God done it."*

"Maybe He did, maybe He didn't, I'd say. Saved by the Lord hisself. Just gotta clean up a bit," he puffed. "Scrap steel, them rusty old beams, we'd get maybe twenty, thirty bucks a ton. Hmm, it'd take fifteen, twenty minutes to yank it out of there, maybe a couple of hours at most. Could clean up a bit with my D-4 if I get 'er goin'. The injector pump's pretty near finished, I'd say."

"Couple hundred bucks for a new one, too."

"Could've fallen in any time, 'pears like," Charlie responded lazily, squinting at the rubble.

Floyd would have said that was a typical Charlie response.

Actually that was exactly what Charlie said when they found A.A. Jr.'s cow in the water. It took all week to fill in the swimming pool, too, but A.A. said it was because he had to pump all of the slimy water out with a rented 2-inch pump which took nearly two days. And then he had to haul the fill all the way from Yunchie's Gravel and Sandpit over on the Seventh Line. And the D-4 could have pushed a lot more dirt a lot faster, if it had only been delivered on site on time, that is, not in 2-ton truckloads; but Yunchie's ten-ton dump was broke down with a cracked driveshaft yoke.

A.A. had to use his converted, inefficient cow-hauling truck and shoveled most of it by hand too, because the hydraulic pump was leaking and the little box wouldn't lift more than three feet. That figures. *"God done it, too,"* he said.

I have to admit that the biggest event ever in Waterland was certainly not lost upon me, either. After all, I had, only the day prior, stuck my nosy and foolish head through the dusty, cobwebbed factory doorway that had been clearly posted "**CONDEMNED NO ENTRY**", the notice that I nailed on the door myself. It was not a mistake. It was speculated that the owners may have even done themselves grievous and irreparable harm by being inebriated on a Saturday afternoon, inviting the building inspector into the place for a drink in the office, after hours, on a whim. He admitted it was a grievous error. The inspector saw the rusted and failing truss bolts between sips of *Catcher's*, it seems, and went home and wrote up an official full three-page report condemning the place. On Monday, it was all over.

Only in retrospect, after observing the big event, the community finally had to admit wholeheartedly that condemning the building was probably a good idea. Less than 24 hours after I saw it intact, it was a scene of mass destruction, inexplicably no taller than a pile of matchstick kindling and bent beams, covered with a few holey sheets of rusty sheeting draped carelessly over the old machines.

The Fires of Waterland

Maybe I closed the old door too hard or something. Maybe I was closer to God than I thought. Maybe I should have put a ten into Tommie's collection plate last week instead of the five. Maybe it was my fault. Maybe I didn't sing loud enough last Sunday.

Floyd would not have allowed me to think anything like that. Floyd knows.

Sometimes I think about the *boys*. Faded memories of those boys vex me, but there are wonderful memories of good friends too, boys that I tussled with and threw snowballs at and pushed into Wilson's creek off of the railroad bridge in the buff; boys that grew up to become solid, important men, firefighters, policemen, carpenters, cartoonists, doctors, even a psychiatrist, professors at law and a judge. Some joined the everyday lunch-bucket brigade and went off to work in the dynamite factory; others went to work in Shoemaker's boot factory that got converted and ended up making cowboy boots for Texan cowboys instead of army boots.

There had to be some *no-goods* too, do-nothings; bums, some of them: a rapist, a car thief, a wife-beater, perverts, men washed only with a mean streak the width of a bellowing yellow steer, and the lowest of the low, pin-striped, high-priced lawyers with forked tongues, fat bank accounts and bad eyesight. There were used-car salesmen with water-pump handshakes pushing thin white-walled tires, and genuine, hardworking but tired-looking cash-croppers and dairy farmers. The rest of them were just general store folks, as well as some other uncategorized, drunken, and pitifully misplaced souls. *The boys.*

We ended up covering the whole spectrum in addition to the fact that back in those days we were mostly sunburned skinny-dippers when there were no girls around. We played hooky from school on hot sunny days, sometimes with the explicit approval of Mr. Dorchester and other teachers on extra hot days. The greater proportion of us was also dollar-a-day potato-pickers, apple-filchers in season and trout-ticklers in June.

Bottom line, as Floyd would say, a quizzical smile on the lined face, a few of us grew up good; some were even semi-respectable, if recalcitrant individuals of varying magnitude. Curiously, many of us

15

came from poverty and the same boys' home up the way, an unusual place that drifted into oblivion like too many of us did when we left there, spending our lives getting adapted to being orphans forever. Some of us were adopted, shipped, graduated, but sometimes run off, never to return, and too conveniently forgotten.

I notice that *the deviant escape from reality*, as Floyd would call it, was never boasted about; perhaps acknowledged, in uncomfortable stifled silence by most otherwise well-intentioned people, and only if pointed out. *Not by me.* I never cared much for that idea, using selective memory. I try hard not to forget, at least never on purpose. It is a fact that someone has to remember; even if it seems like a contradiction of Floyd's good idea to leave memories alone.

That's why I have to tell you. It was a long time ago.

Three

The little girl skipped down the new sidewalk, strumming a stick against the white picket fence making a *rat-tat-tat* hollow sound that echoed from one side of the street to the other. She wore a fluffy white dress that seemed too clean for anyone to play in, and it seemed out of place for summer-time. She was very tiny at the waist, even for a little girl. The wispy blonde hair was long, and suspended itself in a shimmering golden fan in one of the tiny, warm breezes that often visit the village of Waterland in the north corner of Waters County.

She froze instantly, as did the echoes resounding on the houses across the street, when she noticed me bent over in the garden behind the tall tomato plants. I tried to rub some of the red dirt off of my face before I stood up to look at her.

I think it must have been August, just before school started, and it was the first time she met a *new kid* in Waterland. She didn't move, and we eyed one another in a fashion that reminds me of the manner of a scruffy alley cat watching a dog that has just discovered it too far from any tree or other convenient escape. I always think about escaping. To me, it is important to think about escaping. I think hard about that, other things, too. When I think hard about it, *I know I have to be right.* I'm old, but I know I'm still right *sometimes*; and I remember *everything*.

I *was* a *new kid*; and it was cool the first day that girl saw me; even if it was a hot summer for the most part. It may have been cool other times, like in the evenings just after the sun went down, and like inside the ice truck, when Mr. Mogginfort would let us get up in there for a minute and give us ice chips to get cool with if he wasn't in too much of a hurry to get home and feed his scruffy sheepdog, see his crabby wife Belinda, and get some fried potatoes and sausages for supper; but when it was hot back in those days, it was *really* hot. And there were always rackety crickets and the smells of pine sawdust from new houses being built; and white paint and dust balls under the bed and sleeping dogs on porches and slamming screen doors too. I remember it so *clearly*.

"Don't slam the screen door!" my mother called for the hundredth time as I wandered outside to explore my new surroundings instead of doing the work she so carefully assigned to me every day. *That* day, a Tuesday it was, it turned nice and cool outside, perfect bean-picking weather, my mother said, not hot and muggy and smelling like used soap-water like it did inside the stuffy house on washing day. For my mother, everyday was washing day, Tuesday or not because that's what she did. The customers came and went, and I watched them and tried not to let them see me. Some of them I knew and some of them were strangers that stayed too long, so I stayed outside most of the time. I like cool better.

Out in the yard, the clean, cool, fresh air that didn't smell like soap water was like a drink of fresh water with ice. The clouds were white; the door was white; even the house was painted white like foam on clean soap-water. For that matter, all of the houses were white. It seemed like the whole world in this town was white, except for the fact that the houses fresh with that sticky white paint were surrounded with new lawns that had grown unevenly: patchy lawns, green grass patterns in the dirt that was really nothing but raw clay. As sticky as fresh paint, it was a sort of gummy, red mud that stuck to your shoes and everything else when it rained, but hard as rock when it was dry. It would have made better bricks than gardens.

Everyone had a brick garden anyway except Mr. Cross, who was a bachelor that didn't like girls one bit, and always said he was a real gold miner from the Yukon, but had bad lungs from silicosis. He said he couldn't work hard because it made him gasp for air, but I know he had only one gold nugget stuck on a tie-clip, not a bag of gold anywhere in sight, not like he said. So, he got all of his vegetables from the neighbors when they had some to spare, and ate beans from a can when they didn't have anything ripe in the gardens to give him.

"Maybe I'll be a gold miner and get some gold nuggets too, *big ones*, and maybe I'll fill up the trunk of the old Pontiac with them, and I'll eat beans from a can and say *'howdy do'* and fart like you do. I won't even bother to have a garden either. I'll just buy vegetables in a tin can sometimes, if I feel like it too, wait and see." That's what I told Mr. Cross when I met him. He laughed out loud that time and gasped for more air.

I looked down the empty, dusty road on the other side of the white picket fence. Nobody else was in sight, or maybe everyone on the street was hiding behind their lace curtains waiting to see if anyone would get out there in the garden and start weeding Mrs. Dormally's garden first, I don't know.

Nobody else ever got there to help her *first*; I wondered why.

There are seven gardens in the front yards along our street. Rows of nice gardening sticks made of white pine have droopy broken strings and sinner's crosses nailed on them; they are standing in crooked rows like cemetery sticks and are decorated with faded upside down empty seed packages. Mr. Wilkinson, three doors down on the other side has a scarecrow made of straw, and it has dirty *long johns* on it, and a black hat and an old jacket that knows how to flap in the wind because he uses it every year. He said it has *experience*, that's why he uses it every year, and the neighbors have to admit that scarecrow is trying hard to look like he's protecting all of the new vegetable gardens, even if he only has long johns on.

Mr. Wilkinson's garden, which is a big mess of crooked rows of peas, stringy yellow beans, weeds, grass and tomatoes, is the saddest garden I ever saw, even with the scarecrow. Some of the other gardens had no tomatoes or beans at all, just corn and potatoes or peas and grass, but they were neat and straight. Our garden and Mrs. Dormally's garden are the nicest looking and have the fewest pigweeds too, I bet. The rows of corn are straight as arrows. Peas always fall over and look extra-disorganized with crooked rows out of place. In fact, they look worse than lost in the rest of the scruffy long grass, weeds, wild white clover and other green stuff, just like me.

I feel lost with the peas and beans when I'm lying on the ground in the green stuff too, like somewhere in Africa behind those tomato plants. *Dr. Livingston, I presume?*

I sure felt like it when the girl saw me.

"Hi, you," she said.

Four

Don't ask me why we ever moved to Waterland. I cried. I didn't want to. I am scared to move again, even now. I know I will have to move soon; it's too soon; and I don't like that. The other thing I don't really care to do at all is remember some of those things about that time, that terrible time. I find I can't think about it easily; it seems I have to *force* myself. The truth be known, I guess it makes me afraid, afraid of not knowing where I am going, and sad. I don't know why. It's like being homesick, or maybe I just don't understand it or something like that. No matter.

Old Judge Bending showed up and climbed the creaky wood steps of our rickety old gray wooden house that had a stone chimney, with one stone missing on top and all the rest blackened, and a nice front porch with some boards missing on the rail, making a hole just big enough for me to squeeze through, and an apple tree with a broken branch. He said we had to move within seven days.

"G'Day, Mr. and Mrs. Williams!" he thundered at us through the screen door as we stared out at him. He pulled off his brown derby hat and slapped the dust off of it against the blue paint peeling on the porch rail.

He twisted that hat back and forth for a bit and bent it back into perfect shape and carefully studied the cracks in the pine floor, or maybe he was looking at the popped, rusty nails in the worn-out floor to count them, or commit them to memory for some reason only an old man might offer later as an excuse. Maybe he was just getting time scraped up enough to let him remember something he forgot, like I do now, but don't like to admit it.

He grabbed the porch rail and wiggled it back and forth thoughtfully.

"Kind of loose, isn't it?" He asked himself and tested it again. "Don't matter anyway," he added.

"Well...may as well get to it, I always say'" he said, finally looking at us. He opened his long coat and fidgeted in his pocket for a bit, looking off into the distance.

He didn't take anything out of his pocket that time. He played with his hat some more, picking at some gray cat hair that was on top of it.

After he was finished with that, he looked up and mumbled that he had to give my father some kind of folded-up moving paper because the bailiff was sick and the town council said it had to be done. "For the good of the community, you understand, and I wouldn't be here except that Bill Jeffries was doing poorly in the hospital. He is the bailiff normally, but then *you* would know that, wouldn't you, Mr. Williams? He is the bailiff, now isn't he? 'Ya seen him before, but he can't be here, so I am taking his place, like it or not, since he is sick and ain't likely to get better right away." The old man sniffed as he spoke.

"With pneumonia, he's got *pneumonia*," he added loudly, peering at me through the screen door and then said "sick, doing poorly" again like he thought we didn't hear him or didn't know what sick is or something like that. I did hear him, and he glared at me. I didn't like him looking at me like I was bait.

I thought he was going to say '*boy*' or something like that to me, and I foolishly tried to imagine he didn't really see me through the broken screen, but I know he did.

I can tell that he was going to say something else for sure because he swallowed hard like a cat eating dust, and licked his lips, but he must have changed his mind. He cleared his throat and looked like he wanted to spit instead, but he couldn't because my Mother was right there. He swallowed hard and made a face. My mother doesn't like anyone to spit unless it's out of her sight, like out behind the old Pontiac or sitting grand as you please in the outhouse with the door open just a crack.

He cleared his throat again, and the warm evening summer breeze tried to blow the flies off the screen, but they were hanging on tight with all of their little feet. I know those things. My mother banged on the door and waved them away. I tried to see him better and pay exact attention to what he was going to say by peeking back through the screen door but my mother shushed me up and pushed me back away from the door again. After a little minute, when she wasn't looking, I squeezed in beside her by the inside door and watched anyway.

"The council voted ... made a paper ... an ordinance; Morgan County can't, won't, afford nor *abide* — no welfare deadbeats or drunks, hear?" he said. My father did not smile as the Judge shuffled his feet and avoided looking up at him.

"Well, ain't that *kind* of them? Don't that beat all now, Judge?" my father said, disgusted. "Them busybodies are at it again, are they?"

The judge ignored him. "I been told to serve you notice, seems the new ordinance applies to *you*," the Judge said, suddenly smiling viciously. He blinked with both eyes, like he was suddenly deciding which lies fit best or something.

"Well, Sir, I got it. I got the order —the *order*, right here," the old man said, and then he sniffed and reached under the heavy black coat. He pulled out a paper, pulled the screen door open a crack and nervously shoved the folded paper at my father. He pushed the door shut quick and put his foot against it. My father smacked the door and the judge backed up, startled.

"After this Friday past, 'ya ain't getting a welfare check outta *this* council, Mr. Williams. The council won't be waiting any longer, either. 'Ya ain't paid the rent for the last God knows how long, what did 'ya expect, so... so—that's it, Mr. Williams, and like I told you, sorry I have to do this, 'ya understand? You get yourself all packed up nice

23

and quick, and move real soon, get a gallon of gas into that old piece of junk you got there and move along now, we got us an understanding now, don't we? So no trouble, Mr. Williams, and you'd best be pretty quick on it...they gave you seven days. Well, accordin' to the paper, you got seven days."

He stared hard through the screen at us. "That's seven days from being served, so that's seven days from *today*, that is. So there aren't any misunderstandings," he said gruffly. "*Seven days from today.*"

I heard my Mother gasp, and I know it was her because I looked up at her. She had her hand over her mouth, and I could see her coppery gold ring with the green stone shining in the sunlight.

"Where do you expect us to go?" my Mother asked. "We have nothing, and nowhere to go, nowhere! You're telling me to move on? *You,*of all people! Telling me *that? You – of all people! Where do you expect us to go?*"

The judge looked at the broken branch on the apple tree. His neck got red around the collar. "You got bugs on that apple tree. It is gonna die pretty quick now anyway, broke branch and all," he spoke quietly. "Worms got in the broke branch, see? 'Ya should've painted it."

He shook his head and rolled a leaf between his fingers and looked at me, then at my mother. He picked another leaf that was rolled in a cotton wisp. He squashed it and tossed it over the rail.

"Council voted, like I said!" the judge said in a harsh whisper, and I think he tried to say that only to my mother.

"Please, understand my position here!"

My mother whispered, "Your position? *Your position?*"

My father coughed and smirked and spun around on his heel. "I need a beer," he said. "You musta known that was coming, gal. You musta heard that from your gossips, them tea party friends of yours, *those bitches*. They must have told you that by now, woman!" my father said, and he spun around again and looked at me and laughed right out loud.

"Them blabbin' bitches know everything in town before it happens, don't they, Judge?" He slapped the door hard startling the Judge, and me too. "After all, the *Judge*," he whispered with much hate, "*is real society*. Well, isn't he?" He leaned in to my mother, his eyes flashing angrily. "Most of the time they flap their yap-holes and make it all happen, too, don't they? Well, don't they? And they want you out, don't they? They have us convicted, hung, drawn and quartered, dear, so off you go, get out of town! Haven't you been listening?" He tapped her forehead three times, and hard.

"I have heard no such thing, and don't you dare call my friends such awful names. How dare you?" my mother scolded. Her fingers were white, pressed hard against the door frame.

"Friends? You call them *friends*, those nosy society bitches, after what they done?" my father shouted at her. "They're not your friends! After what *they* done?"

"Please! The boy!" my mother pleaded, her voice tight.

"Where do you expect us to go?" she finally asked the judge.

The old man on the porch cleared his throat and swallowed hard again.

"Well, that ain't any of my business, is it? But like I was saying, Mr. and Mrs. Williams, that ain't our problem. You just gotta move, no doubt about it."

"I haven't heard that from anyone with any *moral* authority either," my mother spoke, and her voice was an angry whisper. "Mr. Bending has some responsibility here, doesn't he?" she said angrily to my father.

"He's the damned county judge, stupid. He's got the authority to kick you in the ass if he likes to, it don't matter who he screwed, you or the queen; it don't matter. He can kick you all the way into a hole in Boker's swamp, and hoof us all the way to hell and right this minute, too, if he wants. That's the authority *he's* got, you should know that already, stupid...You know that already, don't you, you stupid bitch?" my father shouted at my mother.

25

Raymond Alexander Kukkee

She slapped his face hard. "Don't talk to me like that!" she said angrily, "Don't ever talk to me like that again!" my mother scolded him, and to the judge she repeated her question.

"I asked you a question, Roy? Where do you expect us to go, Roy? *Where?* Why don't you just get us out of sight? Why don't you just do what he says, bury us in Boker's swamp and get it over with?"

The judge turned away from the door for a moment. He mopped his reddening face with a red handkerchief.

"That can be arranged too, but that ain't my style," he muttered quietly, but I heard what he said.

"You got a lot of bugs here," he said.

He leaned on the door, black fury on his face. He was watching the flies wipe their little feet together and then pressed two of them into the screen with his big hands, rolling them almost gently and letting them drop to the bleached floor. They spun around and around on their backs. He watched them, and then stepped on them, squashing them flat. He scraped his shoe off on the rail and looked back at the apple tree.

He finally said. "Listen, ain't *my* business where you go, see? You just get yourselves packed up and going down the road, elsewhere. Ain't any concern of mine, Missus!" He turned back to the door. "If it helps at all, I hear say they got some welfare housing in Waters County, no guarantee they want the likes of your kind there either. So you'll be going real quick like, and you go to wherever you happen to like as long as it's outta here real quick, now won't you? And as long as it ain't *anywhere* in Morgan County."

"You could just shoot us, too, — likes o' you don't care at all— you're just running us off like a pack of mangy dogs caught running deer!" my father growled.

"Maybe we'll decide not to go!" he sneered. "In fact, I ain't going, Judge, so *piss off!*"

The judge looked at him directly, and the blue eyes turned ice cold. My father made a face back at him. I wondered if somebody was going to say something, and the judge did.

26

He reached into his breast pocket and pulled out some papers. He indicated the folded moving papers by jamming his thick finger into them roughly. He pointed at my father.

"Be a big mistake, boy, don't be so quick to flout the law, *boy*, these here are court orders, *boy*, wrote it and signed it myself!" the judge said harshly, "I think you don't want to be thinking too hard on the why, Mr. Williams, just make damned sure and get packed up so you're gone in seven days!" He turned and looked out onto the street and then squinted back at us. "Morgan County doesn't want you here! You don't leave peaceful-like, the law will be on you, an' you'll get hog-tied and run out on a flat car. Ain't no genuine choice here." he said to my father.

"*I'll* be deciding if I'm goin' anywhere, judge," he said with disdain.

"Does that sound like you got any choice, boy?" he asked my father angrily.

"I'll be going if I feel like!" my father said and wheeled around; pushing me hard sideways, and he went to the kitchen to get a beer. I heard the refrigerator door slam.

The judge sniffed and looked at my mother and spoke directly to her. He talked quietly, so my father couldn't hear.

"Look here," he said. "We were all drinking a bit too much them days, you know as well as I do, don't you? Remember he knew he sold you to me for that weekend for our party. Can't blame me for taking it, can you? You were quite a temptation, no doubt, me not being a fool. I know I had ideas about you back then, but you shouldn't, you can't hold that against a man forever, can you? Ain't my fault the others did too, not at all, not at all —after you gave your dignity, your husband drank that money up so quick. He's a no-good. You were supposed to take off and get a new start, leave the son of a bitch, remember? What the hell did you stay with him for, anyway!?" His voice cracked.

"You know we agreed!" he said.

"We agreed, dammit, we *agreed!* I ain't doing anything else for you and the boy, much as I'd like to, that's it... You showed me you wasn't treated fair. I paid you extra, and the other boys even kicked in for uh, well, well, *disrespecting,* an' hurting you, but you were there *willingly.* You did what you had to; you got the money; didn't you? Regardless, it's your problem now, ain't it...we agreed. Now I'm doing what I got to, and don't be complaining too much. I've been real patient with you so far, ain't I? I got you all that money like we agreed, and you got a few hundred extra too, so it's all in the past now!"

He squinted at her. His voice hardened. "I don't owe you nothing. The boys don't owe you nothing, *nothing!* No more! It's all in the past now, you blew your chance. I ain't interested in feeling obliged no more! You wasted that money on this abusive drinkin', gamblin' son of a bitch! *You understand?"*

"God will forgive me, you dirty bastard! But *you?* A thousand dollars to get rid of us, save your job, your reputation? Who's making you do this, your society? *Your wife? Or just you, to get rid of your own guilt?"* My mother whispered harshly at him like she was going to spit right through the screen. I couldn't believe my ears because I never heard my mother say bad words.

My mother stared at him, her face white with black storm clouds all over it. My father came up behind us and slapped the screen door again. It scared my mother. *Me too.*

I jumped out of the way.

"Oh, hell, you still here, you senile old man? When you get outta my gate there, head off left to the courthouse. You drive real careful. It's a mile and a half that way, west. Don't forget the stop sign at the corner. Don't be drivin' in no ditches, and pay attention so you don't get yourself lost now!" he shouted through the screen.

"Long as we got ourselves an understanding, *you and I,* Mr. Williams, and I assure you, *we'll* be watching."

My father did not answer. He took a big swallow of beer and burped out the door at the judge. The judge backed away and shook his head and clamped his hat back on. He shook his head again.

"Some folk can't abide living peaceful, can they?" He spoke quietly. "Well, I've said my piece."

My father laughed insanely, "He said his piece!"

"G'day, then," the judge said. "Well, I done my bit here," he said slowly. "*You've been served.*"

Then he wouldn't look up from the worn, sand-scrubbed pine floor on the veranda again. He took off his round, steel eyeglasses and polished the road dust from them with the red handkerchief. He stuffed the glasses back into his pocket with the dusty handkerchief instead of putting them back on. He pulled his brown felt hat down, low over his eyes. He stepped off of the porch and down the walk.

My father spit in the dust after him.

"Don't that beat all? That *sonofabitch.* The big man. He gets what he wants, then changes his mind and gets feeling guilty, and you tell everyone in the county so his cronies and their wives get me fired outta my two-bit job. All because of *you,* you got yourself drunk and screwed at that party, you stupid bitch, now we got to move again, goddam him! *And it's all because of you!*" He added, driving his fist into the screen door.

My mother turned white hot.

"It was *your* doing. *You made the deal.* You never would have raised that kind of money for that shark, I didn't want to do that, *ever.* They did it, not me, but I did it for you, and I am not some common whore. You were drunk all the time. You bastard, calling me *that* now. Maybe I should have let them break your knees instead, remember that?" My mother hissed at him, white and shaking. "And you calling me a whore, you miserable bastard—I should have taken off like I was supposed to and let them break your legs instead!"

"*You shouldn't have acted like one,*" he said, laughing. "Who gives a shit anyway? Not *them!* They're all laughing at you!"

"I didn't mean it to turn out that way, I did it for you, for us...to get away and start over, and I thought if we just paid him off, we could start over, *we deserved a chance! Can you never forgive me for that?*" She whispered harshly.

29

My father swore as he watched the judge walk away and punched the screen right out of the door, and it made a loud noise clattering on the porch; maybe that's why the judge stopped walking.

He looked like he was scared off for good, but he stopped in his tracks when he heard the noise, looked back, and then turned, like he was coming back to the porch for a moment. My father barged out onto the porch angrily with his hands on his hips.

"What the hell do you want *now?*" he demanded.

"No!" my mother said, moving out to grab his arm. "No! Please! Come back in!" she asked him, her face white, as she looked up at him and tried to hold his arm.

"Shut up, woman!" my father said angrily, shaking my mother's hand off of his arm.

"You're threatening *me*, boy?" the judge asked, squinting. "Don't threaten me, Mr. Williams, I'm a county judge. I can get you put away real quick like, remember that!" The judge spoke coldly, quietly and put his right hand into the pocket of the black coat. I don't know if he had a gun in his pocket or not, but when my father saw that he backed toward the door.

"You'll do well to remember what I said, sir... *honest* mistakes get made and they're in the past and they'd best stay there. Forget about it now. Too bad she saved your ass, and you ended up drinking the difference. *Didn't you?* It ain't my fault, is it? You had a chance — so now you pack, and get yourselves moving along quick, Mr. Williams, sir — good day!" to my father.

My father didn't say anything else, and the judge watched him for a minute, then he touched his hat and squinted strangely at my mother again.

"Angelina, for what it's worth, I... *am* sorry, I really am," he said gruffly. "It might not look like it to you, but I really am. *I cared about you.* Too bad things weren't different."

He didn't look at us again, and I thought that was just fine with me. He shuffled right down the flagstone walk and ignored the old lady that peered and frowned at him from behind her rose bushes on the other side of our garden fence. She threw her garden hoe at the fence. It whacked the fence with a loud crack. I didn't know that old Mrs. Mulligan could pitch anything that hard.

"*You goddamned hypocrite!*" She shouted after him, red-faced, wringing her hands together and wiping them on her garden apron. She leaned over and picked a ripe tomato and stared at it. I think she was going to throw it right at him but changed her mind.

The judge paid no attention to the flying hoe or to what she said until he was safely outside of our fence. Then, he turned back to her, and when he finally spoke it was like nothing happened.

"And a good day to *you*, Mrs. Mulligan!" he said politely. He kept going. He slammed the door of his shiny black coupe. The motor hummed and the gears clattered, and the judge of Morgan County left a haze of blue smoke to mingle with the road dust.

"*Godamned hypocrite!*" She screamed after him, and threw the tomato after him. It splattered. Part of it bounced off of the roof and into the dust of the road on the other side of the car. A car passed going the other way drove over it. I think the wheels squashed it flat.

"Waste of a damned good tomato!" my father commented loudly and shook his head and tipped up his beer bottle.

I know the judge didn't see the tomato splatter the car or hear what she said then because he didn't stop, and he had the windows rolled up tight to keep out the dust. Maybe it was his best idea: Keep the glass between you and the shame of being scolded by a nice old lady.

Mrs. Mulligan watched the dust settle and then peered through the bushes at my mother and father. She brushed garden dirt off of the inside of her glasses with one gloved finger.

"Well that's what he is, a goddamned, chicken shit hypocrite!" she glared angrily after the dust cloud and then clammed up and ran into the house without looking at us again.

"*So are you, you old bitch!*" my father shouted after her. "Ya ever offer to help, even once, you nosy old bag? You ever stand up and tell the other ladies to stop gossiping about my wife here, did ya? No, you did nothing of the sort, like a bunch of cackling vultures, you kept right at it with all the rest, you nosy old bitch!" He kicked a tin pail off of the porch. It went flying with a clatter.

"It's empty, see? Tomato-waster!" he added, right out loud, too. "I have never had any tomatoes like that to waste, have I, you old bitch?"

My mother looked up at my father and clamped her hand over her mouth and ran into the bedroom crying. My father spit right out the broken screen door onto the porch and glared at me.

"*That's* what you got to do, see, Fetchie boy. You got to say *piss on 'em all!*" and he kicked open the screen door and did the worst thing I ever saw my father do. He opened up his fly and salted the front porch and the wooden steps. It splashed on some flowers. He stumbled and threw the empty beer bottle over the front fence. It broke on the road. "Imagine that!" He sneered.

My mother came back and banged the screen door wide open. "Have you no shame?" she asked my father angrily. "Urinating in public!"

"*Urinating?*" My father hissed. "I said *pissing,* didn't I? I said *pissing, pissing* and *pissing!*" he zipped up his fly angrily. "*Pissing!*" he shouted again.

"So you did!" My mother said, stone-faced white. "You hurt her! *You hurt her!* That is inexcusable; she's been a good woman, a good neighbor to us!"

"Well, *piss on her, too.* How easily we forget, she's nothing but an old tomato-wasting busybody, and *piss on the judge, too.* Hope he gets a flat next time he drives by. *Piss on 'em all!*" he said.

My mother scolded him, white-faced, with her lips clamped into a skinny white line. "*Stop that,*" she whispered.

He stumbled against the door. "*Piss on 'em all,*" he said thickly.

"Come inside!" she ordered my father. She put him to bed and then rinsed the porch off with a pail of clean water. I could hear

somebody laughing down the street. I think it's nice when people are happy. I went to bed and my mother said, "Don't you mind anything you hear, do you understand Fletcher, dear? Go to sleep now."

I went to sleep.

Five

I never heard old Mrs. Mulligan say bad words like she did that time, just before she ran into the house, but she knew how to bake peanut butter cookies just fine. I like Mrs. Mulligan. I should ask her to play baseball some time because she can throw stuff really hard; not like Mr. Mulligan who died because he was always sick and pale, even if he was an outdoors man and had a real wolf skin he got from an Indian chief for giving him a spare tire on a fishing trip.

Mr. Mulligan's ashes are resting themselves on her fireplace mantle in a green glass bottle with a lid. It looks like a cookie jar. I got on my tiptoes and lifted up the lid a bit and looked at the ashes once when I was waiting for her and she wasn't noticing what I was doing. They were grey and lumpy, not green like through the glass.

"Don't be disturbing Mr. Mulligan now, dear." I jumped because she talked suddenly and came up behind me, and then she wrapped her fingers around the knob of the lid. She carefully set the lid on the mantel and took the jar down. She let me study them for a minute and then peered into the jar to inspect Mr. Mulligan herself.

"Well, Rupert, you sleeping well? You look just fine to me," she said into the jar.

"My Rupert," she said to herself. She reached in and stirred the ashes 'round and 'round with one finger and rubbed some ashes between her fingers, then tapped her fingernails against the inside of the jar to dust them off.

"Best he's looked in a long time! He's doing just fine, isn't he? He enjoys having visitors." She smiled at me and put the green jar cookie jar gently up on the mantle again. She clunked the lid back on.

"*Goodnight, Rupert,*" she said to Mr. Mulligan in the green jar, and "Want some peanut butter cookies?" to me.

He died with cancer of the balls; that's what my father said. I don't know why that happens, and he didn't get all dallied up with his best suit on, but he got burned up the next day in the burner at Egansville instead. Mrs. Mulligan told my mother she gave the Sunday suit to the Salvation Army lady instead, and my father said Mrs. Mulligan just collected some ashes down at the incinerator with a regular corn broom and stuffed them into Rupert's favorite cookie jar. He said that when he was drinking whiskey. He kept saying, "*Rupert, he's lucky, nobody can piss on Rupert no more,*" but he was drinking whiskey when he said it, so I believed Mrs. Mulligan instead.

I never saw ashes of people before. I was only there because I was collecting tins and glass and rags that time into a cardboard box with triangle holes, one that used to have oranges in it and pictures of orange trees on it. The peanut butter cookies were warm, "Just out of the oven," she said. They tasted better than usual that day, right after we talked to Mr. Mulligan and inspected his ashes good, but don't ask me why. Maybe it was because Mrs. Mulligan gave me extra cookies to keep in my jacket pocket for later and *four* empty tin cans that used to have peaches in them, and two dozen brown beer bottles that didn't have caps on or even smell like beer anymore. They were old. It was a long time ago.

My father did not drink for a couple of days after we got the moving paper. I think my Mother hid the whiskey on him, but I didn't ask her where she put it. For a few nights after Judge Bending showed up, the crickets and my parents whispered and spoke in hushed tones, but then he found the whiskey under the linen in the closet.

Then they argued, and he got angry and got to drinking again. After he came home from Wally's Watering Hole that night, my father finished off three bottles of beer from the refrigerator. And drank a lot more whiskey, too. He drank too much whiskey, and it made him start singing bad songs and talking loudly and saying bad words again. He looked outside through the screen door and saw the judge's car speed up as he was driving by in a cloud of hot dust.

"There's the sonofabitch! Here he is again, royalty himself, the royal pain in the ass!" He shouted angrily.

"Shshsh!" My mother tried to quiet him. He yelled that the judge was a horse's rear end, again, and he reminded us *that's not the end you feed the hay to.* He jumped up and opened up the screen door and shouted.

"Hey, Judge! Did you hear that, Judge?" he shouted loudly down the street, "you are a *genuine* ass, and I don't mean a donkey!"

He laughed loud enough to wake up the world and stumbled out through the door. He fell down on the porch and swore again. He looked up at me.

"What are *you* lookin' at?" he asked.

"Gimme a drink, Fetchie boy. Gimme a bottle, you little bastard!" I got away from the door and didn't get him any bottles, but I know what he said after that. He got up again and fell down the stairs into the dirt.

"See, Fetchie, you little bastard. Where are you, you little bastard? Get me another beer!"

"Shshsh!" my mother said.

"Well *that's what he is,* isn't he, honey? *A little bastard welfare bum!"*

"Get in here!" she scolded and helped him get up.

My mother scolded him and hushed him. She carried him into the house and put him to bed quick. After a bit she came back outside on the porch, and we sang *Row, Row, Row Your Boat, gently down the stream* real quiet, and *merrily-merrily, merrily-merrily, life is but a dream!* real loud.

The Fires of Waterland

I saw Mrs. Mulligan peeking at us through her curtains that were pinched tight shut like the lines in her face when she called the judge a *goddam hypocrite*, but she must have thought better of coming to our sing-a-song on the porch that wasn't wet anymore. She didn't come outside to help us sing any verses of *Row, Row, Row Your Boat* either, not even one round. I like Mrs. Mulligan even if she doesn't come out to sing on the porch.

The next night in the quiet, batting away at the mosquitoes, my mother and father talked about his worse-than-terrible headache, and he said he was making new plans about far places to go and interesting things that we could go see, but just as it was getting interesting I got tired. I had to go to bed, so I couldn't tell what they were saying about everything.

I sneaked downstairs after a bit and peeked through the screen door. I kept my eyes open and listened as carefully as a spy. I saw my father stumble into the kitchen to get a new whiskey bottle. I can't help it if the screen door made a noise when I touched it, and my father tripped and fell down when it scared him. The whiskey bottle broke, and I could smell it.

"Now see what you done!" he screamed at me. He tried to slap me, but he missed. I got away from him right away. "Clean up this goddam mess, you little bastard!"

"It was not his fault. It wasn't his fault!" she yelled at him, and then said "Go to bed like I told you," to me. He said more bad words and slapped her, and she turned white and tried to back away, but he grabbed her and sat her down hard. Then he shook and fell on his knees and put his head in my mother's lap and shook more until he started to swear out loud and cry.

"I'm sorry, Angel, my head...my head," he cried.

"I know," my mother said, and then she saw me watching that, and she ordered me to "get back to bed like I told you," again, and she stroked his head as he shook and that scared me, so I went back upstairs in the quiet and dark.

37

I made myself think I didn't see him do anything like that before, so I felt lonesome and scared. My mother made me go to bed early every night after that.

I know I have to go to bed when my mother says *go to bed*, but I don't have a big headache, and I'm not a welfare deadbeat bum. I am *five*.

Six

We packed everything but the mice and the dust and some junk into dusty old wooden pop boxes, and we even used a few nice new whiskey-crates. We stopped and ate cheese sandwiches made of brown bread for lunch and for supper, too. That was because the electricity got shut off three days ago, and my mother cried because she couldn't read to me or make hot food. My father said bad things to her again and said she was a stupid bitch to care anyway and that made her cry more. She said, "I can't help it!" He said more bad things. I didn't like that. I put my arms around her, and it made her feel better. My father took off to Wally's bar to visit with his friends and complain about having to move, and he didn't come home that night.

"*Never mind, Fletcher, everything will turn out just fine,*" my mother whispered to me as she tucked me into bed.

I went to Wally's bar one time with my mother to get my father from the back room. In Wally's bar there is a stuffed bear standing up with a snarl and a cowboy hat on, and I saw deer horns on the wall behind the bar with all of the shiny whiskey bottles, all shapes and sizes, and two of them were full but the rest of them were almost empty.

But he told us to get back home where we belonged, so we did. "You go back home now, and don't be hanging around here where you don't belong, boy!" He said to me, and "What the hell's the matter with you, woman? Get out of here, you stupid bitch!" he swore at my mother. I didn't like that. We went home right away.

On the last day, we made the big fire in the old garden to burn the junk, the papers, rags and dusty useless family relics of gray and mostly forgotten times. My father let me light the fire, and I took two tries to get it going. "Don't waste matches!" he warned. His voice was crabby, probably from eating too much cheese and getting bunged up, my mother whispered, or maybe from all the hard work, carrying our lives and the junk out of the old house. She rubbed my hair hard with her knuckles and tickled me to make me feel better, but I still should not waste anything. Not even a match.

We toasted the cheese sandwiches on the smoky blaze. They turned black and smoked a lot, and mine even caught fire. My mother cut off the blackest part because I said it tasted horrible. I stuck my tongue out. My father said, "Don't be a smart ass," and said we better eat them anyway because a bit of carbon is good for you. I didn't know what carbon was except that it doesn't taste good. My mother said not to stick my tongue out. "It's going to get stuck that way," she said that a lot when we played and stretched our mouths with our fingers to make funny faces.

"This is just like camping, isn't it, Fetchie-boy?" my father asked me. "This here's how you do it, boy, you make yourself a fire, cook something up just right, tastes better than anything the old lady makes on the stove, don't it?" he said.

My mother looked at him funny. He made tea in a coffee can hanging on a rusty wire over the fire just like a hobo bum because my mother said it would make the pots black and burns the handles off of her cook pots. He poured whiskey in it to give it some flavor. I didn't have whiskey in mine. I don't like whiskey. Billy McCaudry and I tasted some once when my mother wasn't looking, and we choked a lot and spit it out fast. We didn't try it again too soon, but Billy said that Morgan Catcher's Rye whiskey is his favorite now, and that when he gets big, he's going to drink a whole bottle every day. Not me, I'm never going to drink whiskey again.

My father's eyes sparkled from the flickering fire in the dark, and when he poked at the fire, it made a blazing shower of sparks that winked out on their way to see God, one by one. His eyes reminded me of the stars in the sky that night. Maybe it was because they had the fire in them and the black parts were big and black as the sky, not tiny and mean; blinky and bright blue like in the hot sunny October afternoons when he dug potatoes in the garden, and wiped the sweat from his sunburned face, and swore at God because digging potatoes is hard in the sod and the quacks. He took a big drink of whiskey from the bottle he had and put the bottle back in the spud pail.

"*Goddam sod and quacks!*" he muttered to himself quietly, but I heard him say that. My mother wasn't listening that time because she was busy in the kitchen, canning yellow beans and ripe apples in a hurry that I helped pick from her tree by the porch.

My mother looked happy, only for that one night, gazing into the fire, sitting with her arms around me and her head on my father's shoulder. She did not speak as we sat there. I never saw that before. I mean her sitting with her head on my father's shoulder. That was the first time, but I don't know why. I miss her now.

Even after we moved to Waterland, my mother did not talk to me about the Judge coming by and giving us the moving paper and whispering to her. I saw her crying with her head down. I bet I know what she was crying about. Maybe she was thinking about the day we had to tie the box of dishes on the roof and borrow a gallon of gasoline from Mrs. Mulligan in a shiny tin pail. That was the day we had to pump up all of the flat tires on the old Pontiac and check the oil before we could start her up.

That might have been a different day, but I tried to help pump the tires and nothing worked right and the rubber hose kept falling off of the pump. I was too little and got in the way and when my father let me try, I got too tired and hot too fast. And it was my fault the hose fell off of the pump *again* so my father had to do it all by himself. He got mad and kicked the car and hurt his foot and got a bottle of whiskey from under the driver's seat and took a drink. He winked at me and spit. "That's better," he said, and had another big drink. The amber whiskey gurgled in the sunlight.

"Damned junk!" he said later when he got back to fixing the old Pontiac and found a broken spark plug, and then he said "*Seven of the little bastards* will have to be enough, won't they?" My mother didn't like him talking like that, and he knew it right away. *"One little bastard ain't going to make any difference,"* he muttered. She looked at me, and I knew that she wasn't going to smile that time.

He didn't say anything after that. My mother frowned at him; she didn't say anything, not like Mrs. McAllister when Floyd swears, but I'll explain that later.

Maybe my mother just misses her broken apple tree that grew beside the old porch. Maybe I did something wrong, like when I broke the big branch on the apple tree. That was the time the branch snapped off so I crashed on the ground and broke my arm. She never scolded me because my arm hurt too much, and Doc Winkins said I had to wear a plaster cast for six weeks and said it cost twenty-two dollars. And then he suddenly listened out the window right through the screen and looked at my mother and smiled. He said he knew what would fix me up real fast.

"I know what'll fix a boy's broken arm *real fast* and quicker than anything! There won't be a charge here for that either," he said to my mother on the way out to the ice truck.

I know my broken arm must have got better faster than usual because he ran outside and stopped the ice truck and got ice cream for me, and some for my mother with chocolate on it. I think it made her feel better too, but I still don't know if she misses her apple tree. She never told me.

I waved out of the back window of the Pontiac at our old house and Mrs. Mulligan, and Mr. Mulligan, too. I pretended that Mr. Mulligan was waving even if he can only see out of the green cookie jar sitting on the fireplace mantle. I was stuck between the black, cracked leather suitcases that smelled moldy and the lampshade wrapped up in newspaper and some blankets and boxes of pots and pans, so I couldn't wiggle around much. I felt trapped and stuck there and got hot. When I get hot, I always want to escape, but my father wouldn't let me have the window open. He says it lets the bugs into the car.

The Fires of Waterland

After a thousand miles through the desert we had to stop anyway, so my mother wiped my face with a wet cloth, and I felt a little bit better. That was the time we drove over a hard bump at a swamp culvert and one of ropes holding the whiskey-boxes broke. It made the boxes slide off of the roof of the old Pontiac and I saw the whiskey-box bounce on the road and split open. It smashed my mother's good dishes, even the ones with roses on them. All except for one. It bounced and rolled into the ditch and got in the water. My mother made my father get it out of the mud. She washed it off and then she cried and held the last plate tightly to protect *it* from getting broken too, I think.

I hugged her to make her feel better and whispered *don't cry* to her, and my father saw that and swore and kicked the box and rest of the broken dishes into the ditch and said a lot of bad words again. *Get used to it, Jack.* It was a long time ago.

Seven

Maybe it was because she thought I was still outside working in the garden or maybe she just didn't see me, but she didn't know I was standing there behind her. I guessed it was because I came in quietly and closed the door without making as much noise as a mouse wearing sneakers like she always said I should, so it's not my fault she didn't hear me creeping up on her.

She stood, crying, leaning, bent over in her work, her sick, white skinny hands in the laundry-water, and every so often she thrashed the wet cloth angrily against the glass bumpy thing, the scrubbing board that hung over the edge of the rusty tub and into the cold soapy water. Her teardrops fell in the water, but they didn't make any noise. I waited, and I watched her for a minute until she started scrubbing again, then I made a little noise on the wall with my jackknife, so I wouldn't scare her. She pretended not to see me for a minute and looked away and honked her nose into her apron.

I put my arms around her, and she started scrubbing hard again. She turned around after a bit and blinked a lot and blew her nose again and pretended she wasn't crying. "Silly me, I've got soap in my eyes," she said, but I never saw any soap in her eyes. She asked me if I had finished picking the stringy, yellow beans from the garden. "How about it, Fletcher, are you finished picking those yellow beans yet? They'll be too stringy if we don't get them picked and jarred up soon and nobody will want the darned things will they? So, please, Fletcher, there's a good boy, you help me so much, and I'll help you read some later, okay? Maybe we'll read about Jonah and the whale, would you like that?" She turned on the tap and splashed some clean water at me and tried to laugh.

Picking yellow beans is even worse than eating them. I'm not a *bean man.*

"We're not *bean men,* are we, Fetchie boy? Ain't cha got any *real* food in this house, woman?" My mother didn't like that.

"We'll eat what God has given us," she said.

"Yeah, yeah!" my father said. "My head is hurting. Those beans are giving me a headache." My mother just looked at him.

"*Yeah, yeah!*" he said again.

Whenever you're picking yellow beans, you lean over and it's hot, then your head hurts and you feel funny or sick and think you see black lights and want to throw up when you get up fast. You get dizzy, too.

I said *no I didn't finish yet,* so she said I better get to it, but before I went out again I asked her what was wrong, but she never told me. She never tells me about what is wrong. She clammed right up and stared at the clothes that were trying to float in the soapy water. She poked at them with a wooden wash stick. Then, she suddenly splashed right at me again, and we had fun and I got my shirt wet.

"I'm going to wash that mud right off of that face of yours with laundry water!" She teased me.

"Oh, no you're not! You can't catch me!" I said and escaped up the stairs and walked back down. We laughed some more and then settled down.

My mother dried her hands. She suddenly grabbed my face with both hands and looked directly into my eyes. Her eyes are gray, like mine.

"I love you, Fletcher. You're a good boy, and you're always going to be a good, kind man, and I'll *always* be proud of you," she whispered. She suddenly turned back to the soapy water and started scrubbing. *"No matter what!"* She whispered fiercely. Then, she hugged me hard with both arms and danced me around. We laughed.

"You'd better get along, now, smarty-pants. You get out to the garden right now, Fetch!" she said. She patted soap suds on my face like my father's shaving cream, so I splashed back at her and gave the glass scrubber-thing a couple of twangs with my folded-up jackknife with the ivory handle, and it made a rat-tat-tat sound, too, just like the girl's stick on the picket fence.

I laughed at her and made a face and ran outside. But now, I wish I didn't get her apron wet. It got wet, but I hope it wasn't my fault. Nothing's my fault. That's what Floyd told me. I hope Floyd's right. Floyd's always right about everything. That's the Floyd that you don't know about because I didn't tell you about him yet.

Eight

That *rat-tat-tat* reminds me, I was telling you, that's where I was when I first saw the girl. That's what I was doing when she came along: picking yellow beans behind the tall tomato plants in the new garden. I mean the one at Waterland. I didn't like picking them any better in the new garden than the old one in Morgan County; in fact, it was usually hotter and worse than you can imagine. I get dizzy when it's hot.

The new garden was in the front yard because, like in the other yards along the street, the old Pontiac had to be parked in the back yard away from the road dust. Now, the Pontiac is sad with all of the tires finally gone flat and a field mouse even built a nest with babies on top of the motor. You can still smell gasoline if you take off the filler cap and smell it, even though we didn't use the car for almost a year. One of the back windows got broken by a punk. That must be how the mouse got in.

The problem with the garden trying to grow itself in the front yard is that any of the kids going by can see that I am picking yellow beans. It's a good thing they don't know who I am, at least not just yet.

I pulled my brown tweed hat down over my eyes and squinted at the girl when I thought she wasn't looking. But she was, every time I looked. I pretended I was doing something else by standing the white row sticks up straight and pretended I was lining them up dead-eye-dick straight. I squinted down the row carefully and didn't look at her. *It's better if you don't see what you want to look at sometimes.*

I didn't know where she lived, except I found out it was over few streets or maybe only one or two, but I hadn't got that far in my exploration of Waters County just yet. My mother told me to mind my manners; stay off of the railway tracks; keep out of the hardware store and not make a nuisance of myself just yet.

Thinking about that didn't stop the girl from staring at me through the picket fence just like Mrs. Mulligan staring at old Judge Bending when she called him a *goddamned hypocrite* that time. Maybe it was a bit like somebody staring at a monkey in the zoo, or something.

I went to the zoo once. It seems like everything in the zoo is in a cage like I am. I'm not really in a cage, I just feel like I am. No matter, I don't like animals being in cages either. I thought about that when I looked through the fence. I don't know why I thought about it when I saw that girl looking through the pickets. I didn't know if it was her or me that was on display.

"Hey," the girl said again. I pretended I didn't hear her, but I did and I think God considers that's lying; At least that's my opinion. That's what my mother said, too.

The stick rattled on the fence again. I tried not to look. She rattled it more, trying to get my attention. She didn't go away, I don't know why. I didn't look dressed up that day because I only had old baggy shorts on and a red shirt with no sleeves. I cut them off with my ivory-handled jackknife that's not really ivory, it could be bone. One of the ivory bone handles fell off and got itself missing. I don't know where it went, but I think the neighbor's dog ate it. My shirt was still wet too.

My mother didn't like me cutting any sleeves off. I thought she was going to laugh, but she didn't. We had lemonade with no sugar instead. We put the sleeves in the rag-bag. When you see little curves on someone's face that means there's always a smile starting even if they have sour lemonade. She giggled.

"Oh, Fletcher!" she finally said, looking at my raggedy shirt. She giggled again. "Maybe you should be a tailor," she said it's not my fault if cloth cuts crooked with a dull knife. I was cutting straight as an arrow too. My jackknife is dull because I dig in the sand and peel dirt off of carrots and carve hard wood sticks. I practice circus knife-throwing at targets on the fence and in the grass too. My father doesn't like me doing that because you hit stones. It's not my fault if one of the bone handles came off and the dog ate it. I'm not good at sharpening knives, but Mr. Weller at the hardware store said that he sure would sharpen it for me *right smartly*, and show me how, too, for nothing. My father said *get home and don't be a pest* that time.

I knew that girl wasn't going away, so I acted like the boss of the world and went to the fence.

"What do you want?" Since I was boss of the garden last year too, I had to be as bossy as possible. Six-year-old boys don't even *like* girls, that's the *law*. I left the wooden basket hidden smartly behind the tomato bushes so she wouldn't know what I was doing. It didn't work; she knew anyhow.

The stick stood straight up against the fence and two red shoes stuck through the fence to stand on the whitewashed two-by-fours. I saw two rows of squeezed-white fingers on pink hands reaching through the boards pulling pretty hard to hoist the blonde head to the top of the fence. She was pretty strong for a girl.

"What do you want?" I asked her again, but she was too busy climbing up to see over, so I guess she didn't hear me.

"Hey," she finally said again. The blue eyes peered from between the pointy white pickets.

"Hey," I said after that. I had to say something.

"What's your name?" she asked. I realized the blue eyes had hooked on me like ice water shooting at you from a garden hose a foot away. I couldn't escape. Seeing that I was the official owner of the garden, I asked her what her name was instead of answering.

"I asked *you* first...it's not polite to answer a question with a *question*." She spoke very clearly, as if she was certain she was right.

49

She must have been talking to my mother because that was one of her rules too.

Some manners must have soaked into me somehow, and I felt foolish when I saw the brown tweed cap in my hand. It jumped off my head without my even knowing it. I pretended to swat flies with it. I remembered what my hair looks like whenever I take my cap off and became embarrassed. I swatted flies harder. Pirate hair is usually all stuck down at the front and the back sticks up nearly as high as the picket fence the girl was hanging on. I wished I had a real sword.

"What are you *doing?*" she asked and watched with more than a little curiosity.

"Bugs," I said. I stuck my cap back on quickly. She was only a girl. She probably didn't notice. *You don't have to have your hat off if it's a girl and if it's outside.*

"There are no bugs." She looked all around. "I don't see any bugs," she stated matter-of-factly. "Your hair's messy!" She did notice. Rooster-tails always need combing and never lay down slick like they feel.

I swatted some more bugs that weren't there.

"No wonder. That's 'cause I chased 'em away from you." I offered information on the bugs thinking firstly that it might distract her, and secondly that she might believe it.

"They're gone now ... got 'em!" I rubbed the imaginary bite on my face and ground extra dirt into the sweat without realizing it.

"Your face is dirty," the girl said. I couldn't see her mouth. "What are you doing?" she asked again.

"Working," I replied quickly. "Yard work for my father..."

"What's your name?" I asked to change the subject.

She shifted her hands around to get a better grip on the white pickets.

"*Livvy.*" The stick clattered to the ground. "Oh!" she exclaimed, almost falling as she tried to grab it. "*Livvy Manlin,*" she added, fastening her eyes on the mud on my face as she retrieved the stick.

"That's no fair!" she exclaimed as she regained her hold on the fence.

"What's that?" I pretended I didn't know what she was talking about, but I did. I still didn't tell her my name, and she asked first. God probably cleared his throat that time too, especially since I had put my cap back on and that was bad manners in front of company. She was on the other side of the fence, so maybe that doesn't count. Maybe people aren't really visitors if they're on the other side of the fence, especially if they are girls. I can even put my cap on backwards if I want to. So I did. The blue eyes rolled.

"You! Your name! You never answered me!" The voice was determined. I gave up. I wasn't getting to boss her away, and she wouldn't quit asking me what my stupid name was until all the cows in the world turned purple, she was so stubborn.

I gave up. I told her. I had to. Next thing she'd probably want to do was kissing and get married and make me get a yellow convertible or something. I couldn't take a chance on that. I'm never getting married.

"Fetch." I didn't say it too loud. The blue eyes blinked. "*Fetch!*" I repeated. Fetch was my nickname because when I was little I couldn't say *Fletcher*.

"What?" she asked.

"*What?*"

"Fetch!"

"*What?*"

"That's weird!" she exclaimed. "My dog Gordon *fetches* sticks if I throw them, he *fetches* them, and so what kind of a name is that for a boy? That's not a *name.*"

"*Gordon?* What kind of a name is *that* for a dog?" I shot right back at her and got the upper hand right away.

I didn't want her to ask what my second name was. *I'm not even going to say what my second name is.* "That's a dumb name for a dog!" I added for good effect. I clammed up and scuffed the dirt around the whitewashed fence post. There was no dust on her red shoes.

"Your *real* name must be *Fletcher* then," she concluded. Her blue eyes blinked again.

Like I said, there was no dust on her red shoes. I squirmed a little bit. I still wasn't going to tell her my second name no matter if she was an alien and did experiments on me and tortured me with hot wires under my fingernails. Nothing could be worse than having my heart cut out and cooked with a ray-gun, except if I was forced to eat nothing but parsnips and yellow beans. For three years straight. I'd escape somehow. Even if I had to sew myself into garbage bag like the *Count of Monte Cristo* did or tunnel my way through eleven miles of solid rock with bleeding fingers. That idea was almost too good to forget about for a minute.

I squinted into the bright sunlight and made my eyes blinky and small just like they'd be if I was coming out of the tunnel, and she wouldn't be able to look into them to see if I was telling the truth. *The eyes are the mirror of the soul* or something like that. My mother read it to me from a book somewhere.

I thought that she'd probably stay glued to the fence with her eyes stuck on me until she grew roots or I grew new fingernails and was able to escape again, so I finally decided that I had to make the first move. I gave up right away, hands up.

"*Fletcher Carnival Williams* at your service, Ma'am!" I bowed and swept the brown tweed cap off of the picket-fence hair. She giggled. "Hey!" she said. She probably wouldn't believe it anyway. I was glad I took the chance.

"Gordon's a better name than *Carnival*. It's a little bit funny...don't you think?" Her nose crinkled back into her freckles, making little white lines. She sounded honest.

See? She took the bait. Nobody would have a name like a three-ring circus. *Except me.* But she wouldn't know that.

"But *it's a very handsome* name..." she continued, very thoughtfully. That stood me up straight, and I sucked in my stomach

52

real hard and stuck out my chest and smacked the cap against the fence to get the imaginary dust off of it.

"Made it up myself," I said and swatted another fly.

"I don't think so," she said, and smiled in the funniest way.

"So what, *I'll* call you *Fetch*," she offered. I was relieved at the truce. For about eleven seconds, I felt like I had escaped from a horrible, mad torture. I checked my fingers to see if they were still bleeding from all the tunnel digging. They weren't. I started to relax.

"That's nice," I said, but I said it to the alien torture lady. They always wear red shoes. That's a secret. I found out later that there are torture ladies all right, but they aren't aliens and they don't always wear red shoes.

I heard the screen door bang behind me. The blue eyes moved in tandem and fastened themselves on the skinny woman standing on the porch, so I looked too. My mother stood with her hands on her hips. There was a big wet spot on her apron from my splashing her or maybe it was from smacking the clothing on the scrub board in the tub.

She blinked in the bright sunlight and then put her hand over her eyes like an Indian scout and that's how she saw us standing at the fence. She brushed her hair away from her face and looked back and forth from the basket hiding behind the big tomato plants to me and back and forth an extra few times. My mother knew how to put two and two together and get four right away.

"You done picking those yellow beans, Fetch?" She just had to do it. "Fletcher?" She just had to say *picking yellow beans*. Especially after I just finished saying I was doing *important yard work*. I jammed my cap back on my head and tried to avoid inspection by Livvy's gaze.

"*You lied,*" she stated matter-of-factly, speaking quietly and looking over to see if my mother had noticed what she said. "*You lied. God hates liars,*" she whispered. She looked back at my mother and waved.

My face flushed. I hate that when your face gets red. My ears get red too, and they feel hotter than the sun. I had no choice. You have to answer your mother, no matter what, and I had to answer my mother no matter if they burned to a crisp like my cheese sandwich in the memorable junk fire or not. I hope they don't have to get *trimmed off* too.

"Fletcher, are you finished picking the yellow beans?"

I saw Livvy watching me. She nodded at me.

"Well, she's waiting, so answer!" she urged.

"Only a few more yellow beans to go!" I said, and I pledged the holy truth as if I was teetering on a pile of hymn books thirteen feet high. My ears felt cooler already. The blue eyes peered across the fence at me. They got squinty.

"It takes a real man to admit he picks beans for his mother!"

That amazed me. I tried to look nonchalant if that's possible with hot red ears. I felt them. They were starting to cool off just a bit. My mother said "*nonchalant*" is when you pretend and act like a man of the world, like in the movies, and have a fancy yellow convertible or something. I casually turned my brown tweed hat backwards.

"Oh, I pick yellow beans regularly," I declared officially. "That is, if I don't have too much yard work for my father," I added quickly just to be on the safe side. She squinted at me as if to warn me not to tell any more lies.

"Bring that basket of yellow beans into the kitchen when you're done, I need to start them right away!" My mother stretched her neck up about eight feet high and looked over the fence to see who owned the red shoes that had no dust on them.

"Oh, hello, Livvy!" She called.

"Hello, Mrs. Williams!" Livvy's eyes squinted again.

"You're not supposed to be talking to strangers, young lady!" my mother scolded.

"Oh, I know who he is," countered Livvy. "He's your son and he told me already, his name is *Fletcher Carnival Williams!*" She giggled. I hate giggling. I couldn't see her mouth. She was probably sticking her tongue out at me. I didn't know Livvy knew my mother, at least not yet. But she did. I wanted to pry her fingers off of the pickets and stamp on her toes and make her dustless red shoes get off my official whitewashed fence, but I didn't make a move because she didn't tell my mother that I lied to her, so I guess I liked her all right even if she had red shoes on.

My mother smiled at us, waved and walked around the side yard, disappearing behind the house. I looked again to be sure she was gone before I talked to the girl again.

"I didn't know you knew my mother!" I might have sounded a bit grumbly to God when I said it. I probably did.

The blue eyes glued themselves on me again like stickweed. "I saw her at the corner store yesterday. I talked to her," she said excitedly, "she told me that you're new here, and she told me her name—and she's nice, too" she added carefully, as if she knew what I was going to say next.

"*You're not supposed to be talking to strangers!*" I said, sort of mimicking my mother.

"She reached a brown bag for me," she said, "to get apples, green ones. And she told me I should come by and see you!" She looked at me and smiled.

"I don't think my mother did that."

"Well, she did!" the girl said, sticking her tongue out at me. "I bet she forgot."

Why would my mother do that? She knows I don't even like girls. I was surprised and my ears started to get hot again. I don't care about it, but I guess it's okay. The girl wasn't watching me now anyway. She was reaching up with her stick to poke at a tall sunflower that leaned against the fence. She was trying to scratch off the yellow flower parts to see if the seeds are ripe black yet, but everybody knows the seeds are still white. Her arms were too short.

"Oh," I said, shrugging and looking over my shoulder to see if my mother was coming back yet. *She wasn't. I never saw her again.*

Nine

There wasn't any reason for it. She walked over to the edge of town with the wet spot on her apron and waited in the tall white clover by the tracks with the wild honeybees for the 3:15 freight to drive over her. *It did, and right on time.*

"We couldn't stop in time."

That's what the engineer told the police officer and the police officer told the coroner man with the shiny black car and they all told my father when he got home. It made him cry. He thought I didn't hear them tell him, but I did. I listened and watched through the heat grate in the floor of my bedroom. I wanted to cry too, but I didn't. *I don't know why.* I can see dust balls hiding under the bed when I have my cheek pressed on the fancy iron grate to listen. I wish I had swept the linoleum better when my mother asked me to. She couldn't ask me again, could she?

My father drank whiskey all that evening and beat me hard that night. He said I didn't *stop* her from going to sit on the railroad tracks and get run over, so it was my fault. I told him I thought so too, but that didn't stop him from lashing at me again and again with his belt. The stinging blows didn't hurt much that time because my mother was gone.

They can't hurt me because she isn't here to make them feel better. She will never be there again to make them feel better so it doesn't matter.

The Fires of Waterland

The dishes on the table smashed on the floor when he got drunk and stumbled hard against the table and pulled the oilcloth to the floor. He got up and cried and fell over again and then shook himself quiet and went to sleep. I put a gray wool blanket on him and cleaned up the mess. The bottle was almost gone so I poured the rest in the sink and threw it in the trashcan. He slept on the kitchen floor, and I cooked yellow beans and potatoes in water for supper, and I didn't burn them. Not even a bit. I shook him to wake him up to eat but he said, "Get lost you little bastard, leave me alone, I'm not hungry — go away 'fore I give you a proper beating, *you little bastard*."

So I did. I don't know what happened after that because I left him alone and went in the other room and cried and missed my mother and fell asleep on the Chesterfield.

I got cold in the night. When I woke up in the morning, it was still summertime, but nobody was in the house but me. I made a cheese sandwich and went outside to drive the old Pontiac, even if it had flat tires. "Gimme two bucks of gas," I told the guy at my pretend Texaco gas station. I talked to him through the window, even if it was stuck and I had to talk through the *no-draft* part. I started 'er up again and drove everywhere in the world until it got dark. The sun was blazing all day, and it made the car hot like a desert, but I stayed in there anyway. I rolled down the dusty windows except for the one that was stuck and the one that was broken by the punk and listened to the crickets buzzing in the dry grass. I think God likes crickets. I do.

More dust came in every time a car went by racing to nowhere. The speed limit on our road is fifty miles an hour. My Pontiac always goes exactly at the speed limit. I was going to drive over and see Floyd, but my father said it wasn't good to bother the neighbours everyday, so it was a good thing I had the Pontiac to drive everywhere else in the world and not bother the neighbours. When it got dark, I packed her in and turned the light on over the back porch and watched the moths get dizzy going 'round and 'round for a while. It cooled off a bit, and the crickets stopped singing.

I went upstairs and got my pillow and blanket to get on the floor and keep my eyes stuck open with my head sleeping by the heat grate, so I would see if my father came home. My father didn't come home that night, and I must have been sleeping when he got home the next morning. I didn't dream, not even a bit, but I heard my mother's voice telling me not to sleep on the heat grate.

He waited until all of the people were gone the day of the funeral, and got another shiny bottle of whiskey out of a new wooden whiskey box, and drank it all. It was funny that he didn't think to give *them* any, and they all left with their hot, black, shiny button, wool suits and serious frowns on their faces and didn't smile, not even a bit as they shook my father's hand up and down like a water pump.

That reminds me of the baby-sitter: the one that was sent to stay at home with me the day of the funeral. They wouldn't let me go because I was too young. I was going to cry, but I didn't, even though I wanted to go and my father said no. I saw everybody get their cars into lines and follow each other. I heard the man say everybody had to turn on their headlights. I saw them leave in a line of dust and headlights.

Everybody went that time except Tina McQueeny and me. That's what her name was: *Tina McQueeny*. We played checkers, and she won every time. We looked at picture albums of people and drank sour lemonade. When we got tired of doing that, she undid her buttons and showed me her tits.

They were white and the bumpy middle part was pink like dusty red clay. She said I was sad, and it would cheer me up.

"You look sad, Fletcher. *Maybe this'll make you feel better, Fletcher,*" she whispered to me. She got them close to me and touched them on my face and wanted me to suck on them just a bit, but I lied and said I didn't want to do that. I think I might have wanted to so I could feel better, but I didn't. After that she pulled my hand in between her legs and squeezed it hard. She sighed and said, "Oh, my God..." After that she took my shorts down and tried to see if my wiener would go up and down like a water pump handle, too. I got a red face, and my ears burned. I told her to *stop that right now* and pushed her away and ran out into the garden fast.

"Don't you call them tits, Fletcher Williams! They're called breasts!" Liv giggled as she rubbed a tiny hole in the fog on the car

window. She peered into the darkness to see nothing, and then nestled her heated face against my bare chest. Tina McQueeny had tits, I thought to myself. Big ones. Only mothers have breasts. Tina McQueeny was a slut.

I stayed outside until everybody came home. *"Fletcher!"* Tina called me, but I wouldn't answer. I stayed hidden in the old Pontiac in the back yard and pretended I was driving fast, maybe back to the old house with my mother and father, and I was old enough to drive. I made them sit in the back seat and be king and queen. My mother told me not to drive so fast, and my father said I could go as fast as I want to, so I drove as fast as I could for a minute and slowed down to the speed limit the next minute to make them both happy. Then, I heard them whispering and kissing and tried not to look, but I did anyway. I saw the mouse nest and the moldy suitcase in the dusty back seat, and my mother and father weren't there anymore. I tried honking the horn to bring them back and stopping at the Texaco to see if I forgot them in the washrooms by accident on the way to Regina, but when I banged the horn button it didn't work, not even a peep. The mouse nest was empty, so I honked the horn some more and smelled my fingers. *They smell funny.*

The next day visitors came again, and they looked hot and sweaty in black suits, and after a while they all went away except Tina. My father said bad things to me, and I cried. He made me go upstairs to bed before it got dark outside, so I stayed quiet and watched everyone down through the heat grate. Nobody knew I was there, but I knew what everybody said. It's so sad. I saw what they *did*, too.

I even saw Mrs. Mulligan from the old place, but she didn't bring Mr. Mulligan with her. I heard her tell another old lady that Mr. Mulligan was sitting at home in Morgan County right on the mantle over the fireplace pretty as you please in a green jar. She gave my father a hug. "We're going to miss your Angelina. She was a *good* woman," she said to him and put her hand on his shoulder. After that she left and went shopping for a new garden rake or maybe she just drove back home to see Mr. Mulligan on the mantel. Soon everybody went away except Tina.

"Stay awhile," my father said to her. "Look after the boy for me."

She smiled at him and put her hand on his face. Maybe that was to stop his headache.

When night came Tina made me a cheese sandwich and put me up to bed, then she helped my father drink another bottle of whiskey and laughed a lot and made him laugh too, and then she sat on him with no clothes on. She played *water pump* with him, and they slept in my mother's bed that night, and I could hear the bed springs squeak a few times. I shut my ears with my pillow and didn't listen any more except for a little bit before I got into bed, when I was looking down through the heat grate. I wasn't going to watch, but then I did. I got out of bed and got on the floor so that I could see them through the heat grate. *I want to be there instead of him. No, I don't. Yes, I do. No, Fletcher, God will know.*

I wanted to be there instead of him. I hated my father for doing that in my mother's bed. I got out of bed and looked down at them again. I didn't make any noise. I watched. I don't know why I watched. It reminded me of dogs that run around and play jump up and hop along. Tina McQueeny must have had quite a bit of fun because she laughed a lot, and then they fell asleep. I got tired of watching them sleeping, and I fell asleep on the floor and forgot to get back into bed.

A few of the people that came to our house the last day were from Morgan County, the old place, the one we got kicked out of with a moving paper and where we had to pack our stuff in whiskey boxes and now my mother's dead and I wish we never moved from there. Mrs. Mulligan came again and brought peanut butter cookies for me. "I made them especially for you, Fletcher," she said, and she said she didn't bring Mr. Mulligan in the green jar because the whole affair would have disturbed him *immensely.*

I didn't ask her what affair, but maybe it was something to do with whiskey drinks and Tina McQueeny and my father sleeping in my mother's bed, so I thought it better not to ask. Maybe it was an *affair of the heart* that happened when I was at school or maybe it was one time I went over to Mrs. Mulligan's to collect her cans and bottles in the old days, and I wasn't watching, but I know *something* made my mother sad and Mrs. Mulligan mad enough to throw garden tools around. It made my mother get driven over by the train, I'm sure of that.

Ten

It was hot. The wind was hot and whistled through the screen on the kitchen window. I was alone and my father was sleeping from drinking another bottle of whiskey to almost empty, so I went outside and walked. All the way to the Waterland cemetery, that's at least two miles on the other side of the bridge. I had to go. I wanted to go. I was afraid to ask if my father would take me but I did anyway.

"No! —Forget it! Where's my belt, boy? I'm gonna smack some sense into your head, what's the matter with you? Gimme that bottle, —not *that* one, *the full one, stupid*! Get outside and play on the tracks or something! You stay away from the cemetery. She's dead, you ain't gonna help her a bit, are you? You don't need to go over there, you don't have to bother! She's dead! You're too young to understand anyway, go out and play or something, *get lost!*" I ran outside and sat in the old Pontiac and cried. I thought about it for a while, and I decided I am not too young. I know I'm not. I can understand, too.

I found the place they put her in by reading her name on the wooden cross. It was painted white, just like the clouds. "**Angelina Williams**" and the cross was new wood and shiny, not dull silvered and old like most of the others. There was another newer cross there too in a shiny spiked iron fence, but it said "**William Yakafluic,** *Beloved Husband — We will miss you*". The flowers on William Yakafluic were wilted and dried up. I mean on the dirt, the flowers were all over the pile of dirt, they were heaped up there in a big pile on top of the dirt. The paint was sticky on the wood too. I got in and touched it, and it left a fingerprint on it, and I rubbed some dirt on it hard as possible to get it the paint off of my fingers. The paint on the new crosses smelled like the inside of the kitchen hutch when my mother painted it at the old house. I went back to my mother's cross and read it again. It said:

"**Angelina Williams — 1932-1952**" and *"I Am with God"*.

I sat on the pile of sand covered with wilting flowers and didn't know what to do next. After a while I went all the way back to the edge of the railroad tracks and picked black-eyed-Suzies that look like yellow daisies. I made a bunch and came back to put them right on top of the pile of sand they covered my mother up with. They are my mother's favorite flowers and don't get too wilty for a long time even if you pick them and forget to give them to your mother until the next day.

I wasn't going to cry but my eyes got wet all by themselves, and the water made sand balls that rolled down into my shoes. I didn't have any socks on because it was hot. I remembered at the last minute to take off my brown tweed cap. The sand balls reminded me about the dust balls that I didn't sweep when my mother asked me to. It made me sad again, so I ran past William Yakafluic and his spiked iron fence and got out of the cemetery fast. I stopped by the fence and looked up into the big tree and stood by the white picket gate for a while. I stopped crying by looking into the bright sun. It made me sneeze. And I saw her smile at me and I knew she liked the flowers and I knew it didn't matter about the dust-balls I left on the linoleum under the bed. I guess she must have asked God about it. I heard them whispering. I listened for a long time.

The Waters County Social Services lady pounded on the screen door. It rattled like a loose tooth. Mrs. McAllister smoothed her white apron as she answered the door. "Is the boy here?" she asked. She brushed her coat like there was a cobweb stuck on it.

"Yes, just a minute. Please come in." I was escaping when I heard her drive up, so I crept silently to the corner of the house. I got there just in time to see who was pounding on the door hard enough to scare everybody in the world. I hid between the scratchy raspberries and the fence so she wouldn't see me, and she didn't. She disappeared into the doorway and the screen door slammed behind her. I didn't hear anything else until Mrs. McAllister went to the back door and shouted.

"*Fletcher!*" She had a pretty loud voice. I guess she thought I was gone down the back lane to play with the strays. I wasn't. I was on the side of the house, watching my father's house. I am looking to see if he is coming back to get me or not, just like a priest watches the people in church to see if they are putting money into the basket, or maybe watching to see if God is watching *him*.

I heard her and headed for the back door, and I scared her. Mrs. McAllister is a nice lady, but she gets scared too easy. No wonder. Her husband Floyd has no legs. He said some big rocks fell on 'em, and they turned all green and stunk, and the doctor said he had to cut 'em off or Floyd would be a *goner*. He said he didn't care much for that, but the doctor insisted on doing it right away. Now Floyd drives around the back porch on a creaky high-backed wicker chair that has two bicycle wheels on the back and two baby carriage wheels on the front, held on with two bent nails. He told me he gets down the stairs by *bumming it*. He pushes the chair off the edge and it bounces down all by itself. I helped him to get it back up on the creaky wooden porch quite a few times.

"Hey," I said, coming around the corner of the house. She almost jumped out of her skin. She wasn't the only one. Floyd woke up and almost jumped out of his chair too.

"The boy's right here, woman!" He sucked on his sunburned lips and closed his eyes against the sun. "No needs to wake up the dead! He'll be in there soon enough. You make that lady a nice cup of tea, will you?"

"*Social services have come for the boy!*" she said to him in a harsh whisper that anybody for ten yards and with one good ear could hear.

The Fires of Waterland

"Oh...*oh*...*damn*," Floyd said, and blinked in the brightness as he pushed the gold-colored round steel glasses back up on his nose. He needed a shave. He looked directly at me.

"Boy, after a bit you're gonna have to go inside with the missus." He had the sorriest look ever on his face. Just like the looks the people had at our house the day of the funeral, except Tina McQueeny. Tina smiled most of the time, especially when she was cheering me up. I sat down on the wooden step.

"Come on, Fletcher, I want to feel real good and if you touch me you'll feel real good, too, I promise, you'll see". She slid the silky blouse down her shoulders and reached out to me and pulled my face in close to her tits. I smelled the perfume on her skin and wanted to be close to her. "You're going to be a real man. Wait 'til you grow up, you'll really like me!" she whispered. She looked out of the window to see if my father was coming home yet. He wasn't.

"Fletcher," she said. "Fletcher?"

"Fletcher?" I blinked, and Floyd was looking at me.

"What are you thinking about, boy?" Floyd cut in, and I had to answer.

"Nothing much, Floyd," I said. *"Just stuff."*

"I see." Floyd puffed.

She squeezed my face against her soft skin, and I pushed hard and tried to get away, but it was soft like my mother's skin, soft with perfume on it. "You can touch, me, honey, it's all right, baby..." she whispered, and I don't want to escape now. "Run! Get away, Fletcher!" whispered my mother, maybe it was my mother. I don't know. I don't know. I don't know, and I don't want to know, not now! You! You, boy! Fletcher!

"You, boy! Fletcher Williams! Are you paying attention to me or not?" Mrs. McAllister demanded from the doorway.

"I don't think he much cares to go in just yet!" Floyd said.

"She came all the way over here just to see him; you know she has to see him, Floyd!" Mrs. McAllister shook her head. I tried to pay attention, but I couldn't. Floyd puffed hard on his pipe, and then tapped it on the wheel of his chair. Some of the ashes glowed brightly as they fell on the porch. They winked out all by themselves. Most of the time, I put them out for Floyd, so he doesn't have to worry about burning the floor. You can't put out sparks if you don't have shoes on, and you can't have shoes on if you don't have legs, like Floyd.

"Someday, you're going to burn this place to the ground doing that!" Mrs. McAllister said.

"Not much of a loss, woman!" growled Floyd.

I felt my back against the wall, and she took my hand and put it under her skirt. Stop that. I tried not to feel anything, but I did it even though I tried not to. My face is in the soft skin again. It is soft and too hot. She made noises softly and held my arm and pushed against me. I pulled away. Don't do that. She undid the shiny tin cowboy buckle on my leather belt. Her hand was hot when she reached into my shorts. No. My mother can see me. Tina kept talking, whispering, convincing.

Fletchie, honey, you'll like it. She's gone, and she ain't here. She can't tell you nothing, so it must be okay now. It doesn't matter anymore.

She kneeled in front of me, and her lips were hot when she did things. She put her own hand under her skirt. While she did that she made more noises. Stop that. My mother will see. No! I am trying to push her away. She is a slut, and I have to push her away, but no, no, no, I don't want to push her away, but I have to. I have to run away. My mother can see, and God won't like this, not a bit.

Come along, Fletcher! My mother said. How can she say that? She can't say that. She's dead, and her apron is wet and the freight train ran over her right on time. She looked at me. She smiled at me. I'm scared. Come along, Fletcher. She called at me from the wild white clover and the honeybees. I ran out and hid under the blanket in the old Pontiac. I cried.

Tina is looking for me, but I'm hiding. And I'm never coming out again. I can't. So I didn't answer. I smelled my fingers.

They smell like her now. I want her to do it again. I don't want her to do it again. I can't do it again. No, no, no. Tina McQueeny's a slut. I am hiding. Tina is calling but —

I can't answer. Fletcher...

My father will be home soon. Now he'll take off his belt, "C'mon, Fetchie, you little bastard, get what's comin' to ya, boy. You — gimme that whiskey, boy. Look what you done now, boy. You, Fetchie, gimme that bottle 'fore I come and get it and brain ya with it. Come along, boy, do what I said. *Don't hit me. I'm afraid of my father when he's like this. I'm hiding. Fetchie, get out here!*

"C'mon, Fletcher, honey, where are you?"

Fletcher, your father's just under the weather now, he's bunged up — too much cheese, he'll feel better tomorrow, son. Come along, Fletcher, dear." I can't move.

"Come along, Fletcher, dear."

"Come along, Fletcher dear!" Mrs. McAllister said, holding the door open for me. I jerked suddenly when it wasn't my mother talking, and it wasn't Tina McQueeny calling either; and I wasn't under the blanket in the old Pontiac, at all, and my Father wasn't there. So I got awake by jerking and shrugged at Floyd instead. You always jerk suddenly if you're thinking about something else and Floyd knows that. Floyd winked at me. I like Floyd.

"Fletcher!"

He said I could call him *Floyd* because I was taller than him even though he was a lot older than me. He told me he was six-foot five until he lost his legs. Mrs. McAllister scolded him when he told me I could call him *Floyd*. He always called me 'Fetch' or 'boy'. I didn't mind being called anything by Floyd.

"Shush, Arnold. He's a boy and must learn to address you *properly!*"

"Well, I don't like being called '*Arnold*' much, myself!" Floyd said. He scratched his chin. "Personal addressing, that's a *personal* issue, now, isn't it, Fletcher? And there's a matter for two men to discuss and settle between themselves!" he shot back at her quick as the wink he gave me.

"It's a sign of mutual respect, how men measure up to one another," Floyd said, and winked at me again. Mrs. McAllister saw him that time, so he pretended he had some dust in his eye. Mrs. McAllister looked at him sideways and winked back at him.

"We'll see about that!" she sniffed. "... *Arnold!*" she added huffily. She was drinking tea that time at the dining room table with her little pinky finger stuck straight out and her teacup rattled when she said it and she looked to see if there were any chips out of her good china cup. Floyd winked at me.

Out on the porch we drank some sour lemonade. I wanted more sugar in it but Mrs. McAllister said she didn't have any, so I drank it like it was and made a face. Floyd finished his and got quiet, and said it was sour and then said I was his equal and I had to call him *Floyd* and that was that.

"Fletch, I think you can call me Floyd or whatever you like, your choice," he said smiling at me. I agreed, I like calling Floyd his real name, and it's *Floyd*.

"That's decided for once and for all then," he announced. He clicked the ice cube on his teeth while he sucked on it. Mrs. McAllister told him not to chew on ice cubes, and he said store-bought choppers are made to chew anything you happen to like and don't hurt either, and she got mad again.

"Do as you wish!" she reminded him. "They're dear enough at forty-two dollars without you breaking them again chewing on your ice!" She sent me into the kitchen to get melon slices. I didn't know you could buy new choppers for forty-two dollars. I'll have to remember that. Sometimes even Mrs. McAllister is full of good information.

I chopped up the orange melon slices and listened to Mrs. McAllister giving him a good talking to after that, but a couple of minutes later out on the porch Floyd told me to call him *Floyd* no matter what, even if hell freezes over and new choppers cost *a hundred and forty-two dollars* and Indians are scalping us in a black lightning-storm at the same time, so I did. Mrs. McAllister heard that through the screen door, and I saw her make a face just like I did when I drank the sour lemonade.

Raymond Alexander Kukkee

Eleven

I came to live at Floyd McAllister's eight days after I put the bunch of black-eyed Suzie's on my mother's grave. My father told me to never come home again. I think he made a mistake telling me that, so I did anyway, but after he beat me up and kicked me, and made me drink whiskey to make me into a man quite a few times, I didn't want to be there *at all*.

> "*Ya disobeyed me, I told you not to go out there, you little bastard. I'll show you who's the boss around here; gimme the belt, boy. Go on, get it. I'm gonna teach you a lesson you'll never forget, gimme that bottle there, while you're up, soon as I have me a drink you're gonna get a whippin'. Fetchie, we'll see if you like havin' your arse whipped black and blue, talking back to me an' disobeying me an' all. You won't be walking out there no more, boy, disobeying your daddy. You're going to learn a lesson, boy!*"

I was going to go to Texas, but I got too tired, so I had to sleep in McAllister's wood shed instead. It was pretty cold, and Floyd saw me sneak in there when the door creaked the second night, so he ordered me to come into the house. Mrs. McAllister was standing on the porch watching him when I came out of the shed. She had her hands over her mouth like she was trying not to say anything.

"Floyd," she said, "*you have to call*. You *know* what you have to do."

"There won't be any argument about this, Elizabeth. I have my mind made up," he said. "I'm taking the boy in, Elizabeth. I'm not

70

calling anyone, and a boy can't stay by himself, can he? So, we'll be doing what we can and certainly won't be leaving him to be abused and whipped and left on his own!"

Mrs. McAllister dragged me into the kitchen and washed my face and all over like a bath with a wet cloth and Floyd scrubbed me dry with a towel. "Kind of chilly out there, isn't it, lad? We'll need a little wood for the fire. Come on, Fletcher, you can help!" We went back out into the yard even if my teeth were chattering, and I helped Floyd by getting big armloads of firewood and kindling up onto the porch from the shed while Mrs. McAllister made us hot food. I loaded the firewood onto Floyd's lap, and he wheeled into the kitchen with it.

"That'll do 'er. That's a big help, Fletcher."

We put the wood in the box behind the kitchen stove. The fire smoked and crackled a lot and sparked when we put more wood in it. It was warm by the wood box, and I stayed there for a quite a few months. I don't know how many months, and I mean at Floyd's, not by the wood box, and Mrs. McAllister made good biscuits and beef stew.

"You'll never starve if you got biscuits and beef stew!" Floyd always said when we sat down to eat. He winked at me. Maybe the first time, he knew that I didn't eat since my mother's funeral. That time and most of the other times we ate, Mrs. McAllister's face was red from the heat of the stove. The biscuits were nearly as good as my mother's, I bet. I ate six and slathered extra butter on the last one for good measure, and Floyd winked at me.

We wheeled out onto the porch, and the fire-bugs were blinking everywhere, when we saw Tina McQueeny walk through the garden gate and into the front door of my father's house like every night. She didn't knock on the door either.

Floyd looked kind of disgusted and *harrumphed* a bit, but he didn't say a word, so I watched the smoke from his pipe floating into the sky instead. He wheeled himself inside. I sat there and swatted bugs.

I watched again the next day. I think she saw me that time because Floyd wasn't in sight.

"Come home, Fletcher! There's a good boy!" Tina called to me across the fence.

"Is my father home?" I asked her.

"He won't be back until tonight!" I walked around the fence and stopped.

"I have lemonade with sugar for you!" Tina teased. "It's sweet, Fletcher!" She added. "*Real sweet!*"

I looked back at Floyd's porch. Floyd was gone to town with Mrs. McAllister to go to the dentist. Floyd hates the dentist. "They drill more holes in your wallet than your teeth!" He growled. "Now I gotta pull the rest out, too. *Shoulda got all store-bought the first time!*"

I like lemonade, and Floyd and Mrs. McAllister weren't there to tell me to stay home or anything so I walked around the fence. The black housecoat Tina wore shone in the sun. It was open at the top and I saw her white skin. She opened the door and I walked in. I heard the door close behind me.

Her hand was hot on my shoulder. "I want to show you something first."

"What?" I said, and she giggled.

"*You'll like it, you'll see,*" she said, and she licked her lips.

I saw *that.* "*In here!*" She led me into my mother's bedroom.

"*Sit here!*" She patted the bed. I sat down. I got up again.

Floyd struck a match and puffed hard on his pipe. I like pipe smoke. The door on my father's house slammed behind Tina. Floyd squinted into the setting sun. "Huh!" he said to himself. A pot banged in the kitchen behind us. "That woman! Noisy, ain't she!" he muttered. "Wonder what she's cooking?"

The Fires of Waterland

She pushed me down to sit on the bed and stood close to me so I couldn't get up. She slowly opened her robe. I saw the shiny brown hair and her bare legs. "I'm showing you this, 'cause in no time at all, you'll be a man already, Fletcher, and I like you, and do you like me?" she asked me in a whispery voice. Her tits were white against the black robe. She leaned over and pulled my face into them and made me suck them again. "C'mon, baby..." She called me a baby again. I'm not a baby. I think only babies do that. I am closing my eyes, but I want to see them and taste them more. No, I can't do that, but they taste good, and I'm scared because I think God and my Mother can see me now. She made a soft noise like cats meowing, and I don't know why she does that, and then she suddenly stood up beside the bed and tried to push my face down into the soft hair. It smelled like my fingers did, the day of the funeral and all of the people wore hot black clothes and looked sad and hot and were choking and squinty and had to drive in a line with their headlights on.

Floyd cleared his throat and scratched another match on the arm of his chair. A black car whizzed down the street past us and raised dust. Floyd coughed.

"Fools... too fast, *too fast!*" he looked at me and shook his head. "Seems to me nobody in the world needs to go so fast as that. Everybody's in a damned hurry, right, Fletch?" I nodded and swatted a mosquito. "*Everybody's in such a damned hurry!*" he said, again, but I think he said it to himself because he already told me once. Nobody has to be told more than once, that's what Floyd said *once* and I remembered that. He didn't have his headlights on, either.

They didn't let me go to my mother's funeral, and that's why Tina had to be the babysitter and cheer me up and show me her tits and I liked that. And that's why it was my fault, so I had to run out and hide under the blanket in the old Pontiac and smell my fingers and that's why, that must be why. And now I want to do it again, but I'm not supposed to do that, and I have to push her away again. I pushed her away hard that time, but she sat down and rolled over. She pulled me between her legs and tightened them around me. I was trapped like in a wrestling match. She pulled my

73

shorts down. She was hot and it made me sticky and hot and now I feel sick. Her face was red as a radish from my mother's garden, and she screamed quietly with her eyes shut, but her mouth is wide open. I can see all of her teeth, and they are shiny and white and perfect, and why is she puffing like running and racing and playing tag. She stopped holding her breath all at once and gasped. "Oh..." she said, breathing hard.

Mrs. McAllister dropped a pan on the floor in the house. I jumped pretty high. "*Again!* Oh, that woman, she's got dropsy or worse, I swear!" Floyd grunted. A light flicked on in my father's house. "Shush up in there, woman! You got the dropsy or something?" Floyd asked. "*Shshsh!*"

"Shshsh!" Tina warned me. "What?" I said. Suddenly the back door rattled. "Oh, no!" She pushed me off of her and jumped up and pulled the robe tightly around her. Her face was red as a ripe strawberry. She straightened her hair up and went to the door. I listened. I know it's wrong to listen. My mother said so, but I heard them anyway.

"Oh, it's you!" she said coldly to Mrs. McAllister. "Do ya always listen at people's doorways? Nice day, huh?"

Mrs. McAllister charged through the door and past her. "Is the boy here?" she demanded.

"It's his home, isn't it, Mrs. McAllister?"

She pushed Tina aside and stared into the bedroom and saw me. She shook her head angrily. I think it was because I was sitting on the bed and pulling my shorts up when she appeared in the doorway. I did up my shiny tin belt buckle. She put her hand over her mouth. Her eyes opened up wide. She looked at Tina and back at me. "Fletcher! What's going on here! What on earth were you doing?" She yelled at Tina. Suddenly Mrs. McAllister gasped and turned all white. She hissed angrily.

"Go see Floyd — now!" I ran out on the porch. I looked in through the screen door, and I listened. Mrs. McAllister was mad as a wet chicken. I found out that she doesn't like Tina McQueeny, not even one bit.

The Fires of Waterland

"Bitch! You, little bitch! Perverted slut!" Mrs. McAllister leaned towards her and slapped Tina viciously. She stormed out onto the porch and almost ran over me like a freight train. "I told you to go see Floyd!" she yelled at me. I didn't move.

Tina followed her to the door and screamed at her. "It's none of your goddamned business, none of your goddamned business, you old busybody!" Mrs. McAllister slapped her again and slammed the door in Tina's face.

"Go see Floyd, I told you!" she shouted at me. I ran.

"What's going on!" Floyd asked. "What's going on over there?"

Mrs. McAllister came home right after I did and made me go peel potatoes while she talked to Floyd. I heard her say Tina McQueeny was a slut and a bitch and a pervert, and she should spend the rest of her life in jail. If she was doing that she was a slut, Floyd agreed. After things cooled off, Floyd and I sat on the porch together. Did she do things to you, boy? Some things done aren't right, boy. Don't you never go near that woman again, hear?

"You'll be staying here with us, boy!" then he looked at me kind of funny and knocked the ashes out of his pipe on the arm of the wicker chair. "You don't be going there anymore, no matter what happens! You won't be going near that woman any more now, will you?"

A dog barked in the distance. Some more dogs barked and answered like they always do.

"You'll be staying away from there from now on," he said.

"Why, Floyd?" I asked just as Floyd lit another match and puffed slowly on his pipe until it glowed red.

"Because some things are right and some things are wrong and mostly things are wrong over there". He pointed at my Father's house and looked sternly at me. "That woman's trouble, boy, she's out of control right now, leave it at that for now. We'll talk about it some other time when you're a bit older, and it'll make it easier to understand."

"Okay, Floyd," I said, and batted some mosquitoes into Floyd's smoke. They buzzed off pretty quick.

Mrs. McAllister came out and frowned at Floyd and knitted her black eyebrows together like the stitches on a baseball, black and orange stitches; some good and some broken and sticking out, like on a worn out baseball that has been in the mud for a while. I tried not to listen, but I did.

Mrs. McAllister sniffed and tightened up her face. She looked across at my father's house and said, "She should be in jail like somebody else we know! That girl's a proper slut, Floyd!"

I didn't know what she meant, but I remembered to ask Floyd after things quieted down.

Floyd told me all about it a couple of days later when Mrs. McAllister was busy. Floyd and I were sitting on the porch having a smoke. When I asked him what a *slut* was, he cleared his throat and looked at me kind of funny, but he puffed and said, *"That's a woman that does things with anybody. And shows her tits first thing to everybody too like she does. Like her,"* he replied quietly. He puffed. *"Like her,"* he said again, and nodded toward my father's house. I like Floyd. He always tells me the *facts*.

"What's a *bitch*, Floyd?" I asked him, a couple of days later.

"A female dog, that's what!" He swatted at the mosquitoes. "Sometimes it's improperly used…*that* word, it is used to describe certain women—for certain things they do. It's not appropriate language for a boy any age, even me."

I wanted to ask Floyd if sluts always did certain things like playing *water pump* up and down to cheer you up and did things with their lips and catch you with their legs and make you smell their bum, but I don't think Floyd wants to talk about it anymore now.

"—I told you, *not now, boy!*" Floyd suddenly warned quietly, jerking his head toward the screen door. I clammed up. He cleared his throat. "We should be doing some reading every day to learn some more new words, that's what," he said, "and maybe some Wild West cowboy stories and sailing adventures too." He looked at me and touched the side of his head with his finger. *"There's always something interesting to learn by reading."*

The problem was that Mrs. McAllister *always* shows up at the wrong time. I think she must have heard something through the screen door. She sounded mad enough that she probably would have spit furniture tacks if she knew how. Floyd raised his eyebrows high and glanced at me. I was listening to see what he was going to say, but I didn't hear anything. Mrs. McAllister's eyes were staring through the screen door and were big and had white all around, the same color as a new baseball. The crickets stopped singing for a minute, and so did Floyd. Maybe Floyd expected war to break out any time.

"Too many mosquitoes out here for you, woman?" Floyd finally asked and the glow of the match he struck to light his pipe was brighter than a whiskey bottle full of fireflies.

She grunted and swatted and said, *"Harrumph!"* I didn't know ladies could say that. My mother never said *harrumph* or *slut* or anything like that.

Just then I sort of wished I could see down through the heat grate again. I don't know why I thought about that, but I looked at my father's house and back at Floyd quick as a wink. "You *gotta* go in, Fetch."

"Okay, Floyd," I said, and looked at him. He nodded without saying another word. Sometimes Floyd said a lot of things without saying a word. Sometimes he did say a lot. I remember.

"A fella ought not to use that name for women at all, but sometimes it fits, don't it?" Floyd leaned over to me and looked at me funny. He cleared his throat. *"Some sluts will do different things and some don't, near as I can tell,"* Floyd whispered. *"Thing is, I never saw a slut before that would bother a boy your age, so I think she might be a bad one."* He nodded. I pretended I knew what he meant. Maybe, I really did.

I didn't get to discuss that situation with Floyd again, not last time or this time either.

I got up from the porch and went inside.

Twelve

"Are you Fletcher C. Williams, young man?" the Waters County Social Services lady asked me first thing, before I even had a chance to say anything or even take off my hat and be polite. I don't think the screen door had a chance to bang behind me twice before I knew she was a woman that was a bit too crabby. It's probably because her hair is too tight. She had a piece of cloth tied in it. Yellow, and the knot looked tight like my shoelaces when I make a mistake and pull the wrong string. They never come undone.

"Take off your hat!" Mrs. McAllister firmly demanded. I *almost* had my brown tweed hat off before she said it but not quite. I wear it all the time in the evening. It stops the mosquitoes from biting my head. Their pokey little noses are too short to get through the thick cloth. I figured it out. Floyd said you can figure anything out if you think hard enough about it. I thought hard about mosquito noses.

"Are you Fletcher Carnival Williams?" the woman shouted at me before I had a chance to answer the first time and get my hat off and think up some more good ideas about mosquito's faces and everything.

"Fletcher...*Fletcher!* Will you answer Mrs. Zeban, boy?" Mrs. McAllister said. Her face was getting red, and she wasn't anywhere near the stove or a pan of hot biscuits.

"Yes, ma'am, I'm Fetch," I answered. There was mud on my shoes. I felt my face to see if there was any mud. It didn't feel like there was too much on it. Mrs. McAllister didn't like me having mud on my face. The first night she scrubbed it all over with a soapy washcloth until it hurt, and my ears were stinging. I tried not to cry.

"You mean '*Fletcher*', don't you?" the woman corrected me. I hate being corrected. I can't help it if everybody called me *Fetch* for two hundred years.

"Yes, ma'am, *Fletcher Carnival Williams,* that's me, ma'am," I boldly said. I didn't bow to her like I did to Livvy that time in the garden. You don't bow to crabby people. I just fiddled with my cap instead. The cloth feels like the escape bag from the *Count of Monte Cristo.*

"*Good boy!*" she exclaimed. "He knows his full name!" she nodded happily to Mrs. McAllister. Maybe she thinks I don't know how to breathe, too, I thought to myself. I started breathing heavily just to show her that I could get lots of air and hold my breath until they threw my limp body into the sea. "So many of *them* don't even know what their real names are!" Mrs. Zeban said to Mrs. McAllister as she poured herself a fresh cup of tea.

"You don't mind if I help myself, do you?" I heard Mrs. Zeban babbling again about how orphans don't know their own names most of the time, and she has to give them one. *She doesn't have to do that with me; I'm not an orphan.*

She didn't notice. I tried stopping breathing, but the lights started going out and I had to start again. I felt like I was hot, like I was picking yellow beans and got all dizzy. The buzzing in my ears started to go away.

"*Fletcher,*" Mrs. McAllister warned.

"*I have to take you with me!*" Mrs. Zeban spoke sharply. She was writing fast in a gray folder-thing with red snaps on it. She closed it and held it in front of her tits. They didn't seem to be as big as Tina McQueeny's. I didn't look at the red snaps again right away. It's not polite to stare at something you really want to look at, but you always end up looking at it even if you try not to. I tried to think about the *Count of Monte Cristo* and escape bags and things, and ended up thinking about the mouse nest in the back of the old Pontiac, and driving Mother and Father everywhere in the world, and always going *fast and slow, fast and slow, fast and slow*. That makes everybody happy, and I think everybody should be happy as chickens in an oat bin.

"*Boy!*" Mrs. McAllister scolded.

I came to attention very smartly, just like in the army. "Yes, sir," I said. "I mean, *yes, ma'am*," I mumbled. I'm going in the army some day and march away, and I'll march well and wear a tin hat just like Floyd has on in his old picture in his room, you'll see.

"Floyd said I was staying here with him!" I proudly informed Mrs. Zeban. I looked at Mrs. McAllister, and she looked back at me and nobody said anything for a minute. I could hear the clock ticking.

Mrs. Zeban looked at Mrs. McAllister, and they both looked at me and then back at each other some more. "This is difficult, I know," she said.

Mrs. Zeban sighed and blinked right at the light and fumbled for her pencil. She fiddled with the papers in the folder.

"I'm...afraid that's not possible," she said quietly. Mrs. McAllister looked at me to see if I was still holding my breath. I wasn't. I caught myself looking at the red snaps again. I dropped my hat on the floor so that I could be distracted and would have to pick it up. I got a little bit dizzy again. I felt cold all at once. *I'm not leaving Floyd.*

Not me. I'm never going away from Floyd. He lets me smoke his pipe, but not too much, only to chase mosquitoes away.

"But *Floyd said...*" was all I could say.

I would never agree to move away from Floyd's, no matter *what* she said.

She looked at me and shook her head.

"No matter *what* Mr. McAllister has been telling *you*, young man!"

"My father is going to come and get me as soon as he feels better, and Floyd and I watch every night to see if he's coming!" They looked at each other. "He's coming soon, no more than a week!" I offered. *I think God knows if you have to lie to stay at Floyd's it's all right.*

80

The Fires of Waterland

I waited and didn't fiddle with my brown tweed cap or drop it or get dizzy. That ought to do it. She'd understand that and everything would be all right. She'd get into the Chevy that was parked beside the curb and drive off, and Floyd and me would go back outside and watch fireflies and swat mosquitoes, and he'd let me puff on his pipe to chase mosquitoes away more efficiently with smoke, but only when Mrs. McAllister wasn't looking.

The thin woman didn't accept that for an answer. She sipped on her tea for a moment and the chair creaked when she stood up. She stepped to the door and turned back to Mrs. McAllister.

"Could I speak with your husband, Mrs. McAllister?" she asked, but I don't know why she asked because she didn't wait for an answer. You're supposed to wait for an answer if you ask a question. At least that's what Floyd said. She spoke out the screen door like she was talking to herself.

"Mr. McAllister, would you like to come in for a moment please?" She smoothed the dark blue dress against her skinny bones with her left hand while she held the door open for Floyd with her right hand. Her skin was white like my mother's. If you cared to look closely it wasn't exactly white; more like skinned almonds. I ate some skinned almonds once. *Skinned almonds are kind of slippery when they are wet, too.*

I didn't care to look any closer, and then light shone from the ring on her hand. Floyd wheeled in backwards through the door with the bicycle wheels first. The baby carriage wheels rattled. I think that was because they were loose. Floyd said they'd fall off some day when he was in a real hurry, or sometime when he least expected it. That was one time we were talking, and he was bumming down the stairs.

The thin woman extended her white hand to Floyd. He looked at it and hesitated for a moment. Mrs. McAllister didn't see him hesitate, but I did. I studied how Floyd does things in the last two months, and Floyd hesitated for a moment. He took her white, tiny hand in his big brown one and pumped it up and down a couple of times. Floyd must have squeezed it hard too, because he told me that if you have a soggy handshake it shows you might be in possession of a puffball brain too.

"When you shake somebody's hand you take their hand and squeeze it good, boy. You don't break it, but squeeze it and make them know it's shook! You want them to know you're paying attention right now and not decayed away up top. You don't want everybody to think your mind is made of wet puffball mush, do you, boy? That's a bad thing to show right off before folks even get to know you."

That's how Floyd shakes your hand and does everything, so I just knew Floyd was going to make everything all right, but he didn't. No, that's not exactly right. Floyd couldn't make everything all right. But I know he tried.

"I'm Flora Zeban from the Waters County Social Services Department, Mr. McAllister."

"I know who you are, Mrs. Zeban. Used to work with your father —*John*, wasn't it? At the dynamite factory." Floyd squinted up at Mrs. Zeban and worked the big wheels on his chair so that it went this way and that way quite a few times. He smiled at me. Floyd could change direction in a flash or spin right around. He let me try his chair so I took it for a spin a few times too, but only when he was sitting on the Chesterfield or in the kitchen drinking coffee, *two sugars, no milk, woman!*

"Milk is always better for you than sugar, Floyd!" Mrs. McAllister always told him. "And leave that chair alone!" she always added. "The boy won't wear the chair out, now, will he?" Floyd always told her the same thing.

Mrs. Zeban nodded. "He died last year, Mr. McAllister," she said and got a faraway look on her face.

"Sorry to hear that, Mrs. Zeban. I liked John. I liked your father. Good man he was, *yup.*" Floyd came right out and asked her what he died from. *"What got him, his ticker?"*

Floyd said you should never beat around the bushes too long or you'll forget which direction you're headed.

"Floyd!" Mrs. McAllister looked like she was shouting at Floyd but it only came out as a loud whisper. She shook her head.

82

"Leukemia..." Mrs. Zeban's voice trailed off. "He had leukemia, cancer of the blood."

"That'll get 'em every time." Floyd said, "He was pale, last time I saw him," and thought better of it after he caught the glare from Mrs. McAllister. "Mrs. McAllister's confused, a bit sensitive about subjects like that, I prefer to get them right out in the open," he added cautiously. She shook her head at him again and gave him the subtle *we have to talk about that, don't we* look.

Floyd read between the lines right away and fiddled for his pipe thoughtfully. He shook his head.

"He was a good man," he said again. "I'm going to have to pay more attention to the missus," he said, forgetting his pipe, "but I really am sorry to hear that. Nothing nice about that at all," Floyd said quickly and raised his eyebrow just a hair when he felt brave enough to look back at Mrs. McAllister again. Mrs. McAllister gave Floyd the tiniest nod, so I knew they weren't going to have a big fight after Mrs. Zeban went home.

Mrs. Zeban sat down heavily and fingered the rim of the saucer under her teacup. The teacup rattled. *"Life goes on, doesn't it*; we all have to persevere, don't we?" Mrs. Zeban finally said and put the cup and saucer carefully on the table. She opened the file and snapped it shut again.

"That's right, Mrs. Zeban, life makes fools of all of us sometimes, and the best thing we can do is hitch our pants right back up and *get to it again − quick as possible!*" Floyd puffed, and must have forgotten that he didn't have his pipe in his mouth. He patted his shirt pocket and latched onto his pipe again. He looked at me and winked and shrugged.

"Then, you *know* why I'm here, Mr. McAllister."

Floyd dug into his shirt pocket for his tobacco. He examined his pipe carefully and showed it to me and winked and smiled. He took his time, tucking the briar pipe into the pouch and wiggling tobacco into it and packing it just so with his first finger. He clamped his teeth on the bit and struck a match, waiting for the sulphur to burn away. The pipe glowed as he puffed, and Floyd's eyes narrowed and he looked like he was far off, maybe in Spain where there's bullfights, or Moose Jaw, or someplace good like that.

"Nice man, your father was," Floyd said, noticing that they were waiting for him to talk, but he was taking his time on purpose. I know that's how Floyd makes people listen to him.

> *"Do everything methodically and carefully like you know what you're doing, Fletch, you remember that. People like that when they think you know what you're doing, it makes them sit up and pay attention, see?"*

Mrs. Zeban glanced impatiently at Mrs. McAllister.

"Floyd..." Mrs. McAllister started to say something and stopped.

The smoke drifted toward the ceiling. It smelled nice, not like the dry grass and weeds Archie McKinley and I tried to smoke; rolled up in newspaper, when we were in hiding, sitting down in the long white clover along the railway tracks. Archie walks over from his father's dairy farm sometimes to go trout fishing or go swimming and try smoking. When I get old like Floyd, I'm going to smoke a pipe instead; same kind, same shape, and I won't smoke old dry weeds from the railway tracks. I'll bet I'll have real tobacco.

Floyd glanced at me and winked. He cleared his throat. "The boy could just stay here as long as he wants." He sucked on the pipe again. "Seems simple enough to me."

"Floyd!" Mrs. McAllister exclaimed. "He can't just *stay here*. It's more complicated than you know! Do you know who you're talking to? Do you understand what you are saying, the responsibility you would be taking on?"

"*Woman*, Mrs. Zeban here didn't have to tell *me* who she is, or what her office does, or why she's here. I'm not a fool. I know why she's here, it's all too obvious!" He spun his chair around and faced Mrs. McAllister. "And I got news for you, woman. Your husband, you know, *the one with no legs, you remember him?* He's still got a working head on his shoulders!"

84

Floyd patted himself on the head. "Is it still there, Fletcher?" He looked at me and winked. "Had my hat on it only yesterday. My gosh, what did I do with it?" I laughed. Floyd was funny sometimes.

"Oh, here it is. Yes, that's the one! It's still there! Got hair on it too! The head, I mean!" Even Mrs. Zeban smiled a bit at Floyd's joke. Mrs. McAllister didn't. He snorted and looked back at Mrs. Zeban and then rubbed his chin hard, like he was suddenly irritated. *"As if you don't know it already, Elizabeth,"* he said quietly.

"Mrs. Zeban, sometimes I think this woman of mine thinks I lost my thinkin' ability when my legs got themselves sawed off!" He puffed on his pipe hard. "The two ain't even related, are they?"

I looked at Floyd and nodded at him for a change. Even I know that if your legs get chopped off you can still use your noggin. Now, she'll understand better.

Mrs. McAllister got a little bit red and looked at Floyd and knitted her eyebrows together like thick gravy, but he was talking again before she could say anything.

"W-e-ell, woman...if you can keep that in mind now, you'll understand that I'm right on top of this thing, and I have been from the start; I already knew she'd be comin' and I checked it out, I knew *who* was coming and who she was before she ever got here and y-e-s...isn't this amazing? She's from the Social Services Department just like I knew all along would happen sooner or later, and now, *what a revelation,* she shows up here like *an order from God.* She says she gotta take the boy away, but you might as well hear me right now, *I say no, she don't gotta take the boy away*...nope, she don't *gotta* take the boy away!" Floyd's voice went stone cold, the only time I ever heard that. *"And she ain't takin' Fletcher Williams away, not while I have anything to say about it!"* The only sound in the kitchen was the clock ticking on the wall until Mrs. McAllister spoke.

"Floyd!" Mrs. McAllister's face was all red.

Mrs. Zeban cleared her throat and looked at Floyd and blinked fast with both eyes at once. Then, she did it again. I hate that. It looks like you're lying when you blink too much. Just like the old judge. I

85

reminded myself to remember to ask Floyd if all hypocrites blink a lot when they tell lies.

"May I remind *you*, Mr. McAllister, the father failed to respond to our advertisement in the *Waterland Sentinel*? We are obliged to intervene if the parent fails to respond! The child automatically becomes a ward of the county."

"Well, to hell with your damned obligatory policy, Mrs. Zeban! Boy's fine here!" Floyd wheeled his chair a little closer to Mrs. Zeban. Mrs. Zeban backed up. "*This boy's doing just fine right here!*" Floyd's eyes glowed with fire just like in the bowl of his pipe. I was getting proud of Floyd. "I kind of like having young Fletcher around!"

"*Floyd!*" Mrs. McAllister was getting excited.

"He ain't been allowed to get close to the — the slut, excuse me, — the *woman* next door. We watch over him just fine, and he doesn't take much to feed. And he helps me a lot, and *he can go off to school and he doesn't have to be hauled off anywhere, and that's final!*"

Floyd puffed furiously on his pipe. I know Floyd's winning method will best the argument. I just know, because it always works with Mrs. McAllister. I had a question, but didn't want to interrupt the interesting talking. *How come nobody is asking me or looking at me? I'm the one they're arguing about.*

"*Watch your language in front of the child!*" Mrs. McAllister snapped at Floyd angrily. I sat down on a chair and watched everything and tried not to listen, but some got in my ears anyway. *And I'm not a child either. I hate being talked about and called a child.*

"*Language?* Well — she is a slut and I don't mind saying so, and if I go to hell for it, you remember that *hell's a state of mind*, woman, and it's mostly from *your* state of mind!" Floyd exclaimed loudly. Mrs. Zeban's face started to get red just like my ears. "And just so you know, *Fletcher knows what that means.*"

As they argued Mrs. Zeban looked back and forth from one to the other like a kitten watching a clock pendulum that goes back and forth while it's ticking. I fiddled with my cap. The ticking gets louder in my ears, and I can see the kitten jumping back and forth after the shiny thing. The little white paws almost catch it, but it keeps getting away. Shiny things are usually slippery, but slippery things aren't *always* shiny. I thought about it. Take for instance mud. It doesn't always shine, but it's always slippery. It pays to think hard about things. That's what Floyd said, and I always do what Floyd says.

Mrs. Zeban undid the red snaps on the folder again. They sounded loud. The kitten and the mud went away. She pulled out a paper. She spoke like her voice was stretched too tight. She cleared her throat first and blinked again and looked at me and then went to look out through the screened door into the dark for a minute. She turned to face Floyd.

"I didn't want to have it come to this, Mr. McAllister," Mrs. Zeban finally said.

Floyd puffed furiously. She opened up her file folder snaps and pulled out a piece of paper with a lot of writing on it. It looked just like old Judge Bending's walking paper from Morgan County and I wondered if Mrs. Zeban wrote it herself like the judge did.

"This is a court order, Mr. McAllister. It's not just county policy, it's provincial policy, *it's the law*, Mr. McAllister...whether you like it or not!" Her hand shook. She fiddled with the empty teacup.

"With the abuse, and the improprieties next door that were reported..." She looked at Mrs. McAllister and dropped her voice almost to a whisper and glanced at me to see if I was listening. *"There's not much choice, it was reported,"* she said.

"And who the hell reported that, may I ask?" Floyd demanded. He looked at Mrs. McAllister and raised his eyebrows, his face looking like an angry storm cloud.

Mrs. Zeban looked at Mrs. McAllister and said nothing. She looked back at Floyd. "That's privileged information, I cannot tell you that, but *the boy has to be moved*. You know we have no choice." I heard her say. "He's officially abandoned; it's almost eighteen months, Mr. McAllister. He's a ward of the department now. There's a *procedure*, Mr. McAllister, we have to go through official channels!"

I'm not abandoned, I said to myself and rubbed my nose pretty hard. Floyd said so. "The boy's not abandoned, Mrs. Zeban, not by any means!" Mrs. McAllister interrupted him.

"Floyd, listen to reason for God's sake!" Mrs. McAllister's face was all red. She pleaded with him.

"He can't stay here with *that* going on next door, for God's sake!" She pointed to my father's house. "The boy's father..."

> *I knew what she meant. I'm only seven, but I know. My father sucking Tina McQueeny's tits every night and drinking whiskey, a new bottle every night, tits and whiskey, tits and whiskey, suck them both and get real frisky. That's what Archie McKinley said when I told him, and he laughed and I laughed and we said tits are funny and whiskey tastes horrible, but no matter, you can't fool me now that I'm seven. I know. My father wants her and doesn't want me anymore. He doesn't want me at all. Maybe that's because I saw them doing it but maybe that's not it because I did it too, the time Mrs. McAllister slapped Tina McQueeny. I know my mother wouldn't care to hear about that, but I think she already knows about it and maybe that's why I heard her talking and that's why my fingers always smell funny.*

"That *shouldn't* make any difference at all; Fletcher already knows what is going on, *what difference can it make now?* Moving him around now is only going to make things worse for him, not better, so I don't care if I get in trouble with the law or not, this is not right and you know it, — both of you."

"*It's the law,* Mr. McAllister," Mrs. Zeban said firmly. She closed her file. She looked at Mrs. McAllister and then at Floyd. She lowered her voice and sounded like a Sunday-school teacher that time. "I'm sure that other arrangements can be made later, perhaps we could make a temporary arrangement of some kind, but I'll have to look into it for you. If you would allow me to—maybe we could get *visitation* for you and Mrs. McAllister, but he has to go to the home *today, I have to take him with me now.*"

"She's right, Floyd," Mrs. McAllister said gently, "We can make arrangements of some kind, can we not?" Mrs. McAllister smiled at me and nodded.

"I'm so sorry dear, I know how you feel," Mrs. McAllister said quietly.

"It's okay, Floyd..." I said, but I almost choked. Floyd was shaking and clamped his teeth down on his pipe and his mouth went a little bit crooked. He blinked pretty hard and spun his chair away from us. Mrs. Zeban and Mrs. McAllister looked at each other. I didn't look at Mrs. Zeban again until later. I sat down on a chair and closed my eyes hard. I wished I was *eight*.

Thirteen

My dormitory is on the second floor. There are sixteen beds in one room, all in a row. The floors are yellow wood that is hard and hurts when you fall down on it. It was slippery as mud yesterday again. It is always slippery when the cleaning man waxes it once a month, and we run fast down the hallway and slide as far as we can on it when nobody is looking, but the cleaning man likes us and he whispered to us that he doesn't mind us sliding on it, because he says it polishes that floor better than any scrubbing machine could ever do and he doesn't have to work so hard. But he's only there on Wednesdays, so we get scolded and thrashed and have to do *slops* if we get caught working hard polishing the floor, especially if we're having fun and making noise doing it.

There is a big dining room with eleven tables, and everyone has to stand up and sit down at exactly the same time. The older boys have to take care of the younger boys like me, to make sure we get to the dining room on time for breakfast.

We had porridge first thing in the morning but I wanted sugar on mine, and there wasn't any left by the time the bowl got to me because I am the newest boy, and I have to sit on the end of the table furthest from the sugar bowl. I cried. Jack scraped some off of his porridge and gave it to me and said, "Don't cry, Fletcher." I hate porridge with no sugar. It's worse than sour lemonade. I want to go back and live with Floyd. At Floyd's place we always have sugar in our porridge, and if there is only a little bit left in the sugar bowl, Floyd always gives it to me. I love Floyd. I want to go back and live with him and Mrs. McAllister, even if she scrubs my ears too hard. I never had biscuits and stew with gravy like hers, not even once, *never even once* since I got hauled away from Floyd's like a sack of green cabbages.

Mrs. McAllister gave me a hug and then seemed to want to hold onto me for a long time, the night Mrs. Zeban took me away and brought me to the Waterland Home for Boys. *I'm not an orphan,* but they brought me here anyway, and I told all the other boys first thing that I wasn't an orphan. I just said that Mrs. Zeban had to bring me here because my father decided to suck Tina McQueeny's tits every night instead of taking extra good care of me. The boys laughed, and sang *teeny, mackweeny, wanna pull-a-weeny,* and I didn't even tell them about *that* part yet. I don't know how they heard about it, but it sounded funny, so I sang it right out loud, and laughed with them too.

I didn't tell them anything else about the day of the funeral or even what happened after. It wasn't any of their business, and Floyd told me you should always mind your own business: So I did. He winked at me when he said it, too, right there on the back porch while we were swatting mosquitoes, so I *knew* the business he was talking about.

I wished I had never told them about anything, but after a few weeks everybody forgot about it anyway.

Mrs. McAllister held on to me tightly, and then she cried a little bit too. When I went away I thought she was inspecting my ears in advance for next month, so I pushed her away and went with Mrs. Zeban. I didn't like that, but she always inspected my ears, every night, even the first night that Floyd found me in the woodshed, and she scrubbed them a lot harder than I cared for.

Mrs. McAllister cried and honked like a goose when she blew her nose. She used her apron that time. Mrs. Zeban stayed at the door and pretended not to see us crying. Even Floyd cried. I never saw Floyd crying any other time except that one. He told me one time he cried when he woke up and found his legs were all gone and the nurse told him he'd better get used to it. She said *amputees got no choice about it whatsoever, so get used to it, Jack.* Floyd said she was worse than a drill sergeant.

Floyd gave me a hug and kissed my neck, and I never got kissed on the neck yet except by my mother. His whiskers tickled. "It'll be okay, son, you go along with her...I'm getting you back here soon as the law lets me. We'll see you soon!" I saw Floyd push his glasses back up on his nose. His eyes were full of tears.

I got into the old black Chevy in the front seat with Mrs. Zeban, and she started it on the first try. My father's old Pontiac never started on the first try, and sometimes my father had to get out and crank it. Most of the time it wouldn't go at all because either the battery died or the motor has water in it or maybe the gasoline got stolen by some punks. When that happened, he always got mad and hit me or my mother that's dead now.

I don't think I hate him too much, except for his hitting my mother.

We went all the way to the other side of Waters County. I think it was at least a thousand miles, farther than here to Regina or even the next county before we stopped. I looked in the back seat to see if there was anything interesting to look at, or something that somebody forgot last time, or any mouse nests, but it was too dark to see. Mrs. Zeban said it was a long way, more than forty miles, and we had to stop for gasoline. It cost a dollar and ninety-seven cents, and Mrs. Zeban got a tea-cup with roses on it free. The gas man said she had to make *two* bucks worth of gas before she could get the saucer to go with it.

"I've got the three cents right here in the ashtray," she said to him.

"Oh, no matter, we don't do that, company policy, ma'am," the attendant said.

"That figures," Mrs. Zeban said and I knew she was mad. The roses on the cup were pretty. I held it carefully for Mrs. Zeban, so it wouldn't get broken like my mother's dishes. She said I was a responsible boy, no wonder Floyd wanted to keep me, so I told her

92

that I didn't mind if she turned around right away and took me back. She didn't.

The sign in front of the building had lots of lights on. I know how to read. The sign said "**Waterland Home for Orphan Boys**", and I knew I wasn't an orphan and wouldn't get out of the car but Mrs. Zeban made me. I was scared, but Mrs. Zeban put her arm around my shoulder and said *be a brave boy* and that she would let me ring the big shiny brass bell by the gate. I thought that was all right and got out of the car. I noticed she smelled like mothballs when I followed her. My mother had mothballs in the old wooden trunk with the wedding dress and old pictures, but everything got mixed up, so I blinked hard and I pretended it didn't matter, but I know it did and I might have hated my father for doing that, and it made me sad.

I grabbed the scratch rope and rang the bell loud enough for God to hear. A light came on outside the building and a door slammed.

"Who's there?" A door slammed. "I say *who's there!*" an angry voice shouted from up at the home. "Stop the damned bleeding racket now. Stop ringing the bleeding bell! You'll be waking up the world, won't you now?" A tall man yelled angrily at us as he came around the corner of the building. "*Stop ringing that damned bell!*"

I stopped ringing the bell right away. Mrs. Zeban put her hand on my shoulder.

The man came to the gate and unlocked it with a key. He smelled like whiskey just like my father did, not nice like Floyd's pipe tobacco. He glared and squinted at me.

"Oh, it's you —evening, ma'am!" he finally said.

He was as tall as my father, but not as tall as Floyd before the doctor chopped his legs off with the hacksaw. His black shirt and trousers made him look scary in the darkness and through the bars of the gate the light made stripes. He looked like he was in jail when he looked through the bars. I feel like I'm going to jail too. I hope there are escape bags available. I hung onto my tweed cap tightly.

"Another young lad, I'll be! Is there no end to them?"

He looked at me like he was going to weigh me and sell me for bait. He had a shiny steel tooth. I didn't want to go with him, but Mrs. Zeban said I had to. I wish I was still at Floyd's on the back porch smelling Floyd's pipe tobacco. I even prefer getting my ears scrubbed by Mrs. McAllister with brown lye soap.

I hung onto my brown tweed cap with my sweaty hands and waited for the man to say he didn't have any room for me, and I'd have to go back to Floyd's and live there the rest of my life and eat gravy and dumplings and test drive Floyd's chair around the kitchen when he wasn't using it, and puff on Floyd's pipe a bit, but only when Mrs. McAllister wasn't looking, because me and Floyd use the smoke to chase mosquitoes away on the porch.

I waited, but the man didn't say it. Instead, he held out his hand. I thought he was going to pull me through the gate without opening it, so I didn't want to shake hands.

"So who's *this* fine lad, here?" he asked, but I still didn't shake hands. I think it's a trap. They always want you to reach through the gate and when they get hold of you they never let go.

Mrs. Zeban gave the man some papers out of her folder and snapped the red snaps tightly on it again.

"It's the Williams boy from Waterland—his real name, not like most of them," she smiled at me, then back at the man. He was still holding his hand out through the bars. She frowned at me and nudged me toward the jailer. "The one I called you about yesterday."

"He's the boy what's been dallying next door," the man said. *"Poor lad, he'll be safe with us now."*

"Yes —say hello to *Mr. Tupper*, Fletcher!"

I said, "Hello, sir," and then I clammed up.

The gate clanked open and the man looked like he was coming to get me when he stepped into the light. "He's legally *abandoned*, Mr. Tupper, a ward of the court, and you'll be getting your check next week from the office." He held out his hand like a waiter getting money.

She backed away quickly. "In the mail...like usual, Mr. Tupper," she added, watching him carefully.

The man smiled deviously and rubbed his hands together. "Very well, ma'am, it's a genuine pleasure doing *business* with you, Mrs. Zeban."

He put me inside the gate before Mrs. Zeban had a chance to hug me or anything. That was okay because she smelled like mothballs anyway, and I didn't want her to hug me or anything. If you get hugged by old ladies you start smelling like moth balls, too.

"It's always a pleasure doing business with you, too."

That's what the *Watkins* man said to my mother when she paid him for the stinky ointment. Now, I remember what she smelled like, that's what Mrs. Zeban smelled like, *Watkins* ointment, not only mothballs. *Now I remember.*

"You get along now; he'll be fine here, won't he!"

"I do hope so, Mr. Tupper," she said politely.

"Fletcher, you be a good boy now, we'll see you again, I'm sure," she patted me on the head.

"The lad will be just fine here, Missus," he said. "We take good care of our boys here," he said.

"Good evening then," she said and smiled at me when she finally turned away and left me trapped on the wrong side of the gate. The Chevy chugged off into the dark with only one headlight. Maybe it would be better if Mrs. Zeban stays here too. No wonder I feel like bait. I am. That's the way I feel. Bait. Just waiting for a big fish to eat me and chew me up with pointy steel teeth. Like Tina McQueeny. If I'm lucky I'll get spit out like Jonah did when he got in the whale. I wonder if whales have shiny steel teeth like Mr. Tupper? I don't think so.

"Come along then, no time to waste, boy!" Mr. Tupper sounded crabby.

"Mrs. Zeban should know better than this, she shouldn't be showing up so late, disturbing all the others, so get a move on, we'll get you up to bed right now, this is your new home!"

We walked through the dark and into the home. It had a big hallway and a desk and dark hallways with all of the lights turned off, and Mr. Tupper said I have to call it a home, not an orphanage, and that suits me just fine because I'm not an orphan anyway.

"I'm staying here tonight and Floyd's coming to get me home tomorrow," I told Mr. Tupper, and it sounded loud and echoed in the empty hallway.

"Yes, I'm sure, he's coming for all of the other boys too," he sneered.

"Floyd will come and get me, you'll see!" I said.

"Shush boy, you'll be staying with us long as they pay the bill, makes no difference to me if your Floyd is foolish enough to take on a dozen brats or not."

"Floyd will get me, you'll see," I said.

Mr. Tupper hushed me quiet, walked me up some creaky stairs and put pajamas on me that he got out of a closet that were too big for me but smelled pretty nice. Then he patted me right on the bum a couple of times and stuffed me into a tin bed with a grey-striped blanket and squeaky springs. He stood in the dark and looked at me for a minute, then turned away.

"Go to sleep now!" he gruffed at me.

Fourteen

I didn't like Mr. Tupper, not even a little bit. I'm going to keep my eyes open a long time and figure out how I can escape. I looked around in the dark after he left but all the other boys were sleeping in rows of beds, same as mine, and I didn't see their faces until the morning. Then I wished I *didn't* see them. I opened up my eyes and saw about a hundred eyes staring at me. *They* are orphans, I said to myself. They were all skinny boys. "What's your name?" one boy asked.

"When did you get here?" another one asked. I thought he sounded fine enough.

"I'm not here, I'm at Floyd's," I said. They all laughed.

"Who's Floyd?" Another asked.

"He's coming to get me right now," I said. They laughed again.

"Yeah, Santa Claus and the Easter Rabbit are both coming to get all of us right now," somebody said.

"He is, you'll see!" I said. "What are you all gawking at?" I asked them as bossy as possible, and I covered up my head. When you're the boss, nobody is supposed to gawk at you.

They stood around looking at me like I was a food display or something, and didn't talk loud enough for me to hear. I pulled the blankets over my head again and didn't come out, until Mr. Tupper brought a big boy that was already dressed, to see me.

97

Raymond Alexander Kukkee

"He's in your charge, Jack. You'll see to 'im from now on." Mr. Tupper disappeared down a long hallway.

After he was out of sight the boys laughed. "He's gone," Jack whispered, and stuck his tongue out and stuck his thumbs in his ears and waved bye-bye to Mr. Tupper who wasn't there anymore. The boys all laughed, and so did I.

"Hello, Jack," I said.

"Nice to meet you, Fletcher," he said, and covered my head up with the blankets and laughed out loud. "Okay boys; get a move on, *chop-chop!* Get dressed Mrs. Tickner doesn't want you to be late for breakfast!" Jack said. He tapped on the blankets and shook me a bit. "*Hey, you,* come out of there. I want to take you to meet Mrs. Tickner, you'll like *her!*"

I liked Jack Whittaker right away because he searches under the blankets until he finds you and tickles you until you laugh. He won't pull the blankets off until you agree that only scared rabbits and mushrooms live in dark holes. The first time he stuck his head under the blanket to find out where I was. I was in there, but I was planning to go to Texas.

"You're going to turn white as a mushroom if you stay under here!" he said. He got under the blanket with me, and we played soldiers in foxholes. "Okay soldier, we have to march to the mess hall right away before the grub is all gone!" he said.

"Floyd was a soldier," I said to Jack.

"We're all soldiers sometimes," Jack said, "and I'm getting hungry in this foxhole!" He made a funny mushroom face, and I laughed when he tickled me. We let in a little bit of light under the blanket, so I wouldn't turn too white; then, we got up and dressed and had to go to the kitchen for porridge because everybody else ate already.

Mrs. Tickner wasn't very happy we were latecomers; she said "Latecomers again! You're late this morning, boys!" She rattled some dishes and turned to look me over.

98

"Just so long as you don't do it again, Jack, me boy!" She scolded Jack and sounded just like Mrs. McAllister.

"*Dear* Mrs. Tickner, however do you survive without us being late *once in a while?*" Jack teased her. She swatted him with a tea towel. He didn't tease her after that. That's because, after that, we were always on time. Jack is fourteen. He told me. "She's not so bad, you'll see!" Jack winked at me.

"Fletcher Williams, *eh?*" she looked me up and down and scrambled around the kitchen, looking for something.

Jack winked again. He was right. I ended up liking Mrs. Tickner because she gave me some canned peaches to go on top of my porridge the first morning. I never had canned peaches before.

"You eat them," Jack explained to me when I looked at the wedge-shaped, slippery yellow things sitting in the bottom of the bowl. I tasted them carefully. You can get poisoned to death if you taste poison things a whole lot at once.

Mrs. Tickner raised her eyebrows and looked at Jack, and then clucked loud just like a mother chicken, and pushed the bowl closer to me. I knew chicken noises because Archie McKinley's mother had some in a big cage in the back yard.

"Eat them, they're good for you!" she said. "—Special treat for a new boy, only once, you understand!" said Mrs. Tickner, looking at Jack menacingly. I stopped thinking about Archie McKinley's chickens and tasted the peaches again. I like canned peaches. I tried not to eat them too fast because I found out I liked them quite a bit, and discovered they slide down your throat by accident even if you don't chew them. Jack sat patiently while I ate, and didn't even try to grab any peaches from me, but he admired them quite a bit. Maybe that was because Mrs. Tickner watched him like a hawk, and she had the big wooden spoon from the porridge pot ready to whack him on the head. She gave Jack a cup of tea.

"Don't go telling Mr. Tupper about these peaches, now, will you?" She warned Jack and me, or maybe it was just me, because I ate them.

I never did get a chance to figure that one out, but Jack winked at her just like Floyd used to wink at me. I can wink with both eyes. I wonder what they were winking about. I winked back at Jack. He laughed. I like Jack and peaches and Mrs. Tickner, too.

Jack told me, while we were bed-making, that Mrs. Tickner gave him peaches the first day *he* got to the orphanage, too. Jack said Mrs. Tickner was Mr. Tupper's sister that got married, and that's why her name is different, but her husband got killed in the war by a German bomb that whistled loud; and then the whole place got blew to smithereens when she was at the market getting potatoes and spinach. All because of that, she was homeless and she had to live somewhere, so after the war she got on a ship and cooked herself all the way to Canada and found out she liked cooking all right; so she got a job to cook food at the orphanage, and lived in the pantry between the bags of oatmeal and potatoes.

Mrs. Tickner said she likes me, and I like her too. So do all the rest of the boys. I even remembered to say I liked her and that it was too bad her husband got killed by the bomb. That was when I got kitchen duty for a week to scrape the plates and get the *slops* out to the hogs.

"I'm sorry to hear your husband got killed by the bomb, and you had a hard time, and had to set sail across the whole world just to be a cook for Mr. Tupper," I said.

"Oh, Fletcher" she said. She stopped working and looked at me for a pretty long minute. She looked like she wanted to say something. Her eyes got shiny, but then she just laughed. "It's been so long ago that...I don't think about it much anymore." She reached up on a shelf and got a big mixing pan. "It was a long time ago." She was thinking out loud. "Besides..." she said, "now I have more *men* than I know what to do with!" She reached over and ruffled my hair backwards.

I hate that. People rubbing your hair off, except when my mother did it. That's why I liked wearing my brown tweed cap and that's why I got kitchen duty, because I wouldn't take my cap off at the dinner table, and Mr. Tupper grabbed it off of my head and put it in the high cupboard where I couldn't reach it.

"That'll be teaching you to wear your cap at the table, young man!" he shouted at me. I looked at the other boys, and they grinned and made noises like a whole flock of hungry McKinley chickens, and Mr. Tupper got bright red in the face and hit the table with his wooden yardstick and said *that wasn't* funny and hit some other boys on the head. One of the smaller boys started to cry.

"What's so bleedin' funny?" he screamed at everyone. "No hats are to be worn in this bleedin' dining room!" he shouted loudly.

"Yes, Mr. Tupper, *kind sir*," I said. The other boys split their Sunday-school faces and laughed out loud. Mr. Tupper got mad.

"Bein' a bleedin' smart ass, *you, boy —Williams?*" he swore. *"I'll teach you respect, boy!"* He said angrily, and clanked me right on the head with the yardstick. It stung, and I got tears in my eyes. I didn't laugh anymore.

He gave me kitchen duty every day for a week because I made them laugh. I learned how to clam up that time.

Jack sneaked my cap back to me one night but made me put it under my mattress and hide it. I'm going to run away and never come back if that ever happens again. *Right back to Floyd's.* As soon as I can figure out how to get there, but first I decided that I'm going to help Mrs. Tickner a lot. I stayed in the kitchen every day and worked.

I saw her start mixing stuff right away and looking quite like my mother sometimes, so I clammed up while I scraped dishes. She didn't look at me for a little while. Then, I tried telling her I was sorry about her husband again.

"You are a good boy, aren't you?" she said thoughtfully. She became quiet again and even if I waited quite a while, she didn't say a single word after that so I hauled the slops out and bombed them into the hogs' trough.

I told the pigs they were in jail just like me, and they grunted at each other and pushed and squealed loudly to get at the slops. They reminded me of Mr. Tupper, but I better not tell him that. The pigs seem to be in a big hurry to get fat and go to the bacon factory. Jack said that Morton and Bomber were already in *bacon heaven* for more than a month. Jack had names for all of the pigs, even the one that looked like Mr. Tupper. He called it *"Tupper the Terror"*. I laughed when Jack told me that and told Jack that T.T. didn't have any silver teeth. Jack laughed back. He said I was right.

"Maybe he'll get some in bacon heaven" I said. Jack laughed loudly.

I'm getting to be just like Floyd and Jack, too. I was *right*.

Fifteen

The other boys didn't care to spend time with Mrs. Tickner even if she was a good cook. They said she was really a miserable old lady pretending to be a good cook and that sooner or later she would cook us all in the big oven and feed us to Mr. Tupper for supper in his office with the shiny oak desk and brass clock, so they preferred to play baseball or something. Jack says they just say that to scare the new boys.

They were wrong. She is always nice to me. She gave me peaches one time when nobody was looking, and I wasn't even the littlest boy any more. Joe Coleman and Eddie Peters and Ronnie Gates and Marvin Pychinsky that came to live here after me were assorted sizes but *they* weren't the littlest. Murvie Klinder was the *littlest*. He came here six months after I did, and right after Eddie.

Murvie wears thick glasses and his face is too white and his hair is missing in spots. He looks like a mushroom from being sick. Mrs. Zeban brought *him* too. I remember it was her that brought him that time because she said "Hello, Fletcher, how are you doing?" I wanted to ask her if she got the saucer for the tea-cup with roses, but I didn't get to talk to her because Mr. Tupper jostled me away. The sky had black clouds, and it was cold and windy, and Mrs. Zeban held her collar over her almond-colored neck.

"Get along, boy!" he ordered me with a mean look. "Ain't you got your chores to do? Get back to helping Mrs. Tickner now, before she skins you alive."

I went away, but I heard him ask her for the money for taking in Murvie before I got around the corner. I waited and listened, and I think it was wrong to try and hear it but I did anyway.

"We're an orphanage here, not a damned hospital, woman!" he said.

"It won't be for long, will it?" Mrs. Zeban snapped back at him. She stopped talking for a minute, and her voice was so quiet I almost couldn't hear what she told him. "We have no choice. The parents won't... They've been dealing with it too long. They've split, the mother's run off, and they can't deal with it. They know that he—"

"—Well, you people better pay this one up front then, won't you?" I ran outside. It was raining. I knew what they were talking about. I don't know why I knew, but I did.

I had to share Jack with Murvie. That was all right because Jack is big enough to help more than one small boy. We got him a folded bed right out of the storage room and got a blanket and a rubber pillow. I never saw a rubber pillow before.

I asked Jack if I could take Murvie down to see Mrs. Tickner, and he said yes I could so if I really wanted to take the responsibility. So I did, and I did it right away all by myself.

Mrs. Tickner was peeling potatoes and making stew at the same time. She got up and washed her hands. "Another boy, Fletcher, they just keep coming, don't they? And who do we have here, Mr. Williams?" Mrs. Tickner asked me just like I was the boss.

"This is Murvie," I said. Murvie stuck his white hand out to Mrs. Tickner and wouldn't look at her. "He just got here," I said.

"Well, nice to meet you, Murvie. Let me see, are you hungry?" Murvie nodded, still not looking up from the floor. Maybe he saw a mouse or something. Mrs. Tickner scurried around and got a bowl and a spoon, and opened a tin.

She gave Murvie peaches and said *"Special treats for a new boy, only once, you know!"* to Murvie, but she winked at me and I felt big, just like Jack. I was getting big, just like Jack. Murvie said so. I like Murvie. He has a watch that loses five minutes a day and stops sometimes unless you wind it every day. Murvie keeps it on a chain in his pocket, and it's real gold. Jack said so.

"What's the matter with him?" I asked Mrs. Tickner. Murvie looked at the bowl of peaches and wouldn't touch them. "What's the matter, Murvie?" I asked him. He just looked at me and swallowed hard.

"They're good, eat 'em," I told Murvie. He didn't want to eat them, and I found out why.

Murvie doesn't like peaches, so he said I better eat them and gave them to me. Murvie told Mrs. Tickner and me that peaches don't agree with him because he has cancer, and his hair is falling out. Now, I understand why he is getting patchy bald. He said his father doesn't want him, just like mine.

"Peaches make me barf," he said.

Mrs. Tickner looked at me and said, "You can have the peaches then, Fletcher. We'll see if we have something else for Murvie." She got another bowl from the cupboard. "How about some nice chocolate pudding instead? *A special treat for a new boy, only once, you know?"* Mrs. Tickner asked Murvie. He looked at me and nodded.

"I like chocolate pudding just fine," he said to Mrs. Tickner. She got the pudding for him and gave him a spoon, and I watched him eat it and Murvie seemed to like chocolate pudding fine.

"I had peaches when *I* came," I said to Murvie. "I like 'em. They don't make *me* barf," I said.

"You don't got cancer. It hurts your stomach." Murvie said, and then clammed up.

I saw that Mrs. Tickner was crying when she turned around, and she started to wash dishes all of a sudden, and she stood at the sink like my mother does when she is fiddling with soap-water in the laundry. Mrs. Ticker's apron was wet too.

Murvie was going to say something, but when I saw that I shushed him right up, and he ate the rest of his chocolate pudding quiet as a mouse and licked the spoon clean while I ate the peaches pretty fast. Then, Murvie and I went outside and let her cry things out by herself. I told Murvie that Mrs. Tickner is probably crying privately about her dead husband and everything else, so just be nice to her and don't pay no attention to it. I showed Murvie around and told him all of the important things and introduced him to Tupper the Terror and all of the other squealers, just like Jack did.

"She cries all the time?" he asked as we threw Tupper the Terror some oats. He oinked at us. I think he was telling us *thank you*.

"Yes, she cries lots," I said. "*Thirty-seven* times a day." That was a lie. God doesn't like that, but new boys don't have to get to know *everything* right now.

"Why does she cry all the time?" Murvie asked, and threw T.T. another handful of oats. He scared off the other oinkers.

I slopped some water into the watering trough. Jack said pigs need lots of water, too. I noticed T.T. is getting bossy, so I decided to try it out too. Trying it on a new boy is fine because they don't know everything just yet.

"Never mind, you'll find out soon enough," I said, feeling superior, looking at Murvie. He didn't seem to mind right away, being sickly and all, but I don't think God liked what I said because there was some rumbling thunder, and then a flash of lightning.

"Oh," Murvie said, looking white and pale. He started to shiver. "Okay."

After a bit, I thought it would be better to tell Murvie the truth and explain things a bit better to him since he got cancer, and he promised he would swear to die if he told anyone. I said okay, and I wished after that I didn't make him promise. I showed him how to find four-leaf clovers instead, and we sat in the grass for a while.

"Her husband got bombed in the war, and all she got is us." I explained it better to Murvie as we watched the other boys playing baseball. When I showed Murvie the pigs and told him all of their names again, he remembered them all, even T.T.'s real last name. Then, I told him about the whole world and about Mr. Tupper and that he wasn't so nice all the time. Murvie wanted to know everything about Mr. Tupper, so I told him how he got his steel tooth from an old blacksmith in a welding shop, and I even started to tell him about the porkers heading off to bacon heaven just as soon as they got big enough, but just at that minute Murvie said he wanted to go in and have a rest.

We went inside right away and got a drink of water, but it was too late. He threw up the chocolate pudding all over the floor. Mrs. Tickner cleaned up after him and sat him in the kitchen and gave him some hot chicken soup.

"That's a good boy," she said to him as he tried to eat. He threw up all over the table. She cleaned the mess and put him up to bed for the rest of the day.

After a few months, I got to know him just fine. He was my best friend except for Floyd and Jack, but he got more sickly and whiter every day, and all of his hair fell out, and he had to stay in bed all the time and play with his watch and read comic books, but everyone gets tired of that sooner or later. So I told him about Tina McQueeny to make him laugh. He laughed and then grabbed his stomach and threw up. After that, he didn't smile, not even a bit. I heard him throw up more in the night. Murvie had to throw up every night right on time, and Jack had to clean up the mess.

Murvie died the next week just after lunchtime, because he didn't even touch his pea soup and had to go lay down. And then Mrs. Tickner tried to feed him some warm chicken soup and sat with him. She came down the creaky stairs slowly. Jack and Richard Bordon and Mrs. Tickner gathered us all in a straight line, and Mrs. Tickner told us right out loud that we all expected that Murvie would get tired of living and throwing up, and being bald, and now he went to heaven and wouldn't be staying with us anymore.

"You all know that Murvie has been very, very sick, boys," Mrs. Tickner said. "I know this is bad news," she said quietly. "He passed away. *He's gone to heaven. He died a few minutes ago.*" Some of the boys looked at the floor and started to cry.

"He was very ill from cancer. God loves him and will take care of him now. I know we are all going to be very sad for a while, but there's not much to be done about that, is there? So we must carry on with our lives and remember that Murvie was a fine, fine boy whose time just came, no matter how we feel about it. So, that's all, boys. I'm so sorry," Mrs. Tickner said, like she was the most tired person in the whole world. "You can go out in the yard and carry on. It's a sunny day out there, so go get some exercise. Heaven knows we don't want any more of you boys sick," she said, scatting us outside. Mrs. Tickner was right: It was sunny outside.

"He died, his stomach and guts were all gone," Jack said. "That's what happens when you get *that* kind of cancer." We sat quietly in the dry grass by the fence, away from the other boys that were making a racket and playing baseball. I never saw Jack cry before, but he was, and I was too, but I pretended I wasn't, just like he did, and we stood watching the crows getting chased and pecked at by some smaller birds.

Mr. Tupper made us stand in another straight line when the coroner came in the shiny black car to haul Murvie Klinder away. His father didn't come, just Mrs. Zeban. I think Mr. Klinder didn't like Murvie being bald. Nobody was allowed to go to the funeral the next day because Mr. Tupper got mad.

I was sad and cried, and so did Mrs. Tickner. She gave me a hug in the kitchen after a bit and opened a can of peaches.

"No matter what anyone tells you, it's okay to cry about people you love. It's okay" she said quietly. She put her arms around me and squeezed. "*It's okay.*" she whispered.

I told Mrs. Tickner that I don't think I love Murvie, but he was my best friend, and I didn't think about it too much just yet, so I'm not sure. He had a good idea about getting to Texas and being a cowboy, bald or not, so I guess he was all right. He asked me if I had a watch one time but I said no, so he let me try his on my belt a couple of times and even let me put it in my pocket and look at it. I know how to tell time on Murvie's watch, and Mrs. Tickner helps me tell time on the clock in the kitchen. Mrs. Tickner said that Murvie didn't have too much time when he came, and I said he had a lot of time because he had a gold watch. Mrs. Tickner said that wasn't what she meant. "I meant that Murvie was very sick and close to dying when he came, son."

I said, "Oh," and a piece of peach slipped down my throat. I like peaches even if Murvie didn't. *I don't like chocolate pudding much anymore.*

I dried dishes for Mrs. Tickner and took out the slops to feed Tupper the Terror and the other porkers that didn't know that Murvie died even though they got to eat his pea soup. T. T. Oinker squealed and pushed the other pigs away. I said, "Don't do that!" but he didn't pay any attention. I whacked him with a stick, and he oinked. I don't think I should have whacked T.T. Oinker that time.

I finished the slops and went out and sat on the slippery buffalo grass. I didn't want to cry, but I thought about my Mother and the freight train and William Yakafluic and God and dust balls, but my father charged into my thinking, and I had to cry quite a bit more no matter what I did before I went to sleep that night.

A couple of days later after the funeral, I nearly choked. Mrs. Tickner was telling me stories about when she was a girl and her mother died when she was nine and she had to go live with her crabby Aunt Lily in Dorchester. The door in the dining room banged hard. I slid the peaches down pretty fast. She whispered that Mr. Tupper was coming down the hall, and I'd better pretend I'm busy or else, even if it was only a couple days since they hauled Murvie away.

The swinging door slammed hard against the wall, and Mr. Tupper charged into the kitchen like a mad bull.

"And what's going on here, then?" He demanded. "What's he doing here?"

Mrs. Tickner looked at me like she was going to get hit, but she stood still, brave as a bullfighter and didn't back up. She had the big wooden spoon in her hand, the same one she was going to crack Jack on the head with back in the days when I was the newest boy and if he snitched my peaches.

"Cat got your tongue, *Eileen?*" That was the first time I found out what Mrs. Tickner's first name was. I bet I'm the only boy that knows that her name is Eileen.

"What's he doing here? Why is he not outside with the other brats!? He growled again.

"As usual, Albert, just the usual, like every day, he's one of the good boys that does the slops every day without being told. Don't they have to go out, the slops?" she replied.

"See he does a right proper job of it then, and don't be giving him any favors!" He leaned toward me and his shiny, steel tooth made me stare at it, just like when he was going to sell me for bait. I dropped the spatula and the cracked plate I was holding, and it would have been his fault, if it broke, I bet.

"Awful clumsy and slow, ain't he?" Mr. Tupper glared at me. He was wearing his horn, black glasses and his short fat fingers yanked at the collar of his shirt. His scratchy black suit looked like the funeral clothes the visitors wore to our house at Waterland. His eyes were red and so was his nose, and he smelled like whiskey, just like my father. He got closer. I backed away. He picked up the bowl that had my peaches in it and an ugly black storm cloud crossed his face. He turned to Mrs. Tickner.

"*What's this, then? Peaches, eh?* Ya been givin' 'im *my* peaches, eh?! I said no treats and favors unless I authorize it, now, didn't I? Never learn, do you, Eileen?"

I said *oh-oh* to myself.

"It's bad enough we have to feed the brats and bury them and not make a damned penny, too, isn't it? Without you givin 'em my choice bits for treats, too!" He leaned over me. The veins stood out on his red neck, and it looked like he was going to bite me with his shiny, steel tooth. "Treats are *earned*, Eileen, it's time you learned that!' He walked over to me and breathed whiskey breath on me.

"You, boy, you bleedin' brat, get out of here this instant!" I backed up.

"You'll leave the boy alone, Albert!" Mrs. Tickner said firmly. She pushed him away and moved between Mr. Tupper and me with her big wooden spoon. She must have whacked him before or something because he just looked at her and turned around and started to the door. He stopped and pointed at me and shouted angrily

"You never learn, do you? You always have to have a favorite, don't you?" He snarled. "Well, that one will be leaving, too, just like the Klinder brat!" at Mrs. Tickner. He pushed his lips together into a tight, skinny line that was all white. He kicked his way out the door, and it swung back and forth making a screechy, wonky noise. Mrs. Tickner followed him out the door, yelling at him. Maybe she whacked him with the spoon because they had a terrible argument. I didn't see it because it isn't my business, and I put my hands over my ears and ran outside fast.

I stood by the iron fence in the back yard and wished I was back at Floyd's. The other boys were playing a game of baseball and yelling and screeching the same as Mrs. Tickner and Mr. Tupper. I tried not to hear it, and looked up at the sun to see if my mother and God were talking to Murvie yet, or whispering. I didn't hear anything up there even though I listened hard as possible. I looked through the droopy wire squares on the fence and wondered how far it is to Waterland. If I had the old Pontiac I could pump up the tires and get a gallon of gas in a tin pail and drive there. I would go fifty miles an hour with the windows wide open and let the air in and be a man of the world. Me and Murvie—and Jack. Maybe we would even rescue Tupper the Terror and the other porkers from going to bacon heaven. We could keep 'em in the red mud in Floyd's back yard and feed 'em weeds from the garden and stale biscuits.

Jack came up behind me suddenly, and it made me jump. He tickled me a lot, but I didn't laugh until he made a funny face. He threw me down in the long grass, and we had a wrestling match on the slippery buffalo grass.

Jack lets me win. I sit on his stomach and bounce up and down until he makes me stop, then I tickle him. I picked a horse-tail and tickled under his nose with it, and it made him sneeze. He stuck his tongue out, and I tried to grab it, but he put it away before I could catch it. I tried a couple more times but never had any luck. Then, he wouldn't open his mouth anymore.

111

"That's enough, Fetch!" He tried to throw me off, but I hung onto his belt for dear life and pretended I was a cowboy on a bucking horse in Texas and the world champion rodeo rider. I got tired and fell off.

I rolled over on the grass and chewed on a straw and put my hands behind my head just like Jack. I squinted into the clouds. They looked like animals and changed into faces and trees and lakes. "Jack," I said, "did you know that Mr. Tupper is going to send me away?" He must have thought my face was sad because he sat up right away and spit out the straw he was chewing on. He stayed quiet for a minute and stared into the sky. "Mr. Tupper doesn't like me because I ate his peaches, and he says that I'm Mrs. Tickner's favorite".

Jack turned his face to me but didn't look right at me right away like wise people seem to do all the time. Like Floyd. Jack stayed quiet for a long time and didn't want to talk or wrestle on the buffalo grass. He told me to leave him alone, so I told him "It's okay, Jack." I kept quiet with Jack.

Jack always has the answers to my questions. That's because I'm his charge, and he *has to* take care of me, that's what Mr. Tupper said the first day. I'm glad Jack's in charge of me instead of Arnold Thackery or Richard Bordon. They're big boys like Jack, and they seem to be all right, at least that's what Elton and Dickie told me, but I said *Jack's better*.

Elton and Dickie are the newest boys that came a few days after Murvie got hauled off. They both came at the same time because they are twins and both nine years old, and their parents got killed in a plane crash in Halifax. They were brought to the orphanage on a black day that got windy and rainy, not at night like I was.

Mr. Tupper told Jack that he better let Arnold Thackery and Richard Bordon help him take good care of Elton and Dickie, not Jack by himself, because Jack didn't take good enough care of Murvie that's dead now. "Just you make sure these two don't die like the other brat!" Mr. Tupper yelled at Jack.

I remember that day they came because we stopped playing baseball and ran to the fence and stood in a line to watch when we saw the car stop at the bottom of the hill. The two boys were being dragged toward the gate by their Aunt Sally that was bigger than an oatmeal factory, and she chugged herself up the hill dragging them and she turned steaming red like the boiled lobster I saw in a book one time. She didn't let them ring the bell, not even once.

She shoved the boys through the gate and rang the bell herself and didn't even give them a hug. We ran to the gate in the wind and the rain and all the boys had just started to tell the new boys our names and welcome them, but Mr. Tupper ran over and swore at us and made us go away.

"You get in out of the rain, you bleeding' dough heads!" he screamed.

"Where the hell do you think *you're* going, you *bitch?*" He shouted after the red-faced woman.

He held onto the twins by the ears and shouted again. *"Come back here, damn you!"* at the fat lady as she ran away to the car. She didn't look back. She dusted herself off and climbed into the car without even looking. The rusty car took off in a cloud of blue smoke. *"I'll have the law on you!"* Mr. Tupper screamed after her. The car didn't stop and the thunder started and it was raining hard.

Elton tried to kick Mr. Tupper's knee, but his legs were too short. Mr. Tupper gave his ear a hard twist. That made Elton yell, so he gave them both twisted ears for good measure.

"What are you all looking at?" he screamed at us. "I told you brats to get along! Get out of the rain, you want to get sick and die too?" he raged. We ran inside and got out of the way.

He dragged the twins into his office by himself and told them they had to sleep in the same bed and share food for one because they were a sad case, and nobody was going to pay him anything for so many extra useless boys, especially two at a time.

"Double nothing's still nothing, ain't it?" he said to them. "Double trouble, that's it, ain't it?" He made Richard Bordon and Arnold Thackery look after them.

They told me a few weeks later that the fat woman wasn't really their aunt, just their old neighbor, and their Uncle Cornelius and Aunt

Beatrice in Halifax didn't want them either, just like Murvie's father that didn't want him because he was going bald and had cancer and couldn't eat, and when he did he threw up all the time making messes on the bed and the floor. That must be when he told Murvie he couldn't stand it anymore, maybe while he was mopping and cleaning up the puke.

I asked the twins if they minded living in an orphanage, and they said they didn't really mind if it was just for a little while because they were going to run away to Texas. They said cowboys sleep on the prairie and learn to yodel to the cows as soon as they get escaped from all the orphanages.

I said I'd go with them and show them the way to Texas and show them how to ride bucking broncos too, but they said no I'm too little and won't let me. I wish I was nine *like them*. I'd like to be a cowboy. Thinking about being a cowboy made me pretty near as happy as the time Floyd came to visit me but I'll get to that after.

I told Elton and Dickie that if they weren't going to let me be a cowboy with them I'd take Murvie with me so there, but they laughed and said there aren't any bald cowboys in Texas. I said there was so, but we had to go slop the hogs so I didn't have time to prove it. Murvie died and got himself plunked in a potter's grave, so it was too late for him to be a cowboy anyplace, except in *cancer hell* like Dickie said.

I poked him hard with a sharp stick, the one we hook the pail out of the slops with. "I'm going to get Jack! *He'll pound you good!*" I shouted at him, but Dickie stuck his tongue out so I threw slops at him. I think it served him right, and Elton laughed at him, too. Now I don't have to prove it, either.

Jack sneezed again from the dust in the buffalo grass. Jack always sneezed, and sometimes he said *yahoo* just after a big sneeze. I think cowboys say *yahoo* a lot, so it's a good idea to practice if you want to be a cowboy sometime. I thought about asking Jack to go to Texas with me since Murvie got himself in a potter's grave and can't go anywhere now, but he said he's going to be a doctor or an insurance salesman, not a cowboy. I don't care about that; Jack's still my best friend even if he doesn't want to be a cowboy. Jack said cowboys eat too many beans and they give you gas, and he proved it just then, too. He made a bad noise and I laughed. *"See?"* he said.

I told Jack maybe I'll be a doctor too. I bet if Jack and I were doctors we could have fixed Murvie. Jack didn't even seem to mind cleaning up when Murvie barfed all over the dining room floor and the barf had blood in it.

"Remember that, Fetch, it had blood in it?"

Jack said he didn't ask me to go tell Mrs. Tickner because she was busy in the kitchen, and it would just make her worry even more, and maybe she would get sick if she saw that mess on the chair and on the floor. And we shouldn't bother telling anyone else because Mr. Tupper was busy too, drinking whiskey in his office.

Jack always knew what to do. He cleaned up the mess quick as a wink and pretended he was getting extra napkins out of the cupboard when Mrs. Tickner poked her head out of the kitchen door. Jack was smart, just like when he rescued my tweed cap from that cupboard.

He turned over in the grass and looked up at the sky, and then sat up. "I never heard anything like that yet!" he exclaimed. He pulled up his shirt and scratched his back. I saw funny long white marks all over and across it. Maybe from lying in the grass. Maybe not, and I found out. They were *not.*

"Those are just scars ..." Jack said when I asked him about them later. *"From the whip."* I didn't ask him again. I got too scared, and I told him I was scared about being whipped, too, or being sent away, and he didn't say anything else about it. He went quiet.

"You can't get *sent away* until you get viewed on 'doption day and somebody visits and says they want to take you home. And they have to bring a suitcase to put your clothes in and pay Mr. Tupper some *more* money to let you out of the gate." That's what he said.

" — But there's no 'doption day until next month that I know of..." Jack said, as he finally talked the silence away and picked another straw to chew on. That was the first time I heard about 'doption day." Jack told me.

"Me too!" I said.

That night I dreamed about 'doption day, *and I lined up just right and asked Jack to check me over. He looked into my ears to see if there was any wax. Everybody got 'dopted except me because I had too much wax in my ears.* When I woke up, it was morning. The other boys must have got wax in their ears or dirty faces in the night too because they didn't get 'dopted. They were still standing by their beds and stretching and fooling and pushing each other and getting their pants on. "Hurry up, boys!" Mrs. Tickner called up the stairs.

"There's three adoption days a year and everybody has to be on their best behavior and nobody can have any dirt in their ears." That's what Mrs. Tickner said when I asked her about it that evening and she told me it's *adoption day*, not like Jack said, *'doption day.*

Mrs. Tickner said *that's what comes of not going to school like regular kids.* That was when she started making me read books in the kitchen when I was finished taking the slops to T. T. Oinker. "I'll help you learn as much as I possibly can, Fletcher," she told me, and she looked worried.

"I'm afraid there aren't many families interested in adopting boys right now..." Mrs. Tickner said. "Tough times and no gas money to bus all of you to school...and there are so many like you."

"Why don't they want boys?" I asked, scraping another plate into the slops bucket.

"They don't want boys, except on farms. There are some boys being taken on to work on the farms, but for everyone else, they eat too much and they're too much trouble, and a lot of the farms are closed down with their men killed off in the war, I guess."

"It's not like that with the girls...in the city girls can do housework and such — get put doing other things, when they get old enough." Mrs. Tickner paused at the sink and looked into the water, just like my mother did the day she decided to sit down on the railroad track with the wet spot on her apron. I think she was going to cry, but she rattled some dishes loudly instead.

"What other things?" I asked her, expecting an answer. Mrs. Tickner always answers my questions. She didn't talk until I scraped three more plates.

"Things that they don't want to do sometimes, and I'm afraid, even *bad things*," she said quietly. She went into the pantry and got a bucket of potatoes.

"Everybody has to do bad things they don't want to do, like me; I have to do stinking slops!" I told her. I knew I shouldn't have said that, but I did, and it was too late to take it back. *I wished I didn't say that.* Mrs. Tickner was nice.

"That's right. *That's* enough from you, so get finished and be off with you. I'll peel these potatoes and have the kitchen to myself tonight!" she said harshly. She wouldn't say anything else out loud, so I finished the slops, and I don't understand why she got so mad. I never saw Mrs. Tickner mad before and I even rinsed the bucket out nice and clean before I left.

I asked Jack about why Mrs. Tickner got so touchy a few days after that. We were all finished catching the pigs that got out of the fence, and Mr. Tupper was mad and red in the face and his steel tooth shone brightly in the sun as usual. He said Tupper the Terror was going to the meat factory right quick next time he tried to escape.

"Next time that troublemaker gets out, it's off to the meat plant with him!" He growled. "And you too!" He looked right at me. "Well, what are you waiting for, get yourselves cleaned up!" he yelled. "Damned filthy brats!" he said. I know he was talking about us, not the pigs, because we fell in the mud catching the squealers and had to have a wash. We smelled like the pigpen, Mrs. Tickner said, and she held her nose.

"A fine, stinking bloody mess you are!" Mr. Tupper shouted and laughed at us. "Look at the lot of you! A fine, stinking mess!"

"That's quite enough from you, Charles!" Mrs. Tickner scolded. She marched us to the garden tub to get cleaned up. Mr. Tupper followed, holding his nose.

"Leave *that* little bastard 'til last. He's the dirtiest, ain't he? Spoil the water for the others, now, won't he then?" Mr. Tupper said, and pointed at me. I only fell in the pig muck a couple of times, too. We got ourselves in a line.

"Well, Mrs. Tickner, what are you waiting for? Either clean up these fine, stinking little piggies of yours immediately, or toss 'em out to the pig pen, and feed 'em some slops too, while you're at it!

"*Charles!*" Mrs. Tickner objected, throwing the bar of soap at him. It missed him, and I went to get it out of the grass.

Mr. Tupper clammed up, but I heard him slam the door and his scratchy laugh came out the window when he went in his office to drink whiskey. Mrs. Tickner got out another bar of soap when Mr. Tupper got out of sight. Mrs. Tickner got us hot water, too.

When the smell was gone from all the other boys, and they were clean and smelling like roses and lye soap, she left Jack to clean me up. "Clothes and all!" she ordered. She brought out another kettle of hot water, and we got clean water into the tub just for me because I fell in the mud the most.

"You'll be clean as a whistle in no time, won't he, boys?" She said happily and went back inside. Jack helped me get my muddy clothes off, and I sat in the hot water.

"You're our prize pig-catcher!" Jack said proudly. Jack scrubbed me up good with soap. He said that Mrs. Tickner was an orphan herself.

"Just like us?" I asked.

"Just like us!" Jack said. "No different, not at all...she's had a hard time, her mother died of the fits, and she got living with her Aunt Lily that beat her with a stick every day, and she had to eat dandelions. And then she lost her husband and all, in the war, it was."

"She wouldn't tell me about what girls do when they get to be orphans and are too big to do housework." I think Jack probably knows about that. Jack knows everything.

"She might be talking about things you're too young to know about." Jack stopped scrubbing for a minute and splashed some water over my head.

"I'm not too young either!" I shouted at Jack and splashed some water back at him out of the tub. He jumped. I'm not asking Jack anything else. He thinks I'm too young, but I'm not. So what if I smelled nice and clean and he did a good job scrubbing me, that's what Mrs. Tickner said. I didn't talk to Jack until the next day.

He was slopping the squealers, and I told him I wish Murvie wasn't dead, so he and I can go to Texas, bald or not. I could let him wear my brown tweed cap, so he wouldn't get sunburned. We'd stop in and see Floyd on the way and get some money from him if he had any and get Mrs. McAllister to feed us beef stew and biscuits. I have to stop thinking about that right away now because Jack grabbed my shirt and shook me up and down and yelled at me because Murvie's dead and got planted in a goddam potter's funeral.

"You forget about that right now. He's *dead*, and that's all there is to it!"

"It's *okay*, Jack," I said, and walked away. I didn't even look back that time.

I sat by the fence all by myself. Jack was finished in no time and came over to sit down on the grass with me and make me feel better. "Hey, Fetchie...oh, *come on*, Fetchie, I didn't mean that."

He tried tickling me first, but I got away and said, "Stop that."

"I know something you don't know, Fetch," Jack offered. He picked up a straw to chew on. "You wanna know what it is?" I tried to ignore Jack for shaking me up and down and yelling at me, but it's pretty hard to ignore Jack when he's holding your face and looking right in your eyes like he's studying a grasshopper.

"Maybe," I said finally and I almost looked at Jack, and then I looked at him and he was making a monkey face at me. I laughed. Then, Jack told me that Mr. Tupper said *goddam* one time when he was mad at Mrs. Tickner. God wouldn't like that, I know.

I told Jack *don't say that* but he said it again. "*Goddam*, Fetch, *goddam!*" Jack laughed. "*Goddam-goddam-goddam!*"

"Don't say bad words, Jack!" I said. "*Don't say bad words.*" He just looked at me. I ran away to the other side of the yard and sat on the grass to catch crickets for bait. I saw Jack watching me with his hands on his hips and shaking his head and laughing. Maybe Jack didn't hear God whispering to his mother in the sky like I did. Maybe Floyd will come and get me and take me home.

That reminds me. Floyd came to see me not too long after that. It was a couple of weeks before adoption day, but after the pigs escaped, I remember that. I remember it because it was my birthday. They came in the red truck; it was the same truck, the one with the rattling chains hanging from the tailgate. It was Floyd's red truck.

When I lived at Floyd's, he had the red Ford pickup truck. And even though she said she hated trucks, Mrs. McAllister had to drive it all over the place for him because he didn't have any legs and feet to push the pedals with, thanks to the doctor and his hacksaw. He couldn't have a car because he had to take his wicker chair with the loose wheels on it wherever he went.

"Gotta take my other set of wheels with me no matter where we go!" he told me the first time I helped Mrs. McAllister throw the chair into the box at the back for Floyd.

I always got squeezed in between him and Mrs. McAllister, and I shifted the gears for Floyd sometimes. Floyd put his hand on top of mine to make sure I did it just right. "This boy will make a good driver, he's got the rhythm!" Floyd said, puffing his pipe smoke out the open window. I like driving.

"Takes three drivers to handle this truck!" I said proudly.

"Yup! This here's quite a truck!" Floyd said and winked at me. "Three-speed!" He said.

I could smell the pouch of pipe tobacco in his jacket beside me. The kind I'm going to get when I grow up. Maybe I'll get a red truck with a stick shift instead of driving the old Pontiac, too.

"Just take 'er and trade 'er in down at the garage," Floyd suggested. "You'd get, oh, maybe forty, probably, oh, fifty bucks for the old Pontiac," he said.

"I'll get a new red truck, just like yours," I told him.

That must have been the time Floyd took us to a baseball game. After the game we went to Woolworth's Five and Dime, and me and Floyd waited in the truck and smoked his pipe a bit and listened to the old radio while Mrs. McAllister took all day and went in the store *for a minute* as she said.

"Just for a *minute*, missus?" Floyd asked her innocently when she came wandering out about two hours later, and Floyd and I had already had a nap and discussed going to lunch at Orli's restaurant and try and get back on time and pretend as if she still wasn't gone for more than a minute.

She smiled sweetly that time. "You men were at the baseball game for two hours, weren't you?" Floyd winked at me.

"I got you some long pants, Fletcher," she said and opened them and handed them right to me.

"Try them on." I put them on as soon as we got home. They were brown cords and had a matching belt.

"See, Floyd?" I said.

"Man needs long pants. I'd say...those sure are handsome," Floyd smiled at Mrs. McAllister.

I was proud and even gave Mrs. McAllister a hug. I gave her a hug another time too, the time she bought me a red shirt on sale for my birthday. That's why she and Floyd came to the orphanage. Just to see me on my birthday. The day I turned eight.

Sixteen

When I saw Floyd's red truck chugging up the road with the wicker chair bouncing around in the back, I couldn't believe my eyes. Jack was helping me bat a home run but I dropped the baseball bat and ran. "Hey!" the boys shouted.

Then they followed me but I was running faster than the wind and they couldn't catch up.

My dreams were coming true. Floyd was coming to get me, so I could live with him and wouldn't have to be an orphan anymore. Mrs. McAllister would feed us beef stew and dumplings and biscuits with gravy every night and make sure we wouldn't swear and spit or talk about things on the back porch that she didn't like, and she would even scrub my ears with soap, but I wouldn't mind that, not even a bit.

I ran to the gate as fast as I could go. The other boys couldn't keep up with me because I had to see Floyd right away. Jack stood beside me at the gate. He was puffing. I might have been, but I don't think so.

"So *that's* Floyd McAllister," Jack commented offhandedly.

"He's my best friend, and I'm going to live at his place just like I told you!" I advised Jack. "He might even adopt me!"

"Nobody's gonna 'dopt you. Get it out of your head!" Ricky Tenberg said sarcastically.

"Yeah, stupid*!*" Timmy added.

"Shut up, cricket-brain!" Jack warned. Ricky jabbed Timmy in the ribs with his pointy elbow.

"Ow! Stupid!" Timmy retorted.

Timmy was Ricky's little brother. They both had stick-up short blond hair and freckles. They came to the orphanage a long time before I did. They were always in trouble, and Mr. Tupper got them both by the ears and made them sit in the corner on high stools in the dining room when they started fighting over a bowl of custard.

"You ate yours too fast!" Timmy shouted at Ricky.

"I did not!" Ricky punched Timmy hard on the shoulder and grabbed the bowl from him.

"Dunce!" Timmy said.

"You're the one should be wearing a dunce cap, stupid!" Ricky said.

"Here, here!" Mr. Tupper separated them and grabbed the bowl. "There's no fighting here, so into the slops this custard goes, now, doesn't it?" It went in the slops. Both boys cried when he sat them in the corner.

"See what you did now?" Timmy wailed.

"Quiet! And let that be a lesson to all of you!" he bellowed at the rest of us. I hung onto my bowl of custard tight so nobody could take it and put it in the slops. I saw Ricky stick his tongue out at Mr. Tupper when he wasn't looking.

The red truck pulled up in a cloud of dust, and the dust went into the driver's window that was open. Mrs. McAllister waved her hands in front of her face to chase the dust away and got out after Floyd leaned over and jerked the door handle hard for her. I think Floyd forgot to oil it for her again. He always said he was going to oil it for her, and I helped him do it once, but Floyd forgets if I'm not there to remind him.

"Forgot, that's it. I plain forgot 'bout that. Maybe I could find somebody else to take care of it for me this time." That's why I should live at Floyd's all the time — to help Floyd remember to oil the truck doors and other stuff.

"We can't have the missus stuck in the truck!" Floyd said. He said I could squirt oil on everything with the special oily pump can, so I did all the hinges and the doors and the tailgate, and even the wheels too. I had to wipe the oil off of the red hubcaps that time, but Floyd said he never saw the hubcaps so shiny, and reached into his pocket and pulled out a shiny quarter.

"Fellas that do a good job ought to be well-rewarded and get lemonade, too." We mixed up a good batch and put lots of sugar in it that time.

Mrs. McAllister pushed the truck door open, stepped out onto the dry ground and looked at us. We waved through the fence, and I don't know if Mrs. McAllister saw me or not. She looked like she might be smiling, but you could never tell with Mrs. McAllister if she was trying not to breathe in the dust or smiling at the people because her smiles all looked about the same.

She wore a hat with red and yellow flowers on it that looked like the same kind of cloth that the flowered collar on her dark Sunday dress was made of, and there was a dust pattern on her back from the seat. I saw that when she walked around to the back of the truck and rolled Floyd's wicker chair, the one with the wheels, out of the back.

"My, oh my!" she said to us as she rattled the chains on the tailgate and banged it shut again. Floyd was waving and turning around to look at her and hurry her up with his chair, and I think he saw me, but I'm not sure.

He pushed the screechy truck door wide open and bummed his way down onto the chair by hanging onto the special handle he bolted onto the truck by the door. "Hold the chair still, woman!" he said, just loud enough that I could hear it for sure that time. He got in the chair and wheeled himself to the gate so fast that Mrs. McAllister was left behind.

"Hello, boys!" Mrs. McAllister almost caught up, and her face was getting red.

"Hey there, Fetch, how you doing, my lad?" he came right to me, and I reached through the iron bars, and he shook my hands, both of them at once. I didn't feel like fish bait that time.

"Hi, Floyd!" I knew Floyd would come for me.

"*Ahem!*" Mrs. McAllister cleared her throat and looked at me, and I remembered my manners and took off my brown tweed cap.

"Hello, Mrs. McAllister," I said, and I think my face was getting hot.

"Hello, Fletcher. You've grown, boy!" Floyd's eyes twinkled in the brilliant sunlight. His face was sunburned and brown. That must have been from falling asleep and snoring on the back porch. My eyes were nearly crying from being happy to see Floyd so that made me feel better. I stood up tall, right beside Jack, but I didn't really know what to say, so I said "This is Jack. *Jack Whittaker.* He's my best friend, and he's in charge of me!" When I introduced Jack to Floyd he squinted up at Jack and puffed his pipe.

Jack straightened up and cleared his throat. "Nice to meet you, sir!" Jack said, shaking his hand.

"*He doesn't have any legs!*" Dickie whispered to Elton. Elton jabbed Dickie in the ribs. That shushed him right up, then the other boys lined up to be introduced to my best friend Floyd.

"Near old enough to go out into the world, eh, Jack?" Floyd grinned at Jack.

"*Almost* sixteen now, sir," Jack said and looked at me and stood up tall as he could go and puffed out his chest.

"Ring the bell, Floyd." I suggested. Floyd pulled the cord and the bell rang the loudest I ever heard it. Floyd grinned at me.

"Let me look at you, boy." Mrs. McAllister puffed and glared at Floyd as he rang the bell again. I saw Mr. Tupper running toward us from the office as fast as he could go.

"Mr. Tupper's coming to let you in, Floyd." I pointed at Mr. Tupper.

"Get away from the gate!" he yelled angrily at the boys. We all backed up and the line flinched and wavered.

"Floyd's here!" I proudly informed Mr. Tupper. He glowered at me. I put my hat back on since the waving was all done.

"This *isn't* a visitation day, boy!" he snapped back. *"Get back!"* he ordered me again but I didn't want to get back from Floyd. Mr. Tupper grabbed my ears and made me get back with the others. I wanted to kick his leg but I didn't because it's not polite. "Hold your ground against me, will you, boy!" His voice crackled angrily as he leaned over me. His steel tooth was pretty shiny in the sun.

"What do you people want?" He shouted angrily at Floyd and Mrs. McAllister. Floyd and Mrs. McAllister looked at each other, frowning. "Oh, it's *you two*, is it? Not that it's likely for anything good, then, but what is it?! This is *not* a visitation day, I'll have you know!" He gave my ear a sharp pull. I stepped back and watched Floyd through the gate. *"No one's allowed in here unless it's a scheduled visitation day!"* He sneered at Floyd. *"Some* people *still* have no sense of propriety, I say!" Mr. Tupper added, glaring at us to make sure we stayed back. He sniffed in disdain as he looked at Floyd's wicker chair, and saw that Floyd had no legs and feet. I saw that and I didn't like it, not one bit.

"No need to be rough with the boy!" Floyd spoke menacingly. Floyd pushed Mrs. McAllister behind him and faced Mr. Tupper himself. "*Charles,* we've come to see the boy! Young Fletcher Williams there!" he said gruffly to Mr. Tupper. "All the way from Waterland!"

"I'm sure you'll appreciate the fact that it isn't a *scheduled* visiting day then; last day of the month only, that's the rules, like it or not, I don't care who you are, Mr. McAllister!" Mr. Tupper spoke huffily, looking around to see if we were listening. We hung on every word. I'd bet that Floyd would get the best of crabby Mr. Tupper any time.

"...*Nope"* Floyd said, squinting up at the red-faced man glowering at him. "Don't reckon I do, matter of fact."

Jack almost giggled beside me, and I knew it was my duty to jab him in the ribs and maintain silence. That's what Floyd would have wanted. *Dignity*. So I did, and hard too. *"What'd you do that for?"* Jack whispered, rubbing his ribs.

Floyd spoke quietly. "We come to see the boy, young Fletcher there, and want to spend some time with him. We're his neighbors, Charles ...we came to be good friends. He spent some time living with us, and we kind of miss him." He wheeled closer, sizing up Mr. Tupper. *"We kind of miss him,"* he repeated matter-of-factly, as if it was going to make some kind of difference. Mr. Tupper elevated his nose and sniffed.

"It is *not* a visitation day, is it?" Mr. Tupper said arrogantly. "We really can't have everyone visiting just anytime they wish, you know!" His almost non-existent jaw got smaller and pretty near disappeared as he pressed his lips together into a mean, angry little red line. Floyd looked up at Mrs. McAllister and made his puzzled face. Floyd was always good at looking puzzled.

She drew in a big breath and looked back at Floyd like he wasn't going to get any air from now on because she had it all.

"Mexican standoff, Fetch!" Jack whispered to me. I nodded. I knew Floyd was going to win. *He had to.* If he couldn't visit, I didn't want to be an orphan anymore and that's it, and I'd have to escape in a garbage can and make a run for it.

"Well, I never!" exclaimed Mrs. McAllister, walking around Floyd and approaching Mr. Tupper. He backed up, and must have blinked twenty-seven times in a row. I knew Mr. Tupper was lying right away. I remembered that from before. *Whenever you lie, your eyes blink a lot, and you don't even know you're doing it.* That's what Floyd said. Floyd's always right, and his eyes don't blink very much even when he smokes his pipe.

"We have *rules*," he said. "Upsets the boys having visitors for one and not for the others!" Mr. Tupper sniffed again.

"You mean it upsets *you*, sir, because it's too much of a bother, isn't that what you mean, *Charles?"* Mrs. McAllister said it like she was about to start a huffy-match with the man standing in front of her.

Mr. Tupper almost snorted his head off.

"I'm sure that all of the boys will be encouraged by a visit if it makes even *one* a little bit happier." Mrs. McAllister said, and raised her eyebrows and placed her hands on her hips.

"Dear lady, I'm quite sure you *know* what it is I mean; now if you'll kindly get that...*invalid*...back in the truck, I'll get on with the business of taking care of these miserable little beasts, here...not a penny in it for me, for all the bother, is there? To have to take charge of these brats and to take abuse from people like you is unbearable, to say the least! Nothing has changed, has it! Visiting day is the last day of the month, Mrs. McAllister, like I said!"

Mr. Tupper opened the gate and began to push Mrs. McAllister back from the gate. I don't think God likes that when people push each other. I know Floyd doesn't.

"Now, *now!*" Floyd spoke loudly. Mr. Tupper ignored him and continued to push Mrs. McAllister backwards.

"*My goodness! What are you doing?*" she spoke sharply and brushed his hands off of her. "*Charles, take your hands off of me!*" She scolded.

"Get out, now, and come back on visiting day!" He grunted. His face got red.

"We've driven over fifty miles, and I'm not leaving until we have a visit with the boy!" Mrs. McAllister stood her ground. Mr. Tupper pushed her hard again, and his face turned sideways when Mrs. McAllister slapped his face.

"*Well! I never!*" she almost said *harrumph*, but I think she bit her tongue. Mr. Tupper pushed her backwards.

"*Bitch!*" he hissed.

"*How dare you!*" she snapped at him and slapped his face again.

Floyd growled. "*Hey!*"

"You have a lot of nerve, *you hussy!*" Mr. Tupper yelled.

Floyd wheeled around Mrs. McAllister to get in front of Mr. Tupper. I knew there was going to be trouble as soon as Floyd wheeled in front of Mrs. McAllister, and there was.

"Sir Charles!" he warned Mr. Tupper. *"Enough!"*

"The *nerve* of this man!" Mrs. McAllister said.

Floyd lifted up his hand and motioned Mr. Tupper to approach him.

"I wish to speak with you *privately*, Sir Charles, it...won't take but a minute!" He beckoned to Mr. Tupper and showed him a ten-dollar bill. "Would *this* help?" he asked Mr. Tupper. He motioned to the red-faced man to lean over close so he could talk in his ear.

"We wouldn't want the boys to hear what we're saying, now would we, Sir Charles?" Floyd said. *"I owe you one anyway, remember?"*

Mr. Tupper smiled and closed his hand over the ten dollar bill. Floyd put one hand behind Mr. Tupper's head and pretended to speak into his ear but the other hand punched Mr. Tupper's nose smartly before Mr. Tupper could move. The boys laughed. Mr. Tupper sat down in the dust right away, and had to clean the blood and dust off of his nose and glasses.

"Look at that, will you!" Jack laughed.

"Smash him, Floyd!" Arnold Thackery shouted.

"Kill him, Floyd!" One of the other boys yelled through the fence. Everyone cheered.

Floyd wheeled to the bell and rang it loudly. *"Round one!"* he said. The boys laughed.

"Look who's gettin' the beating and bleedin' now!" Jack shouted.

The boys laughed. Mrs. McAllister had her hand over her mouth. Mr. Tupper scowled at Jack.

"You'll be getting the whip again, you little bastard!" he swore at Jack and that was when I figured out the funny marks on Jack's back. He pointed at me, too.

"*You!* You'll be having a whipping, too, boy, for bringing this trouble on me!" he shouted.

"Not if the lot of us pile up on you and pound you to blazes first, sir!" Richard Bordon called out bravely. "You're not being fair, not being fair at all, and you know it! They drove fifty miles to see Fletcher."

"There's nothing wrong with the boy getting a little visit from these nice people," Arnold put in his say too.

"*You little bastards, you two-faced bastards, all of you! After all I've done for you lot!*" Mr. Tupper screamed at Richard and Arnold. Mr. Tupper got up but stumbled and sat down in the dust again, red-faced and angry as a wet rooster.

Floyd wheeled closer to him. "*C'mon — Charles!*" Floyd's voice sounded quiet and dangerous, and his eyes glinted like ice-covered steel at the man as Mr. Tupper scrambled to his feet and dusted himself off. "*For old times* — never mind the boys, they'll revolt on you soon enough, won't they? Right now, you just pick on somebody your own size, don't you worry none about the legs," Floyd challenged, and raised his fists.

"*Floyd!*" Mrs. McAllister tried to hold Floyd back, but Floyd's my hero, and nobody can hold him back. I got closer to the gate and was getting ready to help Floyd just in case.

"I'm just going to show this *gentleman* a lesson on how to whip boys and be pulling their ears off!" he glowered at Mr. Tupper.

It would have been a good idea to warn Floyd about Mr. Tupper's tricks, but there wasn't time; it was already too late, because Mr. Tupper leaned over quick as a blink and picked up the little front wheels, dumping Floyd over backwards.

"I'll teach you to interfere in *my* business, will you?" he swore and kicked Floyd. It was a hard kick because Floyd grunted out loud.

"*Don't you kick Floyd!*" I screamed. I don't want Floyd to get hurt, no matter what.

I got through the gate and ran past Mrs. McAllister real fast, but I didn't get there fast enough. Mr. Tupper picked up a long stick and started to hit Floyd. Nobody can hurt Floyd when I'm around; I made up my mind about that.

"*Leave Floyd alone!*" I screamed again, and I charged Mr. Tupper. I punched him as hard as I could in his fat belly and kicked him right on the leg even if it isn't polite.

"*Ow! You little bastard!*" Mr. Tupper swore at me and backed up to swing the stick. It hit me on the head with a crack, but not too hard because my brown tweed hat has a thick top on it. He kicked at Floyd, and Jack tackled Mr. Tupper at the same time. I heard the boys cheering.

"I'm going to whip every one of you, and good!" Mr. Tupper got up, grunting hard, and leaned over to pick up the stick again. "Every damned one of you, you snot-nosed brats!"

"You'll do no such thing!" The woman flailed at him like a madwoman, the big wooden spoon hitting him again and again on the head, like a Dutch windmill happily going round and round. Mr. Tupper turned away but looked back just in time to get one flat on the nose from Mrs. Tickner.

"*You'll do no such thing!*" she screamed angrily, and hit him again.

"You stupid bitch!" he yelled in pain and charged her with the stick. "*You broke my nose!*" He started to slap Mrs. Tickner, so I kicked him again and tried to push him away, but he was too heavy. He slapped me hard, and I fell down.

I told you Floyd was my hero. Even though he was lying on the ground gasping for breath from getting kicked in the ribs, Floyd grabbed Mr. Tupper's leg and pulled him down on the ground.

"*Goddam you!*" Mr. Tupper scrambled like a madman trying to get up, but Floyd grabbed him around the neck and held him tight and punched him twice, once with each hand before Arnold and Jack and Richard got there to help us. Mr. Tupper stopped fighting and fell over. He closed his eyes. I think he was unconscious for a minute. The boys cheered loudly, and Jack took control of the stick.

"I think we should give him a *good* beating, *one for every boy here!*" Jack yelled. The boys clapped and cheered. Mr. Tupper didn't move.

"Look at that, ladies! Look, boys, Floyd's punched his lights out!" Jack shouted and laughed. I was proud of Floyd and was glad he never got hurt too much.

Mrs. Tickner was shaking, and Mrs. McAllister helped straighten her up. Jack and Arnold went to see if the ladies were all right. Richard and I picked Floyd's chair back up straight and helped Floyd climb up into it, and found his glasses in the dust. They were bent and Floyd had to twist them straight just a bit to make them fit behind his ears just right.

"What do you say, boys?" Floyd said, soon as he fitted them and cleaned the dust off. The boys cheered. I cheered the loudest. We jumped up and down, too.

"Think we can have a visit now?" We cheered again, and I hugged Floyd hard, and Mrs. Tickner. And I even hugged Mrs. McAllister very hard, too.

"My goodness!" she exclaimed.

"And a nice long one too, you'll be having a nice *long* visit today!" Mrs. Tickner said, her hands on her hips, the wooden spoon held menacingly over Mr. Tupper's head, ready to whack him again if he moved an inch or said a word.

"This is Mrs. Tickner," I introduced her to Floyd and Mrs. McAllister. "She takes care of us and cooks food and gives us treats, and I do the slops for her!"

Floyd reached out with his sunburned hand. "Ma'am," Floyd said. "Nice helpful bunch of boys you got here."

"Yes, we couldn't be more pleased to meet you," Mrs. McAllister's voice shook bravely as she straightened her hat and dusted off her dress.

"Are you all right?" Mrs. Tickner asked the shaky visitor and helped brush her off some more. I didn't see any dust on her, but maybe I missed some.

"Quite fine, thank you. One doesn't expect to be attacked by a gentleman, does one?" Mrs. McAllister regained her composure.

"That one's hardly a gentleman!" Mrs. Tickner indicated Mr. Tupper as he lay on the ground panting.

"See?" I said proudly to Dickie and Elton. "Floyd's my hero!"

"Mine too!" said Jack. I decided it was okay to share my hero with Dickie, Elton, Ricky, Timmy and all the other boys —and especially Jack.
We cheered three *hip-hip-hoorays* just for Floyd. He laughed. "That's good, boys!" He wheeled over to the bell and clanged it louder than it ever rang before.

Now I wish Murvie was still here, because Floyd winning the fight was even more exciting than being a bald cowboy in Texas.

Mr. Tupper sat up in the dust after a little bit, his face bloodied. His shiny steel tooth was missing. His nose was bleeding. "Wha—?" he said, sounding like he swallowed a bag of feathers. Mrs. Tickner stood over him with the big wooden spoon.

"You'll be packing your bags now and leaving!" she warned him.

"Wha—?" he mumbled, red-faced, and scrambled to his feet.

"You heard what I said, Charles, you're leaving—*now!*" she said. The boys cheered. Floyd clamped his pipe hard between his teeth and looked straight at Mr. Tupper.

"You'll be doing as the lady says, now won't you, *Charles!*" Mr. Tupper's face was getting bright red, but I know he was scared to talk back to Floyd. He turned to Mrs. Tickner.

"You have no right," he hissed at her. *"You have no right!"* She waved the spoon at him menacingly.

"I have *every* right! I've already spoken to Mrs. Zeban about your treatment of the boys, and your drinking problem, and your stealing the funds for food—so you'll be packing up now." She approached him with the wooden spoon, and his face turned white. *"Brother?"* She hissed at him. *"You're an animal, abusing these boys like you have!"* Mrs. Tickner brushed the dust off of him smartly as if she was beating the rug from the entry hall. He backed away. She threatened him with the spoon again. *"Now!"* she said.

133

"You heard what the lady said!" Floyd spoke quietly as he wheeled his wobbly chair toward Mr. Tupper.

"I'll have the law on *you,* sir!" Mr. Tupper whined at Floyd. "*Trying to bribe a county official!* You all saw that, this *cripple* attempting to bribe a county official, you all saw it! I'll have my lawyer on him, I will!"

Floyd narrowed his eyes like he was staring at the devil. He lifted his hand and pointed a finger right at Mr. Tupper. "Do your best, Mr. Tupper. I'd be guessing you won't be a public official for long, sir. You can mark my word on that. Last I heard, beating and abusing children was against the law." Mrs. Tickner moved toward Mr. Tupper with the spoon raised.

"I'd bet you'll be the one behind bars, mister ...*whipping boys and accepting bribes, Charles ... in a public institution?*" Floyd warned and moved closer. Mr. Tupper backed away.

"*You'll be hearing from me again. I warn you!*" Mr. Tupper hissed.

"I can hardly wait, Mr. Tupper," Floyd said, smiling.

"And as for you, you ungrateful bitch!" he swore at Mrs. Tickner. "I should have let you be a scullery maid back 'ome!" Mrs. Tickner advanced again and whacked him on the side of the head again with the big wooden spoon.

"Never use language like that in front of me again, Charles Albert Tupper!"

"Hit 'im again!" Jack yelled. The boys cheered again.

"Thank you for your concern for your own sister, Charles!" Mrs. Tickner said, angrily. "But now I never want to see your face again! You'll be moving on! You aren't needed here anymore! You've got five minutes before I send the boys for the cops!"

"*Starting now, Charles!*" Floyd commanded, looking at his dusty gold watch. Floyd used to let me wind his watch, as long as I didn't wind it too tight. I told Floyd that when I get big, I'm going to have a watch just like his, but he said maybe he could just give me his instead. "You're still a mean one, aren't you?" Floyd filled his pipe carefully and measured Mr. Tupper as he spoke coolly, watching him like a dangerous animal. *"You haven't changed a bit, Charles!"*

Mr. Tupper swore under his breath and glared at everyone. He backed away three or four steps then suddenly turned and strode angrily toward the office. When he got there he turned and looked back at us, then scuttled out of sight backwards like a crayfish.

"Oh, glory, I think I knocked his tooth out with my spoon!" Mrs. Tickner spoke breathlessly.

"It must be here somewhere in the dirt." I looked around, and the other boys helped me scuff around in the dust to find it. It was shiny and had dirt and blood on it.

"We'll give it to him on the way out!" Floyd grinned widely and puffed on his pipe hard. Everybody clapped and cheered. Floyd grabbed the stick from Jack and wheeled over to the bell. He thrashed it again soundly, and the big bell rang the loudest I ever heard it.

"Round ten and the winner is ..." Floyd made his hands like a megaphone and his voice sounded just like a fight announcer.

"Floyd!" the boys shouted, but I cheered the loudest, and Jack and I held Floyd's hand up proudly, like fight managers with the winner.

"Now we'll have our visit, and a good one, too!" Floyd said loudly, looking toward the office. "C'mon, boys, let's go up and have a baseball game! I'll pitch for you!"

"Okay, Floyd!" the boys yelled, pretty much at the same time. Floyd winked at me and started wheeling his way up the hill. The boys got right behind me and helped drive the chair so me and Floyd wouldn't have to work so hard. Mrs. Tickner and Mrs. McAllister followed along behind, talking quietly.

Mr. Tupper roared down the path to the gate like a mad bull, glaring at all of us as he passed. "You ain't heard the last of me, not a one of you!" He paused in front of Mrs. Tickner. "You'll be wishing you were never born, you bitch!" He swore a few more bad words at Mrs. Tickner. "And that goes for the rest of you too!"

Mrs. Tickner waved the spoon at him. "It serves you right, Charles! *Abusing and whipping defenseless boys, and ... women too"* Her voice chilled.

"You're a dirty man, Charles, I am ashamed of you, some of the other nasty things I've heard..."

"I only had to do what was necessary to keep order!" he shouted at her.

"No, Charles, you did what you had to — *to profit from their misery,* and I've a good mind to have the authorities after you for all the *improper* things you've done!" Mr. Tupper's face got red.

"I...I'll be going now, but mind you, *you haven't seen the last of me! You —"*

Mrs. Tickner cut him off and shook the spoon at him again. "— In fact, I might change my mind yet! *Your time's up. Don't come back! You're not my brother anymore!"*

Floyd looked at Mrs. McAllister and raised his eyebrows. I never saw him do that before.

"*Aaagh!* Who wants to bother with a dumb bunch of brats and a mindless bitch anyway?" he snapped at her. She lunged at him with the wooden spoon, but he got away that time.

Floyd got in the way and stopped and wheeled his chair around. "You'll be moving on — *now,* Charles, — like the *lady* said, your time's up!" Floyd glanced at his watch and moved toward Mr. Tupper.

"Floyd!" Mrs. McAllister said.

"Never mind, woman!" Floyd brushed her off. "Mr. Tupper's a bully and can't whip anyone his own size, can he? Let him try again, and this time I'll give him a *proper* beating, *just like twenty years ago!"*

Mr. Tupper backed away and picked up his moldy leather suitcase. I knew Floyd could chase him away.

"And here's your tooth!" Mrs. Tickner threw him the bloodied steel tooth. He caught it but his hand shook as he stared at it. "And be remembering that next time I see you *I'll knock it down your throat, instead!"* she added, waving the wooden spoon. Mr. Tupper backed further away.

"Aa-aagh! This is the thanks I get?" he shouted angrily, pitching the shiny tooth as far as he could over the fence and into the bushes. Me and Floyd and all of the boys laughed. Mr. Tupper looked funny without his tooth, like a toothless old hag. Mrs. McAllister tried not to laugh, but she saw us laughing and did too, just a bit.

"I don't need *that* stupid thing or any of you!" he screamed, and huffed away through the gate and down the hill. He kicked Floyd's red truck when he passed it and swore again.

"He kicked your truck, Floyd!" I yelled at Floyd. *"Stop that! Don't kick Floyd's truck!"* I screamed at Mr. Tupper. Mr. Tupper looked back and kicked Floyd's truck again.

"You'll be sorry, all of you!" he screamed, and then stormed off kicking up a huff of dust.

"Can't hurt *that* thing!" Floyd squinted and watched, puffing on his pipe casually. "Hope he didn't break his foot!" Everyone laughed.

"That's *that* then, isn't it?" Mrs. Tickner watched the madman walking away for a minute. She smiled, and generously took Mrs. McAllister by the arm.

"Shall we have tea? — And I can have dinner made in no time, so we'll celebrate and have peach cake for dessert. You shall be staying for dinner, now won't you, Mrs. McAllister?"

"I wouldn't miss it for anything," Mrs. McAllister laughed shakily.

All of the boys raced ahead, up to the baseball diamond. I went too, but I always want to keep my eyes on Floyd. He's my hero.

I saw Floyd and Mrs. McAllister and Mrs. Tickner talking and hugging while we were playing catch. I threw the baseball to Jack. He threw the ball to Timmy, but it went over his head and ended up back down the hill into the weeds by the gate where Floyd was talking. Timmy chased down to search for the ball, then stopped to listen.

"It really was him, wasn't it, Floyd? No wonder Sarah left him."

Floyd smiled. He nodded and stopped to light his pipe. "It was a long time ago, Elizabeth. This is the *second time* I whupped the daylights out of Sir Charles Albert Tupper with good cause."

"*Eileen?*" Floyd asked Mrs. Tickner cautiously. "Elizabeth, this is Charles' sister. *It looks like we have finally met our one and only sister-in-law after all these years.*"

"Oh, my goodness!" Mrs. McAllister said, clamping her hand over her mouth.

"Floyd and Elizabeth! Finally, *finally!* It is so nice to meet you!" Mrs. Tickner said, hugging them both at once.

Timmy ran back up the hill and threw the ball to Jack.

"They're gabbling away about Mrs. Tickner's old sister-in-law or something," Timmy said.

"I'll ask Floyd; he'll tell me," I said. The trouble is, I forgot all about that because we got to playing baseball again.

"They're just happy they whupped Mr. Tupper's sorry ass out of here!" Jack said. "*Batter up!*" The boys laughed.

"*Strike ten!*" Timmy and Ricky shouted together. We laughed and whooped a lot.

"I suppose I am not your sister-in-law any longer," Mrs. Tickner said quietly, "after *today*, it seems, at any rate—and Charles is not my brother anymore either—I will never see him again—not that it makes any difference now, estate or not." She smiled happily, then shrugged.

"*No matter, Eileen, we can still be good friends,*" Floyd said.

"We're right there in Waterland, Eileen, please *do* come visit any time," Mrs. McAllister said. Floyd looked at Elizabeth cautiously and turned his chair to Mrs. Tickner.

"About *Sarah,* too, I don't know if you already know or not; Sarah was remarried, her name is *Dormally* now, she lives in Waterland, too," Floyd said quietly. "I'm afraid her late husband, George—he went and died on us before you came over. It was a few years back. She's by herself again."

"I'm so sorry," Mrs. Tickner said. "Charles paid my passage here nine years ago and put me to work here. *I've never even been to Waterland*...that's life isn't it?" She sighed and shook her head sadly, her eyes flooding with tears. She started walking. Mrs. McAllister came up behind her and gently put her arms around her.

"I'll call the boys for you." She clapped her hands sharply. "*Boys!*"

"That's not how you call *boys*, Elizabeth. *Here's* how you call boys!" He wheeled over and rang the bell loudly. "*Boys!*" Floyd bellowed.

"Shall we make dinner, boys?" Mrs. McAllister called out very loudly. "*Let's go peel some potatoes!*"

When we got back down to the gate to help Floyd get up the hill, I saw Mrs. Tickner wiping her eyes, but Mrs. McAllister got in front of me quick and put a finger over my lips to clam me up.

I forgot all about that part.

Seventeen

We got our hero Floyd pushed the rest of the way up the hill and into the hall in no time. He raced us down the hall and spun around in his chair on the slippery floor. The wheels left a black mark on the yellow wood.

"I'm in trouble now, boys!" Floyd said grimly, clenching his pipe between his teeth.

"No matter!" Mrs. Tickner said, laughing. "Albert's not here to complain about it!" She scuffed her heel on the floor herself, leaving another black mark. "Who gives a hoot!" she laughed harder. "Do it again! I'll race you now, *I will*, Mr. McAllister!" She challenged.

"If you're betting your peach cobbler on your winning, get on your mark, then, Mrs. Tickner, when you're ready!"

"*Get ready, get set — and go!*" Jack yelled, laughing. Floyd wheeled his way down the long hallway over the shiny yellow wood as fast as he could go, with Mrs. Tickner hot behind him. Floyd spun the wheelchair around and lost control. All of the boys roared with the excitement. I was worried about Floyd when he smacked into the wall, but Floyd's the best wheelchair driver I know, and he turned around and got going the other way pretty fast. Mrs. Tickner touched the end wall first, and Floyd was hot on her tail on the home stretch. It was a tie. All the boys laughed and clapped.

"Atta boy, Floyd!" Jack yelled.

Mrs. Tickner was flushed. "We won, didn't we Mrs. McAllister? —I mean *Elizabeth*, to be sure!"

"My goodness, I'm sure we *did* win, Eileen... *the ladies won that time, and I'm sure too!*" Mrs. McAllister laughed and beamed happily. Mrs. Tickner patted Floyd on the head fondly.

"You may have some peach cobbler at any rate, my winning or not!"

"That means everybody wins!" Floyd chuckled. "I almost wiped out—and all that effort and endangerment wasn't even required!" He laughed and shook Mrs. Tickner's hand.

"Oh, my, look at the skid marks all over the floor," Mrs. McAllister pointed to the marks where Floyd's wheelchair had skidded into the wall.

"Not a problem at all, is it boys, Charlie will have them polished up in no time!" Mrs. Tickner said, and laughed. We all cheered, even Mrs. McAllister.

"We can all help Charlie polish those runty marks out of the floor in no time," said Jack, boastfully.

"We'll help Charlie!" Some other boys said.

"Well then, is anybody hungry?" Mrs. Tickner had to shout pretty loud to be heard over the cheering.

"*Yay!*" And there was another round of cheering. We headed down the hallway, and Ricky held the doors open for everyone.

"My, aren't *you* a polite young man," Mrs. McAllister said. Ricky got as red as a cooked beet and studied the knots in his shoelaces.

"He's a quiet one for the most part," Mrs. Tickner said quietly to Mrs. McAllister.

She leaned down and hugged Ricky hard, and then hugged Mrs. McAllister, and we all went down into the kitchen to peel potatoes with Mrs. Tickner, even Floyd.

Mrs. McAllister peeled the carrots, the boys all peeled the potatoes, and Mrs. Tickner made peach cobbler and apple pie, too.

For the first time at the orphanage, we ate all we wanted. I was happy. Floyd was back. We sang songs after we ate, and Mrs. McAllister played the old piano that was a bit out of tune and no wonder, because it was made in the old days when all they had was wooden nails and horse glue; that is what Jack said. For a special treat, Floyd and I sang *Home on the Range* and everybody clapped for us.

After that, I showed Floyd everything in the place, and the other boys started to help Mrs. Tickner get the slops out for a change, even though they used to think she was a miserable old lady and getting kitchen slops out wasn't a job for any boy except *me*. I helped Jack feed T. T. and the other porkers even though it was my special day. They squealed more than usual. When we got back in, we ate some more peach cobbler.

"Time for a baseball game, boys!" Floyd winked at Mrs. Tickner.

"Head 'er outside now! Time to run off some of that food!" He winked at Mrs. Tickner.

"Never mind the rest of the slops, boys. There will be plenty of time for that, won't there? Get on outside and play!" Mrs. Tickner smiled. All of us headed outside right away, but I was the last one, helping Floyd, so I saw Mrs. McAllister rush around, preparing more tea and cutting wedges of apple pie to set out on the table for after the game.

I was batting, and when I saw Floyd watching, I whacked the ball really hard and ran around the bases as fast as I could go. Floyd clapped and cheered.

"Way to go, Fetch, way to go!" he shouted. Floyd started out watching the game, but we got him to join in after a few minutes. We put him to bat right away because he's our hero. He hit the ball on the first pitch like I knew he would.

Floyd raced around the baseball field like a madman. The ball went down the hill by the gate and over the fence, and I had to go find it. Floyd can hit a ball farther than anybody I know, even if he has no legs.

The Fires of Waterland

"Hurry up, Fetch!" Jack yelled. I climbed up and over the creaky wire and flopped onto the grass on the other side. I couldn't believe my eyes. The ball was in the weeds right beside Mr. Tupper's shiny steel tooth. I wasn't going to pick it up, but I looked at it in the dirt, and I stepped on it instead, like Jack would have, I think.

"C'mon, Fetch, whatcha doing?" one of the other boys yelled. I looked at the tooth in the dirt and kicked the dirt away from it.

I changed my mind, I don't know why. I picked it up and was going to take the time to clean the dust and blood off of it but Jack yelled at me so we could hurry up and finish the baseball game before the sun goes down, so I stuffed it in my pocket and got the ball back up the hill. That's why I still got it; *the tooth*, not the ball.

Later on, when everyone was sleeping after Floyd went home back to Waterland, it was nighttime and dark. Everyone was gone to bed, lights out, but I had my eyes open and the moon was shining. I took the steel tooth out of my shoe to look at. It was a little cleaner that time because I washed it off in the hog's water trough again when Jack and I slopped T.T. the porker *extra good*, to make him happy since he was next to be heading to the bacon factory.

I'm glad Mr. Tupper is gone for good because the last time I woke up and the moon made the steel tooth shiny in the dark, it was still his tooth. And because he had his hand under my blanket playing water pump just like Tina McQueeny, and now I know that he must be a slut, too. I got myself too tired watching the moon and fell asleep.

He clamped his hand hard over my mouth. I smell whiskey like when my father gets in new whiskey crates... "Keep quiet boy. Quiet, you little bastard, if you know what's good for you," Mr. Tupper whispered at me, and I can smell his breath. If I keep my eyes shut tight Mr. Tupper will think I'm sleeping. Why can't I breathe? Just go away, just go away, just go away, just go away...I'm shutting my eyes tighter, nothing is happening now. "You'll do what I say, won't you now? Or I'll burn this place up with all you little rats in it and you'll get a whipping like Jack, you bleedin' brat." He turned me over and pulled the blanket off and sat on my legs, and it hurts and I can't breathe and I'm cold now, cold,

143

cold, and cold. Don't do that. Pig noises, pig noises, he makes pig noises like T.T.Oinker, don't do that, shut up, shut up, shut up, you pigs, "Shut up you little bastard, don't you make a sound now. Now, you little bastard, you tell a soul our little secret I'll kill all you brats, every one, you understand?" He hisses loud into my ears like an oiled snake and now he's gone. I'm keeping my eyes shut now, but I didn't shut my eyes tight enough and that's why I'm crying. I'm too scared. I have to cry and Jack might come and put his arms around me and cover me up again. He's back, no, it's not him. It's Jack, it's Jack. Jack's in charge of me because I'm a smaller boy, and there's no sugar left for me in the bowl, I'm too far from the sugar bowl.

"Dirty bastard!" Jack shouted out loud, "Goddam you, you dirty, filthy bastard!" Jack screamed again, and some of the boys were scared, but Jack made them be quiet right away. I cried more, but I got stopped after a while because now I'm the same as Jack. I said dirty bastard too in my head and then I said, "Dirty bastard, filthy bastard," out loud just like Jack did, but I know God didn't like that. I know because the thunder sounded like He cleared his throat, and it started to rain. Jack stopped me from crying again, and we listened to the thunder and the rain on the tin roof and pounding on the glass windows and watched the blue lightning. I wish God would make the lightning hit Mr. Tupper, the filthy bastard snake slut. I'm sorry, God, but that's how I feel. Stop it hurting and kill Mr. Tupper the filthy bastard, with a blue bolt of lightning. Now I know I won't have to tell Jack about that, Jack knows. Jack knows something, now he knows. He knows that I won't tell anyone, not that. Jack will know what to do. Shush, be quiet now, he might come back...sshhh... He can't come back because Floyd punched his lights out and Mrs. Tickner beat him with her wooden spoon and sent him packing.

I got myself awake again. I still had the tooth in my hand. I will never go to sleep now. *Never.*

I put the tooth back in my shoe, and I might have gone back to sleep, but thought about whether I have to ask Floyd if he knows anybody else that is a slut and a dirty bastard, too. Maybe I don't have to ask right now, because I don't want to know, but I do know what a dirty bastard slut snake *does*. We always kill the snakes in the baseball field and feed them to the pigs.

"Don't use bad words, Fletcher," my mother whispered from heaven right beside God or maybe from the sweet clover and honeybees by the tracks and the little wet sand balls that run down into my shoes and the white wood, behind the white picket fence not silvered gray like the others. If I wish hard enough, I can see her.

Before I see Floyd next time I'll make up my mind whether I should ask him, or maybe when I see him I won't ask him, or maybe when I see him I'll *have to* ask him. *Floyd will know. Floyd knows everything.* I shivered myself back to sleep, and it was morning before I knew it. Maybe I was dreaming. That's it, I was dreaming like being a cowboy out riding the lone prairie with Murvie even if he's got cancer and the pukes and is bald and got a potter's funeral. I'm glad Mr. Tupper got a beating and got sent away for good.

Eighteen

I tried to give the tooth to Jack. For getting whipped and things he knows, and for giving his sugar to me, and things that happened to him. That is why I tried to give the tooth to Jack, because now I know that things happened to him, *just like me.*

"Keep it. *It's yours,*" Jack said when I showed the steel tooth to him a couple of weeks after Floyd and Mrs. McAllister went back home. So I did. I tried to give it to Jack for getting whipped all his life, but he shook his head and wouldn't take it.

"No, *you* found it, Fetch, you keep it. *It won't do me no good, will it?*" he said, and spat into the grass. "Besides," he said, waiting for a minute and spitting again, "I... don't want *nothin'* to do with that old bastard pervert Tupper," Jack told me as we walked around the yard in the dark. Mrs. Tickner said it was alright to walk around in the dark if we wanted to. Not Mr. Tupper. He made us get to bed before the sun went down every night. "Never wanted anything to do with him! Never! The filthy *pervert!*" Jack sounded disgusted. "I'd as soon kill him as look at him now," Jack looked angry and black *like a storm was coming.*

We sat on the cement cover over the water well and listened to the pigs oinking quietly and looked up at the stars. Jack stayed quiet for a long time. I saw a falling star.

I wished Jack would take the silver tooth. Mrs. Tickner told me it was silver, not steel. It just *looks* like steel. *Sometimes things are not what they appear, boy.* That is what Floyd said.

"Maybe I should give it to Mrs. Tickner. *Hey, see that?*" I pointed out the falling star to Jack in case he missed it.

I asked Jack if giving it to Mrs. Tickner was a good idea. "So she'll have something to remember her brother by." I spit. "Her husband got killed and bombed and blown to smithereens all over the place, not even a tooth left, and she has nothing to remember *him* by," I reminded Jack.

"She hates her brother's guts like I do," Jack said finally. "She hates him more than I do!"

It was that time I saw that Jack was a lot like Floyd. He hesitated wisely and jerked his head toward the hogs. The hogs snuffled in the trough looking for some more food, but I know they already ate everything, so they must be hungry like I am.

"What he done to you, and what he done to me, 'n' some of the other boys, he's no better'n them pigs!" he said eventually. He spit pretty far. "In fact *those pigs is more human than he is!*" He said, "*I like pigs better.*"

The moon came out, and I saw tears in Jack's eyes. He must have got a bit of dirt in his eyes because Jack doesn't cry, not even when he gets whipped. That's what he said, but maybe I'm wrong because I never saw Jack get whipped, but that's what he said, and I believed him. He turned away.

Jack got up and paced around suddenly. "I'm going to tell you, Fetch," he said quietly. "You gotta know, *somebody's* gotta know, so... *You're old enough to know, ain't you?* What he's done to me, and you, and Eddie, and the others — I feel like I might have to go find him!" He sat down again. "Maybe I'll just kill him myself an' get it over with, kill him and nut him and skin him like a gutted pig!" I don't know why Jack laughed, but he laughed and stood up and threw a stick at the pigs. I know Jack doesn't want to hurt the pigs. He always took care of the pigs nicely and gave them clean straw and made sure that all of the pigs, even the runts, got some slops every day, just like him making sure I get sugar for my porridge, even if I'm a new boy and down at the end of the table. One of the pigs squealed loudly in terror. It sounded like Tupper the Terror.

"Shut up, you pigs!" Jack yelled harshly.

"Jack!" I almost fell over. "*Find him?*" I asked, not believing my ears.

"You know I'm going to be sixteen, right?"

"*Find him and kill him?*" I asked quietly, but out loud, looking to see if the pigs could hear us. Maybe not, because I heard quiet oinks. I picked a straw to chew on. The lights in the kitchen galley went out.

"Boys! Time to come in now!" Mrs. Tickner shouted from the porch and went back in, letting the screen door slam as she disappeared.

"Coming, Mrs. T.!" Jack shouted. He scratched his head and looked at me in the dark. "You never know what's going to happen, do you?" he said to me. "Look what he done to *you, because I didn't tell anyone what he done to me and the others!* I was a *coward,* Fletch. I should have told somebody a long time ago, and see what happens? He did it to you too. It was *my* fault," he said bitterly.

"He's gone, Jack," I said, picking another straw and chewing on it. "Here Jack, chew on this straw, and we can be farmers instead. We got the pigs already."

He picked a straw and chewed on it. Moonlight glinted like steel on his eyes and that reminded me of the shiny tooth.

"I ain't a farmer. That's why I decided I gotta get out of here. *I gotta get away from here and...*"

"What?" I shouted almost out loud because it was a big surprise to me that Jack would even *think* about leaving.

"*Shush!*" Jack whispered. "I didn't tell you, but I'm leaving in a few weeks... Well, you know I'm getting to be sixteen, and *I don't have to stay here no more...* The law says I can leave when I'm sixteen, come hell or high water, so I'm going!" He scratched his head. "I'm gonna run off and join the navy. That's where I'm going, the navy."

"*The navy?* I never heard of any orphans running off and joining the *navy,* Jack," I said. Somebody has to tell Jack that. Jack looked like he didn't believe me.

"I'm going to try, anyway," he said finally.

"Can I come, too?" I asked. I like being in the navy. It's almost as good as being a cowboy in Texas even if you're bald like Murvie, wearing a white uniform.

"No, I gotta go by myself."

"You can't stop me. I'm going in the Navy, too!" I said to Jack. He laughed.

"You're going *everywhere* fast, Fletch!" He pushed me off of the well lid. I got back on and didn't say anything. I pushed Jack's hat off from the back instead. I thought about it for a minute and decided that I don't like that. *I can go in the Navy if I want to.*

"You'll have to help Mrs. Tickner with the smaller boys when I decide to go, won't you?"

"I know that, Jack. You don't have to tell me that, I know."

Jack picked up a straw and chewed on it. He spit. I spit too, just like Jack. We forgot about Jack leaving for a while because we were just about to have a big fight. "I bet you can't hold me down now, can you?" I challenged Jack.

"Want to have a wrestling match and see?" he asked.

Jack and I had the biggest wrestling match we ever had in history, and I won right away. Jack let me win. He always lets me win. We sat in grass and then flopped backwards and laughed a lot and looked up at the moon.

"You don't have any money, Jack," I said. I just thought of it. Now Jack won't have to go because he doesn't have any money.

"Don't need much. I'll hitch all the way there," Jack finally talked. "When you get to the Navy they pay you right away," Jack said. "And drink rum every day too. It's the rules. You have to drink rum every day in the navy".

I want to join the navy too, just like Jack. I don't like Catcher's Rye whiskey like Billy McCaudry, but I like rum. I chewed on a long grass stem instead and practiced being a farmer listening to the pigs grunting quietly. Just for now.

"It's a long way to the Navy, Jack. Why don't we go to Floyd's? He'll know how to get you there."

"Can't be bothering Floyd, now can I?" Jack snapped. He was getting a bit crabby. I think he doesn't really want to go in the Navy. He wants to live at Floyd's and eat beef stew and dumplings just like me. I know. I know a lot. Now, I know what to do. Take Jack to Floyd's with me.

I reached into my pocket. "You can take this silver tooth with you and sell it at a jeweler for cash," I suggested. "Take it, Jack!" I held it out to him. Jack shook his head.

"Then take me with you, Jack, and I'll show you how we can get ourselves all the way to Floyd's and live there and we'll get a job in a dynamite factory!" I suggested. Getting a job in dynamite factory is better than killing Mr. Tupper or going in the Navy, even for a minute, I bet. Better than the Navy, except for the drinking rum part. That's almost as good as being a cowboy in Texas, I bet. I got thinking about Murvie for a minute, but Jack interrupted before I had a chance to think very long.

"Go to Waterland?" Jack looked at me like he thought I was crazy. I'm not crazy. Not me. Jack knows it, too.

"Me and you can stay at Floyd's as long as we want, he said so. We can work in the Shoemaker factory. It's just over the river. We can take turns, boots and dynamite, dynamite and boots. We need cowboy boots to get us walking to Texas, and it's not far from Floyd's! Only six miles, I bet. That's not far unless it blows up. We can run to work every morning. We'll get stew and biscuits at Floyd's—even Mrs. McAllister said so, remember?" I said excitedly. "We can make our own real cowboy boots, brown with stitch stuff. We can make 'em, Jack!

Jack leaned over and picked a timothy straw and then chewed on it and smiled and chewed some more and spit just like a bald cowboy. Jack would have made the best cowboy in the world. I know Murvie would have liked to learn to spit like that out in the moonlight too, but don't forget Murvie died and got buried in a potter's funeral by

Mr. Tupper. I think Murvie would have liked to work in a dynamite factory and the cowboy boot factory, too, like us.

"Maybe that's better than being a bald cowboy out on the prairies *without* a *real* cowboy hat, Jack."

"I'll think about it, Fetch. Thinkin' about Tupper, a stick of black powder is what he needs..."

Jack and I went in because Mrs. Tickner called us again and said we were supposed to. "You boys were supposed to be in here a half hour ago!" she yelled. We went in and went to bed like the other boys. We whispered about things for a little while, but my eyes got tired, and I forgot everything Jack said, even the navy and drinking rum and the admiral's daughter, too.

A couple of weeks later that must have been the reason Mrs. Tickner was crying when she dished out the porridge for us on a rainy morning. I had to do Jack's work and take care of the smaller boys that morning. Jack was gone. *So was the silver tooth from my shoe.*

Nineteen

Three days after my sixteenth adoption day I got to be thirteen years old. It was the most important adoption day I ever had, not because I was thirteen years old and not because I was adopted. *I wasn't.* It wasn't because Floyd and Mrs. McAllister came to visit. They came on every adoption day just like clockwork and every visitation day, ever since the time Floyd and Mrs. Tickner gave Mr. Tupper his beating and royal toothless send-off. Too bad Jack wasn't still here to see what happened, but he wasn't, so too bad.

Arnold Thackery opened the gate and let Floyd's old red truck chug right up the hill and through the gate and right up to the door. Floyd and Mrs. McAllister are first to get here on adoption days every time because they are in a hurry to see me, and I'm in a hurry to see them, too. Sometimes, there are no old black Fords and Dodges and Pontiacs following them, and sometimes there are quite a few, all eating Floyd's dust like usual. Today there are four cars following Floyd up the hill.

"I want all of you be on your best, now!" Mrs. Tickner straightened our collars one after the other, and inspected our ears. "And stand off of the parking lot so you won't get yourselves run over!" she added, brushing the dust off of her sleeve.

"Yes, Ma'am!" most of the boys called back. We line up nice and neat on the grass for Mrs. Tickner, so that everybody can see that we're not brats and punks and no-goods.

The Fires of Waterland

I always stand right in front, so that Floyd can see me right away, even before they get all the way up the hill. Floyd always waves right away, and even Mrs. McAllister saw me and waved too, and that's when I saw the girl they had with them.

I ran to the truck even before the dust settled and helped Mrs. McAllister haul Floyd's wheeled chair out of the back and held it steady for Floyd while he bums down into it. The girl stayed in the truck and watched carefully. She kept watching me, and I don't know why.

"Well, lad, how are you doing?" Floyd said, as he spun his chair around to face me.

"Fine, Floyd!" I said, as I held my hand out and gave his a good shake. My hands are getting big and strong just like Floyd's. That's from hauling the slops and big pails of water to the pigs, and doing all kinds of hard yard work too, at least that's what Floyd says.

Mrs. McAllister gave me a big hug. "My, you are growing, Fletcher!" My face got pretty red and that girl noticed right away, too. I think she was going to look into my ears for dust too, but I backed off right away.

"I bet you don't know who *this* is," Mrs. McAllister smiled, indicating the girl. The truck door squawked loudly when she opened it. I don't think Floyd likes to ask Mrs. McAllister to oil the hinges, so it didn't get done lately. That's because I haven't had a chance to oil it good, and Floyd can't. "*Fletcher?*" Mrs. McAllister reminded me.

Now the girl climbed down out of the truck, since Floyd's dust was settled down, so her dress wouldn't get dirty, and his chair was out of the way.

I shrugged and squinted at the girl. She was about ten or eleven and had long blonde hair and blue eyes. She wore a white dress and had white gloves on. She turned to face me and smiled. Her teeth were as white as daisy petals. She didn't have any shiny steel ones.

She said "*Fletcher Carnival Williams, what do you mean you don't know who I am, anyway?*"

153

I shrugged. I saw her face before, but I forgot who she was, but I can't help it. And how did she know who I was anyway? I looked at Floyd and felt pretty silly but the other boys didn't notice because they were all getting looked over by the other visitors and being told, "*Stand up straight, young man,*" by a tall skinny man with a fancy hat and a hot, black wool suit on.

I shrugged and I squinted at her again for another try.

"*Picked any yellow beans lately, Fletcher?*" she asked.

'*Only when there's no important yard work to do for my father' I told the girl over the fence. I brushed off my brown tweed cap and saw my mother coming out of the door with a wet spot on her apron. "Oh, hello, Livvy" my mother said. "Fletcher Carnival Williams at your service, Ma'am."*

"You remember *Livvy Manlin*, Fletcher—from Waterland?" Mrs. McAllister charged in on my remembering and interrupted, but I knew who the girl was before she reminded me, so there. I reached for my brown tweed cap, but it wasn't on my head now. I forgot to put it on. It was still under my mattress where I hid it from old Tupper and always stored it nice and safe from anyone else getting it, too. I always get it when I need it, but this time I forgot about it just when I need it the most. I don't know why, but I felt like the *Count of Monte Cristo* again, but this time I didn't have any escape bag or time to dig a tunnel, and certainly not enough time to escape. I looked at my fingers. They weren't bleeding too much, yet.

"*Fletcher?*" the girl asked again.

I started to smooth my rooster tail hair down and caught myself before the girl started to giggle. I hate giggling.

'*You're not supposed to talk to strangers, young lady' my mother said.*

I could hear my mother talking. I don't know why. But then it wasn't my mother talking, it was Mrs. McAllister.

"Are you going to say *hello?*" Mrs. McAllister hurried me up as if I would not have remembered to.

"Hello," I said. I scuffed my shiny shoes in the dust. I don't know why people always think you should have something to say when you really don't, and I don't want to say anything, but I did, just for Floyd.

"Hey, Fetch, nice to see you again," she offered. My ears were burning. I don't know why. Maybe I do know why. She wasn't on the other side of a fence. She's a girl, too. I don't know which one is worse, being on the wrong side of the fence or being a girl. I looked at Floyd to get *saved* because I didn't know what to say, but he was busy stuffing his pipe with tobacco and lighting up and chatting with other visitors.

"Fine bunch of lads, aren't they?" He commented and puffed at the man standing next to him. The man rubbed his chin. I don't know why, because there were no mosquitoes. That man had a tight black suit on too: the funeral kind that gets too hot and makes your neck all red. The glasses sitting on his nose are big and black like his suit.

"*Harrumph!* All small and spindly, aren't they?" he said.

"Finest bunch of boys around, I'd say!" Floyd said. He was right. Floyd's always right.

I got distracted from listening to Floyd by a woman visitor putting her arms around Joe Coleman. He tried to get away, but she squeezed him harder, and his face got red just like mine does. I hate getting squeezed. It makes you too hot.

Mrs. Tickner came and saved me from having to talk to Livvy. She dragged everyone in for tea and cupcakes with icing on, so Livvy followed Mrs. McAllister and Mrs. Tickner and the other ladies. She turned around and watched me as she walked. She waved. I feel better and a lot braver now, so I waved back at her.

I told Floyd that I had to go see the pigs, and he wheeled his chair up along beside me. He puffed on his pipe, and the smoke swirled behind him. The other boys went for cakes with the visitors too, but not me.

"Nice girl, that Livvy," Floyd commented. He didn't look at me because he was too busy watching T.T and the other porkers. They squealed and grunted and snuffled through the fence at Floyd's chair.

"What'd you bring *her* for, Floyd?" I asked. He squinted up at me and took the pipe from his mouth slowly. The sky reflected in his eyes, and he looked wise. He hesitated. Just like Jack and me. I hesitate now, too.

"Nice girl, that one, and she likes you. I can see that, looks like *she has plans for you, boy,*" he puffed his pipe back to life with only one match. The flames jumped up high when he puffed in the flame of the match.

I felt my face getting red again. I threw T.T. Oinker some loose green grass. The other porkers tried to get some, too. They squealed. "Let's go sit over by the well cap over there," Floyd suggested.

We moved over and got away from the pig smell and the oinking, and I sat on the concrete well cap, and Floyd did too because I helped him get out of the wheeled chair. The wheels looked pretty wobbly. I showed Floyd that the nut on the wheel was loose again, just like last time. I promised that I would tighten it up for him before he went home. "Thanks, Fletcher. The spanner's in the glove compartment, just like usual," Floyd said.

"What'd you bring *her* for, Floyd?" I asked again, after the important mechanical things were talked about. He squinted into the sun and back at me.

"That girl's been hounding the missus to come up here and see you for quite a while," he finally said. "She does seem to like you quite a bit, doesn't she?" Floyd smiled, but still didn't answer the question I asked. Sometimes Floyd does that, and the answer gets in my head all by itself.

"Oh."

"Near a year, I guess. Got trouble at home, that one, spends a lot of time with us now," Floyd scratched his neck and reached into his jacket pocket. He took out his wallet. He opened it and handed me a picture.

I could see it was Livvy and Floyd and Mrs. McAllister, Floyd smiling right at me with his pipe in his mouth, and Livvy with her arm around Mrs. McAllister. "Nice picture isn't it?" Floyd asked.

"Who took the picture?" I asked. I knew from the picture that it wasn't Floyd. When you're in the picture, you can't take it.

"Well...it was that... young lady next door, you know..." His voice faded, but he turned to look at me. "You know, the woman that was staying with your father?" I was so surprised that I didn't say anything, not even a word. Floyd finally talked again. "Tina McQueeny." My ears started to buzz. I remembered the name.

Tina McQeeny, wanna pull a weeny, Tina McQueeny wanna pull a weeny, Teena McQueeny wanna pull a weeny...

Now, I know who that woman is. I forgot about that part. I don't know why I forgot about that part. Good thing. God wouldn't like that, and neither would my mother, I bet.

"Tina McQueeny?" I asked. "She's still there?"

Floyd stirred and looked up at the clouds. "Something else I gotta tell you, boy. You ain't too likely to care much to hear, but you and I have always spoke straight up front, ain't we?" I nodded.

"What, Floyd?" He watched as some pigeons landed in front of the pig house and pecked at spilled grains in the muck. T.T. oinked at them, but they didn't take off. T.T. oinks at everything, and soon he'll have to go to the bacon factory, too. Everybody has to go to the bacon factory sooner or later. Mrs. Tickner said so one time, and I didn't like it, not one bit.

"I'm sorry, love, but it gives us money to run the place, doesn't it then?" she told me. I ran outside and cried that time. I sneaked T.T. extra slops, but Jack saw me and told me to get used to the idea no matter what. It doesn't matter because Jack's gone. *Get used to it, Jack.*

Floyd hauled out another picture but didn't let me see it right away. "I took this picture, somebody you might want to see."

"Give me the picture, c'mon, Floyd!" I said. He held it away. He held it up high in the sky and even if Floyd doesn't have any legs, he can hold a picture high. I couldn't reach it.

"First..." Floyd hesitated. "I gotta tell you that your father ain't been seen around for a few months now, quite a few months." He sighed. "Fletcher, my boy, I never lied to you or nothing like that, have I? Lies don't pass between men that are friends."

"That's right, Floyd. I know that, Floyd. So, my father isn't around?" I nearly said *so what* but I didn't mean to, honest.

"Last three times we were up here I meant to tell you, but I didn't know *how* to." He stuffed his pipe again and puffed it a few times until it was going again. He clamped his hand over the top of the bowl and kept the smoke in. I know how to do that, too.

"Mrs. McAllister and I talked about it an awful lot and decided. Since you're thirteen now, you can understand things that are tough to take, but being the truth, see?" I nodded and reached for the picture again, but Floyd held it away and smiled.

"I took this picture just for you, before *you find out by yourself.*" Floyd handed me the picture. *A woman.* The sun felt hot, and I got dizzy from looking at the picture. It was Tina McQueeny that smiled at me from the picture, but she looked different. How did she get in one of Floyd's pictures? I didn't hear what Floyd said, and I stared at the picture some more.

> *She's a slut and I have to push her away now. I don't want to push her away but I have to. I have to run away. My mother and God will see. "Come along, Fletcher!" My mother said. How can she say that? She can't say that. She's dead, and her apron is wet, and the freight train ran over her right on time.*

I looked at the man in the picture, too, but I had to look at Tina again. She was still smiling at me. *So was the man.* He was wearing a hat. He looked at me. *Jack was looking at me out of the picture.* He wasn't in the navy drinking rum and wearing a uniform, he was looking at me out of the picture. *It can't be Jack, but it is Jack.*

"Come along, Fletcher!"

"Come along, Fletcher!" Mrs. Tickner shouted from the doorway. "Let Mr. McAllister have some refreshments." I shook my head and looked at the picture. *It can't be Jack, but it is Jack.* The screen door banged shut. Floyd didn't say a word. I didn't talk out loud. I want to run away now, and I don't know why because Floyd's here with me, and Floyd always knows what to do. Floyd cleared his throat.

"Boy? *Fletcher?*"

I don't want to look at Floyd. *He knows. He knows it's Jack. I know who she is, too. I don't want to remember, but I do. I do remember. Tina McQueeny, the slut.* I looked up in the sky and watched the clouds. I smelled my fingers. I forgot about her. How did she come back? She can't be back, how can she come back? She's in the picture. Jack's in the picture. Jack can't be there. He went in the navy to drink rum. Yes, he is in the picture, not in the Navy, and she's got him. Jack's in the navy drinking rum, it doesn't smell like whiskey my father drinks.

I smelled my fingers. They smell funny. I want to do it again. I don't want to do it again. Tina McQueeny's a slut. I'm not going to answer. My father will be home soon. No, he won't. He's never coming home. Your mother can't see you, silly, she's not here, so come on Fletcher, you'll like it, you'll like it, you'll like it, stop that.

They smelled like soap-water. That's what it was, soap-water. I jumped and looked at Floyd again. He watched me closely, then scratched his head and put his wallet back into his pocket, watching me. I looked at Floyd and tried not to think. I can't think. I *have to* think.

"Something on your mind, Fletcher?" Floyd asked casually, puffing on his pipe thoughtfully. "You look a little upset." I shook my head, but it didn't make any difference, I was thinking no matter what.

I wish I had my Pontiac here. I'd drive over as fast as I can go and get Jack away from her right now. I know he's looking at her tits, too. She'll do things to you, Jack, like old Tupper; she'll make you do things, Jack! Jack — Watch out, Jack! She's a slut, like that old bastard Tupper. Don't say that, Fletcher, it's bad. It's bad to say that, don't say that. Jack? Jack? What? Oh, no, it is Jack! No, it's not Jack with her, it isn't Jack, it can't be Jack with her. Yes, it is; he is with her; it is Jack with her. God, don't let him do that! Leave Jack alone! Oh, Jack, she got you now!

I nodded. I looked at Floyd and nodded.

"She got Jack, Floyd; she's got Jack now, too!" I stared. I remembered to look at the picture again. The man that was standing with his arms around Tina was *Jack. Jack was smiling.* He had a hat on, like my brown tweed hat, and he was *smiling.* That's where my hat went. No. It's under the mattress where I keep it.

"That's Jack!" I almost shouted. The blood was roaring in my ears, and I couldn't hear anything. *Nothing at all.* I shook my head. "What's Jack doing there?" I demanded angrily. "*She got Jack!*" I shouted. "*She got Jack now!*"

"Don't get yourself worked up about it, now!" Floyd grabbed my arm and sat me back down because I was almost to my feet. "What's the matter, son?" Floyd asked. "What's the matter?"

I sat down hard. I shook my head quite a bit, and I don't even know why. I looked at Jack again. His arm was around Tina. *Oh, no. Jack, you can't escape now.*

"C'mon, Fletcher, let's walk a bit." Floyd ignored me and hoisted himself off of the well cap and slid onto his chair. He started wheeling away. He turned around. "Coming?" he asked quietly. I got up. I didn't want to, but I did.

The gravel crunched under my feet and the wheels of Floyd's chair as we started moving slowly along. I caught up with Floyd, but not right away because I was staring a lot at Jack's picture. He was smiling a lot. No wonder. Tina McQueeny was wearing a blouse tied up tight under her tits, and her shorts were cut off real high. I could see them again, just like the first time, outlined under the thin yellow blouse in the sunshine, not like the first time.

I wonder if Floyd noticed her tits too. I couldn't miss them, so how could he? He didn't say anything; he didn't say *anything* about it. Maybe his eyes are worse than he said. Floyd never gets his eyes tested once a year like he is supposed to because it's free, and he doesn't have to pay for it, not a nickel, that is what Mrs. McAllister said. Maybe he doesn't want to know his eyes are getting older, or maybe it wasn't important to him. Floyd only notices and says *important* things.

"Wondered when you'd notice that Jack was in that photo," he smiled. "You should have seen the look on your face. Mind you, with what happened back then, it ain't no *surprise* you missed him. No surprise at all," he spoke a little slowly, as if he was thinking a lot. "Must have been quite a surprise to you. And rightly so, I'd say!" he spoke gruffly but smiled strangely at me. He didn't hesitate that time, either. Not even a bit. I looked at the picture again.

"How'd Jack get there?" I asked Floyd. I couldn't believe my eyes.

I bet Jack's seen her tits and everything else all the way to Regina. Probably. She probably showed him right away. She's a slut. She has to show them to everybody and does everything right away to *everyone*. No. Floyd doesn't want to see them. He said so. Floyd's always right about everything.

"Got him a real job at the broomstick factory, first thing the day after he showed up on our doorstep."

"No, I meant with *her*. How she grabbed Jack so fast like that?"

I am mad at Jack. Jack should know better because after what that old Mr. Tupper did to him, Jack should have been watching. That's it, Jack wasn't watching. That's it, Jack wasn't watching, he wasn't paying attention. When you don't watch what's happening, that's when things happen, I know. It's like putting your hand through the gate, and Mr. Tupper grabbing your hand right away without giving you a chance to get away, and never letting go, and selling you for bait, or burying you in a goddam potter's funeral without letting you know. Just like Mr. Tupper did to Murvie Klinder, my friend Murvie; and now he'll never get to Texas and be a bald cowboy and camp out in the tumbleweeds, and learn to sing and play the guitar like Gene Autry. I know that's what happened to Jack. *No, Murvie.* But me and Floyd have to save Jack as soon as we get to Waterland. *We gotta save Jack right away.*

Floyd looked around for a while before he answered. "Wasn't *she* grabbed *him*, lad. *He* grabbed *her*—"

"—No, he didn't, not Jack. Jack's not like that. He doesn't want to grab anybody or get married at all, never, *never*, and he doesn't even *like* girls, and I bet he hates sluts!" I looked straight at Floyd and I'm

161

not sorry I said that, either, no matter what. Floyd just looked at me for a minute.

"I'm sorry, son. I think you're having a hard time with this, aren't you? I shouldn't have showed you that picture, but I thought you'd be happy to see that Jack's just fine."

Floyd watched the pigs for a minute. I think Floyd likes pigs, too. "It's good to be concerned about your friends, boy, but they have to make their own way, and you'll find out eventually that you have to make your own way too. And things will happen to them, and things that you don't care for; *that's life*. We all live it, we all run into people that are bad people, sluts in more ways than one. The worst kind being the ones that pretend they are your friend and deceive you and take advantage. So, you get used to the idea quick now, because your hating people isn't going to *change* them. In fact it might make them worse." He scratched his chin.

"For instance, maybe that young lady Tina really isn't as bad as we think. She just let her physical wants get ahead of her using common sense. Maybe that's what happened with her...on more than one occasion. Jack seems to like her just fine, and she's quite a pretty young lady. So, what's really so wrong with that, as long as Jack's happy with her?"

I turned away because my eyes were starting to burn, and I thought that I might want to cry, but I better not because Floyd will see me. *You don't cry when you're thirteen. Boys don't cry.* That's what Jack said back when I got to be eight, on my birthday, and Jack was in charge of me, and so I better do what Jack said. I picked a straw to chew on instead. I don't care anyway. Jack can do what he likes, but I don't want him to have Tina McQueeny. No, I don't care, but Floyd said it's always right to be concerned about your friends. Anyway, it's better to chew on a straw and think hard about things instead of letting Floyd see you cry.

"We have to go see Jack right away and make sure he's happy then, no matter *who* got him!" I finally told Floyd.

"That's the spirit, lad." Floyd said, "That's the *important* part. That Jack's happy."

The Fires of Waterland

The hinges on the screen door squeaked. Mrs. Tickner stepped out into the sunshine. She had her hands on her hips and was looking for us everywhere at once. She must have thought we were wheeling around in the backyard, but that's not where we were. "Over here, Mrs. Tickner, we're over here!" Floyd shouted.

"Fletcher! Bring Mr. McAllister in for tea now, will you?" Mrs. Tickner called again.

"We're coming right away, Mrs. Tickner!" Floyd yelled to Mrs. Tickner. The door slammed behind her as she disappeared back into the kitchen. "We'd better head in for now, lad..."

"Not me, I'm going to do the slops," I told Floyd indifferently. "I have to feed the hogs." Floyd's never wrong, but maybe we still have to save Jack. Right away, too, but Floyd didn't seem to think so. Maybe Floyd didn't really care about Jack like I do. "I think we better save Jack right away, just to be extra careful, Floyd."

He shook his head. That made me mad, but I didn't tell Floyd that. I clammed up and headed off the feed T.T. and the other porkers. T. T. was oinking quietly and snuffled in the trough and then at me for something new to eat.

Floyd called after me. "Fletcher, you're wrong this time." Floyd followed. I thought he was getting ready to tell me he changed his mind, but then he said, "Boy, you're wrong this time."

"I'm going to save Jack all by myself. I'm going to save him by myself if you don't help me!" I called back at him. He must have changed his mind about going in. He wheeled over.

"You don't have to save Jack, Fetch. He's a man now, and he's deciding for himself, just like you're going to be doing pretty soon now, too!" I saw smoke puff out of his pipe when he got up behind me, but I pretended I didn't see him. I tossed T.T. Oinker a handful of grain. The other porkers pushed in and squealed wildly. It hurt my ears.

"I'm going to Texas then, to be a cowboy and rope wild bulls and brand them."

163

I will, you'll see, they'll be branded just like me and Jack with stripes on his goddamned back. Jack, goddamned Tina McQueeny. I hate you, too, slut, slut, snake-brained Tupper, silver-toothed lying slut. I have to rescue Jack. Don't talk like that, Fletcher Carnival Williams, don't you dare talk like that. It can't be my mother talking. She can't say anything; she's dead, just like the dusty stuff and pictures and such we dumped in the memorable junk fire and all them dead glass soldiers. Fetchie, boy, it's empty they are, Fetchie, dead soldiers, gimme another live one. Goddam you, boy, be quick about it, too. Hand me that bottle of whiskey! I'll be taking the belt to you, boy, soon as the old lady's gone 'ta town, too. No, she's dead, ain't she? She's gone to town for good, goddamn her, and goddamn you too, you, you little bastard. It's all because of your mother, goddamn her, gimme that goddamned bottle, boy. Ya know what's good for you... Gimme the damned bottle, Fetchie. I need a drink — gimme a drink. No, don't hit me, no, no more.

You hit my mother. I hate you. I'm running away soon. I'm never coming back, me. I'm going to be a cowboy and ride my horse with Gene Autry, and Murvie Klinder's coming with me. He doesn't care if he's bald and dead and buried in a potter's grave. We're getting to Texas now, we're running off.

Floyd smiled. "Maybe I should go to Texas, too, but neither of us can go, right?" Floyd reached into the pail and threw the oinkers some oats too. "No, Fletch, running some place, or running off to do something else isn't going to help you sort this thing out. You have to face things *as they are*, not like you think they *should be*," Floyd said quietly.

He puffed on his pipe and scratched the top of his head. He turned his chair and went a few feet. I heard him sigh as he stopped for a moment, then he clamped his pipe in his mouth and pushed himself along, and the smoke curled behind him. The wheel on the back wobbled when it went over the ruts. He paused and turned around to look at me. I saw the setting sun shining in his glasses, and the glass things looked red-orange and orange-red just like the sun. I couldn't see his eyes to tell if he was saying the truth, but I am mixed up.

Floyd said it *before*, that Tina was a slut, but *now he says she might be all right* because her common sense got left behind, and she got Jack and now it's *okay* for Jack to be there. *Jack needs us to go save him.* I know. Maybe it's not me, it's Floyd that has got himself all mixed up looking at Tina in the picture because she is so pretty. Yes, that's it. Maybe Floyd's common sense got left behind too. No, it can't be because Floyd is always right; he's never wrong. I never saw that before.

He waited before he spoke. "Coming?" he asked. I didn't answer, but I looked at him for a little bit. People like it if you answer them right away, and think you're not mad at them. I scuffed my sneakers in the dirt and studied the way the sand piles up and falls over. I looked to see if T.T. Oinker was watching me study sand, and he must have been because he grunted about it. Floyd turned away. He got it right away. It doesn't take Floyd long to figure things out.

"Don't be angry, Fletch. Doesn't do a man any good to burn himself out over things that can't be changed, does it?" I watched him as he wheeled away, and I thought about whether I really should be mad at Floyd and decided I was. Floyd stopped and waited. I am mad at Floyd because he doesn't think Jack should be rescued. I know Jack needs rescuing.

And even if Floyd changes his mind and decides that Jack needs rescuing, I don't really want to go with him and his wobbly chair and chopped off legs. Maybe everyone in the whole world feels like they are chopped off like Floyd's legs that really were hacked off, and Mrs. Tickner is cut off from her husband because of a bomb; and my mother was killed by the freight train too, and God is looking after her right now because I can hear them talking. It doesn't surprise me that I'm getting chopped off from Jack, right now, too, but *maybe it's okay.* Maybe I better *get used to it, Jack.* Look what happened to Murvie. *See what happens?*

You have to face things as they are, not like you think they should be. That's what Floyd said in my head again, and how can he say that in my head when I'm looking right at him? He told me that a long

165

time ago when my father was drinking whiskey and doing things like Mr. Tupper, and the freight train ran over my mother.

I don't want to hear that. I don't want to hear that, no, no.

Hey, Fetchie boy, gimme that bottle, you little bastard. It's all your fault the old lady had to kill herself, that stupid bitch. I'm going to whip the ass off you soon as I have another drink, boy!

It's all my fault, I know it's my fault. I know, I'm a little bastard, my father said so, he said it, now I know. Stop talking like that. No, no, don't think bad words like that. Come along, Fletcher, my son, your father will feel better soon, you'll see, honey. It's from eating too much cheese and he's all bunged up, and he's got a terrible headache again, that's all. He'll feel better soon, my son.

I blinked hard and my mother and father drove away in the old Pontiac with the mouse nest, and God sitting in the back seat whispering quietly, and they went fast, then slow, then fast, then slow, with a gallon of gas from Mrs. Mulligan, and Mr. Mulligan's ashes in the green jar and peanut butter cookies too.

Don't disturb Mr. Mulligan, dear. No, Floyd said that God doesn't call me that, and Mrs. Tickner doesn't even call Mr. Tupper a snake even if he acts like a snake slut with a silver tooth. That's right, isn't it, dear? Don't say those words, not now, not now. Think hard about it, boy. Remember you can't change everything, no matter how you might like to. Get me another bottle of whiskey, Fetchie boy, 'fore I whip your arse black and blue like your mother, that stupid bitch, her acting like a whore and all. I hate you, you 'n' her. It's all your fault. No, no, honey, he's sick and tired and bunged up from eating too much cheese, and his headache is back, he'll be okay soon, you'll see...

Floyd turned again and looked at me and didn't say anything at all, not a word. He nodded and winked at me, so I changed my mind and followed him. I don't agree with him just now, and I might go to Texas; or maybe me and Dickie and Elton will team up with Ronnie Gates and Marvin Pychinski to rescue Jack sometime or go somewhere, but I know that Floyd is right, or maybe I am just hungry. I want to go home with Floyd. I belong with Floyd. That's it. I belong with Floyd, because Floyd knows everything.

The Fires of Waterland

We sat in the dining room after we had spaghetti with tomato sauce and three meatballs each, and Floyd told jokes to the other boys, but I'm still thinking hard about why Jack is like he is.

I wonder if Jack still chews on straws and says yahoo a lot and has wrestling matches. No, he has Tina McQueeny now. Don't make any noise, Fletcher, "Shshsh!"

Mrs. Tickner gave us hot peach cobbler and added ice cream that Floyd and Mrs. McAllister brought with them in a cooler pack that had ice in it. Mrs. McAllister helped dish it out with the big wooden spoon she borrowed from the rack in the kitchen, the one Mrs. Tickner whacked Mr. Tupper with, and Livvy handed out the bowls to each of us along the table.

I like Livvy. She made sure I got one of the bowls with a big scoop of ice cream and extra peaches. "Here, Fletcher Carnival Williams. *Eat this,*" she said to me.

"Thank you," was all I said, and didn't look at her too much. I look at her when she's not looking, but I make sure I look away fast when she looks back at me. Her eyes are still blue as ice water. I think she's pretty, like my mother.

The boys always laugh at Floyd's jokes, but the best one was on me that time because *Floyd said I could go visit him at his house*, and I didn't even hear him because I was watching Livvy Manlin. She was talking to Richard Bordon. I was daydreaming about being a man of the world.

Get away from her, Ritchie, she's my girlfriend, leave her alone right now.

"Fletcher Carnival Williams at your service, Ma'am!" I take my cap off right quick to ask if she would kiss me. *"How about a kiss, Livvy, just a little one? Nobody's looking, honey!" "Fletcher! You are a naughty boy, aren't you?" "Only when you're around, honey!" I can smell her perfume and her hot breath close to my neck. "Fletcher!"*

Mrs. Tickner came over to me. *"Fletcher?"* she said. She put her hand on my shoulder, and I stopped watching Livvy. The boys laughed. My face got hot. "Fletcher, my goodness, are you daydreaming again?"

Mrs. McAllister looked at me and smiled like she expected me to kiss her or something. I looked at Floyd and back at Mrs. Tickner.

"He is one for daydreaming, Mrs. McAllister, but you won't find a better boy anywhere. All of our boys are good boys. You won't be sorry, not a bit. Shall *we tell him now?*" Mrs. Tickner asked Floyd. "We have a surprise for you, Fletcher...you're going to go visit with Mr. and Mrs. McAllister for a week!"

I jumped out of my chair. "I'll get ready fast as a wink!" I shouted. I laughed.

"Go up and get a clean shirt and pants to take with you, and don't forget your toothbrush!"

I ran upstairs fast that time. I got a bag and took my red shirt and long trousers and even my best socks. I forgot to get my brown tweed cap from under the mattress where I always keep it, but it doesn't matter because it's always safe when I'm not using it, and I am going home to Floyd's, my *real* home. I want to be there even if it's only for a week, and I'm never leaving there again because Floyd's place is always in my dreams.

Twenty

Mrs. Tickner gave me a hug and my ears got all red, I know because I saw them in the mirror on Floyd's truck when I climbed up on the running board. We tried to squeeze into the old truck but it was too tight for Mrs. McAllister to shift the stick shift and drive with me and Livvy and Floyd all jammed in beside her, so I climbed into the back with Floyd's chair and watched how fast we were going through the back window. I waved at the other boys. It was the first time I was away from the orphanage since Mrs. Zeban let Mr. Tupper pull me through the gate like a piece of bait.

"Pull over to the bell, woman," Floyd said as we approached the gate. She stopped with me right beside the bell. Floyd turned around and looked out the window.

"You ring that bell hard as you can, boy. *This is a special day.* You can ring it hard as you want!" he said, and smiled at me.

"Oh, Floyd, don't be so childish!" Mrs. McAllister scolded at him like a blue jay yakking at a chicken.

"*You ring that bell hard like I said!*" Floyd said to me, and "*I said this is a special day for Fletcher!*" to her.

"Ring it, Fletcher!" Livvy yelled. "*Ring it!*"

I grabbed the rope on the big bell and rang it almost as loud as Floyd could. I saw Mrs. Tickner and the other boys clapping and cheering. They waved to me from up at the orphanage. Mrs. McAllister honked the horn five times and stepped on the gas and ground the gears, and I watched the boys and Mrs. Tickner waving and clapping and getting smaller and smaller like ants and disappear. *I miss them.*

Mrs. McAllister went 45 miles an hour making a lot of dust and didn't even crash, and I saw Floyd help Livvy change the gears for Mrs. McAllister, just like when he used to help me. We drove past my father's house and wheeled into Floyd's back yard. I can see the old Pontiac sitting in the weeds in the back yard next door, but I don't see Jack. When I got off of the truck, I pulled Floyd's chair down and wheeled it close to the door so he could bum his way onto it.

"Atta boy," Floyd said. "Nice to be home, huh?" We wheeled over to the porch and Floyd bummed his way up to the top of the stairs.

"It's a long time ago you left here, Fletcher, so *welcome home!*" Mrs. McAllister said. She gave me a hug.

"Cat's got his tongue, Elizabeth," Floyd said to Mrs. McAllister. "Can't think of anything at all to say."

I looked over the fence, and now the garden isn't there anymore and there are weeds in my father's yard, thick and uneven, mostly rusty brown like the old Pontiac with the broken window.

I didn't say anything that time and I don't even know why, and Livvy and Mrs. McAllister dusted themselves off and climbed up onto the porch and sat on the swing. Everything looked exactly the same except for the weeds and peeled paint, and I helped Floyd put his chair up the stairs.

"Good to have some help with this thing," he said. I noticed that the wheel was still wobbling.

"We need a wrench, Floyd, the wheel's loose," I said.

"In the truck, boy, there's a wrench that fits everything under the sun, you go get it, it's under the seat." I went back to the truck and got the wrench and tightened the wheel as tight as it gets.

"Thanks, lad, get the oil can too, right there on the porch on the shelf there. You can oil 'er up for me too!"

"Right, Floyd, we'll have 'er fixed up in no time!" I said.

The Fires of Waterland

The two ladies laughed and swatted mosquitoes as Floyd and I took care of the important mechanical things, and hauled my clothes up to the spare room. I even oiled the hinges on Floyd's truck while I was at it. I'm home now, and a good man always helps take care of his home.

There was another surprise I had and I don't know what to think about it yet because I haven't had enough time to think hard about it like you're supposed to. Floyd must have forgotten to tell me when we were at the orphanage feeding T.T. Oinker and talking about Jack getting rescued — that is it, he must have forgotten.

Mrs. McAllister and Livvy went in to make supper and left us out to feed the mosquitoes. It was dark out and the lights in the other houses were blinking on and off, too. A car went by with blue lights on the windshield.

"Look at that, Floyd!" I said. "I never saw that before!"

"All the rage now, kind of nice, aren't they, Jack says they call them *'love lights'*."

"I like 'em," I said. "I'm going to put lights like that on the old Pontiac!"

"Better get the motor working first."

"We can do that right away, can't we, Floyd?" I asked.

"First things first, always do the most important things first, better organized that way" Floyd said.

It smelled nice on the wooden porch and I put Floyd's match out and we chased mosquitoes away with the smoke again, but that didn't change the *surprise* I got. It wasn't like it was before. I don't know why.

"You might like to know that the girl lives with us all the time now, Fletch." I thought I heard Floyd wrong.

"Livvy stays here with you and Mrs. McAllister?" I asked. I feel funny now, just like getting a needle or something. "She's got a mother and father, Floyd; she can stay with them, can't she?"

"She's got trouble, see, well, to make a long story short, she's got an aunt and uncle, but there's some problems *there* too, so Mrs. McAllister kind of...took her in, you might say, keep her off of the street, you know. She's a cousin of Mrs. McAllister's anyway. Fourth or *fifth*, I think." He said.

"Oh". That's all I can say about that; I want to stay here.

Floyd, how come she can stay here, and I can't? I belong here with you.

I clammed up and stayed quiet. Sometimes it is best to not to say things out loud. Floyd said so.

"She's been here for about six months now, Fetch, and her mother and father aren't together anymore, she left him for a bit, and off to California he went, and nobody heard from either of them for—"

"—Now they don't want her back, Floyd?" I interrupted.

Just like Elton and Dickie's Aunt Sally that dragged them up the hill and chugged like an oatmeal factory and Murvie's father that doesn't want him anymore because he got cancer that made him puke all the time and turn white and get as bald as an egg and got him not to like peaches one bit and that's why he gave them to me.

"...That's about it. We never heard from them since, so we got permission from that nice Mrs. Zeban, you remember *her*, Fletch? The lady that took you to the orphanage, —yup, that's her, she said because we're already *sort of related* we could be Livvy's foster parents, if we wanted to, not even any paperwork to do; she's family. She's a nice girl to have around to help the Missus out a bit, wouldn't you say?" Floyd took off his glasses and polished them with his handkerchief.

I had to think about it for a minute but it seemed to be all right with me just then. Nothing mattered because I was home. "Okay, Floyd." I watched my father's house to see if Jack was there, but nobody showed up and no lights came on.

Mrs. McAllister sent Livvy out to get us for supper, and it was the best supper I ever had in my whole life. Mrs. McAllister had my favorite on the table, beef stew and biscuits. We sat down and prayed to God and dished up.

and thank you, God, for bringing me home to Floyd and get me to stay here, quick, before I have to go back to the orphanage, I'm not an orphan, not me, Floyd and Mrs. McAllister could be my foster parents too, please, if you let them, and Livvy's here, and they are her cousins and get to be her foster parents. Can they be mine too, please God? That's what I want, that's all I want, that's...

"Amen," Floyd said.

"*Amen?*" Mrs. McAllister said to me. I forgot I'm supposed to say "*Amen*" too, so I did.

"Amen," I said. Livvy looked at me, and I thought she was going to laugh but she didn't. "Amen."

"Dig in!" Floyd said. We dug in and ate too much.

"My tummy's tight as a bongo drum!" Floyd said.

"You'll never starve with delicious beef stew and wonderful biscuits," I told Floyd. Floyd laughed and Mrs. McAllister turned red with happiness.

"That's for sure, Fletch, and these women sure know how to cook, don't they?" Floyd said. "Best beef stew and biscuits in the country!" His voice was loud as thunder. The clock ticked quietly in the next room, but I could hear it.

"You gentlemen are always teasing us ladies, aren't you?" said Mrs. McAllister, looking very happy and pleased with herself. "Livvy made the biscuits, too, all by herself."

I looked at Livvy. She smiled at me quickly and then looked away. I can see her face getting red, too. I saw her steal a look at Mrs. McAllister, and they smiled like they had a secret. They did, but we didn't get the apple pie secret until afterwards.

Livvy got up to take more biscuits out of the oven and then poured Floyd a glass of milk, and I noticed that she was helping Mrs. McAllister a lot, I can see that. Then I chewed a little bit and I thought the biscuits tasted funny for a minute, and I looked at Floyd and he lifted up his eyebrows at me and winked. They really didn't taste funny, not even a bit, I just thought they did, but they didn't. They were as good as Mrs. McAllister's. I remember that.

Livvy smiled at me and I saw her look smug and pleased as a pink punch bowl as I slathered extra butter on the next one.

"These ladies always have secrets," Floyd said, "sometimes it's best not to know them."

Floyd is always right. Mrs. McAllister and Livvy have lots of lady secrets all day but I couldn't tell Floyd that I got one at night with Livvy a few days later. I can't tell anyone, not even Floyd, even if God knows.

Livvy got into my room when I was sleeping. I don't know why.

"Fletcher?" she whispered.

"Shhhhh" she said. "I just want to sleep with you. You know I like you a lot. When you like someone a lot, it is okay to tell them you love them and sleep with them." I didn't say anything for a minute. I clammed up for a minute and she stood in the moonlight.

"*Livvy!* You shouldn't be here; they'll hear you," I said, almost out loud.

"Shhhhh... they're sleeping," she said, snuggling closer.

"I think *I love you*, Fletcher," she whispered. Her eyes flashed in the moonlight.

"I like you too," I said, "but ... you shouldn't be here! Mrs. McAllister will kill us and God won't like it and Floyd will get mad too!"

"They can't hear us, and God can't see us either, silly," she whispered, and then she giggled. "*Everybody* does it, Fletcher... Mom and Floyd do it. I saw your father and Tina McQueeny doing it right out my window, silly. I saw them making love just like I saw my mother and father doing it when I was little and I was in bed with them. Your father and Tina were doing it, she gave him her breasts, she sat on him, she sat right up on him and put her breasts in your

174

father's mouth. Fletcher, *I want to try that.* I want to put my breasts in your mouth now. Do you want to touch them, Fletcher?"

"No!" I said. "—Yes, —I want to, but I don't think I should do that, I can't do that now, we shouldn't do that. God won't like that, he won't like that, I know."

"I want you to just touch *them* then, *no more...* do you want me?"

I said, "No, no, — yes, —but not if you are a slut like *Tina.* Floyd says she's a slut because she does things with *everybody* and shows them her tits."

"No, don't you dare say that about me, ever, don't you say that about me or I'll hate you forever, and ever and ever and ever!" she said. "We can do it, but—"

"No, you can't do that, only sluts do that, *sluts, she's a slut.* She's a *slut.* You should go to your own room right now. Don't make noise."

"*I love you, Fletcher, if they can do it, so can we.* Okay, Fletcher— for now, promise me I'll always be your only love," she whispered, "I'm going now..."

"I promise, Livvy, *I promise,*" I said. "I don't want to be a slut either. *I love you,*" I whispered. "Maybe my father will go away again, we can go in the Pontiac in the backyard."

"Maybe we can get married, too," she said, giggling.

"I don't want to get married yet, not yet, silly," I said.

"I mean when we grow up and my breasts get bigger, silly."

She kissed my face quick and crept to her room.

I felt strange. I *wanted her to come back. She did.*

I was watching the moon, and the door closed silently behind her. She snuggled against me tightly. "Shhhhh," she said. I closed my eyes to see if God was looking.

"*Livvy!*" I said. I can hear her breathing in my ear. Whether God likes it or not, I didn't try to make her go away.

"See? She whispered. I'm sleeping with you and I'm not a slut and you can't be a slut either if you love me and she took my hand and put it on the soft bumps. I like that, Fletcher, I like that, you can touch the other one too, we can do it again tomorrow night, when they're sleeping, okay, if you love me, Fletcher, do you love me? And they're not called 'tits', Fletcher Williams, they're called 'breasts'. Her eyes flashed at me in the moonlight coming through my window like sparks in a fire and her face was hot, and don't you say 'tits', do you want to touch them, Fletcher?"

"No! Yes I want to, but I don't think I should do that, I can't do that now, God won't like that, he won't, I know." Her skin was warm.

"See? It's okay, Fletcher. I'm not a slut, you're not a slut, nobody's a slut when you love somebody, my mother told me when you love somebody you sleep together, that's why I'm here with you , and I love you. It's okay, Fletcher. I love you."

She closed her eyes, and the moon was gone, and I went to sleep.

In the morning I was surprised. I saw that Livvy was still sleeping with me and her head was up against me, and she was holding her teddy bear tightly around its neck. I looked at Livvy and wanted to get the blanket down from her neck, touch her breasts again, but I didn't. God didn't kill me, and I didn't ask her to be there, so it must be all right to sleep with someone you love.

I didn't wake Livvy up. I remembered I saw down her neck, she wanted me to see down her neck that she doesn't have big tits like Tina McQueeny, just little bumps. And now I am trying not to think about our secret, but I did anyway.

I got myself up before anybody else because I didn't want to look at Livvy with the blanket up to her neck and the choked teddy bear, and I wasn't sleeping, so no point in puffing to myself and laying there doing nothing. Get up and around and get to it, that's what Floyd said.

Twenty-One

I woke up the next morning in the big bed and smelled bacon and coffee. The sun was shining hot on my face and I didn't know where I was, but it didn't take me long to remember. I jumped up quick as a flash, and I had my shirt on and was just pulling my trousers on when the door opened. I turned away fast.

"*Sleepy head*" Livvy teased. Her blue eyes looked at me from behind the brown door, and she clicked the door shut quickly before I could say anything back at her. I heard her going down the stairs, and I got sidetracked and looked out the window for a while. There was a black Chevy pickup parked in front of my father's house. I tried to look in the house window to see who it was, but the curtains were in the way. I could see smoke coming from a high brick chimney at a big building down the street and there were quite a few cars in the parking lot in front of it. I didn't remember seeing that building before. Floyd said it was a new broomstick factory and *that's where Jack works*. Maybe I'll get a job there too, and then Floyd will keep me here.

I opened the bedroom door to see if Livvy was peeking at me, but she wasn't, so I smelled the house for a couple of minutes. I remembered every minute of living at Floyd's and the smells made me remember it better. I like living at Floyd's. I walked down the stairs.

"Good morning, young man!" Mrs. McAllister said as she turned the bacon over in the frying pan. Livvy looked at me like she was

177

being cautious, and smiled. She polished each fork and knife as she set them carefully on the blue-flowered tablecloth and adjusted the roses in the jar on the table. She poured orange juice in each glass.

"You go out on the porch and drag that sleepy Floyd in here for breakfast, will you now, Fletcher?" Mrs. McAllister smiled at me.

"Yes, Ma'am" I said, and now I know I'm glad I'm here to see Floyd and Mrs. McAllister and even Livvy, it's like dreaming or something, but it's real, so I really can go outside on the porch and get Floyd, just like before. I smelled the bacon again and before I opened the door, I scuffed the screen just a bit to get the flies off of it first because they must have smelled the bacon too. I went outside. Floyd was snoozing in the sunlight, and his glasses were lying on the newspaper on his lap.

He snorted and woke up. "Well, it's about time you hauled yourself out of bed, boy," he said. He put his steel glasses on his nose and squinted up at me. He smiled. "Nice morning isn't it!"

"Sure is, Floyd." I looked at my father's house. Floyd distracted me by rubbing his hands together like he was anticipating something special.

"Something smells good around here, it must be time for breakfast."

"It sure does, Floyd, because Mrs. McAllister has bacon and eggs and biscuits ready for us and she wants me to get you in right away," I said.

He patted his pocket looking for his pipe. He squinted up at me. His eyebrows went up like he was going to say something important. When somebody's eyebrows go up, they are *always* thinking something important even if they don't *say* it, but Floyd said it after he cleared his throat and fidgeted for a minute. He spoke quietly.

"Maybe you could consider calling Mrs. McAllister *Mother* from now on, young man, Mrs. McAllister is getting kind of tired of getting called *Mrs. McAllister* and I think she'd be pleased as punch if you'd call her *Mother* from now on, maybe you could *consider trying that, why don't you?"*

The Fires of Waterland

I only have one Mother and I know she's buried but she's gotten right up there with God and I gave her black-eyed Suzie flowers to help her get up there and I'll never have another mother that got a wet spot on her apron from splashing water at me but she is there and talks to God in whispers.

I didn't say anything but I think Floyd must have knew what I was thinking or read my mind because he looked at me for a minute before he said anything.

" ...if you *want to*, boy, a man has to decide for himself when he's ready to do things, so when you want to, but I don't think your real Mother would mind you borrowing Mrs. McAllister to be your Mom for a day or two when you're ready, lad, she would understand that, I'm sure."

I sat on the wooden steps and thought about it hard. Nobody can make you have two mothers if you don't *want* two mothers, and I got one already, so there.

"Besides, she's already got some practice being a mom with Livvy here now—and you from before hasn't she?" Floyd added when I wasn't paying attention.

"*What?*" I asked.

"You mean *pardon me*, don't you, son?" Floyd cleared his throat again.

"*Pardon me?*" I said quickly. Floyd always teaches me to say things correctly, like '*thank you* Sir' and '*pardon me*' but I forget sometimes and Floyd reminds me. I learn more at Floyd's, even if Mrs. Tickner does her best.

"I was just speculating that the Missus has experience in being a mother already, you having been here for quite a few months, and now Livvy's here too."

"Oh, I see." I got up and walked down the stairs and picked a long piece of grass from beside the wall. I bit off a piece and chewed on it just like Jack showed me. I looked through the fence at the black truck to see if Jack was there yet.

179

"There's no *obligation*, Fletcher, maybe it'd make the Missus happy, maybe even more comfortable with you, see?" Floyd looked toward the screened kitchen door and back at me. He lowered his voice.

"Maybe you could ask her if that might the right thing to do, seeing as you're getting older and such," he said, and looked back at the door again. "She's missed you a lot more than she lets on, lad. Some women are like that, they got their minds made up about something, but they don't say much about it, and it seems to me that might be the thing here."

I don't know what Floyd's talking about. *I pretended I did.* I nodded. I heard pots banging in the kitchen and the women's voices chipping away at the morning quiet, but I couldn't make out what they were saying.

I thought about it some more and picked a ripe raspberry and ate it. It was sweet. The honeybees were trying to eat some too and buzzed around the red fruit.

I leaned against my father's fence for a bit then I got myself back up the stairs and sat on the wicker chair right beside Floyd. I brought Floyd a raspberry too. He ate it slowly. Things taste better when you eat them slowly.

We both pretended to watch my father's house while we thought hard about it together. The air was quiet, dead quiet. *"Okay, Floyd"* I finally said.

Floyd smiled and looked away quickly. I don't know why. Maybe the raspberry was sour.

"Breakfast is ready!" Livvy said to us through the screen.

"We'll be right there" Floyd said. "Give me a push to the table there, lad." I got up and wheeled Floyd through the door to the table.

Floyd buttered the last biscuit and gave it to me. Livvy watched as I ate it.

"Good biscuits" I said, and looked right back at her. She blushed and pushed the jam-pot a little closer to me. I saw Mrs. McAllister's eyes flash across at Floyd's, but they didn't say anything that time.

Floyd sat back and patted his stomach after we finished eating. He finally looked at me and cleared his throat. "This young man has something to ask you," Floyd told Mrs. McAllister. Floyd stirred his coffee and clanked the spoon on the saucer a couple of times. It sounded like the bell at the orphanage.

"We have an announcement to make," he said, and smiled widely at everyone.

Livvy got up and started to take the dishes off of the table. She put them into the sink quickly and sat back down when Floyd motioned her to sit.

"Oh?" Mrs. McAllister looked at me. I didn't know what to say and I wanted to escape to Texas right away, but I didn't because *I told Floyd that I would do it.*

My mother won't like that, it will make her cry and God might not like it either but I promised Floyd, how can I get out of it? I can't... I started to talk but nothing came out. "Uh..." My face was getting hot.

"Get on with it, lad, personal addressing, and now there's something that has to be settled between two adults themselves, remember?"

Mrs. McAllister looked at Floyd and raised her eyebrows. She looked at Livvy. "Fletcher?" she spoke quietly.

"Floyd told me an idea; he got me to think about it, that... you might like it if I call you *Mother!*" I blurted out. "Or *something,*" I added, my ears burning. I was embarrassed... The girl with the blue eyes had a very surprised look on her face. My face got red. Mrs. McAllister smiled, and I never saw that before, but she smiled a bit like my mother. *How come I never noticed that before?*

"Why Fletcher, that would be ever so wonderful, I'd like that, but..." she paused. I'm embarrassed now. We have to stretch this out forever and a week, and my face is getting redder every second. I looked at the clock. I think it was stopped. I paid a lot of attention to the clock when Floyd spoke.

"That's very thoughtful of you to say it's *my* idea, Fletcher, but I think it's been on *your* mind for quite some time!" Floyd said. Livvy nodded at him and looked over at me.

"I think so, too!" Livvy said. She reached over and put her hand on my shoulder. *I don't know why she did that. What do girls know about things like that anyway?*

"Perhaps you might be more comfortable calling me *Mom* or *Aunt Elizabeth*," Mrs. McAllister said.

"Now there's a good idea, too, Fetch, but maybe shorter's better, you could shorten things up a whole lot by calling her *Mom*." I looked at Floyd and he looked right back at me and nodded.

"*Mom* is nice, sounds nice and comfortable, good for personal addressing, eh, Fletcher?"

I had to study the clock a bit more and the linoleum for a while and the ceiling and the shiny chrome things on the stove and even the curly yellow strips of sticky bug paper hung in the corner of the ceiling by a thumbtack stuck in the white paint.

I felt underneath the edge of the chair to see if there were any wads of chewing gum like under the desks at school. I don't know why, but I have to admit I was uncomfortable that time and figured out that I would look like a man of the world if I scuffed my sneakers around a bit and paused, just like Floyd does, before I decided.

"Man has to take time to make the *correct* decision, Elizabeth," Floyd said to Mrs. McAllister.

Livvy grabbed my arm and shook it. "*C'mon, Fletcher! Say yes!*" I looked at her and tried to ignore her. She was getting too bossy already.

"I call her *Mom*, didn't you notice, Fletcher Carnival Williams?" Livvy prodded me again. I looked at her, and my face must have been as red as a sun-scorched beet.

"*I didn't know that*," was all I could say just then.

"Well, Fletcher, you're getting to be a man now, you can take your time and decide which you would prefer, or can you decide now?" Mrs. McAllister asked. I took a quick look at Floyd. He nodded at me. That's one thing about Floyd. He always helps you make the right decision. I got up and walked right over to Mrs. McAllister. She stood up and looked down at me.

"You sure have turned out to be a handsome son," she said to me. She held her arms open to me, and I don't know whether I answered before I got the hug or after. That's what happens when you grow up tall and get to be a man of the world. I knew I would get a yellow convertible someday. I pretended I did.

I stammered as nervous as I could get "Can I call you *Mom* then?" I asked. She suddenly sobbed and rocked me back and forth for a long time, and she cried and the tears fell on me and got my face wet and I cried too.

"Mrs. —*Mom*, don't cry," I said to her. It felt funny to say *Mom*. I didn't see Livvy and Floyd getting out of the kitchen onto the porch to leave us alone together. I think Floyd escaped on purpose that time.

"Don't cry, Fletcher, you be good for your Mom, my Son, promise me", I will, Mother, I'll be a good boy for Mrs. McAllister just like I am for you, she can borrow me for a little while, God knows, he knows it's only for a little while, doesn't He? *"Yes, my son..."*

"*My son, oh, my son is home again!*" she whispered to me. "I've missed you so much, Fletcher, it is so nice to have you back home! I'm going to love being called *Mom*, now things are going to be just fine again!" She honked her nose into a blue handkerchief and wiped her eyes.

"I think it will be *wonderful!*" she said, finally, and I don't know how long that was because Floyd and Livvy never made a sound when they went outside. They just weren't there anymore; I discovered them on the porch after we washed our faces and collected the dishes, and saved the scraps in a nice plastic bowl to go in the bird feeder. While I was down on the grass putting it into the feeder, I heard Mrs. McAllister tap on the door. Livvy looked up.

"Floyd?" Mrs. McAllister called out the screen door to him.

"Elizabeth?" Floyd answered, and spun his chair around to face her.

"Our *son* is really going to call me *Mom*," she said proudly.

"Well *glory be*, isn't that wonderful, woman? Best news I've heard for months around here," he said. "Personal addressing, now there's something that's been *properly* settled between you two!" Floyd hauled out his pipe and lit it thoughtfully. "Finally!" Floyd added, and winked at Livvy.

Mrs. McAllister blushed and went back into the house, and we heard her singing *Amazing grace, how sweet the sound…*

"You did good, boy!" Floyd spoke loudly to me, and I showed Livvy how to adjust the height on the bird feeder so that the cats can't get the birds, because sometimes girls don't know how to do things like that, and sometimes they do, but I was embarrassed and had to change the subject.

"You did well, Fletcher Carnival Williams," Livvy whispered. "I'm proud of you!"

"You did good, my Son, everything will be all right now", my mother leaned down from up there beside God and whispered to me, "I'm proud of you too."

"I once was lost, and now I'm found…" she sang, and we heard the dishes clinking in the sink.

Twenty-Two

I never saw Jack Whittaker the week I was home with Floyd, not even once. I watched the house, and I saw a light go on; the black truck came and went, but for some reason I never saw Jack. I did see Tina McQueeny once, but it didn't look like her, and I told Floyd that wasn't Tina McQueeny but he said it was so.

"Same woman, it's Tina, no doubt about it, Fletcher. That's her, alright, you just don't remember her looking like that with curly hair and all."

"She looks real different, Floyd," I said.

We were sitting on the wooden porch and were alone. The women were gone shopping and I took that time to talk seriously to Floyd.

"I hear she joined the Ladies Auxiliary at the church," Floyd said, kind of offhandedly. I didn't know what that was.

"What's that, Floyd?" I asked.

"What's what?"

"You know, the Ladies Auxiliary."

"I hear they bake cookies and stuff like that; at least that's what I think they do. I'd be lying if I told you I know *exactly* what they do there all the time, but I know sometimes they put on teas and bake sales and such to raise money for charity. Sometimes they hold suppers in the basement of the church, good food, too. We'll go some time, only a buck a plate, all you can eat."

"I didn't know they let sluts into places like that!" I said matter-of-factly to Floyd.

Floyd got mad when I said that. He huffed up right away and glared at me. I don't think I ever saw Floyd get mad except when Mrs. Zeban came to haul me away the first time and Floyd wanted to keep me home with him. *"Boy! Now you listen well, real well!"* His face was red. "People make mistakes, you hear, and no matter what you think about that woman, you keep it to *yourself* from now on. See, it's in the past and that's where it's best kept, understand?" I didn't say anything. *"Understand?"*

I felt my face getting red and Floyd never talked to me like that before, I never saw that before. I looked down at the worn boards and didn't look at Floyd. He was angry. "We already talked about that at the home, boy. People make mistakes and leave common sense in the ditch with the weeds, but it's only an oversight, things that happen like that are usually temporary, and something that we should learn to forget about, forgive, and overlook whenever we get reminded of them, too!"

"Yes, Floyd," I said when I thought I got over it.

"You get over that real quick, now, and put it to rest," he added. He got out his pipe and puffed angrily. "I don't want to hear you refer to her like that again, it isn't right!" He puffed again, but the pipe was out so he had to light it again. He shook the match out and tossed it onto the grass. "Fella' never knows when God might be listening to him talking, so don't say that again!" He looked at me sternly. "—Or Mrs. McAllister —your *Mom*, for that matter! Don't let *her* hear it again either." He puffed again and his voice softened.

"Your Mom has become reasonably good friends with Tina and the hatchet's been buried for a long time. Let's leave it that way, shall we? There's not really any excuse for what she was in the past other than the lack of common sense and thinking hard about things and coming to the right conclusion—but no point in killing her over it years later either, is there?"

My brains started hurting, I'm sure that's it. I did not understand, but if Floyd said so, I better start pretty quick. *Get used to it, Jack.*

I looked at Floyd and clammed up for a while. After I thought about it some more, I really didn't understand, but if Floyd says it's the right thing to do, then it's the *right* thing to do. *I wonder if God thinks that is lying. Maybe not.*

"Okay, Floyd" I said, finally.

He nodded, and then after a bit, he winked, like he forgot about what we were talking about or something. He pushed and pulled his wheels back and forth and seemed like he was thinking really hard for a long time. I watched him fall asleep in his chair. Floyd's hair is turning white. His head went sideways and his glasses fell on the porch floor. I picked them up for him.

When Floyd wasn't looking, I sneaked around the fence into my father's backyard and opened the door of the old Pontiac, quietly. I sat in the front seat and drove around the world for a few minutes. The old mouse nest was still on the back seat, but there was no mouse. My mother and father weren't there either. The car was hot inside and it smelled the same. I cried and hid under the old blanket. I went to sleep.

After a while I woke up and forgot about crying and went back home to Floyd's. He was in the house reading the newspaper. He shook his head.

"Should tell me when you're going for a walk, boy, so's I know where you are!"

I didn't want him to know that I was in the old Pontiac.

"Yes, Floyd," I said quietly.

"Guess we'll have to take you back to the home on Tuesday, eh, lad? Mrs. Tickner will be missing you, too!"

"I want to stay here, Floyd," I said.

"I know, son," he said to me and shook out a new page on the paper. "I know all too well, boy. I want you to stay here, too."

It took me a long time to go to sleep that night. I watched my father's house but there were no lights on, and the black truck never showed up. I covered up and kept my eyes open until I couldn't see in the dark. I heard Livvy close her bedroom door.

"*Oh, my God!*" Floyd exclaimed right out loud the next morning. I was sitting at the table eating breakfast. "*Elizabeth, come out here now!*" Floyd called Mrs. McAllister, and I know when something's wrong with Floyd because his voice changes.

She ran out the door, and he spoke to her in a whisper. He showed her the paper, I know, because I was watching through the door even if I wasn't supposed to be. She clamped her hand over her mouth. "*Oh, no!*" she said and covered her mouth up again with both hands. She turned white as paint. "What happened, *what happened?*" she moaned.

"I don't know! They say it might be arson, I don't know, they don't know yet!"

"*Oh, my God, my God! Her — and three of them, three! Oh, my God!*"

I opened the door and went outside to see what happened. Floyd folded up the paper, and I could see in Floyd's eyes that something bad happened. I know because his eyes were getting red but he wasn't crying yet. Mrs. McAllister was kneeling and had her face in Floyd's lap. She was sobbing.

"What's the matter with Mom?" I asked Floyd, without realizing that it was the first time I ever called Mrs. McAllister *Mom* without being self-conscious about it.

"There's been a terrible accident, boy, a *terrible* accident, that's...I...boy, I *got to...I better tell you, right up front!*"

"Floyd?" I could see that Floyd was going to cry right away.

"Fletcher, I...I don't know *how* to tell you this!" Floyd started. He sobbed.

"What, Floyd — what happened?" I asked. I got scared right away when I saw Floyd crying.

The Fires of Waterland

He folded up the paper and leaned over Mrs. McAllister in his lap as if to protect her and held her tightly. He looked up at me again and there were tears on his glasses. He took them off. He put them back on and shook his head. "I don't know how to tell you this, Fletcher...son..." He began, and coughed. He looked at Mrs. McAllister. She went to stand behind him and put her hands on his shoulders.

"Fletcher, there's been a fire, lad, *a fire...at the home.*" He almost choked. He coughed hard. He took off his glasses and wiped his eyes

"*What?*" I asked, like watching puppets in a dream or something, it wasn't real. It can't be real, but it is, *it is. A fire.*

> *...and whiskey boxes and old pictures and old clothes and dust and the memorable junk fire burned and burned and sparks winked out on their way to see God one by one and the fire burned the cheese sandwiches and the hobo-bum coffee in a tin can hanging on a rusty wire got whiskey in it and me and Billy McCaudry tasted Morgan Catcher's Rye one time and it's his favorite but I don't like whiskey that's why my throat is burning. Hush, Fletcher, my mother said.*

"*Oh, no!*" I said. *I can see the flames.*

"I'm afraid that some of the people you know, you love —have been *killed*, son...I...I'm sorry, son."

"*Who!?* No, Floyd, it's a mistake, *it's a mistake*, and you didn't read it right, *it can't be right!*" I shouted.

"Not now, son, *not now!* Take a few minutes...you'll know soon enough, it's all here."

I felt the noise in my head get louder. Mrs. McAllister was sobbing, but she stood up and put her arms around me. She was crying and holding me up, and Floyd was holding us both up from his chair. We stood there for a long time and everybody cried on each other. I don't know how long.

Mrs. McAllister put on the kettle, and we had tea. I am glad that Livvy is still sleeping because it is the *worst* news you can get except if your mother gets killed on the train tracks. Floyd picked up the paper and shook it open. He read it out loud.

"Mrs. Eileen Tickner, the manageress of the Waters County facility, and three occupants, Marvin Allan Pychinski, Joe Raymond Coleman, and Richard Egan Bordon..."

"—No!" I shouted out loud. "It can't be, *it can't be right,* that's not right, *that's not right!*" I screamed.

"Easy, son, take it easy, it's happened, we can't change it, can we!" Floyd took my face and held it in his hands.

I shouted *"No, Floyd!"* But I don't know if I really mean it or not, *we should be able to change things that are bad. I don't know why we can't.*

"Mrs. Tickner and Richard Bordon are *heroes,* Fletch, they got all of the other boys out ... and—but...they died, trying to find Eddie Peters and Joe, to get them out. They found Eddie, and somebody threw Eddie out of the window, so he made it, but they went back to try to find Joe and Marvin, the fire marshal said...he reported they found them close by, they said they were hiding under their beds; he thinks they couldn't find them in the smoke, and passed out ... It appears somebody found Ricky Tenberg in time, and got him out, before they all died. He's in the hospital."

I cried a lot and put my arms around Livvy when we told her. She screamed and cried with me, and we all cried together. It was hot and the crickets were singing outside, but Livvy and I didn't pay any attention.

I didn't eat any supper that day, and I don't remember going to sleep. Me and Floyd watched as Livvy cried and hugged Mrs. McAllister to death all day, and Floyd cried with me, and I cried a lot more when Floyd phoned Mrs. Zeban. She said that Ricky Tenberg was in the hospital with severe burns and might die too.

"Third degree burns, oh my God!" Mrs. McAllister said when Floyd told her. I don't like this at all, not one bit. I like Ricky Tenberg, but I didn't tell you too much about him just yet.

The Fires of Waterland

The only good part about this whole thing is that Mrs. Zeban said I could stay at Floyd's as long as he would have me. It didn't make me feel any better. I never thought that could happen. I mean me not feeling any better about being able to stay at Floyd's, not the fire part. I don't want to feel better or know about anything right now, not about the fire and not about staying at Floyd's and not about Ricky Tenberg, either. It's going to make me cry again, and I can't stop crying, and I know I won't be able to stop, but Floyd said *that's all right.*

Twenty-Three

"They're moving the boys down to an emergency dorm they're setting up in the factory warehouse down here?" Floyd spoke on the telephone. It sounded like a buzzing mosquito on the other end of the line, and I listened to Floyd even though you're not supposed to listen to other people's conversations.

"They're setting up a dorm in the warehouse for now?"

"They're getting a disaster grant from the government to set up again?" he asked again. The mosquito buzzed.

"They think it was arson, do they, oh, my God, how could someone do that?" Floyd said. He paused.

"*They have a suspect?*" He paused again.

"*Oh, my God!*" Floyd said. "That wouldn't surprise me at all, not one bit, not *one bit,* after what happened! *I hope he gets what's coming to him!*" Floyd turned around and saw me listening. He motioned me out of the room.

I went out and sat on the porch. Livvy was sitting in the swing on the porch. Floyd built the swing especially for Livvy, so she could have fun in it and swing back and forth to stay cool when it was hot out, but she was sitting there without saying a word, staring at the sky.

"They have a suspect" I told Livvy importantly. She kept sitting there, hardly moving at all. I sat down beside her to make her feel better. It's my job to make her feel better, so I did. I patted her on the head. She did not look at me.

"*They have a suspect for the fire,*" I told Livvy again.

"I heard you the first time," she said, again without looking at me. I always thought that you are supposed to look at the person you are talking to. "Who is it?" she asked, without looking at me again.

"I don't know," I said. I didn't know, either. Right then I didn't know, but I sure did find out fast when Floyd wheeled his way out onto the porch.

"Don't you listen to people's conversations from now on, Fletch!" Floyd cautioned. "*Privacy* is important to people, you'll find that out for yourself sooner or later."

"Okay, Floyd," I said. I am embarrassed. I know privacy. It's when someone wants to do something or say something that nobody else is supposed to know about but sometimes you hear it anyway. "I'm sorry," I said, and scuffed my foot on the worn wood.

"They have a suspect in the fire, I'm afraid. They've proved it was arson, even the barn was burned. It was gasoline, the smell of gasoline, it seems, and the wind was blowing the wrong way for it to catch by itself from the dorm fire, so it looks like *it was torched too!*"

"Did Mrs. Tickner and Richard let T.T. Oinker out too, did he get saved, and the others?"

"I'm sorry, son, they never got to them before they... they were all lost too..." he shook his head and looked at the blackening sky.

"Oh, no!" Livvy said. "*Poor animals!*" She started to cry. I didn't cry that time because T.T. Oinker and the boys were all headed for the bacon factory next month anyhow. So there. *Get used to it.* Mrs. Tickner said so. *Oh, God. Now Mrs. Tickner's chopped off too.* I put my arms around Livvy and made the swing go back and forth for her.

That night the wind came up and dust darkened the air even before it got dark.

"There's a real big storm coming, you two. *Let's get with it you two,* better get the clothes off of the line for your mom," Floyd said. We hauled the clothes in just as the storm hit and the wind howled like a *banshee,* Floyd called it. It got dark and lightning crackled across the sky like God was really mad about the fire. I don't blame him. The electricity went off and we had to go to bed early with no lights except wax candles, and Floyd didn't want to use them too long.

"Fire," he said, "is a great thing when used properly, a terrible enemy when used improperly!" I agreed with Floyd right away and was glad to see the candles put out. It took me a long time to go to sleep. I woke up in the night and I could smell the burned candles, but I didn't hear the wind any more.

I hung around and went outside. I opened the squeaky lid and pulled the new newspaper from the rusty mailbox at the end of the road and came back and sat on the swing on the porch to read it. A dog barked.

It was in the headlines. I know how to read headlines.

"Floyd!" I shouted, even before he came wheeling through the door. *"Mr. Tupper's in jail for burning up the home!"*

"Hush, boy! You'll wake up the *dead!"* I think he made a mistake saying *that.* I don't know why Floyd said that, but he looked at me kind of funny. I think he made a sick mistake and I tried not to look back at him for a minute just like he told me a long time ago, if you know that somebody is uncomfortable, don't examine them too closely like a bug in a jar, let them get their brains settled quick as possible. I think Floyd's brains settled real quickly. I know that because he hesitated, and it wasn't the kind of pause you make when you are trying to be a man of the world.

Floyd cleared his throat. "You'll wake up *the girls,* is what I *meant,* Fletch."

"Look, Floyd! *They got him!"* I handed him the paper. Floyd looked at the headlines.

"Well, let's see... *'Fire Suspect Arrested in Orphanage Fire'.*" He wagged his head, urging silence. He indicated the article in the paper. I took it and looked at it again.

"*See?*" I asked. "Mr. Tupper's in jail, Floyd! *He* burned up the home!"

"Well...let me see that, again, boy." Floyd shook out the paper again, flipped through a couple of pages and studied the headline again. He folded it up and looked at me.

"He's arrested, no doubt, but that don't mean he's done anything wrong, now does it?"

"He did it, Floyd, *I know he did it*. He's sneaky and he said we were all going to get it, we all had it coming to us good, remember that, *remember that*, Floyd? The time we had the big fight and Mom slapped him and you cleaned his clock—Mrs. Tickner smacked him good with her spoon, too, and me and Jack and the other boys helped you?"

Floyd pulled out his tobacco pouch and packed his pipe thoughtfully. He lit a match and puffed on his pipe for a few moments. That's how Floyd thinks. I know.

"I remember that, Fletcher. He did make threats, no doubt about it, but all that means for sure is that we know he made a bad error of judgment, threatening us and all!"

"But he killed them, Floyd, he did it, I know he did it!"

"Maybe he did, and *maybe he didn't* do it, Fletcher, son, but we can't say *he did*, not until it's *proven*, see, there's a difference, isn't there? If he did it, we'll get him!" Floyd shook his head. "I know how you feel, son, but you keep this in mind, no matter what happens, no matter how angry you are, it's the law, Fletch. You have to *prove* that he did it!"

"You and I can prove it, Floyd; we can prove it for sure!"

"Don't be so sure about that, boy, things aren't always quite as clear cut as you might like!" Floyd looked at the paper again. He chuckled. "Well, I'll be!" He looked up at me. "You might be right, boy; maybe they got him, and got him *good!*"

"Why, Floyd?"

"Says right here they got evidence on him, evidence from the scene of the fire left right at the back door, on the porch."

"What evidence, Floyd?"

"Best evidence we'll ever need to hang that man real quick, Fletch! *They found Tupper's silver tooth!*" That was probably the worst thing that ever happened to me in my life. It hit me over the head like being whacked with a baseball bat and a hammer at the same time. I don't know what to say to Floyd now because *Mr. Tupper doesn't have his silver tooth.* I know that because I had it from the baseball game and washed the blood and dirt off of it in the pig trough, and I already told you that *Jack took it* the night he disappeared from the home. I knew right away that there was a problem.

"Maybe you're right, Floyd," I said after the noise settled down in my head. Maybe Tupper the snake didn't do it, maybe it's not so clear cut, and just like you said it's the law, you said so, you have to prove it. I kept that to myself. *You don't want to know about that, not right now,* I thought to myself. "Don't you, Floyd?" I said out loud without realizing it and Floyd looked at me and lifted up both eyebrows.

"Don't you *what?*" He asked.

"Don't you have to prove it?" I stammered. I don't want to talk about this right now. *How can Mr. Tupper's silver tooth be at the fire and how can Jack have it at the same time? It wasn't in my shoe when Jack left, Jack got it, he got it, and now it's at the fire and I didn't see Jack yet and where is he?*

"Don't you believe they got to *prove* he's guilty now Floyd?" I quickly asked, and I know I fooled Floyd this time but why don't I feel happy about it? Because now I won't have to tell Floyd anything just yet? Should I tell Floyd about Jack getting the silver tooth? I don't want to look at him because I know I'm not exactly telling him what I am *really* thinking and that's sort of like lying, that's what my Mother said. "They got evidence now, right, Floyd — so he's guilty?"

"He's *guilty as sin*, Fletch, they got evidence on him! Not only that, son, if there's *some* evidence there, you can be sure there's *some more.* There's more than one way to skin a pig, isn't there?"

Kill him and skin him like a gutted pig. I'll just kill him myself and skin him like a gutted pig.

Maybe Floyd knew what I was thinking, but I clammed up right away and said nothing at all. *Nothing.* But maybe I showed the silver tooth to Floyd and don't remember it. Maybe he's not saying anything about it, or maybe he's forgotten about it, or maybe he's trying to test me and see if I'll tell him what I know about it; *why would he do that?* Floyd always says it's best to be up front between friends, but there's more than one way to skin a pig, too.

More than one way to skin a pig, that's it. I bet Jack is getting even with Tupper the snake for what he did to him and me and the other boys at night in the dark.

"Maybe I'll just kill him myself an' get it over with, kill him and skin him like a gutted pig!"

"Kill him?" Jack can't do that, he can't do that, Jack wouldn't do that, not Jack, Jack couldn't do that, he takes care of smaller boys and saved my brown tweed hat in the cupboard and takes us to get peaches from Mrs. Tickner and gave me his sugar when I was the newest boy and he didn't have any money to get to the Navy so he just got to Floyd's before me so he can work at the broomstick factory and that's why he took the tooth, he sold it. He sold it for money and somebody bad got it, gave it back to Mr. Tupper that snake bastard. Don't say that, Fletcher, that's a bad word. And he burned the orphanage and Mrs. Tickner and the porkers, get used to it, they were going to get sent to the bacon factory, Mrs. Tickner said so, and Tina McQueeny wanna pull a weenie got him now, so get used to it, get used to it, get used to it, and that's it.

I didn't tell Floyd about that idea I had. I didn't get a chance.

"Hey, Fletcher!" I turned around, and *there he was,* standing at the fence and looking right at me and *he knew what I was thinking, too.*

I mean *Jack.* It was *Jack* standing there.

Twenty-Four

Jack Whittaker looked taller and browner, not pale and sickly like at the orphanage. He had a small-brimmed hat low over his eyes, and he had a dusty brown vest on over his white shirt that made his shoulders look taller and skinny and that's what must have made him look like some *other* Jack, not like the Jack that took care of me. I don't even know why I didn't see him get out of the truck, but I didn't.

"*Fletcher?* Is that you, boy?" I stared at him. I wanted to ask him if he had the silver tooth or not, but I know he can't have it because they found it at the home, evidence on Tupper the snake.

"Jack's home!" Floyd said. "*Jack's home,*" he repeated to me, and Floyd pointed to the fence. Jack took off his hat so I could see him better, and then he looked a little more like Jack to me.

"How you doing, boy? You turned into a mushroom yet?" he laughed. "Cat's got your tongue, boy?" Jack asked, laughing again. I think I scratched my head. Jack never called me 'boy' before, I don't know why. I still didn't say anything.

"Hey, Mr. McAllister, cat's got his tongue just yet, but perhaps *you'll* say *good day,* to me, sir!" he said to Floyd.

"Hello, Jack," Floyd said, reaching into his pocket for his tobacco. Jack started walking around the fence to come into Floyd's yard.

"Fletch, boy, what are you doing here?" Jack asked me. I didn't say anything yet because I was too surprised at seeing Jack, and I was just thinking about him hard, and Floyd told me that if you think hard about things you can even *make* things happen.   I couldn't believe my eyes.

"He came home for a bit to visit with us, and now Mrs. Zeban says he can be staying here as long as I care to keep him around now, things being changed all around now because of the fire, Jack."

"*Fire?*" Jack asked. "*What fire?*" he exclaimed, almost like he was pretending like he didn't know what was going on and Mrs. Tickner and Richard and Marvin and Joe and all of the porkers getting killed and the wind wasn't blowing the right way so the porker house and everything was torched too, that's what the paper said.

"*What fire, Floyd!*" Jack asked again. Floyd wheeled over to the edge of the porch and motioned Jack to sit down.

"Me 'n' Fletcher here were just discussing that, Jack." Jack flapped my hair back and forth on my head and sat down beside me and turned to Floyd.

"There's been a serious fire at the home, Jack, the orphanage."

"No!" Jack said. "No! — Anybody hurt?"

"I'm afraid, Jack that the news isn't good —Mrs. Tickner, Richard Bordon, they were killed, rescuing the boys."

" —Oh!" Jack said.

"And you forgot Marvin and Joe, Floyd, you forgot Marvin and Joe, why did you forget Marvin and Joe, Floyd? Jack, Marvin and Joe, they're dead too, they're all dead too, and T. T. and all the porkers got fried too, and they got Tupper in jail and good for him, he's going to be in jail. It serves him right for what he did, and now Ricky's got all burned up too, and *he's* in the hospital and he's going to die, and I'm glad they got Tupper in jail, *he did it, I know he did it*, didn't he, Floyd?"

"*Marvin? Joe? Dead? Oh, my God, no, what about the rest?*"

Floyd and I didn't have a chance to tell him about the rest before his face screwed up and he got red and he took his cap off and flapped it on the wooden stair and I saw his eyes got tears in them. He looked away from us, and I can see that he's ashamed of crying.

"Ricky Tenberg?" Jack asked, "Got burned too?"

"Third degree burns," Floyd said, "and the prognosis isn't that good, they think we're going to lose him, too."

"I can't believe this... *I can't believe it!*" Jack said, trying not to look at me. "How could this happen? How could this happen, Mrs. Tickner, she's better 'en my own mother, she is, and how can she be dead? Oh, oh..." He moaned. He put his face down on his knees, and he shook like the house in the banshee storm.

"Take it easy, boy," Floyd said to Jack. Jack stood up and kicked his hat and made it roll down the steps and into the dust. I went and got it for him, but he wasn't looking at me. He sat down again, and he was not paying attention to anything except crying.

"Don't cry, Jack!" I said.

You don't cry when you're twelve. Boys don't cry. That's what Jack said back when I got to be eight, on my birthday, and Jack was in charge of me, and I better do what Jack said.

I looked at Floyd, and he shook his head at me. I think he was telling me not to stop Jack from crying *because it's all right to cry even if you're a bigger boy*, and I wanted to ask Floyd about it. I don't understand Jack crying because he always told me he was the world's toughest orphan punk, but I cried with him and he shook a lot. I put my arms around Jack, and he put his face in my shirt. I watched Floyd while I did that, and I was going to say something, but Floyd shook his head at me again and then nodded it up and down and kept his mouth in a tight line and frowned and blew smoke from his pipe at the mosquitoes.

I didn't tell Floyd that I saw the curtains move in the big front window at my father's house. They opened and clammed up tight right away.

Twenty-Five

Mrs. McAllister made Jack stay for supper that night even if he told her he was supposed to be going home next door to be with Tina McQueeny. Maybe Mrs. McAllister knew something that Floyd and I didn't because she made every excuse in the book to keep Jack with us.

"Oh, Jack, you'll be wanting to stay tonight, and you and Fletcher can visit for old times' sake, can't you? And my goodness, you'll certainly not staying alone by yourself tonight, will you now? You stay with Fletcher and my Floyd, that's it. There won't be any more argument, will there, now there's a good boy, come up stairs and we'll get you a bath and supper and you can bunk down on the Chesterfield when it gets late, you hear?"

"I'll be getting along home pretty quick, Mrs. McAllister. Thanks the same, but someone's going to be expecting me, isn't she?" I know who they were talking about, *Tina McQueeny*, but I didn't tell Jack he should get rescued from her because he's supposed to make up his *own* mind, that's what Floyd said.

"There's no one home next door, she's not home. So my goodness, you'll just stay here, Fletcher wants you here, don't you, Fletcher?" I think Mom told a lie that time. I know she told a lie because I saw the curtains move. I think I saw the curtains move, but Mom was looking at me funny. I don't know why. You're not supposed to tell lies because the truth always comes out. Mrs. McAllister *never* told any lies. *That can't be right.*

"Sure, Jack, you and me and Floyd can talk about everything and you can tell me where you've been and how come I didn't see you and..."

"—Fetch, I'm sure Jack has a lot of things to take care of, just getting back from his trip, and all—" Floyd said that suddenly but got cut off by Mrs. McAllister. Her face was red.

"—You can stay here, *boy*, there won't be any argument coming from *you* now," she said with much authority, and I could see that it was an *order*, and so did Jack, and so did Floyd for that matter, because he sucked hard on his pipe. She grabbed Jack's hand and pushed him up the stairs to show him some towels and the bath. I heard the water pipes bang and the water running.

Floyd was silent. He watched in amazement as Mom took Jack over from us, and he couldn't believe his eyes either, I bet. "What's got into that woman's mind, I wonder...must be the bad news. That happens, sometimes, Fletcher," he said, "when there's too much of a bad thing for a body to accept all at once, the mind does strange things. Sometimes it shuts down until it's got all sorted into some kind of order; that's what *usually* does it," he wagged his head up the stairs after them and shrugged. "Too much bad news at once, and a body can't take that, and I think that's what's going on with your mom." He pushed his glasses up his nose.

"We'll be heading outside for a smoke now!" Floyd wheeled toward the door and waited for me to open it for him. I opened it and wheeled him outside. It was warm and only took about eight seconds for the mosquitoes to find us.

"My mind's shut down from the bad news too, Floyd, is yours?" I asked, scuffing out a smoking match that Floyd dropped after shaking out the flame, but not *enough*. He just threw it on the porch, casual as you please, and I jumped on it right away because I thought about the fire right quick.

He looked at me kind of funny and said, "Yes, Fetch, I think it is, kind of," and "Sorry about that, son, old habits are hard to kill, aren't they?"

"Some day we'll set this old porch on fire *ourselves* if we're not careful" I said to Floyd.

"As long as you put the matches out for me we'll be fine, don't you worry about that. Besides, it won't be much longer, the Missus is getting me one of them big, tall ashtrays on a stand, the steel kind with a pipe stand and real sand in it and high enough so I can reach it from my chair just fine, won't be no more worry about setting this porch on fire; that we don't need, we already decided!"

"Good, Floyd!" I said, "But I won't have any matches to put out, either!"

"I think you can tolerate that just fine, all things being considered," Floyd commented offhandedly, and glanced over at my father's house as if he noticed something, but he didn't say what. I looked to see and I thought the curtains might have moved again, but maybe it was my imagination. I didn't see anything.

Jack got a bath while Floyd and I talked about things, and then it was dark and it was time to go to bed. Jack looked just fine in Floyd's green-striped pajamas and I noticed that the legs were still on them, but I didn't say it. Mom got Jack a wool blanket and a pillow to sleep on the Chesterfield, and Jack went to sleep right away, but that wasn't until after we talked a few minutes.

"I'm glad you're here, Fletcher. It's just like old times," he said. "All those damned old tin beds, and I ain't seen *anybody* since I took off, not a soul, but a lot of things happened. It's a big world, Fetchie boy, and you an' me are going places, we got things to see!"

We talked a bit about Texas and T.T. Oinker and Jack made me laugh by oinking like T. T., but we didn't talk about the bacon factory or Murvie dying or the fire and everybody getting toasted, because everybody would have to be sadder than necessary. And Floyd overheard us and said we shouldn't overdo things when you're tired or our brains will start smoking and shut down for good, *so go to bed* and we did, but we dragged our feet and held out for a few extra minutes.

"*Fletcher!*" Floyd spoke sharply. I got moving right away that time.

I went up the stairs to bed but on the way I heard Floyd and Mom talking in the kitchen in whispers. I didn't listen because it's not the polite thing to do; there was nothing else to do because Jack was starting to fall asleep while I was talking to him and soon he was snoring like T.T. Oinker, only quieter. I shook him a bit but he didn't wake up at all, so I let him be. I made a note to tell Jack that he, the toughest orphan punk in the world, could catch flies by snoring if he wanted to, and sell them for bait.

Upstairs the door was open to Livvy's pink room and I walked in to talk to her, but I forgot she wasn't there because she was off to visit her Aunt Barbara-Lynne at Egansville for a couple of days. I forgot to tell you that, and it's twenty-eight miles away, but it doesn't matter. I couldn't talk to her anyway if she's at Egansville making cookies with Aunt Barbara-Lynne.

I looked out the window. I forgot about Livvy and her aunt and cookies and Jack right away, and I didn't shout out loud, but I almost did. The curtains were open. That's why I saw them.

It was a good thing Jack stayed with me and Floyd that time because Tina McQueeny wasn't quite by herself like she was supposed to be, and then, there was no doubt; I knew I was right, the curtains *did* move.

I saw them and looked out the window again to be sure because I think my mind is shutting down. The curtains were open, and she was in my mother's bedroom and had no clothes on and I saw her tits again, and she had a visitor and he didn't have any clothes on either. I didn't know *what* to look at. He was lying on the bed, and he had a bottle of whisky in his hand. It was my father.

> *I saw your father and Tina McQueeny doing it right out my window, silly, I saw them, making love just like I saw my mother and father doing it when I was little in bed with them they were doing it. She gave him her breasts. She sat on him, she sat right up on him and put her breasts in your father's mouth. Fletcher, can we try that. Fletcher, I want to do it too, I want to put my breasts in your mouth now. No, you can't do that, only sluts do that, sluts, she's a slut. My mother knows she's a slut.*

I gasped hard and turned away. I didn't watch them. I went back to bed and I was awake for a long time.

Twenty-Six

My father disappeared during the night, because he wasn't there the next day when Jack got out of Floyd's extra green pajamas and had bacon and eggs and went home. Mrs. McAllister hugged Jack and patted him on the shoulder.

"Jack, you come back here anytime you want, young man!" she said. "My goodness, yes, you're welcome to come any time, you know that!" She looked at Floyd. He must know what that was about, but I didn't.

I saw Tina come to the door and grab Jack and kiss him on the mouth, and she had a shiny red housecoat on and she waved to us. Now I *know* that Jack needs to be rescued, I'm sure of it. Jack looked back at us and so did Tina.

"My God, is that Fletcher? *Fletcher?*" I heard her squeal to Jack with delight just like the oinkers when we gave them oat slops. She waved again. "*Hi, Fletcher!*" she shouted. My face got hot, and I felt Floyd looking at me. I did not wave at her and didn't look at Floyd, not once. Tina and Jack disappeared into the house. We didn't look at each other and the screen door slammed behind us.

Mrs. McAllister said *Harrumph!* Floyd and I heard her. "*We* must have something better to do than watch *that!*"

"I think you're probably correct this time, Elizabeth. In fact, I'm sure you are!"

I thought about it hard when Floyd and I went back into the house and had another cup of coffee. I finally suggested that we better tell Jack right away that my father had been there.

"You gotta leave that situation alone, Fletcher," Floyd warned me quietly. "Stay away from her whatever you do, and unless I miss my guess, Jack will find out for himself. A man always has to find about that kind of thing for himself, doesn't do anybody any good to jack his nose into other people's business." He smiled. "No pun intended on Jack's name, either!" he added.

"What's a pun, Floyd?" I asked.

"Don't rightly know, but making fun out of something that's serious business, that comes pretty close to it", he said, "and you're asking a lot of questions, I noticed, Fetch, good thing school's coming up soon."

"I hate school, Floyd!" I said. We never talked about the subject of school before. I don't know why. He shrugged his shoulders up and down. "Law's the law, boy, you gotta go to school, that's all there is to it."

"Not me, Floyd, me and Jack, we can drive the Pontiac around and can see the world, he said so last night, and we got a lot of things to see, all we need is a few gallons of gas, that's what he said!" Floyd laughed.

"Furthest Jack's been is to the broomstick factory over there, and the country fair at Red Deer out west, or was it down east in Bolton, maybe?" He asked himself. He pointed at the new dormitory being built down the street from the broomstick factory. *"Look there"* he said. *"The outside world."*

"It looks and sounds *real* exciting if you compare it to the orphanage, or taking out the slops for T.T. and all the other hogs, or maybe a three-man game on the baseball diamond at your Second Division Public school yard here in Waterland, doesn't it? That's where you're going to be spending most of your time this fall, — in school, but on the overall scale, think hard about that, now, boy, it can be delusional."

"That means it makes a fool of you, and it's pretty small potatoes —with a carrot or two enticing you, to the outside— that's leading you on, if you got your eyes closed up tight. It might *seem* exciting for a bit, but that's where Jack's been and that's what he's comparing *this* place to. Now, you, son, you wouldn't want to bet your whole life on hopes up to here, imagining you're flying higher than a barn roof and then get chopped off at the knees, and learn how short you really are, now would you?"

"Is that what happened to you, Floyd?"

"I told you what happened to me, but I wasn't speaking about my old legs being chopped off; I was referring to doing something successfully with *your* life. That means you got to go to school and make something of yourself, or you'll end up on the short end of the stick!"

He looked around when the truck door slammed. We watched Jack and Tina climb into the black half-ton truck. They honked and waved and Tina said "Hey Fletcher" and smiled silly at me so I could see her white teeth as they backed out and took off out of sight and made a big cloud of dust, too.

"Long and the short of it, boy, you gotta stay in school!"

"I don't like school anyway, Floyd, you can teach me everything I need to know, that's all," I said, and I studied the fuzzy yellow stuff in the middle of a hollyhock flower waving in the wind and leaning itself against the wooden step and watched a bee buzzing in there, getting the yellow pollen on his legs.

Floyd's eyes sparkled in the sunlight and got a little smile on his face. "Well, then, *what's the capital of Ontario*, boy?" Floyd asked.

"Bolton?" I said after I figured out that the fair where Jack went had to be held at an important place, so that's it. It couldn't be Red Deer, because that's too far away, like Regina, so Bolton's *it* because that's the way Floyd works. He hints at things and makes it easy to learn stuff.

"I don't think that's right, Fletcher, but if you think hard about it, you'll probably realize that I don't rightly know for sure either—but, for a hint, let's use logic, could it be Ottawa? That's where all the *government* men go. That could be it, could it not?"

"Well, I bet it can, so now I know, too, Floyd! Ottawa's the capital of Ontario, I can remember that! See? You can teach me, Floyd, so I don't have to go to school."

"Floyd!" I heard the voice coming out of the screen door and Mrs. McAllister came out. "Telling stories, shame on you, Floyd! Fletcher, *Toronto* is the capital of Ontario! Shame on you, Floyd, teasing the boy!" She shook her head and started inside again.

"*Toronto?*" Floyd squinted up at her. "...Hmm, so it is." He looked sideways at me and back at her, but she was still shaking her head.

"You should know Floyd by now, Fletcher Williams, he's *always* pulling your leg!" She flapped my hair. "My goodness!" she said.

"Geography. I was never a whiz at the fine art of geography, but of course it is *Toronto, of course—Toronto it is! Toronto* is the capital of Ontario!" Floyd said it right out loud.

Mrs. McAllister wagged her finger at Floyd. "*And don't you forget it!*" she said and left us alone. The screen door slammed behind her. Floyd lit up his pipe.

"Gotta tease the Missus sometime, don't I Fletch!" he puffed and glanced back at the door to make sure she was gone. "Sometimes that woman has no sense of humor at all, not a bit."

"She knew you were pulling my leg."

"See, I knew that, Fletcher, but I wanted to make a point, which happens to be, on *this* occasion, that I don't know enough about, for instance, say, *geography*—which happens to be a good example, to *home* teach you, boy. You might want to reflect on that for a while too. —Some things in this world make me feel like I'm still in the sixth grade myself." He shook his head. He got a faraway look on his face. "I can't teach you *everything!*"

"Floyd! You know everything I'll ever need to know!" I said, and Floyd *does* know everything. I told Jack that, and all of the boys at the home when I was there, but now I don't think it's going to make any difference because he shook his head again and looked serious. If Floyd makes up his mind, *forget it, that's it, Chuck.*

"Mrs. Zeban says me an' Elizabeth gotta get you enrolled back in school here once the summer's over, that's the law, —if you're going to stay with us, Fletcher. So far as I'm concerned, we have no choice, and that requires your participation like it or not."

"I guess so," I said to Floyd. The bee buzzed its way into another flower, and I saw it escape and scat off home quick as the mosquitoes that zoom away to get out of Floyd's pipe smoke.

"Floyd?" I asked him a couple of days later, when he had no shirt on and wore shaving soap all over his face like a white beard. He smiled and winked and made a face at me. "What's a Master's Degree in the Humanities?" He scraped the soap off of his face and squinted into the mirror. He glanced at me and leaned over the tin basin he had sitting on the bench, and shoved his face into the warm soapy water. He sounded like he was talking under the water and made bubbles. He surfaced like Moby Dick, blowing bubbles and puffing, and I handed him the towel. He hid his face in the towel and rubbed his ears dry.

"Where on earth did you get *that* idea from?" he asked me, but that time he didn't look at me. He scrubbed his face again. A shadow crossed his face as he looked in the mirror.

"Just what is it?" I asked again.

"It's a piece of paper, mostly, son, but where on earth did you get that idea from?"

"Mrs. McAllister —*Mom*," I corrected myself, "showed me your picture with a square hat and that paper in a frame from the bottom of your old trunk under the bed," I said. "She said it was your degree from McMaster University and it said `Floyd Arnold McAllister' and 'Master's Degree in the Humanities' on it, so what's a 'Master's Degree in the Humanities'?"

"*That woman!*" Floyd said, and studied his face in the mirror and took the razor and trimmed off a hair he missed. "That *infernal* woman!" He paused for a minute and shook his head as if he was thinking about something; it must be because I saw his funny hat in the old picture. He smiled.

I saw some bees at the window again. They were buzzing into the flowers again. I opened the screen, and they scatted off to the lilacs.

"Well?" I asked, "*What is it, Floyd? You can tell me!*"

His eyebrows went up. He leaned forward and whispered loudly at me. "*Officially?*" I nodded.

"*Officially*, it's a university degree specializing in specific cultural patterns humans develop in their collective societies, and all of the strange things we do *inside* our cultures; our civil evolution, its influence on how we think and act socially —uh, —and a whole lot of other stuff that's important bunk and shoe polish if you *have* to get that piece of paper, —but say, I got a real good idea, what about between you and me, son, let's keep that paper under the bed in the trunk if that's all right with you? Some things are better left under the bed like dust balls."

"*Right, Floyd!*" I whispered proudly. I left it that way. Between me and Floyd and the dust balls under the bed.

The dust balls in my father's house, the ones under the bed that I didn't sweep when my mother asked me and now I didn't do it, and now she's dead and she can't ask me any more can she? And now, she's like Mr. Mulligan, *don't disturb him dear. 'You get used to it son, you will, too. You'll get over it, you'll see. The dust balls don't matter now,'* my mother whispered. My mother didn't whisper to me for a long time. I don't know why she started now.

I went outside and watched the bees. I didn't even hear Floyd wheel out behind me.

"You're deep in thought, boy," Floyd finally said, and I jumped.

"I was watching the bees." I thought about it hard and I bet that honeybee came from the white clover down at the railroad tracks. I didn't tell Floyd that idea. Mrs. McAllister called us in for lunch.

"Is the Master's Degree in the Humanities like the *sixth* grade, Floyd?" Floyd looked down the street before we went inside.

He puffed. "*Quite a lot.* Seems there are lots of *similarities,*" Floyd said. "Shush, now!"

We had beef stew and biscuits, and right after that Livvy came back home and her Aunt Barbara-Lynne didn't stay for tea because she had to go pick up *Mr.* Barbara-Lynne.

I looked at her when she came to the door with Livvy, and I noticed they looked a bit like each other, except Aunt Barbara-Lynne was tall and skinny and flat like Mrs. Zeban up front, and had a green ribbon in the back of her yellow hair. She wobbled her way back to the dusty brown car and looked shaky. "It's from those spiked heels, stupid invention!" Floyd said it was, "too high and unstable, break an ankle, she will!"

She called, "Soggie's at school, I have to pick him up right away. I'll stop for tea next time!" We sat at the kitchen table and ate apple pie.

"Is he getting a degree in the Humanities at school?" I asked. Floyd squinted at me, something like a warning look. I clammed up.

"She has to pick up my uncle at school" Livvy said, explaining everything to us, "and his name is *Soggie Sweeney*—and no, he's a *lawyer,* remember, he's not going to school, he's just visiting, did you think he's still going to school? You're so funny, Fletcher, he's giving a speech!" She laughed and showed Mrs. McAllister the new dress her Aunt made from scratch and new pink cloth, just for her.

"You men go outside and let us ladies talk some!" Mrs. McAllister said. Floyd and I didn't move, but Livvy helped Floyd get going out through the screen door and Floyd winked at me, so I followed him.

"*Bye! You men go outside and talk, we ladies will talk some,*" Livvy smiled in a funny way as she said that, just like Mrs. McAllister did, and I felt her blue eyes dig right into me.

Floyd had a sleep in his wheeled chair on the porch and crickets buzzed around in the hot air, so I thought about it while I sneaked next door and sat in the old Pontiac and drove around the world.

I won't be hopeless when I'm in the sixth grade and get my degree in the humanities like Floyd, I know *that*. I just didn't bother to tell Livvy about it or say that I saw my *father* the other night, either. I didn't *have* to tell her. I was sleeping and dreaming when she told me. That's it; it *must have been a dream*.

Twenty-Seven

I did not see Jack at my father's house, even though I watched every day when I was working in the garden and doing important yard work for Floyd. "Good job, Fletcher!" Floyd called to me when I finished cutting the grass. Floyd can't cut the grass in his wheelchair, but he can go to sleep, so that's what he did right away. I pulled some weeds in the garden and dug some potatoes for Mrs. McAllister and put them in a six-quart wooden basket that used to have blueberries in it.

I heard the car stop at the gate, and the door slammed. I looked up and there she was, was, bold as brass, Livvy's Aunt Barbara-Lynne. She had a suitcase in one hand.

"Hello, Fletcher!" she said from under the wide-brimmed hat that let sun splotch on her face, making a pattern like little diamonds. "My, you are a hard-working young man, aren't you?" she laughed. "Is Livvy home? I've come to pick her up!"

"What?" I said. *"Pick her up?"* I must have sounded like an echo.

"I've come to pick her up!" the woman said again, "What's the matter, don't you believe me?" She laughed.

I didn't believe her. She's not Mrs. Zeban and Livvy's not an orphan. Her mother and father are just divorced and away from each other, so she's not an orphan that can be hauled around like the scorched furniture from the orphanage that got hauled to the new building at the broomstick factory. And she doesn't have to go where somebody *says,* like I had to, and I'm not telling her if Livvy's home because she's not bait and I don't want Livvy to get hauled away, not ever. I like Livvy, even if she says *'You're so hopeless, Fletcher,'* or *'You're so funny, Fletcher!'*

I didn't like that, *not at all,* but everybody made it so that I didn't have time to answer back.

"Oh, hello, Mr. McAllister!" she sang out to Floyd right over my head like I wasn't standing there with a basket of potatoes.

"Livvy's here, Mrs. Sweeny. She's inside with Elizabeth, getting ready, the room upstairs to the left. She might not hear you, so don't bother knocking, you might like to just go right on up!" Floyd said. Floyd was wide awake, so he must have heard us talking and woke up on the porch and I didn't notice.

I looked at the suitcase. It was not cracked, not even a bit, and had flowers all over it, pink ones, red ones. All the flowers were tangled up in green leaves, something like bean leaves.

She disappeared into the house. I set the basket of potatoes on the porch and sat on the step. I looked at Floyd. He looked away.

"Floyd?" I asked. He kept quiet for a moment or two.

"She's going to live with Mr. and Mrs. Sweeny, her aunt and uncle in Egansville now. Came up kind of fast, never had a chance to tell you, you being off with the boys to the baseball diamond and such!"

"*To live?*" I asked, not believing my ears.

"To live, Fletcher. Barbara-Lynne is Livvy's mother's *only* sister, no reason why she *can't* live with them, nice people. He's a lawyer now, but he used to be a teacher at the high school there. Lots of money, more than I've ever seen with my pension here. *Makes sense, too,* doesn't it?"

"*You didn't tell, me, Floyd!*" I said. I was hot and getting dizzy too. "You didn't tell me, Floyd, *you didn't tell me!*" I shouted. "*You didn't tell me!* I don't want Livvy to go away; I don't want her to go away!"

Floyd shook his head. "It's not that we don't *want* her here, Fletcher, don't you see? We love her like a daughter!"

"But Floyd, *I love her too, I – *" I stopped talking because the cat got my tongue and made my face get red, I can't believe I told Floyd that. My head was talking *inside*, but my tongue wasn't saying anything *outside*. I hate that.

> *If you love me, Fletcher, do you love me now? Fletcher promise me I'll always be your only love, she whispered. I'm going now. I promise, Livvy. I promise. I don't want to be a slut either. I love you.*

Floyd lifted up his eyebrows and looked like he was studying a bee in a flower. He patted his shirt pocket for his pipe. "We all love her, we've all grown to love her, but just because she's going away that doesn't mean she'll never be back, does it, does it?"

"But we're a *family*, you didn't tell me!" I jumped down off of the steps and ran around the house and down the street.

I heard Floyd call me but I didn't answer him. I went through the back alley, ran and got through the white clover by the railroad tracks and the white picket fence looked right at me. It was the cemetery.

"I am not going to cry now," I told my mother when I finally found her. I sat beside her on the ground and my black-eyed Suzie's weren't there. There were no black-eyed Susie's left, or other flowers there, not a one.

The way I found her was strange. Everything was different. I saw William Yakafluic, and then I looked for the hill of sand, the place where I thought my mother was, but the white cross was not there and the sand pile weren't there, just a strange sunken place with patchy grass, and a crooked old cross that was grey and silver-colored bare wood, with only bits of paint, and the paint was peeling off. I helped it a bit; I mean the peeling bits of white paint, I don't know why. I pulled the loose paint off of the cross and threw it up in the air and watched it spiral and fall to the ground. I cried.

> *"There, now, don't cry, son. I'm here, that's better, isn't it, Fletcher?" my mother whispered to me. "Everything is fine, son. I miss you too."*

215

The air moved and the train whistle at the crossroad screeched. It made me jump and the train roared by, and I watched it and waved back at the caboose man that saw me, and I felt better. Maybe I'll be an engineer or a caboose man someday. The wind cooled my face and I looked around. I didn't see very much. I pulled some weeds out of the grass.

The cross still said 'Angelina Williams 1932-1952' and '*I am with God*' carved into the silver wood, and the white paint that was left was stuck in the cracks, and I pushed the cross up straighter and stamped the dirt to make it stay right.

I rubbed the green moss off of the wood, and some old gray moss bumps too. I cleaned the moss out of the lettering with my jackknife and scraped them good to make the wood new again. Even though it was hot, I cut a nice straight line around the sunken ground with my jackknife and trimmed off the long grass that hung down into the sunken hole. It took a long time, but I finished it right. Nobody even asked me to do that, but I did. I sat down and looked over my work.

"Nice job, Fetchie boy!" I heard that voice because it made me jump just like the screeching train did, but I looked up and I couldn't see who was talking and nobody was there. "Didn't expect to see you here, boy!" he said. I heard that voice again, and I knew that voice too, so I stood up fast. I put my dirty hand over my eyes like Indian scouts do when they look into the sun. *He* was there. It was my father standing there, just like a hobo bum.

He stepped out from behind the tree and over the white fence and leaned against the big tree. He stood in the shade of the large branch that straddled the sharp steel picket fence.

"*Cat got your tongue, Fetchie boy?*" I didn't know if I could talk or what to say. He took off his dusty hat and squatted down against the tree.

"Kind of hot, Fetchie boy, kind of hot to be out here working without a hat!"

"You don't belong here with my mother!" I finally said, and I know I sounded angry. "Go away, *go away!*"

"You been at McAllister's all this time, and that Floyd, he's a clever one. He's never said anything at all, eh, *nothing* to me!"

"Floyd takes care of me since the fire at the orphanage I got sent to, but it's burned down now so I live with Floyd, and we're a *family* now — and Floyd doesn't have to tell *anyone!*"

"I know all about how long you been here, boy. I been watching you, you and them *McAllister's* and that beautiful little lady living there; pretty little thing, she is. I been watching *all* of you, eh?" He rubbed his whiskers.

"*Watching us?* You're making that up! You don't know anything about us, and Floyd doesn't have to tell you where I am and who Livvy is, *never, he doesn't have to tell you anything, so go away!*"

"Well, Fetchie boy, it is the truth — but you wouldn't have come to see me if you *knew* I was there, would you, Fetchie boy? You wouldn't have come to *see your old man*, or *even say hello*, across the fence, now would you?"

"No! I wouldn't go near you, not ever! You hit my mother, that's why she's dead, and I knew you were back, I saw you!"

"Don't lie to me, boy, you better not be lying to me, God don't like no kid that lies to his old man, eh!" He slapped his hat against his leg sharply and hung it on the fence. He reached up, stepped up carefully between the sharp pickets on the fence, and hoisted himself up to sit on the big branch. He was higher than my head and looked down at me.

"*You're* the one lying, not me!" I said.

"Don't call me a liar, boy, either, if you know what's good for you! You ain't learned nothing, have you, respect for your parents, boy, *I'm your father, remember?*" he shouted at me.

"You're *not* my father, not now, *not now!*" I shouted up at him. "*Floyd is!*"

I got brave and went closer. "And what do you know about God. Don't you talk about God, I never saw you at church, *never*, He doesn't even like you, I bet! You can't talk about God, you know nothing about God, my mother told me, so you don't know anything

217

about God, not like my mother *you killed*," I shouted back at him, "all you know is being a deadbeat drunk!"

"Don't you be telling me what I know, boy —you don't know me, you ain't never seen me for years, you certainly ain't seen me since I got back here, boy. Don't tell no lies, either, you ain't seen me, eh, and don't judge me, boy, Bible says *don't judge others,* boy!"

"I saw you! I saw you!" I got back to my mother's grave and sat down right beside it. He watched me like I was a monkey with a red bum in the zoo. *I was in the fence, wasn't I, and he was the visitor, and he was throwing peanuts at me.*

"I'm going home," I said.

"*Running away*, boy? Stay and talk for a while."

I looked up at him and I was still being watched, and he rubbed his face and picked a couple of leaves and dropped them. They whirled and the breeze caught them and carried them away. Like me. I want to get carried away right now, right out of the zoo.

"*What do you want?*" I demanded loudly.

"I wanted to see you, boy!"

"I don't want to see *you,* so go away!" I got up and brushed the dust off of my trousers. I kept my jackknife in my hand. He looked away and then back at the cross on my mother's grave. "*You're nothing but a deadbeat drunk!*" I shouted, and kicked angrily at the dirt, some of the dirt splatted toward him.

"Fetchie, boy, I *know* what I am, you don't gotta tell me that, but I ain't had a drink in over a month now!"

"Lies, you're lying to me! *You're lying to me!* You hit my mother, you made her cry *every day* and you whipped me with *that belt, that one, the one you're wearing!*" I pointed at his belt and spit at him. The shiny truck-buckle was the same one, I know it was.

"Boy, if it was the old days I'd be taking it off *right now* and whip you good!" He shouted at me.

"Go ahead, *I'm* not lying, *I saw you in bed with the slut* in my mother's bedroom, drinking whiskey, so *who's the liar? You're nothing but a liar!*" I screamed at him.

"Fetch, boy, that's a lot of water under the bridge, I changed, don't be ugly, boy, *don't be judgmental,*" he said quietly. He looked off into the distance and frowned. "No need to —I need your help now, I need you back, boy!" He shook his head. "I changed, don't you see, now I need..."

"*Changed? You didn't change, not a bit,* you were drinking whiskey in bed with that slut, and you lied, *you lied to me, see? You don't need me!* You whipped me and told me '*don't come home, don't, never!* ' I spit.

"You lied to me about being there and you lied about not drinking, you're nothing but a lying deadbeat drunk, you probably killed my mother too, and said the train did it, and now you're squawking about *God*, so I *know you're a liar, you're a goddamned liar and a hypocrite!*"

"It was the *liquor*, boy, and you watch your mouth, boy! That's foul language for a boy your age, so watch your mouth. It don't do you any good to use a foul mouth —and I don't blame you for being angry, but you got a *wicked* memory," he said quietly. My father looked up into the sky and around behind him and back at me. He licked his lips nervously and looked at the ground.

"*It's not right, that,*" he said, in not much more than a whisper. "I *loved* your mother. *I did, I loved her,* and it wasn't like you think, it was just the *drinking, the drinking was out of control. I was out of control,* so now I get it all back, eh, *I get paid back with all of it?*"

"You deserve *everything* you get! I'm with Floyd now, and I'm *not* coming back, you're still a deadbeat drunk and a liar! *God hates liars!*" I added, "You just said so yourself!"

"You're a harsh judge, Fletcher Williams, or is it *McAllister? Are you changing that, too, Fletcher?*"

"*I'm not coming back to you, ever, so what do you think?*" I screamed. I fell down on my knees beside the neat line of dirt and jammed my knife into the trimmed grass. I cried hard that time.

219

When I stopped crying I looked up at the big branch where he was. The sun was not in my eyes anymore, and the wind died down to quiet. I checked around to see if he was hiding behind the tree and looked up to see if he was trying to get closer to God by climbing up high, but he was not there. I sat on the big branch and sat until it was almost dark, and the silver crosses were dark and I got scared. That was enough time to get afraid, and I did; I thought about where he *might be*, but I didn't figure it out for sure.

He was just gone; vanished, nowhere to be seen. I started for home.

Twenty-Eight

It was dark when I got back home to Floyd's, and he said "Livvy wanted to say goodbye and she cried, but we didn't know where you run off to, boy, and Livvy was worried about you. So, they waited and left just before supper; where were you, anyway?"

I did not answer. "I don't want to talk about it, Floyd!" I said, and I went to bed right away so I wouldn't have to. I heard Mrs. McAllister arguing with Floyd, and I didn't go to sleep for a long time. I looked out my window and saw the moon and the stars instead.

"Boy, wake up, you won't want to miss this!" I woke up, and the sun was shining in my face. It was Floyd. He was at the bottom of the stairs calling me.

"What, Floyd?" I called back.

"Better look outside boy, to the front gate there! Be quick there, now, we ain't got all day, have we!"

"Okay, Floyd!" I said. I scrambled my trousers on and a shirt when I looked out the window. There was a line of dusty boys standing in front of two runty dirt-yellow school buses. I couldn't believe my eyes. *It was the boys from the home*, and they all came to see me. *Me*, Fletcher Carnival Williams!

I opened the window. "Hi, Arnold!" I shouted. "Hi, Eddie! Up here, boys, *up here!*" I shouted loud, and they looked up and saw me

221

and it was the best day of my life. Arnold Thackery said, *"There's Fletcher, boys, there he is!"* and pointed up at me and the boys clapped and cheered.

I saw two bigger boys that didn't get to the home while I was there, and Timmy Tenberg, that's Ricky's little brother, and Eddie Peters and Ronnie Gates and a new bunch of smaller boys that I didn't know yet. I laughed and got myself down the stairs and past Floyd and outside to the porch before Mrs. McAllister had a chance to hug me good morning.

"I'm glad to meet you, Fletcher!" Mr. Fester smiled nice at me and shook my hand hard but I was watching the boys at the gate.

"I'm happy to meet you, too, sir," I said, and then I watched his mouth first thing to see if he had any silver teeth. He didn't. He was very tall and skinny and wore a brown suit with a red tie. His vest was the kind that has silver cloth on the back of it when you take your jacket off and has a gold watch chain hanging across the front so you look important. When Mr. Fester looked at me, I didn't feel like bait.

"All the boys here call me *Wiltie*, so you can call me *Wiltie*, too!" he said.

I looked at Floyd. He said something like it was all right.

"Personal addressing, that's something to be settled between two men, right, Fletcher?"

"Right, Floyd" I said to Floyd, and "All right, *Mr. Wiltie*," I said to Wiltie, and I got a bit embarrassed, but everybody laughed so it made me forget it right away.

I got along the front of the line and shook hands with every boy, after I helped Floyd bum down the stairs and get into his chair. Arnold helped too.

Wiltie hauled me along the line of dusty boys and introduced me to the bigger boys, Nelson McDougal and Tim Winters, and to all of the smaller boys I didn't know just yet. There was Billy McFee who's missing three front teeth, and Parker Drummond, and Lennie Maclean that got a brown tweed hat like mine; and Jimbo, and another Eddie that is a boy with brown skin and black hair, not the

Eddie Peters that was at the home already when it burned; and Milton Laxter, and another boy named Danny that's skinny and got glasses; and some others — too many, and I can't remember the rest of them just now.

After the introductions and handshaking with me and Floyd and Mrs. McAllister, Mr. Fester said, "Now if you'll quiet up — *quiet up*, boys, so we might be able to talk a bit!" just like an announcement.

The boys stopped gabbling right away when Wiltie wagged his skinny finger at us. He walked over pleased as punch and stood right in front of me and Floyd.

"We came to pick you up. We're on our way to see young Ricky Tenberg in the hospital, and Arnold and the boys thought you might like to go with us since you're right on the way!"

"Fletch'd like that, I think he could be persuaded to go along!" Floyd grinned at me. I looked at Floyd to see if I was getting tricked into going away from Floyd's, like *Livvy* was.

"We *would* bring you back, you know!" Wiltie added.

"Okay!" I said. "Can I go, Floyd? Mom?"

"You'll have to get your face washed first and that scruffy hair combed before you go off anywhere, young man!" Mrs. McAllister said.

"Oh, I don't know... well, *maybe,*" Floyd said gravely. "Of course I have a lot of chores that *should* be done *first,* don't I, Elizabeth?" The boys fell silent.

"Floyd! *You rascal!*" Mrs. McAllister said, laughing. *"He's just pulling your legs, boys!"*

Floyd made another funny face. "She's got my arm twisted, boys!" He laughed. "*Of course* you can go, Fletcher! It'll do you good!" he finally added after he wrinkled up another serious funny face for the boys, tooted his pipe at me like *Popeye the Sailor,* and teased me good. Everybody clapped and cheered, and I cheered the loudest. That's why I like Floyd best, he makes everyone laugh.

"How about you, Mr. McAllister, you want to come along with us, too?" Mr. Fester asked Floyd. "I'm sure all of these men can get your wheels up into the bus, Mr. McAllister."

"Call me Floyd, please!" Floyd said, "You call me Floyd, all the boys do, right, boys?" The boys cheered.

"Okay, Floyd," Mr. Fester said, quick as a wink, "How about it?"

"I think I'll just stay home with Elizabeth today, seems like it's *Fletcher's turn* to do something *important*. I'll come along next time with you. Fletcher's going to represent me at the hospital this time!" Floyd winked at me and Mrs. McAllister smiled at him and nodded enthusiastically.

"Aw!" the boys shouted.

"Next time it is, then, Floyd," Mr. Fester said, and looked at me, "Well, then, Fletcher, what are we waiting for? Let's get a move on!" I glanced at Floyd and I knew he was proud of me and I think he knows I can do a good job for him.

"Get a move on, boy. I won't let them go without you now, so you go get ready!"

I never got my face washed and scruffy hair in order so fast in my life. You have to hurry when you're going to do something important like representing Floyd.

I don't want to remember too long about Ricky Tenberg right now because he was blackened and toasted like raw meat, and he couldn't even have bandages on because he didn't have too much skin left. He got upset and cried when he saw us, he couldn't talk, and the nurse said he was going to die soon. His brother Timmy cried and promised to get *to be a doctor some day and fix him, wait and see.*

Floyd told me he was a brave boy and agreed with me when I told him I think he was waiting for us to see him because he died the next night. Floyd told me that's what happens: People wait to see people they love before they die, and that's what Ricky did, so now I have to think about it, like it or not.

The bus ride was hot and dusty and the nurse at the hospital let us go in to see Ricky in two-by-two's so that we would not make too much noise laughing and pushing and sliding down the shiny hospital floor. The walls were yellow just like at the home. We had to wait and take turns. I got sent in last with Timmy. He cried when he saw his brother.

"Hey, Ricky," I said to him and the air in his room smelled terrible. The nurse said yes it was so Ricky, but it didn't look like Ricky, not even a bit, because his hair was all gone just like Murvie's, and his head and lips were burned black. He had to lie on his stomach and his back was covered with a wet sheet.

"You'll get better, I'll fix you some day, you'll see, Ricky!" Timmy said right out loud, crying. "*I promise, I'm going to be a doctor, you just wait and see!*"

Ricky could not talk or shake hands, just cry a lot, and the nurse said, "You two had better go along now, that's all the visitors for today."

I represented Floyd very well, that's what Wiltie told him after, and Floyd told me, after Nelson and Tim got the boys back on the bus.

"The prognosis isn't that good, I'm afraid," Wiltie told Floyd when we got up the steps at home. "*Over forty-five percent third degree burns — he's not going to make it,*" he whispered to Floyd right there on the porch and shook his head sadly. I heard that. After the boys left and waved at me I sat on the steps and stayed quiet for a long time, just for Ricky.

The next time I went on the bus it was to Ricky's funeral, and they buried him at the cemetery where my mother is. I looked up on the branch of the big tree to see if my father was sitting up there. but he wasn't. Wiltie told the boys to *get down off of that branch right away.* It was Jimbo and Danny.

"*Get down from there, you could fall and get yourselves hurt on that fence!*" he ordered, and Nelson ran over there and got Jimbo and Danny down right away.

"*Get down here, you two!* This is a serious occasion!" Nelson said to Jimbo and dragged him and Danny back into line with the rest of us.

225

The rest of us stayed serious, and stood neatly and quietly in front of a pile of sand covered with a green cloth, and the wood box that Ricky was getting planted in was painted white.

The Reverend began, "We have been brought together on this sad occasion to lay to rest a young boy called away from us by God; young Richard Tenberg has been taken away from us because of a tragic, tragic accident..."

Wiltie said we should pick up dirt and drop it on the white box after the Reverend finished reading from the Bible and talking, so we did. "*Ashes to ashes and dust to dust,*" the Reverend said.

That was the second funeral I went to. The first one was at another cemetery in a flat field with no headstones and no trees. That's where Richard Bordon and Joe Coleman were planted. Mrs. Tickner wasn't buried there because she wanted to get shipped collect all the way to England to be buried with her dead husband, and her funeral service had to be held at the train station to get her to the shipping company on time.

That day was too sad to talk about, but it was a good thing she got to go to England, because if she stayed here she would have been like Richard and Joe that got a potter's funeral, just like Murvie did, if it was up to Mr. Tupper that's in jail. When we said the prayers, I opened my eyes and saw the men with shovels waiting.

"*Let us pray, my son,*" the Reverend said, and he looked right at me and I had to shut my eyes quick.

They didn't put up any crosses for Richard and Joe in the long grass. I looked around for Murvie, but the grass was too high and I couldn't find him.

I cried. I don't like that.

Twenty-Nine

"Order in the court, all rise!" the bailiff shouted at us and I think he was looking right at Floyd and me because we were talking. We shushed up right away and I stood up like everybody else. I looked up on the balcony, and I saw Livvy with her Aunt Barbara-Lynne, but she didn't see me. Arnold was sitting with Wiltie and another man dressed in a black suit, and I saw Mr. Tupper with a man at another table inside a fence and the guard watching Mr. Tupper had a cowboy gun.

The oak door opened, and I got the surprise of my life. The old man moved slowly to the judge's chair and sat down, and then he looked up from the paper on the desk.

"Case Number 368!" the bailiff read from a list, *"The Queen versus Charles Albert Tupper!"*

I didn't pay any attention to that part because I *knew* the old man sitting at the front with his black bed sheet on, and he was looking old and white-haired. Last time I saw him it was through a screen door, and I thought he was going to say *boy* at me or something.

It was old Judge Bending that gave us the moving-paper in Morgan County.

He coughed and cleared his throat and looked like he was going to spit, so I think he's going to die soon. He took a glass of water and drank. He cleared his throat right out loud three or four times. I think it was four.

"Charles Albert Tupper, is that you, sir? If that's *you,* stand up, that's it. I'm going to explain this to you in everyday language, so that *you* understand it; never mind the fact you've got legal representation sitting beside you, I always like to make sure the *defendant,* if that's you, that he or she understands what's happening; and in *this* case sir, *it is most definitely happening to you,* since, in this instance, your legal representative is leaving something to be desired. He does not seem to know that he's supposed to be standing up with you. At any rate, *you, sir, are charged with the serious business of arson;* that's intentionally burning something like a building illegally, and that action appears to have resulted in the deaths of several people."

Mr. Tupper interrupted the judge by coughing his head off and looking choked. The judge looked at Mr. Tupper and shook his head.

"You through, sir? Need a glass of water? Here, pass him that glass of water," he instructed the bailiff, and "Sit down now. Yes, I mean *you"* to Mr. Tupper. Mr. Tupper drank the whole glass and handed the empty back to the bailiff. The judge continued talking to him.

"Now you pay attention here, sir, because it appears that the orphanage fire has been linked to you, sir, and if that is the case, it is quite easy to understand that those deaths are also being attributable to you." He looked down at his desk and read something from the papers on his desk. His lips moved but he didn't talk right away. He shuffled the papers and looked at us. "Therefore..." he said.

I saw Mr. Tupper was going to jump up to talk, but the judge shook his head again and held up his hand like a policeman stopping traffic.

"Mr. Tupper, you have been charged with murder in the first degree of Mrs. Eileen Tickner, and murder in the first degree of Mr. Richard Bordon; you are also charged in the deaths of Master Joe Coleman in connection with the same incident. I see, very unfortunately for you, and just recently, too, the name of one Master Richard Tenberg has been added to this horrific list of victims of the fire at the *Waters County Home for Boys...*

"For the record, this charge has been added officially by the crown, it will be first degree murder also, that makes *four* counts of murder in the first degree, so, Mr. Tupper, sir, *how do you plead?*"

I noticed right away that the judge forgot my friend Marvin Pychinski and I told Floyd. "Floyd, he forgot Marvin!" I said it right out loud before Mr. Tupper had a chance to say anything. The crowd bustled.

"Order in the court! *Order in the court!*" old Judge Bending shouted, and banged his gavel on the bench. The bailiff moved up to the big desk and whispered to the judge.

"Is there a *problem* here, bailiff? *The Crown hasn't got its act together, I take it?*" The bailiff shook his head.

"—Oh, my, I see there *is* a problem, too, *another* young lad was also killed in that fire, one Marvin Pychinski, another resident of the Home!" He looked up from his paper and right at Mr. Tupper. "Same charge might be applied to all; murder in the first degree, sir; *we do have them all* now, I take it?"

"Yes sir, your Honor," the bailiff said.

The man sitting beside Arnold and Wiltie stood up. "*Yes, your Honor! Sogman Sweeney for the Crown, your Honor!*"

"Glad to see *we're* paying attention, *Mr.* Sogman!" the judge said.

"*Sogman Sweeney*, your Honor," Mr. Sweeney replied.

"You any relation to that Sweeney fella over in Morgan county?"

"*One and the same, your Honor!*"

Judge Bending looked over his round steel glasses at Mr. Sweeney. He took them off and polished them with a paper. He glared back at Mr. Sweeney.

"Well, I'll, be, *so it is*, it is you, Soggie, my eyes aren't what they used to be!" he thundered. "Welcome aboard!"

"While we're at it, and everybody here except me can see who it is, *just who is that*—sitting down on the job, and getting paid for it, supposedly representing the *accused?*"

"James Ditworth for the defense!" The skinny man seated beside Mr. Tupper stood up.

"Mr. Ditworth, you mean that you finished that plum circuit court investigation already? Why, that wasn't scheduled for completion until December some time!"

"All finished your Honor, and here I am back at my *usual* job, *defending the innocent, spitting mad and loaded for bear,* sir!"

"Amazing, I hear you *got* them, too, you must be good!" the judge said. The skinny man smiled and straightened up his tie. "We'll see how innocent *your client* is, won't we?"

"That's what we're here for, Judge," Mr. Ditworth said.

"Very well then, all the official formalities have been taken care of, haven't they? *Let's get back on track then!"* He slammed his wooden gavel on the bench.

"Mr. Tupper, now we'll get back to *you,* but first," he said, turning to the skinny man, "I am deeply grieved, Mr. Ditworth, to see that you, sir, on your brief sabbatical from real life, have forgotten all procedure and correct protocol that is required in my court! You may have finished your plum circuit investigation ahead of schedule, and been successful, and you might be loaded for bear, spittin' mad and peachy keen too, but that doesn't cut any ice with me, do you understand?

"You, sir, are supposed to be *standing up* with your client, aren't you, sir? What's the matter, can't you remember *anything?* And for your information, this is the official bench *here,* so you don't sit there looking at your client *there* — is that to see if Mr. Tupper's going to pay you, or what? That, sir, if you will allow me to make an observation for you, is a privilege you have to *earn* first, so you better stand up now and look at me — and right smartly, too. Let's do things *right* from now on!"

He banged his gavel again and Mr. Ditworth stood up, red in the face, and mumbled humbly "May I offer my *deepest* apology to the court, your Honor, sir!"

"Very well, then, Mr. Ditworth, see that it doesn't happen again." Mr. Ditworth nodded, red-faced.

"Mr. Tupper, getting back to you then, sir, since everyone is guaranteed an expeditious day in court, we'll get ourselves expediting this process right along —it is said that on June 17th of this year you did deliberately set fire to the *Waters County Home for Boys* resulting in the deaths of these *five* unfortunate people, and also in the complete destruction of the buildings and incidental livestock consisting of a few dozen chickens and fourteen fat market hogs."

Mr. Tupper looked down at his feet. Judge Bending looked at some more papers and shook his head.

"I need a minute here. Sloppy, *sloppy* job, court clerks don't get paid enough to do their jobs properly or something?" He glared at the bailiff. "Says here you were in charge of that institution until some time ago but were forced out because of some *alleged* improprieties."

"*Objection! Irrelevant!*" Mr. Ditworth jumped up and down like the monkeys in the zoo that have red bums.

"Mr. Ditworth, now's not the time —but you are right, these are only *alleged* improprieties, I will instruct the jury to disregard, but Mr. Ditworth, *shame on you,* we haven't even *started* examination of the witnesses or *facts* yet, —is that a fact worth repeating *twice?*"

"Yes, your Honor!" Mr. Ditworth said with a red face.

"Well, then, Mr. Ditworth, *we haven't started up with the witnesses or examination of the facts yet, have we?*" The crowd laughed. "*Quiet in the court, please!* The jury will take a note of that, in this hearing, those are only *alleged improprieties,* and we are not here to address *that* issue; therefore, the jury will ignore *all* allegations of wrongdoing prior to the day of the fire, and, right time or not, let me make that perfectly clear!"

The judge spoke sharply and glared at the jurors. I saw there were six men and six ladies, and they all squirmed like they were sitting in grade five school at test time, or even worse yet, spelling out loud while being watched by the school inspector.

"Counsel, *approach the bench.*" The lawyers squealed their chairs and both walked up to the judge.

"Now, Mr. Sogman —I mean Sweeney, and Mr. Ditworth, do you think you two gentlemen can allow us to proceed *without* turning this into a circus?"

"Yes, your Honor!" Mr. Sweeney and Mr. Ditworth said, both at once. Judge Bending cleared his throat.

"Let me give you fair warning, gentlemen, this is a most serious case, and any attempts to thwart justice will result in the severest of consequences."

The men nodded nervously.

"*Step back.*" The men looked at one another and sat down again, squealing their chairs again.

"Very well, shall we proceed?

"Charles Albert Tupper, to make it *simple*, I can see that these legal eagles can make things complicated even before we get started, but we'll ignore them for now and get to the facts—which is four counts of murder in the first degree for the poor souls you killed right there with the fire, but I'm going to stand down *one count* in preference to one of *attempted* murder for the boy that died after, because he didn't die right there like the others, even though this court could make that first degree murder *too*, do you understand?

"But we'll allow you *some* leeway on that one, so make that *attempted murder one count, four counts of first degree murder,* and *one count of Arson with willful intent to destroy,* and *one count of destruction of County property* that rightfully belongs to the poor taxpayers of Waters County, —and I'm going to add *fourteen* counts of cruelty to dumb animals for *you*, Sir, because it says here you poured gasoline all over those poor hogs too, and you can count your lucky stars I'm not counting all of them chickens you murdered too. How do you plead to the charges? —And stand up again, I see your coughing fit is finished." Mr. Tupper and Mr. Ditworth turned red and stood up.

"Well, *come on*, how do you plead, or do I have to ask you *again?*"

"*Not guilty!*" Mr. Tupper squawked. "I'm *not guilty*, your Honor, not me. I wouldn't 'a done nothing like that, would I, me own sister was killed, wasn't she? Even if she hit me on the head with 'er wooden spoon and got me beat silly by the bleedin' brats, and flung me on the ground and kicked me out of the 'ome, for some minor disagreements of policy and propriety; but of this fire, I'm *innocent, I am!* ...And I wouldn't be burnin' no dumb animals, not me! Pigs, they're my *favorite* animals, they are, —I like pigs—*hogs, I do!* I like bacon, too, *Canadian.* Every morning I eat bacon, fried lightly, not dried out like *some* eat it then, *only the best!*"

"That's all very interesting, but you'll get your chance to tell your side and indicate your preferences, and even defend yourself in good time, sir; meantime, you'll do well to remember that this is undoubtedly the worst crime witnessed in Waters County in over a hundred years, since 1858; that's when a crazy man like yourself who cross-hatched a dozen young girls with a meat cleaver got himself hung good; he burned them up, or tried to, but *he* had *his* day in court, and got his just rewards—and just like *him* back then, *you'll get to say what's rightfully yours to say*—and if you expect cooperation from this court, sir, you will sit down with much patience and clam up! We have due process to observe!"

Mr. Tupper and Mr. Ditworth sat down and whispered to each other.

The judge looked down at his papers and shook his head. "You got a lot of *gall*, sir, but if that's how you want to plead, let that be entered to the record as '*not guilty*'. The judge thundered. "Mr. Sweeney, call your first witness, if you've got any, proceed!"

Mr. Sweeney stood up and turned around.

"*Prosecution calls Jack Whittaker!*" I couldn't believe my ears. I turned around and saw the guard let Jack walk in the front door, bold as brass. He was wearing a fancy dark green, striped suit and had a derby hat in his hand. I never saw Jack look like that before. Jack walked right past Floyd and me. He didn't see us.

"What's Jack doing here?" I asked Floyd.

"Don't know, but I think we're about to find out!"

Jack moved to the witness box and stood in front of the bailiff.

"Raise your right hand on this Bible and state your name!" the bailiff ordered, and offered Jack the Bible.

"Jack Elwood Whittaker."

"Do you swear to tell the truth, the whole truth, and nothing but the truth, so help you God?"

"I do!"

"Be seated then." Jack sat down nervously and fiddled with his hat. He noticed me and smiled at me, and it made me feel funny. Mr. Sweeney approached Jack and looked him over, smiling.

"Not badly dressed for a young man from the Waters County Home for Boys!"

"Yes sir, Mr. Sweeney," Jack said, proudly hooking his thumb under his lapel and adjusting his derby hat on one knee. "I got me a job at the broomstick factory and gets my twenty bucks a week, and I got a house to live at right next to Floyd McAllister, there." He indicated Floyd and me, "And I got a good woman to sleep good with every night, and I eat *real good* too, every day!" I think everybody in the whole courtroom giggled. I hate giggling, just like Floyd, so we didn't.

"I'm not a *dirty orphan-boy any more, not me.* I got myself a pickup truck too; cost two hundred, a black one, fifty-eight thousand miles on it, *vee-eight,* and I put new tires on it, I did, and it don't burn *no* oil, not a drop!"

"Perhaps you could confine your answers to the questions asked, Mr. Whittaker," the judge said, clearing his throat, and I can see he was trying to hide the smile on his face. "Mr. Sweeney, you might want to set a fine example for Mr. Whittaker by asking *direct* questions!"

"Yes sir, your Honor, sir, I was just getting to that, the comment directed to our Mr. Whittaker was one to make note of the fact that the Waters County Home for Boys produces *fine* boys, that turn out to be *fine* young men in the *fine* tradition of this *fine* province!" He grinned toothily, snapped his suspenders sharply, then glanced at the judge sideways, guilty as a snitch.

"At the expense of this fine County and the poor taxpayer, Mr. Sweeney, you might just as well inflict that on this court too, while you're at it," and then the judge blustered loudly, "You keep talking like that, Mr. Sweeney, sir, you'll be a real politician in no time. Meantime, I don't see any soapbox under those feet of yours, so will you kindly get the hell on with what we're here for before I find you in contempt of this court? And while I'm at it, you just try me while everything is so *fine*, and I'll be real happy to *fine* you fifty bucks, now get to it, this is my first, last, and only warning!"

I knew right away that old Judge Bending was a hypocrite, just like Mrs. Mulligan said, because he said *hell* in his court and that's swearing too, just like Jack said *ass*, so he's not doing like he *says*. That's what a hypocrite is, that's what Floyd told me.

"Yes sir, your Honor," Mr. Sweeney answered meekly.

"Mr. Whittaker, upon what occasion did you last deal with Mr. Tupper?" Jack looked at Mr. Tupper and squirmed. His face got red. "Mr. Whittaker?" Mr. Sweeney asked.

"Answer the question, Mr. Whittaker!" the judge said while Jack fiddled with his hat.

"I... I... saw him at the hotel in Egansville, two weeks before the fire, yes, that's it. Two weeks before he lit the fire," he said nervously. His voice cracked.

"*Objection!*" Mr. Ditworth jumped up. "There has been no guilt established, the statement is inflammatory and worse yet, it is only an *opinion* of this witness!"

"Sustained!" the judge said, and "Very good, Ditworth, I see you're doing your job admirably, you might make a lawyer yet," he said to the lawyer. "The jury will disregard the portion of Mr. Whittaker's remark that says the *defendant lit the fire!*" I saw the jurors write things down on their paper pads.

"And may I now ask you, Mr. Whittaker, what you were doing in Egansville?"

"Sir?...oh, I had to...be away from home for a couple of nights, and I went to Egansville, closest hotel, only six bucks a night and the food's good, too!"

"I'm sure it is, but before you tell us what you had to eat," Mr. Sweeney said, looking at the judge nervously, "what were you *doing* there?"

"*I went to meet Mr. Tupper,*" Jack said, cautiously, looking down at his feet.

"And why was that?" Mr. Sweeney asked, strolling over to talk to the jury, and rubbed his hand slowly over the polished oak divider.

"*To ask him for money,*" Jack whispered.

"*Louder,* Mr. Whittaker, the court clerk cannot hear you. Worse yet, I cannot hear what you are saying, young man!" the judge ordered.

"Again, Mr. Whittaker, why would you want to meet with Mr. Tupper, why did you meet with Mr. Tupper at the hotel in Egansville?"

"*To ask him for money!*" Jack said loudly. Jack looked down at the floor.

"And *why* were you asking him for money?" Mr. Sweeney asked.

Mr. Tupper whispered at Mr. Ditworth. Mr. Ditworth jumped up quick as a flash.

"*Objection,* your Honor! Counsel is wasting the court's time with this line of questioning, *not relevant, none of it is relevant!*" Mr. Ditworth yelled.

"Get on with it, Soggie —I mean Mr. Sweeney, you're testing my patience again, but I'll *allow* this line of questioning, Mr. Ditworth. But you'd better show where you're going pretty quick, Mr. Sweeney!"

"Yes, your Honor!" Mr. Sweeney said.

Mr. Tupper was whispering to Mr. Ditworth as soon as he sat down again. "*Okay, okay!*" Mr. Ditworth said, almost out loud. The judge glared at Jack and swore under his breath. I heard.

236

"Answer the question, Mr. Whittaker! Why were you asking Mr. Tupper, the defendant, for money?"

"Like I told Mr. Ditworth, didn't I, I needed some money, and I figured Mr. Tupper there owed me, *he owed me big time* for what he did to me. He did things to me before, when I lived at the orphanage, and I told him I needed some money for some new duds and such. He got all red in the face when I reminded him about what he done to me in the middle of the night and all that, and I knew he didn't want me sayin' anything about what he done, not there!"

Jack continued, but he wouldn't look at Mr. Tupper.

"We was sitting in the bar and I kept talking, he didn't want me to say anything out loud, so he shushed me up and bought me a hamburger and a chocolate shake. He treated me nice and respectful and said we should go up to his room and talk about old times and hockey and ball games and said he wanted to know how Mrs. Tickner, that's his sister that's dead now, was doing at the orphanage without him, and how his boys was doing, and what I thought about the good old times and if T.T. Oinker and the hogs got put to market yet.

"After I finished eating he said I should try a refresher, so he got us a few drinks, rum, or whiskey, it was, the kind that is all mixed up with soda pop, and I thought he got kind of drunk, he did, but not me. I ate, and I didn't drink too fast. He slipped the barkeep a ten and got a bottle into his jacket, and we took it up to his room and first thing he took his pants off and pushed me over towards the bed. He tried to kiss me right on the mouth, too, that old queer, but I said *no, I ain't doing that no more, and how about some money*? So, we had another drink, and then he got me down real tricky, did it by breaking my arm up behind my back, twisted my arm, and tripping me up and pushing me down on the bed.

"He's bigger 'en me, ain't he? An' he *did it, he did it like before*, then when he was finished, the bastard tried to be nice, he gave me another drink and said that was for old times, and he hauled out fifty bucks and handed it to me, *that's* what it was for, it must have been for getting his jollies, because he said, *'you're an expensive slut, Jackie boy, but it's just like old times, ain't it?'* he said."

I saw the judge's face screw up like a pickle, but Jack talked before he could say anything.

"And to prove it, it's all true, it is, that fifty bucks, I put it in my shoe quick, right away so he couldn't get it back, that's the money I got off him and the next day I got this set of duds with it," Jack said, and thumbed his lapel and looked at his shoes again. Jack looked up at the judge. The judge scratched his head for a minute.

"He's lying, the little bastard!" Mr. Tupper yelled.

Jack stood up and yelled back at him. *"He's a goddam pervert, that old Tupper is, a goddam pervert snake!* I didn't want it shoved up my ass. I never did, not me!"

"You liar!" Mr. Tupper shouted at Jack. *"You liar! That's a lie!"* Mr. Tupper shouted to the judge. *"All's a bleedin' lie, it is!"*

The judge slammed his gavel loudly on the bench.

"Order! Order in the court! Control yourself! Control yourself! You be quiet!" the judge shouted at Mr. Tupper, "and *you,* Mr. Ditworth, kindly control your client! I'll have none of these outbursts in my court!" He looked sternly at Jack. "*You,* young man, must learn not to use foul language! There will be no swearing allowed in my court!"

"I didn't swear, not me, your Honor," Jack said proudly.

Maybe Jack is a liar. I think Jack lied that time because saying *ass* is swearing unless it's talking about some kind of a donkey or something like that, just like in the Bible.

"All I said was *he give me fifty bucks, then give it to me up the ass,* well, and he gimme fifty bucks, didn't he, that *proves it,* doesn't it?" Jack said, "And the next day I went and bought my suit—could of got brown, but I like this green better, myself, and Mrs. Finnegan adjusted it perfect for me herself. I only had to sit on my ass and wait an hour, down at Finnegan's Department Store. Oh, and I got the derby there, too!" He showed the judge his hat. "I got the derby there, too!"

The judge cleared his throat and shook his head.

"This testimony is not completely relevant to the case at hand, but it does infer *other charges* may be pending. The jury is hereby instructed to ignore these accusations for the purposes of *this* trial." He turned to Jack.

"And *you*, Mr. Whittaker, you will kindly refer to rear end as your *rear end* from now on, young man!" Judge Bending ordered. Jack laughed and got smug. Floyd told me one time that getting smug was being a *smart ass*. The court twittered, and the judge *harrumphed*.

"I got my rear end down to Finnegan's Department store and bought these duds, then, if that makes you happy, at Finnegan's Department Store —that's what I said, isn't it, that's what I said, isn't it, your Honor?" Jack said, smooth as silk, and he had a smugly serious look on his face.

"Mr. Sweeney, can you instruct *your* client, *please?*" The judge asked sternly.

Mr. Sweeney put his hand over his microphone and leaned over to Jack. "*Your ass is your rear end, Jack*, and you will use only that term to refer to your *ass*, and *only if necessary*, and while we're at it, never mind your hat!"

The courtroom burst out in laughter. Even the judge smiled that time. "No wonder they call lawyers *evil* sometimes," the judge said to himself.

Me and Floyd and everybody else heard what he said, even if he tried to cover up the microphone.

"Soggie, *fifty dollars for contempt!*" the judge shouted.

That made everybody bust out laughing, even Floyd, and the judge slammed his gavel on the bench so hard the papers flew around. Suddenly, it was so quiet you could have heard the pigs getting a sunburn after too much slops.

"This is the *last* time I will tolerate outbursts in my court," the judge scolded us right out loud. "*Any* further outbursts will result in the court being cleared of spectators, is that clear!" I think he was looking right at me when he said that. I thought he was going to say *boy!* again, or something.

239

"Will you *kindly* get on with it?" the judge asked Mr. Sweeney, and looked us over again, sternly, like a grumpy teacher that hates the sound of his own chalk screeching on the blackboard, but he's got to do it. He's got to write down all of the alphabet and arithmetic he can stand, to keep the little buggers busy so he can say 'have them all completed by three o'clock, now, and anyone that's not finished shall remain after school, and get the strap, you'll see!' and he can go into the teacher's room and have a little tipple of rum and a little sleep too. That reminds me of Mr. Dorchester that keeps his bottle of rum under his desk, but I'll have to tell you about *him* later.

"Mr. Whittaker, *we can, uh, understand now* where you got the money to buy your suit and all, but can you describe what happened after that uh, unfortunate incident, on that night you spent with Mr. Tupper?"

"Oh, yes, sir, I can get right to that if it pleases your Honor, sir, I can get right to it. The same time I seen him, the time at the hotel, like I said, your Honor, I asked Mr. Tupper if he wanted his silver tooth back as a matter of convenience because he still never had one since the time it got knocked out and lost in the fight at the home and now he looks damned silly without it. I told him he would look nifty if he'd just give me *another* fifty." Jack smirked at his own joke. The audience shifted, and I saw lots of people smiling.

"I showed him the tooth. It was all cleaned up and real shiny, that tooth, and I told him it would only cost him another fifty to have it back in his mouth where it belongs, ain't doing *me* no good, I said, and I said I'd wash it off with soap and water or even dip it in whiskey for him, too. He got all red in the face. He comes slappin' at me right away...

"He screamed like a madman at me, and shouted, *You, boy, you gimme that tooth, Jackie-boy, you blackmailing little bastard,* that's what you are, a bastard blackmailing orphan brat, gimme that tooth or I'll whip you silly. I owe you one anyways. I owe *all* of you little bastards one; you owe me for losing me position and wasting my life helping the poor and disenchanted and such, or some big word like that— *them's* not maybe *exactly* the right words he said, your Honor, but that's the meaning for sure. I'm telling the truth, your Honor, that's the gospel truth, so help me God!

"Then he punched me on the side of my face and made me see stars, right here, it was," Jack indicated his right cheek, "and said if I didn't give it back to him right now he'd *get even* and I'd be sorry, he said, he said he was going to make 'em *fry and die,* that's what he said, Mr. Sweeney, sir, and your Honor, sir, *that's what he said,* he said they would *fry and die!*

"Then he ran at me and twisted my arm behind my back again real tricky-quick and punched my face and shoved me against the wall. He must have got his hand into my pocket while I was looking at the stars, and that's how he swiped the tooth from me. Then, he kicked me in the balls and I fell onto the floor, and I was hurtin' real bad while he looked at the tooth.

"He stood there looking at the tooth in his hand and smiled ugly-like. He said *'Maybe I will burn the useless little bastards out anyway, maybe I will yet,'* and before I could say anything else, he picked me up by the neck and threw me out of the room, and shut the door on me; and it was the middle of the night and I had to go sleep in the bus station, and Mr. Mudwax, that's the station master, he's gettin' right after me right away.

"He don't want no bums sleepin' in the bus station, and he told me forget goin' down to the train station, the CN cop would nab me right away for gettin' on private property and such, but I explained to the old bugger that I couldn't get a room anyplace and pretty soon he gimme a blanket and let me stay, that nice man; he even gimme a sandwich, fish with onions, *whitefish,* it was, weren't no bones in it either, and a nice cup of tea to wash it down with too. He's a nice man, old Mudwax, *nobody* was ever nice to me like *that* before."

There wasn't a peep in the court. The judge cleared his throat. "Perhaps you'd better get back to the subject of the tooth, young man, and if you'd kindly refer to your elders as *Mr.* or *Mrs.,* you would make a better impression on this court!" the judge said sternly.

"Oh, yes, *Mr. or Mrs. Judge*, sir, that's what I'll call 'em from now on, sir," Jack said quickly and then he got all red, and the crowd twittered. The judge looked at him over his spectacles.

"Mr. Sweeney!" the judge warned.

"Yes, your Honor, I can see that this witness has been a test of your patience, no doubt, so we'll progress right along, your Honor, to the most important fact you'll see in this proceeding!"

"See that it is, Sir. We don't have all day, Mr. Sweeney!"

Mr. Sweeney walked over to the jury and turned around and pointed at Mr. Tupper. He reached into his pocket and pulled out a plastic bag. It held a silver-colored object. He held it up for the jury to see.

"He, *Mr. Tupper—abused this young man and took this silver tooth from him by force. The silver tooth that was found at the scene of the fire!*" he shouted dramatically.

"*Let this be exhibit A!*" he yelled at Mr. Tupper. The courtroom got noisy all at once and everybody was gabbling like Archie McKinley's chickens when we threw them corn.

"*Murderer! You murdering pervert!*" a lady screamed at Mr. Tupper and threw her umbrella across three rows of people, and it hit him, too.

The judge's face got red. He shouted "*Order!*" but that didn't help, not one bit.

"*Hang him!*" another lady screamed.

"*Son of a bitch pervert!*" a man yelled and before you know it, the whole court was standing up, yelling at Mr. Tupper and throwing sandwiches, tomatoes, all sorts of lunch and paper junk and other things too. Mr. Ditworth and Mr. Tupper dived under the table.

"*Murderer!*" The collection of old ladies sitting beside us, and some of them were just like Mrs. Mulligan, raised a ruckus by jumping up and down like scrabbling chickens, screaming their tonsils out right beside me and Floyd.

Floyd said, "Oh boy, there's going to be hell to pay, and right now!" He yelled that right out loud, too, because the noise level was getting worse. The judge stood up, hammering the desk with his gavel so hard that the handle broke.

"Court is adjourned, clear the court!" I think old Judge Bending finally snapped good, because Jack said *ass* and then Mr. Sweeney said *ass* two times, and nobody is supposed to say *ass* or anything like that, or throw food and umbrellas at Mr. Tupper even if he is guilty, but they did. The judge got right to it and barked his orders like a mad dog eating the tires off of a doughnut truck. He screamed right at the bailiff. I heard him swear, too. He said *"Get 'em all the hell out of here!"*

"All stand!" the bailiff shouted, but it didn't make any difference, because everybody except me and Floyd were on their feet hopping up and down, so I stood up quick as a wink. Nobody minds if Floyd doesn't stand up. I saw the judge grab his papers that were left on the bench. He glared at everybody and stormed out the back door and slammed it, too.

"Clear the court!" the bailiff ordered. *"All rise!"* He added, after the fact. Nobody heard him anyway. The bailiff pointed at the door.

We cleared the court like the man yelled, and I got standing beside Floyd in his chair to watch the little old ladies gabble like feeding chickens out on the sidewalk while we waited for Mrs. McAllister. Livvy and her Aunt Barbara-Lynne pushed their way through the crowd with Mrs. McAllister and started talking to Floyd. Mrs. McAllister gave Barbara-Lynne a hug and a kiss then they started examining me like a whitefish sandwich or maybe just bait but I got distracted.

"Hello, Fletcher" Livvy said quietly to me, and examined me with her blue eyes like she was looking at a bug on a green-bean tree. "I've missed you, Fletcher; I haven't seen you for a long time!"

"Hello, Livvy..." I said, and I got nervous because I didn't know what to say. She was wearing a yellow dress that I never saw before, and it had a wide white belt on it that matched her hat. She looked nice, but somehow *different*. I know what it was. I was looking at her breasts. They were a little bigger. I tried not to look at them, but I did. My face got red, and I think she got a pink face and giggled just a little bit because she knew what I was looking at. I didn't notice Floyd wheeling back over to us.

"Why don't you take this beautiful young lady here, to Camson's Drugstore, there, and buy her some ice cream, Fetch?" Floyd said, giving Livvy a big hug. I don't mind if Floyd hugs Livvy because he lets her go right away and doesn't yank her off to Egansville. He let her go, puffing on his pipe, and then he winked at me. He pointed at the soda shop across the street. He pulled out a two dollar bill and handed it to me. "Take your time, son, none of these people are in a hurry, believe me!"

"Go ahead Livvy — and Fletcher, *you* take good care of her, will you, now?" her Aunt Barbara-Lynne said right away. "Don't hurry! We have to wait for your Uncle Soggie anyway!"

"Come on, Fletcher!" Livvy said, and grabbed my hand. I never had my hand held before but I noticed I didn't mind it. You don't mind somebody holding your hand if you love them. We started to walk across the street.

"You dropped some *cash*, there, boy!" a man said. I turned around just in time to see the man pointing at a two-dollar bill blowing around on the ground. I ran and picked it up with one smooth motion and didn't look at back at Floyd either. He always said that if you pay attention and take care of your money it helps take care of you. I know it gets ice cream at Camson's Drugstore and dark green suits with a derby hat at Finnegan's, so it must buy other things, too, things that I don't want to talk about now.

Thirty

"It's okay living with Aunt Barbara-Lynne," Livvy explained. "She treats me fine and makes me nice clothes," she indicated the yellow dress. "She made this dress for me!" She kept her hands neatly folded on her lap.

"How about your uncle?" I asked.

Her face got red, but that must have been because of the wind outside. "He..." she started to say, but we got interrupted before she said anything.

The waitress brought the ice cream sundaes to the table, chocolate with whipping cream and bananas for me and strawberry ice cream, the pink kind, with real strawberries around it in the whipping cream and a cherry on top for Livvy. I ordered that especially for her. I gave the waitress ten cents for a tip; that's what Floyd said to do. She came back and gave me a dollar-fifty in change. We tasted the ice cream right away before she got back. It was good. I ate a big spoonful right away to freeze my nose because my face was still red from dropping the money.

Camson's Drugstore doesn't sell toothpaste and drugs and stuff like that, because that's only a name it has on the front. Inside, it has a little window where the cook jabs his head out and flops the hamburger plates under a set of hot red lights and yells, '*Table six!*' It has green leather on the seats to match the green plastic on the tables in the booths, but there are apple-red plastic tablecloths on the other tables to match the red chairs. Shiny chrome jukebox record selectors are mounted on the wall in each booth, but not at the tables; that's why Livvy and I sat in a booth.

"Let's play a song, Fletcher, a *nice* one" she said, and handed me a nickel out of her purse.

It costs five cents to play a record, any kind of music you like, so I flipped through the selectors and picked a nice song. I think it was a cowboy song, maybe Roy Rogers, but I forgot if that's right because the songs got out of order with everybody crowding in from clearing the court and selecting B-14 or A-22 from another booth before you get a chance, and C-34 from a different booth when it's supposed to be *your* turn, and you don't know if your record ever gets played next or not. Sometimes, the same song squawks out quite a few times in a row like it's stuck. I noticed that right away and told Livvy, but she said I can't help that, so don't worry about it.

"It doesn't matter, Fletcher," she said, touching my hand. I looked to see if anybody saw that.

It was only the second time I was there, I mean at Camson's Drugstore, because the first time I came with Mrs. McAllister and Floyd. That time we had milkshakes and sat at a table so that Floyd could wheel right up close to the table and feel comfortable with us.

"Oh, Floyd, is this your new boy?" the waitress asked Floyd that time. She looked me over like she was going to buy me right there. "What a handsome young man — isn't he, Mrs. McAllister?"

"You may call me *Elizabeth*," Mrs. McAllister said.

The waitress looked at me like she wanted to kiss me and flap my hair all over the place, and my face got red. "Yes, he is a good looking boy," Mrs. McAllister said. Floyd lifted up his eyebrows and winked man-to-man at me.

"Mister, I have a special treat for *you*," she smiled at me and wiped the table off with a damp cloth that smelled like pine trees. "I'll be back in a flash!" She went behind the counter, and I couldn't tell what she was up to, but she brought me a vanilla sundae with coconut and a cherry on top with chocolate sauce poured all around it and the first thing I noticed was that there was frost on the outside of the tin dish. I touched it, and it melted away. I looked at the waitress.

If she was sixteen, I would have been surprised because she was small, not much taller than I am, maybe a couple of years older than me, and she was pretty. She had dark, tightly curled hair with a white leather thing with flowers painted on it and a wooden stick like a pencil jammed in the back. That's where she hid her real yellow pencil, too, in her curly hair at the back. I thought about the cherry. It was the same color as her red lipstick. Her teeth were as white as the ice cream, and the cherry was the same color as her lipstick and it tasted good. I liked Sharon Smithson right away.

The coconut on the ice cream was curly like her hair, but white instead of black. I shouldn't have liked her right away, but I did. I didn't understand why.

"Say *thank you,* Fletcher," Mrs. McAllister said. "Isn't that lovely?" I mumbled thank you and tasted the ice cream again to see if it was old stock or left over or tricky or what. Floyd says that when you get something free you'd better check to see what's wrong with it because you never get something free unless it has got a defect of some kind or has a lot of strings attached. I checked it over and it tasted good, and there were no strings tied on the bowl either.

Mrs. McAllister and the waitress talked about the Waterland Church tea social and bake sale coming up and *la-dee-dah, oh, goodie,* the lady's quilting club was accepting new members and why didn't she come and join, *there's always room for young people.* Her name was Sharon Smithson. It was right there on her name tag, *isn't that convenient, Floyd,* and *why, it would be so nice if she would come and join up, too, next Saturday, for sure,* and all kinds of other things while Floyd drank coffee with a lot of extra cream and winked at me a lot and puffed on his pipe and kept clammed up, while the ladies talked up a storm.

I didn't think so when I started tasting it, but I know now that I ate my free ice cream way too fast. I told Sharon that it was good, and I said, "Thank you, Ma'am," again, too. She gushed at me a bit more but I got used to it, and now I think I even like it a bit, too.

"Don't ever call me *'Ma'am'*, Fletcher," she said, gazing directly at me, "I'm not old enough for that, I'm only a little older than you are, not even a year!"

"Okay," I said, and looked at Floyd. He smiled at me again.

"You *should* bring him here more often, Floyd!" she said to Floyd, and "You're going to be a handsome old man, Fletcher Williams, *just the kind I'm looking for!*" to me. Floyd and Mrs. McAllister laughed, but I noticed that Mrs. McAllister gave Floyd a secret look.

I couldn't wait to get out of there, but then we had to have more coffee, and then lunch. And Floyd had to talk to Mr. Walkerby that just had a new baby girl. She was seven pounds seven ounces, and the wife was still in the hospital and *they were both doing well, thank you.* And then it was *school's starting soon, young man,* that was Mr. Dorchester chewing on a hamburger while he talked to us. He's the teacher I said I would tell you about, and he said today his car motor made a funny noise like *'Pfooof!'* and seized up tight as a bung on a rusty barrel on the way to the courthouse, because of the heat, it *must have been.*

I said, "Maybe the manifold pipe just got plugged up with a mouse nest," and Floyd laughed, and Mr. Dorchester winked at me. Floyd puffed and said, "I'd check that, too, if I was you!"

Floyd said that again, too when Mr. Dorchester was leaving, to remind him about the mouse nest. Then, he shook hands with Mr. McDaltie and Mrs. McDaltie, who blessed our table with the information that she makes wedding cakes, and they just moved into a house just down the street from Floyd's. He said the water wasn't turned on yet, and they couldn't have a bath, not until Tuesday, I think. So, he was borrowing water in tin pails from the Bibbs next door, and it cost sixty-two dollars to pay the moving-truck to haul his grandmother's rosewood player-piano with a split soundboard, her Chesterfield, and a grandfather clock that couldn't tell time since 1888.

They gabbled about eight hundred and eighty-eight more hours about each of their trips to Waterland too, where to stop for lunch and change all the flat tires he got on his '46 Hudson. *New tires too, those tires can't be any good at all.* He couldn't leave the furniture, the piano and the collection out behind the junk shed because the old lady set up such a fuss. He told her he could get seventy-five bucks and a broken lawnmower for the whole works from his neighbor Atlanta Jones, that's really just an antique dealer but says he isn't.

No matter how much Atlanta Jones wanted to give them for the junk, he said they better to move it quick, *no matter what she said*, and he would be free to get her into the *old folk's hotel on the fifth floor*, and he could bugger off and get a job at the new Waterland broomstick factory for three bucks an hour, and no wonder we didn't get out of Camson's Drugstore for a couple of hours.

I watched Sharon serving the customers; and ten or eleven different folks had coffee and French fries and extra coffee, and even after quite a few more customers after that, we were *still* there. Mrs. McAllister finally got tired and said, "We must go now, Floyd!"

Floyd got some extra scolding from Mrs. McAllister, and I heard *"More coffee, folks?"* at least ten times from Sharon who was watching me when she brought the double creams to go along with all that extra coffee and information gabble. I watched her back, too. I like Sharon Smithson a lot, I'd bet. I even smiled at her, and she winked at me.

Finally, Sharon came along again and said, "Will that be all?" and Floyd smiled nice at her and gave her a dollar for a tip.

"Don't forget about our quilting circle, now, will you?" Mrs. McAllister said, and Sharon looked like she was going to pat me on the head, but then leaned down and put her hand on my shoulder instead and squeezed it a bit. I don't know why, maybe I'm getting too big to pat on the head, *doesn't anybody know that yet*, and she looked at Mrs. McAllister and said, "If you ever want to get rid of this one, *I'll have him*," her voice dropping down too low, and I noticed that she smiled sweetly, and she looked right in my eyes, and it made me feel funny. *Kind of like bait.*

Then, she giggled at Floyd and Mrs. McAllister, and Mrs. McAllister made a face at her like she just swallowed a hot onion.

"No, thank you, we'll keep him," she said after an embarrassing moment. "We like him just fine!" and she grabbed me and pushed me toward the door without really pushing hard, just enough so that I would know where I was headed, no doubt about it. I looked back to see if they were following and waited for them at the door while Mrs. McAllister got her purse snapped shut up tight like her lips were.

"The offer's still good anyway!" Sharon teased, whispering that out loud at me when she walked behind the counter and glanced back at Mrs. McAllister.

I started to think that Sharon Smithson's voice sounds a bit like Tina McQueeny and she's short, not any taller than me. I liked Sharon, no doubt about it, and good thing Livvy Manlin wasn't there to hit me on the head. I wonder if she shows her tits around to everyone too, and I bet anything maybe she's going to babysit Mr. Walkerby's baby. No, she can't do that because she gave me ice cream and got a nice easy job already, and you can't see anything, no tits at all, when she leans over to wipe the table. That's good, so maybe she's not a slut like Tina, and I don't know it yet, and Mrs. McAllister just doesn't like her.

That's it, son, my Mother whispered to me, I know she's all right. She's a fine girl, but your Mom doesn't like that girl, not one bit, she's not like Livvy, not like Livvy, not like Livvy,

"...*not like Livvy.*" It was Mrs. McAllister talking. "*She's not like Livvy,* dear." I looked back. Mrs. McAllister smiled grimly like a secret just popped up. I saw Sharon coming back to the table. Floyd stretched his arms up.

Floyd chuckled and cleared his throat. "Thank you, Miss," he said, handing her four shiny quarters one at a time into her hand. Floyd always counts money carefully.

"Thank you, Mr. McAllister," Sharon said, blushing. "It's too much!" Floyd shook his head.

"We'll be getting along now, Elizabeth," he said, and smiled nicely at Sharon. She watched me and waved as I opened the door, but I pretended I didn't see her because Mrs. McAllister was watching, so I cleared out of there fast and waited at the truck that time.

The Fires of Waterland

"You gave her a *whole dollar* for a tip, Floyd; That's far too extravagant!" Mrs. McAllister scolded Floyd in the truck on the way home.

"She's a good girl, she gave us *extra-good* service, and extra coffee, now didn't she?" Floyd puffed, as Mrs. McAllister ground the truck into second gear. "No doubt about it," he said, "anybody that will put up with us for that long *deserves* a dollar tip, that right, Fletch?" He looked at me and winked.

"And she didn't complain about us sitting there for over two hours gabbing with everyone in sight," Floyd said, and nodded firmly to me. "She's taken a liking to Fletcher too, and she's a beautiful, charming girl, a *decent* girl," Floyd said after a minute.

"*She's not like Livvy, Floyd!*" Mrs. McAllister said firmly, and ground the truck into third gear. I clammed up and didn't say a word because Mrs. McAllister's face was getting red.

"Look at those cows, Fletcher" Floyd pointed right at some Black Angus cows. "*Good* stock, Mr. McKinley's, not like *some*," he said.

We were waiting at Camson's after school as usual, and I was daydreaming, then I had to pay attention again because Livvy was smack right in front of me.

"Fletcher? *Did you miss me?*" Livvy asked, plopping her books on the table to get my attention. I was watching cars go by, making dust go west, and the waitress — it wasn't Sharon Smithson this time, it was a big fat grade twelve girl; I think her name is Beatrice Mystern, but nobody wants to know it, and she has thick glasses and bad teeth and she was mopping up the counter with a green cloth. *Spilled milk.* Then I was not really paying attention to her either because I was thinking about just barely escaping from Sharon and listening to the people in the booths around us jabbering about the trial.

"*That old pervert!*" I heard one lady say, and she looked around and said it again right out loud and she looked around. Some people looked at her and gabbled back and forth in whispers.

"Well he is; he's an old *pervert!*" She wasn't looking at me when she said that and that suited me just fine.

"I wish you were still living at Floyd's, where I am," I said, and ate another slice of banana. I always save the bananas for last, except for the cherry. I save the cherry for the very last because it's the best. Even Livvy knows I save it for the last.

"Floyd's keeping me there now, for good," I said, "I heard him tell Wiltie — that's Mr. Fester at the home, the temporary home," and I thought it was important to tell her that I was in the same room. "I still live in the same room, too."

I never thought that could happen, but she reached across the table and touched my hand.

"How *wonderful!*" she said. I didn't understand what was *wonderful*. The room was the same as it was before.

"Never mind!" she said, smiling. She squeezed my hand. I liked it.

"Here!" and she fed me a strawberry, a big, sweet one. I don't think it's polite to feed somebody in a restaurant like a baby. I looked around but nobody was paying attention at all, so I gave her my cherry for a trade.

"Thank you." Her blue eyes flashed.

"Aunt Barbara says I can come and stay weekends. I can come back on the school bus with you on Friday night and get back to school Monday mornings, and all we have to do is get Mom to agree!"

"And Floyd," I said, and I don't know why. I knew that Floyd would be delighted to have Livvy around to keep Mrs. McAllister busy and out of his hair, and she would be good company to her, too. And they could sew and bake and discuss woman stuff and plan fancy cookies and rhubarb pie with sugar on it for the church bake sale.

"Of course Floyd, too, silly, he'd have to agree too," she said, and squeezed my hand. "I can talk Floyd into *anything*." I looked across the street and I could see Floyd talking to some men, but Barbara-

Lynne was walking toward us, and just like the time in the garden, I knew she was going to drag Livvy away from me again.

"Your aunt is coming to get you already!" I said. She looked across the street and touched my hand softly. "It was nice to see you, Fletcher!" she whispered. The big glass door opened and in flounced Barbara-Lynne Sweeney and ruined my day for sure; It always ruins my day, her taking Livvy away. I got a big surprise, and so did Livvy.

"I talked Mr. and Mrs. McAllister into keeping Livvy for a few days, maybe a week-end and maybe a weekend or two, Fletcher!" Barbara-Lynne said happily as she flopped down onto the plastic seat beside Livvy and ordered all of us an orange pop with ice from the machine that bubbles the pop around in circles.

"Your Uncle Soggie and I haven't had much time together since he got *this* job," she said, and the smile disappeared off of her face like a skipping stone dropping into the water. She looked into her purse and scuffled around and paid the waitress thirty cents and a nickel for a tip. Her smile came back.

"And Livvy's told you about our plan for her visits to McAllister's, once school starts?"

"I told him, Aunt Barbara!" Livvy scolded her, "Of course I told him, silly!"

"It's all settled then!" Barbara smiled, and I watched the pop go down in the glass and up into the straw as she sucked up about half of it.

"I already arranged it with your dad," and she stopped suddenly, a little flushed, " —I meant *Floyd*, Mr. McAllister, of course. How silly of me!"

"It's fine, Auntie. Fletcher knows what you mean, don't you, Fletcher!" Livvy said, and pushed her foot against my knee under the table. I know that she means Floyd, so I stayed cool and smiled nice like a man of the world with a yellow convertible car would and sucked up some orange pop without making any slurping sounds instead. Floyd always said to be sure to notice the difference between people that make mistakes on purpose and people that make mistakes

253

by accident because people that make mistakes by accident aren't the same as people that make mistakes on purpose.

"You'll see, sometime, what I mean," Floyd said. *"You'll be finding that out for yourself, sooner or later, Fletch, it's nowhere near the same thing, it ain't the same thing at all, different intent, different purpose, sometimes purposeful accidents hurt people,"* Floyd explained.

So I remembered that, it's not the same thing at all. Barbara-Lynne made that mistake by accident and it is okay and it wasn't even silly even though she said it was, but I didn't say that out loud.

"Oh, there's your Uncle Soggie, I have to run!" she said, not smiling again, and sucked up the rest of the soda pop in a flash, got up and kissed Livvy on the cheek.

"I love you both. We'll pick you up, Livvy—in a couple of days, probably Wednesday!" She grabbed her purse and ran to the door. She stopped suddenly at the heavy glass door and turned back to us.

"Oh, *maybe Thursday*? —See you, Fletcher, *you take good care of her, you hear?"* She waved and we watched her run across the street, her white skirt flying in the wind like my two-dollar bill. She got into the black Ford with Mr. Sweeney and waved at us again. Livvy waved frantically out the window at them.

"I'll take good care of you, Livvy", I said, and watched as Floyd and Mrs. McAllister got his chair into the truck and pulled a U-turn to pick us up.

"I know you will, Fletcher, I love you!" Livvy whispered out loud, and the people behind us giggled and looked at us funny. We clammed up right away, and I felt my ears get red.

"Kids! Isn't that cute, Jonathan? Aren't they darlings, but they're just *babies*, —How old are they, anyway?" the woman, giggling, asked the man, pouring ketchup on his hamburger. He laughed.

"Twelve, thirteen, maybe, see, *hardly* old enough for lovin'. She ain't even got real titties yet, but my, my! Ain't she a *beauty?"* he said.

"Oh, a little heartbreaker—and look at *him*, too!" she said, smiling at me and winking. The woman straightened up her pillbox hat, and put on some more lipstick, bright cherry red, by looking at her reflection in the shiny chrome jukebox selector. I noticed that she was really looking sideways and watching to see if I was looking at her. She put her white-gloved hand up to her lips and blew me a kiss, but I didn't want to catch it. She pouted out her lips at me and giggled. The man took a big bite out of his hamburger, then reached across and swiped the cherry from the top of the women's ice cream, as quick as Jack winks.

"Jonathon, *you naughty* boy!" she scolded at him loudly and giggled. She pretended she was pouting, but she was looking at me. The man held the red cherry up to his mouth and stuck out his tongue to lick the cream off of it, staring at Livvy, and laughing. He popped it into his mouth and chewed it, smiling and gawking his bulgy black eyes right at Livvy some more. Livvy didn't like that one bit. Her face turned pink, then red.

I remembered all at once that I promised Livvy I would take good care of her, and I don't like those people getting cherry-chewing, kissy smart-ass and talking about her like that. I don't like cherries and hamburger mixed together at all, so I stood up right away.

"Floyd's waiting for us," I said out loud, and I know it was lying, too because I could see Floyd jabbering to another man across the street. Mrs. McAllister was still gabbling with some other ladies, and I know you're not supposed to tell lies.

I knew my ears were getting hot and I was uncomfortable, maybe that's what you get for telling lies, and I didn't want to look at anybody except Livvy. I noticed that she neatly kept her head up high like a fashionable magazine lady and ignored the kissy couple like they were a pair of moldy, week-old blue cheese sandwiches that the cat licked or sat on or something.

I looked back at the man as I held the heavy glass door open for her. Livvy put her hand on my shoulder, smiling sweetly at me as though nothing had happened, as she passed through the door. The man back at the table leaned over and said something to the woman, I don't know *what,* and maybe they noticed how red my ears got. She giggled and blew me another kiss that missed, and the man laughed and winked. That one was a different kind of wink than Floyd usually

255

gives. I felt different, maybe like important or grownup or something. Maybe, even like I was doing something important, protecting Livvy Manlin.

Before I had a chance to think hard about it, that idea got bumped out of me. I turned from the glass door and Jack was standing right in my way. "Excuse me!" I said, and I looked up at him, finally realizing who it was.

"*Fletcher, boy, how ya doin'?*" he asked, smiling at me and touching his derby hat and looking cool as a cucumber.

"Hello, Jack," I said to him.

"Been having ice cream with this pretty little lady, have you?" he asked, rubbing his fingernails on his green lapel, and shaking them like they were hot. "*Hot stuff there, Fetchie, hot stuff!*" he teased. "*Catch fire yet?*"

Livvy studied Jack, and her eyes were indifferent, cold, and she kept her head held high.

"You two must have *something* to talk about, I'm sure," she said, "I'll go across and talk to Mom for a minute," she added, smiling to me, and squeezing, then letting go of my hand. "I'll see you in a few minutes, Fletcher."

"Mr. Whittaker," she said politely, "*if you will excuse me,*" she said, smiling, but I think it sounded like ice rattling in a tin bucket.

"That girl just doesn't like me, *she doesn't like me,* Fetchie, me boy, she don't like me at all. I don't know why. I ain't never done nothing to make her like *that,* have I—but look at her, will you?" We watched Livvy cross the street. I noticed that she looked both ways, too.

"Maybe she got some of them dislikes from Mrs. McAllister, there, or maybe she doesn't like *my woman that* might be it, maybe she doesn't like Tina; I don't understand why not, do you?" Jack asked. I didn't say anything, not a word. Not about seeing Tina in bed with my father, and not about why Mrs. McAllister doesn't like Jack Whittaker, either.

I watched Livvy shaking hands with the ladies that were talking to Mrs. McAllister and I paid attention to that until Jack flapped my hair all the way to Mexico. I backed up fast and smoothed out my hair. I hate it when people flap your hair, especially when you're grown up.

Jack stood back and looked at me with a surprised look on his face.

"Well, never mind, Fetchie-boy, you been to Texas yet?" Jack asked me. He took off his derby hat and showed it to me.

"Not *exactly* a cowboy hat, is it?" he said.

"*It's not a cowboy hat, Jack,*" I said.

"You seen me in court, boy?" he asked. "Hell, I done *good* in court, didn't I, I done *real good, I fixed that son of a bitch good, didn't I?*"

I held my breath for a long time just then, and I might have turned black or purple.

"What do you mean, Jack?" I asked. "I saw you. I heard what you said, and you said Mr. Tupper must have lit the fire, he gave you money and whiskey, and it was like old times."

"You missed the *best* part, Fetchie, you missed the best part!" I tried not to look at Jack. He had a funny look on his face.

"I didn't miss anything, Jack. Floyd and I were right there; We were there all day!" I said. I didn't know what Jack was talking about.

"I can't believe you missed that," Jack said, teasing and pushing me backwards like in our old wrestling matches, "Fletcher, *it was a story. I got the son of a bitch,* that old snake, *I got the bastard now. I got him good, too.* He's going to pay for what he done, what he done to you and me, what he done to the others, *he's going to pay!*" He laughed and swung around a steel street light pole like a kid.

"A *story?*" I asked Jack, with my mouth open, like I was trying to catch flies. "*A story?*" I asked again. "What do you mean, *a story,* Jack?"

"*A story, that's all it was,* my boy, Fletchie. We got 'im by the balls, we got 'im, and he's gonna pay, he's gonna pay hard time in jail. It'll be off to jail for that old bastard Tupper, *ha ha!*" He laughed hard and poked at me again. "They don't like *perverts* in jail, Fetchie! *I took the tooth, Fetch. I took the tooth out of your shoe, you were gonna give it to me anyways, remember*, a few nights before I left? The night I left, Fetchie!" he laughed and patted his hat on his head. "The night I left, I took the tooth, *remember that?"* Jack asked, suddenly serious, and then he broke into laughter again. *"I took it* —and with all the excitement there, who *knows*, boy? I might have even—*planted it at the fire by accident, maybe I did*, who the hell knows, who *knows? They gotta prove it, maybe I didn't, but they'll never find out, now will they?"*

"But you said—" I said, and my mouth must have been wide open. I felt dizzy, just like picking yellow beans in the sun.

"Never mind what I *said*," Jack whispered fiercely at me, and leaned closer to me, "The old bastard wouldn't gimme fifty bucks for the tooth *so I kept it*, didn't I? *I kept it, I made up the story. It was all a story—about him belting me and taking it back, 'cause I never even had it with me that time.* I never gave it back to that slimy old snake pervert; I never *intended* to give it back to the old snake. I didn't have it 'cause I said to myself, I can get ten bucks from the jeweler for it, *and I did, too. I need it worse than he does*, the old bastard,—and now look who's gettin' it up the ass! Doesn't that just do your heart good, Fetchie? Doesn't it just do your heart *proud?"*

I saw Floyd waving at me from across the street. I held up my hand like a traffic cop to Jack.

Stop. I don't want to know this, you're a liar, you killed Mrs. Tickner and the boys, you burned the boys and the silver tooth was at the fire and I know you had the silver tooth and you're a goddamned liar. Jack, I know you had the silver tooth.

Jack saw Floyd waving at me and turned back to me. Jack burst out laughing.

"That's not even the *best* part, Fetchie-boy, that's not the *best* part," he said, suddenly giggling, "He never even done me up the ass that time, either, like I *said* he did, Fetchie, boy, *we got him good, I made that up, too. I swear it.* I found the fifty on the sidewalk outside the hotel and went in for a drink by myself, and I seen Tupper in there, and the whiskey-drinking he was doing gimme an idea to talk to him and get him drinking hard, until he's stupid drunk, then wait 'til dark. And I'll take the old bastard out back into the back alley, I says to myself, and after I gets him drunk, I'll pound the living misery out of him, maybe stick a crowbar or a stick of wood up his ass too. *And I'll even kill the old bastard if I want to.*

"I'm sayin' to myself, I'll get the old bastard for all them times at the home, *I told you,* and I done it, *I will yet, see if I don't;* I says to myself, when I see the old bastard was happy drinking whiskey at the bar, the old bastard, I never talked to him that time for more than it took to choke down the rot-gut whiskey he bought me for old times, he *wanted me to go with him,* but it was all a story.

"I told the goddamned judge a *story,* except for the part where Tupper wanted to know his sister was doing' all right, *it was all a story,* ain't that a split? Made me laugh like hell when I first thought it up, Fetchie, I laughed like hell, to myself, *I did,* but when I saw him smiling at me and then him grabbin' my leg under the table again and again, cheap-like for the price of a drink of his rotgut whiskey.

"Smilin' and grinnin' like he was getting his jollies off under the table, too, right there I knew for sure I'm going to nail the bastard to the cross for whipping me, too—somehow if it takes the rest of his miserable life, and I swore to myself I'll fry his balls in hell itself, in real hell itself, and make him know it's *payback,* for all them times he shoved it into me like a dirty priest and *whipped me,* the old bastard pervert!"

Jack grinned, a vicious grin at me and *whooped.* I didn't *whoop.* I didn't say anything. Not a word.

"Well, *whaddya think? I got 'im good, didn't I, Fetchie? I got 'im good!"*

I couldn't believe my ears. Jack was a liar. *He was there at the home. He started the fire. He killed everyone. Jack was a liar and a murderer.*

I turned to run across the street, and I didn't look both ways. I think a car just about hit me because the wheels screeched, and the driver honked his horn right in my face. I saw smoke coming from the tires.

"Watch where you're going, boy!" the driver shouted at me out the window. Some extra car horns honked behind him. I started to run

259

again. Jack grabbed my jacket from behind and got me to a halt and pulled me to the sidewalk, right beside him. I tried to push him away.

"What we done, it's for you too, boy, it's for you too!" Jack shouted at me over the blaring car horns. Jack pulled me close to his face. *"It's for you, too,* boy!" He smiled strangely.

"You better watch what you're running into, what you do, Fetch, boy. *You'll be gettin' yourself killed,* you do the *wrong* thing, see, — Don't go gettin' yourself run over and *killed,* now, will you, Fletcher?" he said menacingly. I turned around and tried not to look at Jack, but he made me look at him. I tried not to look at him but I had to.

"You won't be a-tellin' our stories to anyone, now will you!" His eyes were closed to slits, and his face was smiling, but all white. Just for that minute, I don't think I liked Jack Whittaker any more.

Thirty-One

"I'd say you didn't understand Jack right, that time in front of Camson's!" Floyd said, puffing on his pipe, making it glow in the dark. "I seen what happened, but it's easy for a man to jump to conclusions, the *wrong* conclusions; a man shouldn't jump to conclusions, but you did. *The damage is done. — So now what are you going to do about it?*" Floyd was right, and he lifted up his eyebrows when he looked at me too. I was ashamed of myself and I'm mixed up now and I don't know what to tell Jack to be sorry for thinking he was a murderer and a liar.

"But he *said* he might have left the tooth at the fire, didn't he, Floyd? *He said he might have left it at the fire to get even with Mr. Tupper!*" I tried to explain it to Floyd. This time Floyd will understand, I know he will.

"But he *didn't* — he didn't leave *that* tooth, the one from Mr. Tupper, *the real tooth that was found in the fire,*" Floyd said, "*the one that was found on the scene,* boy, that's a *different* one — *you thought he threw the old one into the fire,* the one you told the judge you had back at the home then, but he didn't!" He scratched his nose.

"When he got picked up drunk and taken into the cop shop that night, he saw the tooth in a bag on the evidence desk, but it was the tooth that was found there under the body, and it give him the idea to get even with Mr. Tupper, so he *told you he threw it in there, but he didn't, get it? He didn't leave it at the fire, boy, he didn't have it. He sold it!*" Floyd explained it some more to me. I got mixed up.

261

"The tooth, the one that was found at the fire, was found under Richard Bordon. I mean it was found with blood on it, and it was in good condition because it didn't melt in the fire, it was under his body. Mr. Tupper, even if he won't admit it, the probability is good that he and Richard Bordon had a fight. Richard had a fight with him, and maybe he got that tooth knocked out in that fight, and that's *why* it was there!" Floyd puffed his pipe thoughtfully.

Floyd knows how to explain stuff.

"Mr. Sweeney hypothesizes that Richard discovered Tupper doing something, maybe stealing the place blind, or maybe even pouring the gasoline on the floor in the hallway, and challenged him, and tried to stop him, but in the scuffle, Tupper popped him over the head with a crowbar or something. The coroner said Richard's skull had a fracture in it, they found a crow-bar close by; and by that time with the fight and ruckus they raised and all, he didn't want to be found there by anyone else — maybe with Richard laying on the floor, maybe dead already, so he had to get rid of the evidence quick. He had to light the fire and get out of there, and they think that's what he did."

"So Mr. Tupper killed Richard first, then lit the fire to burn up everybody." I felt my face getting hot in the dark again. "And Jack just lied about the tooth?"

"No, Mr. Sweeney *supposes* that Mr. Tupper attacked Richard," Floyd said. "We don't know if he killed him first or even if that's what killed Richard or not." Floyd puffed hard on his pipe. "No matter what Tupper said to the court, only heaven knows if he's lying or not, and only God knows what the *real* truth is. Coroner couldn't tell anything definitively about the timing, or what happened *exactly*, the bodies were burned up so badly. The only reason Mr. Tupper was arrested was because that tooth was found and identified by Dr. Yin Mo, the dentist that fitted it. Tupper would have got away with it without that tooth being found when it was."

It was at least the twenty-fifth time that Floyd explained it to me. I can't tell you about what happened in the court after the big ruckus because crabby old Judge Bending wouldn't let spectators back in for the rest of the day to see the trial, even if they brought their own lunch, but everybody got back in the next morning.

"We will not tolerate spectators behaving like common rabble. Spectators in the court disturbing the importance of this official proceeding!" is what the judge said, at least, according to Floyd; he was warning the spectators not to act like rabble. I must not be a rabble spectator because I got back into court one time with Floyd, too.

The only reason I got into the court after the ruckus was because Mr. Sweeney snooped with false information from Jack, and that made Mr. Tupper admit he had lost a tooth fighting with Richard, and so *where was it, Jack?*

By twisting Jack's arm, he found out about the tooth I had. He made me tell the judge about it. Floyd brought me in and waited for me, by special permission.

"You Fletcher Williams?" the judge asked.

"Yes, your honor," I said.

"You have grown up some, boy," he said

I was nervous and I didn't want to look at the judge because there was no screen door to hide behind anymore, and I didn't know where else to look. I saw Floyd and Mr. Sweeney smiling at me, and I wished I had my brown tweed cap to twist at a bit but I didn't, so I planned to look at Floyd until the judge reminded me that I was *in a trial, not on trial,* and had to look at him when I was talking, *young man.*

"You'll look at me and speak up clearly when you're talking to me, *young man!*" The judge said. "This here's an informal part of this trial, *young man,* so let's proceed; you're Fletcher Williams, you go by *Fletcher,* I hear. Fletcher, because you are under age, that means under the age of sixteen; in this jurisdiction, in *this* court, you are still what the law calls a minor. You gotta tell the truth, now do you understand what I'm saying?"

"Yes Sir, your Honor," I said, and I looked right at the judge. He looked like he had the same dusty steel glasses he had on the back porch. He took them off and polished them with at red polka—dot handkerchief and stuffed it under a big book on the desk. He pinched his nose, pushed them back on, blinked and snorted like T. T. Oinker. *He looked like T.T. Oinker.*

"Let's start out nice and easy by saying for the record, where you're from; might it be that you're of the Williams family that lived in Morgan County? As I recollect, you're from Morgan County, just down east—a few years back? *Well, are you, boy?*" The judge gruffed at me. I nodded yes. "*Speak out, boy,* the clerk—see, that lady with the machine there? *She writes down everything you say,* so she has to *hear* what you say for the record!"

"Yes," I said, and I watched the clerk poke the buttons on the machine. She looked up at me so I talked some more. "I live at Floyd's place now, over in Waterland."

"For the record that's Floyd McAllister's place, the boy lives there now," the judge said gruffly to the clerk. She nodded and poked some buttons. "Got that straight?" the judge asked.

The clerk nodded again and started minding her own business and poked the buttons faster.

"I live at Floyd's," I said again. I don't know why I said that.

"I see," the judge said, "and I understand you don't live with your family any more, your family's gone? Your daddy, he's been—my memory serves me right —he was a real hard drinking man in the past, that right?"

"Yes your honor, and beat me lots too," I said to the judge.

"That's irrelevant, strike that from the record," the judge said to the clerk. The judge shook his head. "We ain't interested in *history,* boy," he said, "that's not the business of this court, not now. You don't have to say anything like that about your own *private affairs;* all we want is the *truth,* boy!"

"*That is the truth,*" I said.

"*That's the truth,*" he muttered to himself. "*Strike that from the record,*" he said to the clerk. "*It's always a shame when truth has to be stricken from the record,*" he added, and said, "*tsk, tsk.*"

The courtroom was quiet, and I saw Floyd looking at me. He smiled and nodded, but I had to get back to paying attention to the judge because he was talking to me again.

"I thought you might be the same boy, I was sure I saw you a long time ago. I remember now, you was on a front porch of a condemned house back then. The house was condemned, that means not fit to live in, and you had to move, but my, you grew up some! Grew up good, too! Imagine that! Yes sir, your daddy, he was a hard, hard man! I had a few dealings with him, came across him a few times in front of the Morgan County bench!"

I looked at Floyd and thought about what he said and changed my mind. Floyd said I ought to be proud of my father anyway because everyone had a good part, no matter how many warts were on the outside, like a potato, even lumpy, warty potatoes with scabs on the peel cook up nice and taste good in beef stew with butter and salt.

I looked at Floyd, and he nodded at me from the audience.

"I saw him a while ago down at the cemetery where my mother is buried, and he talked real nice and he said he doesn't drink anymore," I offered proudly. Floyd smiled at me.

"This is all off of the record, Aggie," the judge said to the clerk. The judge shuffled some papers and looked at them. He shook his head, handing them back to the clerk. "I see," the judge said. "That's an interesting idea, not likely it will happen, but good to hear," he added, after he cleared his throat.

"That's got nothing to do with why you live with Mr. McAllister now, and not your father, I take it?" He asked, and winked at Mr. Sweeney.

"Yes sir, I live with Floyd. Mrs. Zeban said it's all right, if we get along good, so he takes care of me now," I looked at Floyd. He winked. "And Mrs. McAllister too,—I call her *mom* now—she takes good care of me too," I added. The judge nodded.

265

"You say you saw your father at the cemetery, is that only once you've seen him since you went into the home? I mean, since Social Services shipped you off to live at the home?"

"No, I saw him *twice,* once through the window," and I felt my face getting hot, "Do I have to say what he was doing?" I asked. I didn't want to tell the judge more private affairs; that I saw him in bed drinking whiskey and getting all undressed with Tina McQueeny sitting on him, because Jack was in court, and *right there*, sitting pleased as punch and looking right at me.

"Fletcher, you don't have to tell what your father might have been doing because it's not relevant to this case, let's understand that," he pointed it out to the jury, "but off the record, between you and me, let me give you some good advice, boy," he said back to me and leaned over to me and said it quietly. "What you *can* believe is, *no matter what your daddy says, alcoholics never change.* You can believe your daddy still drinks hard like he always did, *once an alcoholic, always an alcoholic,* and don't you start thinking otherwise. You gotta face reality, and you just make a point of getting growed up better'n he did. You're lucky, you are, you got a real good chance at doing just that over in Waterland with Floyd McAllister there, and Mrs. McAllister; Floyd's a fine man, and Mrs. McAllister, I hear she's a fine lady too, the best there is, I hear!

"Same thing with your mother, boy. I heard about her, and her, uh, unfortunate accident, no mistake about it. I knew your Mother, she was, she...was a nice lady, got herself into some unfortunate circumstances, *that's* not the business of this here court, boy, and I heard she's dead now. I'm sorry about the uh, *accident with the train,* that was unfortunate. I know she's dead, real unfortunate, but that's *all history,* and this here court's not interested *in history,* so let's get back on track here, *you pay attention now, boy.*

"*You're here to tell the truth, do you understand that?* No matter *what* your background is, *if you're an orphan or not, no matter what happened back then. No matter who your father is or what you seen him doing* through any windows, or doors, or anywhere for that matter, but let's just stick to windows for now, like you said. *No matter what the situation is now or what it was before, what counts is the truth here in my court.* Let's make it clear as glass in your windows, *you got to tell the truth if you're going to sit here in my court.* Now you *do* understand that, don't you, young man?" I looked at Floyd. He nodded to me.

"Fletcher?" he asked again after a minute.

"Yes, Sir," I said to the judge, and looked at Jack and I was relieved, no doubt. Now Jack knows I have to tell the truth no matter what, because the judge said so.

"Let's get on with this proceeding, we're going back on record here," he said to the clerk.

"I understand that you had a silver tooth in your possession at one time that was once the real and personal and private property of Mr. Tupper, the defendant over there."

"Yes Sir, I *did* have it," I said. "I don't now because Jack took it out of my shoe." I added, "From under the bed when I was sleeping."

"I see, and where did you get that silver tooth? By that I mean, *how* did you come to be the proud owner of the tooth that was in your possession? Not every boy in the world has a silver tooth to keep under the bed in his shoe." A lady on the jury giggled. The judge looked at her sternly but didn't say anything.

"I found it in the grass after the big fight when Floyd and Mrs. Tickner whacked Mr. Tupper with a wooden spoon and Floyd punched his lights out, and we all got together and sent him packing down the road!" I said. "That was after Mr. Tupper got mad and pitched it over the fence because Floyd knocked it out and he yelled *ouch* and screamed his head off at us for getting whipped by *everybody.*" I added, "We were playing a game of baseball and the ball got over the fence, and I went to find it."

"I see, there was a fight, and the tooth got knocked out, and Mr. Tupper threw it away and you found it, is that correct? While you were searching for a baseball in the grass, at the orphanage, you found *that* tooth? And we understand that you *are no longer in possession* of that tooth?" the judge asked.

"*Yes sir,* I mean *no,* sir," I said after I looked at Floyd and at Jack, and I had to tell the truth, that's what Floyd says. You have to tell the truth, the whole truth, *so help you God*, or your feet will rot and burn in hell forever.

"Yes, I found it, but no, I don't have it."

"What happened to the tooth, Fletcher?" the judge asked gruffly.

"I don't have that tooth now 'cause *Jack's got it.*" I heard the crowd make a noise. The judge looked at everybody and gave them a warning look.

"And where did it get to, *where is it now, do you suppose?*" the judge asked.

"I don't know," I said, telling the truth, and I think that's really lying because I knew that Jack took the tooth but I didn't know where he kept it or what he did with it, no matter what he says. I can say the truth that I don't know where it is because I think Jack's a liar, but I really didn't say that out loud, *did I*, because Jack was right there looking at me.

"Maybe that tooth you had under the bed in your shoe got itself found at the fire and into that plastic bag on the table over there," the judge said and pointed at it.

"Bailiff, hand me that exhibit bag there on the end of the table. *Is this the tooth you had?*" the judge asked. He got the bailiff to pass me the plastic bag with a silver tooth in it. The tooth looked brand new. It was shiny all over. I looked at it carefully and shrugged. It looked a bit like the one I had except it was bright and shiny.

"This is *Exhibit A*", lad, it's *very important that you look it over carefully*," the judge instructed.

"I don't know," I said honestly, because the tooth I had was shiny on top but got black stuff on the back and the sides of it, and some blood and dust too, from getting thrown over the fence and lost in the grass until I found it and washed it off in T.T. Oinker's water trough, and then with water from the pump in the yard. But I didn't know if that black stuff was from being in my shoe at night, maybe even tar from walking barefoot on the pitch-post fence in my balancing act with Marvin Pychinski and Ronnie, and then getting the sticky stuff off of my feet and into my shoes. I asked Mrs. Tickner how to get the black stuff off of silver, how about that? But I almost forgot about that part, and Mrs. Tickner told me that all silver gets black stuff on it.

"It's tarnish, Mrs. Tickner said. " Silver tarnishes, like old silverware knives and forks and tea services," she told me. I'm glad I remembered that just then because I liked Mrs. Tickner, but I didn't tell the judge. He was too busy getting back to it.

"Does it *look* like the tooth you had?" the judge asked.

"No," I said, telling the truth, and that's the truth because the tooth in the plastic bag was shiny all over, front and back, and on the sides, and never had any blood or tar on it from my shoe or pitch-posts or any tarnish like you see on silver tea-services either. The tooth was the same shape, and had the same square edge like a straight line on the biting side. I studied the tooth carefully so that there would be no mistake about it. It was pretty new and shiny.

"It has the same shape," I told the judge and reached up to hand him the bag.

"It has the same shape. Yes, it does that. Now, *do you think it is the same tooth?"* the judge asked. I looked at Jack. Jack watched me like a cat after a mouse.

"Objection, calls for an opinion!" Mr. Ditworth yelled at the judge. *"The boy isn't an expert!"*

"Objection *overruled!* Could be, but we'll be allowing some leeway here. Think about it, counselor. This boy's the only one that's ever studied that tooth up close enough to know if it's the same one or not!" the judge said. "Doctor Yin Mo—who is an *expert*, I remind you, Mr. Ditworth, only yesterday—testified this tooth—was Mr. Tupper's tooth, *which he made himself and sold to the defendant,* right? -so I'll *allow it!"* he said. Mr. Ditworth sat down, his face red. Mr. Tupper scowled.

"How about it, boy?" the judge asked.

"It's *not* the same tooth I had," I said, after a minute to hesitate and make sure I wanted to say that because Jack was still staring at me. "Mine had tarnish black stuff on the sides and back, it was only a bit shiny on top. This one is shiny and polished. *It's not the same one."*

"Maybe Jack still has the tooth he took from me," I suggested. I didn't say he still had it, I only *suggested* it. Jack's mouth opened up wide.

"Mr. Sweeney, Mr. Ditworth, approach the bench!" the judge ordered. He leaned forward.

"Mr. Sweeney, sir, perhaps we should listen more to our *brains* and less to the bull roar that usually accompanies these procedures? I am annoyed as hell about this, sir, so I am now going to instruct you to recall Mr. Jack Whittaker to the stand, because I think, no, *I know*, *it looks like he didn't tell this court the truth!* I don't like what I've just heard here, Soggie, and I don't like to think that I have to tell *you* precisely what questions to ask him when you get him up here, or is that necessary, too?"

"No sir your Honor, that won't be necessary," Mr. Sweeney said quietly with a humbled look on his red face.

"Step back!" he ordered. The judge looked at some papers for a bit and picked up his gavel. He banged it hard on the desk and pointed at Mr. Sweeney.

"Approach the bench, yes, both of you again!" he bellowed at the lawyers. *"We could have been looking at a mistrial here!"* the judge shouted. "And all because your star witness that said he knew for a fact that the defendant was there at the scene of the crime. When in fact, he didn't know any such damned thing and made it all up because he saw something that gave him an idea for vengeance which rightfully belongs to the Lord, and the Lord only — and Holy Christ, it's going to be a miracle by God himself if there's enough additional evidence to convict this murderous devil. And I *will* tell you, I'm mad as hell about this, because if I didn't have Dr. Mo's testimony that this tooth was made for the defendant only recently, I would have to throw this evidence out, now, and if it weren't for this boy's testimony under those circumstances, there would have been a mistrial, wouldn't there!"

"Yes sir, your honor but—"

"—Damned right I would have had to throw out that evidence, and it would have been all *your fault, and yours alone, sir!*" the judge shouted.

"There's going to be an investigation of those procedures that were initiated in *your* office, Mr. Sweeney, no doubt about that! Your star witness has perjured himself; he's turned out to be a goddamned liar! *A liar!* The defendant *could have been arrested* because of what your goddamned lying witness said, *solely* on what that liar said! That could have resulted in a mistrial, now, or are you so goddamned smart you think you are exempt from the law you can get around that one too? May I remind you that there is *murder one* involved here?" The judge wasn't screaming, but if he got any angrier he might have fallen off of his chair.

"*You* are a sloppy lawyer, Mr. Sweeney, *a sloppy, careless lawyer.* You failed to clarify the statements from your witness, or even bothered to ask him if he was telling the truth, which is unforgivable!" Mr. Sweeney looked down at the floor. Floyd looked at me and raised his eyebrows just a little bit. Mr. Tupper grinned at Mr. Ditworth. They seemed happy and I don't know why and I didn't get to find out because the judge hammered on his desk again.

"And what are *you* so happy about, Mr. Tupper? *I am hereby instructing the jury to find you guilty of all counts before this court!*" Mr. Tupper's face went white.

"Far as I'm concerned, the rest of this trial is a farce and a waste of taxpayer's money! *You*, sir, burned up that home to cover up your murder, and killed people in the process! You are the lowest kind of coward, and you even killed your own dear sister in the process! *This* court shall deal with you appropriately!"

"*You, boy, you're dismissed with the thanks of this court!*" the judge thundered at me. "And you remember what I told you about your father!" I noticed the judge's face was still red as a beet, so I got up before he changed his mind and sold me for bait, and Floyd and I wheeled our way toward the back door.

"And now for *you*, young man," the judge scolded sternly and pointed at Jack. "*You* get your fancy suit and your little lying ass up

271

here. You don't bother to bring your derby hat with you because I might send you straight to jail for *perjury* and you won't need no damned fancy derby hat in the goddamned jailhouse. So, you better tell me the truth starting right now for the record, or I'm going to have you locked up for the next ten years for contempt of this here court, and you can take that to the bank, I swear!" Jack jumped up and headed toward the bench. That was even before Mr. Sweeney had a chance to talk in order.

"*I call Jack Whittaker back to the stand, your honor!*" Mr. Sweeney called out. He saw the angry judge reaching for his new gavel.

"*Just for the record,* your Honor! — the clerk has to record —" Mr. Sweeney said to the judge.

" — *You're trying my patience, Sir!*" shouted the judge.

I looked back at Jack. He was white as whipping-cream as he moved into the witness box. Floyd whispered to me that *we better get out of here while the getting is good.* The guard closed the door tight behind Floyd and me, and we couldn't hear any more. Floyd shook his head and smiled.

"We better get ourselves home and get something to eat. I think we need some ice cream." We blinked our way into the sunlight, and I helped Floyd into the truck, and threw his chair into the back. Then I found out the *truth.* It was the next day, I think, or maybe a couple of days after that. That's right, it was a couple of days.

"Jack got fined fifty bucks for lying to the court and six months of community service. He has to help old folks with their yard work, because lying during a trial, that's *perjury!*" Floyd told me, when we were climbing in the truck after getting groceries at Ifield's Foods. We bought celery and canned beans and apples and three chocolate bars but passed up on the lettuce, potatoes, turnips, carrots and green beans, because we still had plenty to pick in the garden.

"I wish you wouldn't *gossip!*" Mrs. McAllister said, grinding the truck into gear.

"Fletcher has a right to know what happened!" Floyd said. He continued. "After all, he and Jack go back a long ways!" Floyd winked at me and cleared his throat and started anyway.

"Mrs. Ifield told me that she heard someone say that Mr. Sweeney was talking about it in the store last night, and he said the judge almost threw Jack into the clink overnight for telling that story even though bits of it might have been true, see?" Mrs. McAllister stopped at the red light and honked and waved at Mrs. McGillvary walking across the street in front of us.

"Hello, Roweena!" she yelled out the window. Mrs. McGillvary waved back.

"The point is, he lied about the tooth, and the *only* thing that saved Jack was the fact that the tooth wasn't the prime evidence anyway. Seems like they discovered that Mr. Tupper had bought gasoline the same day using that gas can, it was the same one, it had his initials painted on it. That's what the gas station attendant said, and then to top it off they found Mrs. Tickner's silver tea service in his flat in a burlap sack under the bed!

"It seems that he was stealing from his own sister, and maybe that's why he got caught, maybe that's the only reason he got found out; Richard discovered him in the process so he had to get rid of the evidence, and that's what he did. Richard discovered him, he fought with the boy and knocked Richard over the head and started the fire. It does seem he had that in mind to burn the home when he got the gasoline, because he had it with him.

"The judge fined Jack fifty dollars and gave him a suspended sentence with some public service duties and really just let him off in consideration of the *improper* things that were done to him by Mr. Tupper."

"Oh, Floyd, I'm so tired of hearing about this whole matter!" Mrs. McAllister said, pulling up to the house. That was how I found out that Jack wasn't a murderer and a liar. He was just a liar, maybe everyone thought he was a little better liar than average because he had openly committed perjury, and it does sound important, doesn't it? That's what Jack said bragging to me two weeks after, and he was still smirking too.

I said *that's not funny, Jack* but he still thought everything in the world was funny until he got a case of sunstroke and all clammy and nearly fell over from sweating a lot, that's what Mrs. Merlegammi said when she brought a wet rag to put on his head. He wouldn't have been seen dead sitting down in her garden unless he *was* dead, but he was doing his time for the crime, digging Mrs. Merlegammi's potatoes by hand, all sixty-two rows of them, as part of his punishment. The best part was that we had ice cold soda pop, and we fell over laughing when I told him smartly that I am not only a cowboy from Texas but a *witness just like him* too, I said, but the witness part was only *sometimes*.

"You shouldn't have lied, Jack," I said, throwing an old rotten potato seed at him.

"I know, Fetchie," he said quietly. "I couldn't help myself, that old bastard—I wanted to hurt him real bad. *I lied."* He stood up and looked across at McKinley's barn. Brown and white cows were wandering around the barnyard, looking like they were ants.

"I won't lie no more," Jack said, squinting into the sunlight.

"That's good, Jack."

I told the boys from the orphanage the same thing too, when they showed up couple of weeks later, coming to buy all of Mrs. Merlegammi's potatoes, and using the bus for a potato-truck. That was after they arrived on the bus to move into the new dormitory and get settled in time for school. Everybody was in a big hurry and they were too busy moving all the beds and tables and kitchen junk to talk. There was such a rush getting the new orphanage for boys in order that I felt funny and sort of cheated and left out. Maybe I was just a bit out of place, so I clammed up and walked back home to Floyd's.

"Everybody tells little white lies for *whatever* reason" that's what Floyd reminded me that night when we talked about it, just like he said a hundred times before.

"Since nothing you can imagine or dream up can ever take them back, or make them right," Floyd said. "you're better off not doing it; after all, you're not supposed to tell lies at all". I agreed. "You better forgive Jack" Floyd suggested.

"I did," I said.

Thirty-Two

That's why I helped Jack with his punishment with yard work and dig everybody's potatoes, to *forgive* Jack.

"That boy looks kind of lonesome, maybe a bit hot and tired over there, working all by himself, doesn't he?" Floyd asked me one hot summer afternoon. We could see Jack in the field behind Mrs. Merlegammi's shed, cutting brush with a dull axe, and piling it on a smoky fire. "He's got lots of work to do, but he seems to keep right at it," Floyd added.

He hauled out his pipe and stuffed it just right. "I think he's basically a good boy, but got influenced by the wrong people," he said. "Wouldn't hurt if you kept him *company* now and then, would it?" he asked, and lit his pipe, but he didn't look at me. "It's up to you, you might help him out a bit, and it might make the summer go faster."

"Okay, Floyd, but I'll just keep him company. I won't do his work, the judge said *he's* supposed to do it, isn't he, Floyd?"

"Jack's a little prideful, he might not like you *helping* him, but I don't think it would hurt to pretend you're *not* helping him. Just tell him you'll keep him company a bit, pretty soon he won't mind if you pass him a shovel or throw a few sticks of brush on that fire over there, and maybe you could even take him a bottle of that red soda pop right now. I think he might like that just fine."

The Fires of Waterland

Floyd shook out the newspaper and waited to see if I was going to say anything else. I didn't. I got two bottles of cherry pop and went over to pretend to help Jack for a minute, and it took the rest of the summer.

We cut grass and hoed a lot of gardens, and I was too tired, but I did Floyd's yard work by myself at night and Mrs. Dormally's garden and yard work on Saturdays. Floyd said he was proud of me and didn't mind waiting to have his yard work done at night. He said it was for a good cause. My working with Jack was a big help to Floyd too because I got a basket of cabbages and a whole bag of red potatoes free from Mr. and Mrs. Puchenko, two bags of white potatoes from Mr. Bibb, and another bag of red potatoes from Mrs. Swain.

She told us she couldn't eat them all no matter what, and Mr. Swain doesn't like potatoes because they grow in dirt and horse manure for most of their lives, or at least that's what she said.

"He prefers rice. He says, *rice is nice,*" Jack mimicked and then clammed up when we saw Mrs. Swain taking a stroll to get the mail from the little white mailbox at the end of the walk.

"Good morning, Mrs. Swain!" we yelled, polite as can be. She waved at us.

Jack and I were always polite anyway, but we got to laughing ourselves silly after she went into the sun porch to read her letters and probably take up her knitting. She was knitting Mr. Swain a pullover sweater from used green wool, and she said she was going to surprise him if he didn't get back home before she finished. I think she told us he was working in Yellowknife welding chemical tanks every day of his life and his eyes were going bad from looking at the sparks.

"Mr. Swain's going to be coming home on Tuesday!" she yelled happily at us from the porch and waved an open letter at us.

I didn't get any potatoes from Mrs. Merlegammi even if she had the biggest bumper crop in history because Jack already had most of them dug and cleaned off and bagged and put into her root house by the time he had the sunstroke. A couple of weeks later she donated sixty-one bags to the new orphanage, and Jack and I had to carry every one of them right back out of her root house all the way into the bus to haul them to the orphanage, and pile them up high in the cold storage shed.

"Very good, boys!" Mr. Fester said as we stacked the last two bags up near the ceiling. "You've done a nice job, nice and neat! We'll reform you yet, Jack!"

Jack flopped down on the pile of empty bags in the center of the floor and puffed a lot.

"I'm *never* going to tell another lie, I guarantee it!" he said.

"Me neither," I promised.

Mr. Fester hauled up an old wooden bench and sat for a minute, then got up and paced back and forth, deep in thought. Jack and I watched him, and Jack's eyes went back and forth like a pendulum in a grandfather clock. He winked at me and shook his head.

"Smell anything burning?" Jack asked, grinning. I didn't know what he was talking about.

"Wiltie's got smoke coming out his ears," Jack whispered to me quietly. Suddenly, Mr. Fester stopped pacing.

"Jack, I've been thinking," Mr. Fester said. " – *The judge don't mind if you don't. I've spoken to him already, and it's all right with him* – and you're almost finished your probation, and you promised *never* to tell lies and get in trouble again. And I've seen you've been a decent, hardworking, young man all summer, and I've heard from the neighbors that you've *always* been polite and honest, so I've been thinking a lot about you. There might be a place for you in the home here.

"You could help out with the boys; supervise, you know, like you used to do at the old home. You know, you *do* have a lot of experience with boys. I understand you did a really good job at the old home, so now you could be a really big help here. You could help the younger boys, and do repairs! You are handy, I can see that. You can paint; fix doors and shingles, anything that happens to come your way. You seem to be able to do *anything* you try, even dig potatoes, I see!" He laughed. "I bet you could be the assistant cook, too, if you wanted to be! What about it, you interested?"

"No thanks, Wiltie, I got me a job already!" Jack stood up right away and shoved his hands in his pockets and talked without even thinking about it for a minute.

"It's a real nice offer though, isn't it, Fetch? But I spent all of my life in the orphanage; I got bad memories of the old place. I get bad dreams and wake up with the sweats, so I ain't never going back, not me, not if I can help it. I got a place to live and a job and a woman, real nice sometimes, too, so no matter what, I don't need no orphanage job, *not me!*"

"I hear you lost that job because you got yourself on probation," Wiltie looked at me and then at Jack. Jack looked down at his shoes and pretended to rub some dirt off of one with the other. He hesitated. It didn't help. He switched. Shoes, I mean.

"I still got that job. Somebody's tellin' you stories, I'd say!" Jack said. "Right, Fetch?"

"I thought I heard you say you wouldn't be stretching the truth any more, just a minute ago — or was that somebody else I heard? You hear anybody *else* talking in here, Fetch?" Wiltie asked me and winked. I didn't answer. I knew he had Jack by the shorts, but I looked around to see if anybody else was there anyway, just to help Jack out a bit. Sometimes, you can't help somebody even if you want to. I wanted to help Jack, but you can't fool Wiltie.

Jack fidgeted and hooked his thumbs into his belt like a cowboy and scuffed the dirt floor again. He looked at me, and I saw his face getting red. He turned away, and then sat down hard on the bench. He sniffed, and that was the first time in a long time that I saw Jack with no smirk on his face. He pulled off his derby hat and zinged it against the wall.

"You're right. I...I stretched the truth just then, but in general, I ain't lyin' no more, not me. But about that job... that boss, he weren't nice at all, he came right out and told me, he said: *'You get your lying orphaned ass out of here. I don't wanna see you 'round here no more, you slick derby-brained dandy, and I ain't gonna send or recommend any fruit ball dandied-up liar to working for nobody else, either!'*

"That's what he said, and I ain't worked a day since. I just copped a few potatoes and carrots and the like to help out a bit on them yard jobs and gardening and such; you know how many places I get sent to work off my probation sentence? Nobody ever really explained the difference to me, did they? But it was either that or go to jail, that's what that damned old judge give me — some choice eh? And some of them people, they got the facts *wrong*. They think I'm a bad criminal or worse, maybe a dirty rapist pervert bugger or something, even if I'm not the one that done it. They don't even want me around, not even if I'm cleaning up or doing their yard work *free* for them; and you know where I live, next to Fletcher's place there.

Jack got up, walked over and gave his derby a kick, then picked it up and dusted it off by flapping it hard against the wall. It got flat, but he punched it back in shape and jammed it on his head.

"*Derby brained dandy*! That's what he said, Wiltie!"

He angrily ripped his hat off again and smacked it flat some more against the wall but fixed it back nice every time. Then he kicked the wall hard. He got a sad face and started talking again.

"Tina — she works in the dry goods store in Egansville, she buys the food and pays the rent and it *looks* like I'm working, don't it? — Because the rent is paid, but now I can't get no job no matter how hard I tried. Nobody wants to take a chance on no dandy bald-faced liar like me, 'specially since everybody and his barnyard full of stinkin' smelly stock, every bloody swine and damned chicken in the country knows I have a *criminal record,* even if it's only for perjurin' myself already. An' even if that crabby old judge said there was a whole lot of circumstance beyond my control, and especially since I been a victim of that perverted old bastard Tupper, that murderin' sick old queer — and I hope he rots in hell for doin' what he did!"

Jack sat down and took his head in his hands. I don't know if Jack was crying or not because it was getting a bit dark. "Don't cry, Jack!" I said, and looked at Wiltie. He shook his head.

"It ain't fair. *It ain't fair, not a bit,*" he said. He wiped his face. It was still dirty. "It don't matter what I do, does it?"

The Fires of Waterland

"Jack was real honest and took good care of me when I was little back in the old days," I said proudly to Wiltie. "He was in charge of me and made sure that I got everything, even when I was the new boy and didn't have a chance in flaming hell with so many boys there. Jack always took good care of me and got my cap back and gave me his sugar, too!"

"I heard that elsewhere, too, Fletcher. This lad, I know he's a kind lad, that's what the other boys said to me too. That's why I've been thinking about putting Jack to work at the new home. There's lots of boys, small boys, just like you were, Fletcher, scared to death, hungry. They need somebody that understands how they *feel* when they come to us."

"Jack knows how we feel!" I said. "*Jack, you gotta go.* You gotta get to work with Wiltie, it's a good job. It's a good idea, maybe not as good as working at the broomstick factory—but let's see what Floyd says. Let's ask Floyd. He'll say what he thinks, he won't boss you around and tell you what to do, but he'll give you good solid advice. He told me to help you with your probation work and I did, and I'm not sorry, and *see?* We're having *a lot* of fun, aren't we?"

Jack looked at me and snuffed his nose in a dusty handkerchief.

"I ain't workin' no orphanage, not me! Imagine, *me workin' in an orphanage home, after spending my whole life there already!* Now if I do that, I'll be gettin' old and gray and walking around with two stick canes, and takin' care of scaredy cat, snot-nosed, orphan boys, and feeding them porridge every day, and having to give them all my sugar, and cleanin' up puke when they get sick, and keepin' 'em from fighting over the last speck of sugar, even if it's 'supposed to be mine. —And I ain't even got to Texas yet, ain't never been *anywhere else* in the world except to Egansville and that lousy burned-out home for rotten-assed boys like me—my whole life. And so now I gotta *work there* too? And never get anywhere else the rest of my life no matter what? And me with whip marks all over my arse, and *no* damned job and a *criminal record* yet! So, get that idea out of your pea-brained head, it doesn't sound like a good idea to me at all, not a bit, thanks!" Jack wiped his leaky nose on his shirt sleeve.

281

"Jack!" I objected because I don't have a pea-sized brain, and I know Jack *needs* a job at the orphanage. "Jack, I think you're wrong; me and you can work at the home instead of going to Texas, can't we? *Don't say no.* I think you should talk to Floyd, we'll get it right if we ask Floyd. He'll tell us the right thing to do, so let's go ask Floyd first!"

"No, I ain't askin' anybody about what I'm supposed to do with myself. I ain't *never* doin' that. *People that does that* are weak-minded fops!"

"People that seek advice when they *don't* really know what to do are smarter than those that *don't ask,*" Wiltie said.

"That's right, Jack. Get smarter by asking Floyd first, not after you make a bad mistake, like trying to filch potatoes while somebody's watching!"

"Jack, I wish you would reconsider," Wiltie said.

"Thanks but *no thanks, not me.* I ain't doin' *that!*"

"Jack," I said, looking at Wiltie to see if he got the idea I had, "if Floyd thinks it's a *good* idea would you at least *think* about it?" Wiltie smiled at me. Jack shuffled around and pounded on the wall with his fist. He got to the door and looked out and finally turned around.

"I don't want to, but...I don't know. Maybe it ain't bein' a snot-nosed fop quite so bad if we *think* about it, and it might be okay if we ask Floyd."

"It ain't being a pea-brain, either, Floyd knows what's best. He helped you when you showed up here, didn't he?" I challenged Jack. "He got me to help you get over your *jail-escape* work, didn't he?"

"I don't want to say if you're right or wrong, Fetchie-boy, but I have to admit he did right by me from the first. He helped me a lot and give me money and a new shirt so I'd look just dandy for my first day of work. And Mrs. McAllister fed me every day, even for a few days after my first payday, just to make sure I got a good start! He told *you* to come and help me too."

I knew we were getting somewhere with Jack, because he said that last part slow and thoughtfully, after he paused a bit to think about it, just like Floyd does.

He added, "At least until I met that Tina. Now she feeds me, takes care of me good, too."

I wanted to say something else about what Tina does for Jack, but I thought better of it and clammed up and let Wiltie talk first.

"Well, tell you what, Jack, here's the deal," Wiltie proposed. "Floyd already suggested it to me; see what I mean it being a good idea and all, but you go and talk to Floyd yourself. If he says right there it's a good idea, will you try it out for three or four weeks?"

Jack scratched his head and seemed a little bit agitated and didn't answer for a minute, and I couldn't stand it anymore because he wasn't answering. Floyd told me you should never look a gift horse in the mouth.

"Sounds good to me," I said excitedly, "it's like a gift horse, Jack, so does it sound good to you too?" I asked. "*Jack?*" I shook his shoulder. "We'll both get to work right away, too!" I told Wiltie. "We don't eat much, and you only have to pay us each a thousand bucks a week!" I said to Wiltie. He laughed.

"If it sounds good to you, Fetch, it sounds good to me too!"

"You boys come in and have supper now. We're having leftover roast beef stew with extra potatoes thrown in the pot, and we'll top it up with apple pie!"

"You already talked to Floyd about it and he said it was a good idea?" Jack asked Wiltie.

Wiltie nodded. "Ask him yourself," he answered pleasantly. "I don't want you to make a decision right now, tomorrow would be just fine."

"Apple pie and beef stew?" Jack asked. "Now that does sound like a gift horse, a hungry one. It sounds right fine and good enough, *don't it sound good to you, Fetchie boy?*" Jack shouted. He jumped up and went with us.

I think it was nearly the best supper I ever had. Maybe it was from getting two pieces of apple pie because Allie Morgan said he hates cooked apples with cinnamon on it, even if it's in a pie crust with sugar on it. I asked him why, and he said his old man had a big apple orchard before he got driven over by a tractor while he was picking up apples for the old horse, so Allie hates apples, cooked, boiled, baked, peeled, raw, ripe, or green, but mostly he hates them *squashed* in apple pie like he saw his old man. His mom got all the trees sawed down and went on holidays three days after the funeral and forgot about Allie, and she never came back *once*. And he doesn't get any letters from her, either, just like all the other rotten-arsed boys Jack was complaining about, even me.

That's how Jack came to work at the new *Waterland Home for Boys* and stayed there until he died. And he was happier than being a rich cowboy in Texas, because Tina McQueeny gave up her job in the dry goods store right after that, and got to be the cook in the orphanage too, just like Mrs. Tickner used to be, except that she didn't give the boys peaches, and she didn't have to sleep in the pantry between the flour bags like Mrs. Tickner did at the old home. She stayed with Jack in my father's house.

Maybe Jack didn't tell me they got married in the courthouse or something, but they must have, because after that they pulled the curtains over the window every night in the dark. Livvy and I didn't see them doing anything through the bedroom window again, not even once. I watched every night to see if my father was there. That's what I said I was doing, but he wasn't, and Livvy said I shouldn't do that.

Thirty-Three

"What are you doing?" Livvy whispered fiercely from the bed behind me. Bright moonlight washed over her face. I thought she was sleeping when I opened her door silently and crept past her bed to look out the window, but she wasn't. Down below, there was a fragment of light escaping into the darkness from between the tightly closed curtains of my mother's bedroom window, but I could not see anything. I stood there. She sat up.

"Nothing, I was just looking to see if my father came home," I whispered back at her. I know that I lied because I didn't want her to know that I might have been hoping, even if just a little bit, to see Tina, or maybe more than a bit. I'm sorry I lied. Maybe it's not so bad doing things if you're sorry.

"Fetch, you know he hasn't been here for months!" she said. "He's been gone for months now, he's gone *forever* don't you think? I don't think he'll ever come back now, do you?"

She flopped back down onto the pillows and sighed out loud. She wiggled her toes. "You know you're not supposed to be in here. She lifted up her head and shook her long hair, watching me. She flopped back down again and then bounced back up like she was on a haystack with pokey Canadian thistles in it. She watched me like a cat for a minute and that made me shift from one foot to the other. My feet were cold. "What are you *really* doing?" she asked finally, and studied me carefully. I think she knew. Livvy always seems to know what I'm thinking.

285

Maybe I did want to see Tina, maybe I should tell Livvy that I want to see her with no clothes on and that I just want to see her tits; maybe that's why I wanted to look, but I can't very well tell Livvy that. I want to say it. I want to tell her and be honest and tell her everything because I love her, but I can't. Now maybe I'm even sorry I didn't.

I looked at her and she put her head back down on the lace-covered pillow and watched me some more. Hair glistened in the moonlight and made a beautiful shining fan on the pillowcase. It looked like polished gold. It reminded me of my mother's hair that always glowed like gold in the sun. Livvy sat up again.

"Do you want to talk?" she asked. "You could stay with me for a while," she whispered, "if we're quiet, but you can't make a sound." She patted the edge of the bed. I took another look out the window and sat down. I bumped the frame on the bed with my knee. It hurt.

"Ouch!" I said, and right out loud, too.

"Shsh! We'll be in trouble if she finds you in here!" she warned, pressing her fingers to my mouth. "Mom said I'm not supposed to let you in my room any more now that I'm turning into a woman. That's what she said, women need their privacy!" She put her hand on my arm and smiled at me. "Do you think I'm turning into a *woman,* Fetch?"

I didn't answer that. "Don't you think she's a bit prudish — we don't *do* anything, not like Jack and Tina do," I objected, almost out loud again, but I remembered to whisper at the last minute, "Is that what she's so worried about?" She didn't answer so I insisted. I wished I didn't, but I did.

"Fletcher," she started out, and I could see that she was turning red and embarrassed a little bit, "it's hard to tell you this, but I — I got, I get the — *the curse* now, I — I get my p-p-periods, you do know *what that is,* don't you? I get *periods* now. I can get babies if I let boys sleep with me; she told me, we had a talk about it, and you're not supposed to know about it, it's *women's* private stuff and boys aren't supposed to know about it."

"Silly — is that all? I knew that!" I was surprised, well, maybe a little bit, because I didn't think Livvy *could* talk about that stuff, being a proper lady and doing quilting and going to church teas and bake sales. "Me and Floyd talk about *everything*, you know that," I said.

Besides, I knew all about it even before that, a long time ago, because Archie McKinley told me his sister got bleeding right there in her swimming suit, right between her legs. They were down at the pool on Fisher's Creek, and she thought she was going to die and she was scared and crying. She was making a big crybaby blubbery fuss, she thought she was dying or something, and he had to make her get home to her mother *right now*. Archie told her she had nothing to worry about, *big crybaby*.

"A couple of days later we were fishing and only caught two little trout, but he said that Sarah got all *ladyish la-de-dah* just like magic when her mother told her she was just growing up like the birds and the bees and took her shopping to make her feel better. She bought her a booby trainer bra and lipstick to wear all the time and told her that all the girls in the whole world gotta go through *that* and it was nothing to worry about, *so there*.

"See? I know *that* stuff," I explained it to her. "You got your period right now?" I asked her casually.

Livvy looked at me for a minute, and I thought she didn't know that happened to Sarah but it turned out she did.

She giggled. "No! Sarah told me about that—but I slapped her silly because I thought she was just trying to show off. She said she always had bigger breasts than Teri Brownlee, and Teri, she's got the biggest ones around, so I told her *just you wait and see who gets bigger boobs yet*," Livvy giggled again. I shushed her. She looked back at me and pecked me on the cheek. She pulled the cloth away and looked down into her nightshirt.

"Mine are still little," she giggled. "See?" She leaned forward and showed me. I looked down her night-gown and nodded. They are soft and pink, but they aren't very big yet. I reached in and nearly touched one. Livvy giggled again, and that's a bad habit. I mean *giggling*, not touching boobies. She turned away.

I shushed her. "You're not supposed to let anyone touch them now. I'm not stupid, I know those things."

"And you know we *can't* be like Jack and Tina, even if we *want* to!" she said. "Boys don't do that, I mean —*we're* not supposed to do things until we get grown up and maybe get married," she added.

"I'm not getting married until I have a car, and I'm a man of the world, and have a convertible and a job that pays at least a thousand and forty bucks a week," I said.

"*I know,*" she whispered, turning to me. She hesitated. "But you know Mom, she always worries about us. Remember, I told you she saw us, she saw me sleeping on your arm, your hand was touching me, right there where it's not supposed to be just yet, and *'shame on you,'* she said. And *'don't do that anymore. Proper ladies don't do anything like that until they get married,'* that's what she told me the next morning. She came up to get her sewing stuff and saw us sleeping, — we were sleeping in your room that time — she told me she didn't say anything to Floyd.

"He might have just killed us, maybe; she was worried sick. She said it was a big responsibility having two teenagers in the house at the same time that are getting on to the age of making babies, and she had to do *something* about it for her own peace of mind, so she said she had to scold me whether she liked it or not. When she said *proper ladies don't let anyone sleep with them just yet*, three or four times — and then she said it again a lot louder, Fetchie. I thought she was saying that I was an improper young lady, like a slut, and it made me cry a lot, but she said she didn't mean it *that way* and *'there, there, don't you cry now, Livvy, honey. No harm done, sweetheart. Just promise you won't do that again,'* and she made me feel better after.

"I talked to her for a long time about *everything* and made her promise that she wouldn't send me away, send me back, because I *can't* go back to live with Soggie and Barbara-Lynne, *never. I'll run away forever, I won't go back,* I told her! I might visit. I still love Barbara-Lynne, and that's what I told her, but I won't go back to live with them. I wanted to explain it to her, but I couldn't tell her everything, I *couldn't.* She would have a fit or something. She's so prudish and old-fashioned, it would have shocked her, hurt her so much, so I couldn't tell her why. *I just couldn't tell her why!*" A car whizzed by the window and honked the horn. The light shone across Livvy's face and went away. I hate that when people think you're sleeping, and they honk the horn to wake you up.

"I don't want her to send me away, Fetch. I love you and Floyd and Mom, and I'm *always* going to love you. I told her that, and I told her I wouldn't let anything happen. I mean — anything like those things that Tina and Jack do, she thinks things like that are bad, and I sort of promised I wouldn't even let you in my bedroom because she thinks *ladies don't do that, just sluts.* I even said *that* to her, and she made me promise, *swear on the Bible* and especially *promise and hope to die* that I wouldn't turn out to be a slut like Tina McQueeny. You know she told us so many times that she's a slut. I don't know why, but she keeps saying that!

"I said *I can't, I won't be a bad girl.* I won't be a slut no matter what because I want to be here with you and her and Floyd. I'll do anything I have to, *anything* to live here and stay with you, you know that!" She rubbed her face hard, like washing it with sand to get tar off.

"You know I don't want to go live with Barbara-Lynne and Soggie, and now I'm going to have to tell you *why* — what happened, so you understand; *you have to promise not to tell.* You won't like what I'm going to tell you, but I trust you, Fletcher, so do you — do you promise to understand what I have to tell you, *do you promise me?* Promise me not to get angry and *kill* somebody?" Her voice sounded tight and funny, and when I looked at Livvy there were tears in her eyes shining in the moonlight.

"No, I won't promise," I said. "You don't have to tell me if you don't want to, and because it must be bad if it makes you cry." I put my arm around her and thought about it for a minute. She sniffed. "But if you want to tell me and it makes you feel better, go ahead. I'll try really hard to understand." When you love somebody, you understand them, that's what Floyd says. "I won't even kill somebody if you don't want me to."

She took a deep breath and started to talk fast like she was holding her breath.

"Well, then, I have to tell you." She trembled. "I don't know *how* to tell you this," she started, her shoulders shaking.

"I don't like him anymore, I mean Soggie, *I hate him*. You're going to be so angry —he put his hands in between my legs and pretended he was tickling me, he laughed and then he grabbed my hand and made me do something, *something I didn't like!*" Livvy gasped and shook.

"He —oh, Fletcher, I was so scared, he made me touch his... his, oh, you know what I mean. I couldn't believe it, it was so ugly! That *first* time—*we were alone*, Barbara-Lynne was gone shopping with somebody—Aggie Nostawood. She's the old lady that lives next door. She takes her shopping every week because Aggie gets lost by herself and can't find her way home and doesn't give out the right amount of money. It was her, I think—but anyway, *we were alone*. He always seemed so nice, but he locked the door and he took me into the bedroom to show me something. *Pictures*, he said, and made me sit down on the bed, but he turned around and took it right out of his pants. His pecker, I couldn't believe it at first. *I couldn't believe he was doing it,* but he did it, and showed it to me. It was ugly, *how ugly*, and wet, and he squeezed it and pulled back and forth with his hands, then he stood up and pushed it close to my face. I was so scared. I said *'What are you doing?'* and he said, *'I love you, Livvy, darling, I love you so much. It's all right for us to love each other; do you know how we can show we love each other?'*

"I said *'I don't know, I don't know, Soggie, what are you doing? — again,* and *'don't do that—please don't do that, I'm scared,'* and he said, *'We can show love for each other. You can kiss me, right here. I want you to do it, if you do it for me, honey. I'll know you love me, you can kiss it to show me that you love me. Barbara doesn't love me. I need you to prove that you love me, Livvy, darling, I want you to prove you love me!'*

Livvy trembled and looked away from me, embarrassed, and I know she was crying because she wiped her eyes. Her shoulders were shaking. I think it was a good idea to keep quiet and I did.

> *I'm going to kill Soggie first chance I get, that dirty slut bastard. He's just like Mr. Tupper the pervert murderer that done it to me and Jack, that's what I'll do to him for hurting Livvy, I'll drive right over him with a cement truck. First chance I get.*

She finally started to talk again.

The Fires of Waterland

"Fletcher ...I shouted *'No!'* at him, —and I backed up away from him, but he kept getting closer to me. I was scared!

"He kept wanting me to do that, and he kept playing with his hands and trying to get me, and he got his handkerchief from his pocket and groaned and wiped himself off, the dirty bugger. He said *'Don't tell Barbara-Lynne that we love each other because it's our secret,'* and I was scared, Fletcher. And he said *'I'm sorry, honey-buns, I won't do that again. Don't tell'* —and I was so scared. I didn't know what to do, but I knew I couldn't do it. I got away on the other side of the room, and I wouldn't touch him or let him near me even though he started to cry and zipped himself up again.

"I couldn't hardly even *look* at him again, so I ran out of the house and down the street—then he got mad and called me a stupid bitch. *'You're just like Barbara, you stupid little bitch!'* he shouted at me, and I didn't come back into the house until I saw Barbara-Lynne came back home.

He wouldn't look at me and tried to joke and gave me five dollars right in front of Barbara and said *you should go to the movies this afternoon,* and tried to give me a dish of ice cream, but I wouldn't eat it. Barbara-Lynne asked me if I was sick or something. I just said no and ran up to bed. I heard them starting to argue." Livvy wiped her eyes with the corner of the bed sheet. *"I hate him, Fletcher!"* She watched me as I listened, I don't know why she did that.

"I didn't think it would ever happen *again, but it did, he —he did, he did it again!* The *second time* was when I went for the weekend —that time I went and stayed for the Monday holiday too, you remember that time? —just a few months ago, and I thought Barbara-Lynne was going to be there, but Soggie lied when he picked me up. He said she was going to be there, but Barbara-Lynne wasn't there, she was off to Ottawa to visit her cousin, and I didn't know that. I wouldn't have gone if I knew that!" She looked at me for a minute. "*You* believe me, don't you Fletcher?"

"Yes," I said. I waited.

"*That time* he tried to give me wine. It was red wine, but I didn't like it, I didn't drink it, I poured it in a plant when he wasn't looking. I saw a lady do that in the movies one time. He played music on the record player and made me dance sexy, and then he wanted me to take my blouse off, but I didn't, he made me spin around with him. He pinched my rear end and pushed himself against me, he was hard and stuck out again, and I pushed him away and lied. I said—I mean I told him that I felt like I was going to throw up from drinking the wine and getting dizzy, being spun around dancing, and we sat down.

"He put his arms around me and petted my hair, and asked me if I felt better yet, then he patted my knee and pushed his hand under my skirt. He hurt me with his fingers and I had to slap him on the face and make him get his hands off of me..."

"'Little *bitch!*' he swore at me, and slapped my face hard.

"Then I couldn't believe it, he did the same thing *again*, he stood up and unzipped and showed me his ugly thing, he called me a *little bitch* again. He said I should *beg* him to let me do it for him, get down on my hands and knees and beg him to let me suck him, suck him! — and *'kiss it and not run off like last time, you little bitch,'* that's what he said. *That's what he called me over and over again* and his face got all red and he swore at me, and said maybe he should just *kill* me, and he said that it was my last chance. Then when I said no he tried to push my head down, he—he tried to —he tried to *make* me do it, Fletcher. He hurt me again, he smelled dirty, he *was* dirty—I was so scared. *My own uncle* trying to make me do something like that,—and *you know,*" she sobbed.

" – *Oh, Fletcher—you* know, *you* know how many times, Fletcher —how many times we've seen Tina doing that? We thought it was funny, watching your father, and with Jack too. So you know it's not like I didn't *know* about it, and it's not that it's never been done before, people do it all the time, and I won't be afraid to do it when we get married, Fletcher, because I love you. I love you, when you love someone you can do that with *them,* but I couldn't do *that,* not with a dirty, filthy pig, a dirty man, *not my own uncle,* he should know better than that, the dirty bugger, and him being a lawyer too!

"Did you know adults get in trouble for having sex with children? He knows I'm only thirteen. Did you know that, Fletcher,that adults can get in trouble for having sex with *children?* Of course you knew that, because of what the judge said to Mr. Tupper and why he was sending him to jail longer for what he did to Jack, and Mr. Tupper said he was going to jail *forever* anyway, so it didn't matter?" She breathed sharply and looked away.

"I stood up and slapped Soggie's face and he slapped me right back, but I slapped him harder again, and he grabbed me but I got away by kicking him, right between the legs, too. And he squealed like the dirty pig he is, and I know Barbara-Lynne, if I told her now, she'd probably get him hauled to jail too, or maybe she wouldn't say a thing. She'd just get his gun, his loaded shotgun out of the bedroom closet and kill the dirty bastard!" She sat, trembling.

"Now you're going to hate me Fletcher, maybe I shouldn't have told you that." She blew her nose on the corner of the bed sheet and wiped her eyes.

I looked at her for a minute. The moonlight was shining on the tears in her eyes. I thought about it for another minute. "I'm sorry that happened to you, Livvy," I said after a bit.

She shook her head and put her hand on my face. *"Don't be sorry for me, Fletcher, I'm a tough little bitch. I'll kill him myself next time. I'll kill that dirty man, so help me God, I will,"* she whispered.

I nodded a bit but didn't say a thing. The moonlight shone in the tears as they fell, splashing the sheet.

Livvy got out of bed and looked out the window. She stood for the longest time, and then her shoulders shook hard again. She stopped after a while and turned back to me and shook her head and climbed back into bed. She looked tired. I tried not to look at her too much, but then I saw that she was crying again. I don't like to see Livvy cry. I gave her the corner of the sheet to wipe the tears out of her eyes some more.

She snuffled and then she smiled a little bit and grabbed my face with both hands and kissed me. I couldn't believe what she said next.

"How can you love me now, Fletch, how can you love me after what happened? Do you hate me now, Fletcher? *Do you, do you hate me? Now that you know?"*

I didn't know what to say because I never heard of anything like that before. I mean an uncle doing that to his own niece, I had never heard of anything like that except me and Jack and that terrible perverted bastard Tupper, but that's not even normal what he did, so it doesn't count, does it? I kept quiet and thought it to myself. *I don't know why that happened to Livvy but I didn't like it at all,* so I clammed right up and put my arms around her tight and held on to her for a long time.

"I love you no matter what happened, Livvy," I finally whispered. "I'll always love you no matter what happens. I promise, no matter what happens." She cried. I cried too. I don't know why. We kept quiet for a few minutes.

"It's okay to cry, Fletcher, honey, it's okay to cry," my mother whispered to me from the window to heaven.

"I don't hate you, Livvy. I'm sorry you got hurt, I'm sorry that happened to you," I finally said, and I meant it. "It's better that you told me. I can't hate you no matter what, and I'll never hate you, no matter what."

She wiped her eyes and looked at me. "I know, I thought so, but I didn't want to tell you about it, I was so scared, and hurt, and ashamed, and—I'm never going back there, not unless I know that pervert Soggie's away, or maybe I would go if you can go with me, or if Mrs. McAllister—Mom goes too, —or if I know Barbara-Lynne will be there *for sure*—no I'm *never* going back there, no matter what. Anyway, I like Waterland better. I can go on the bus to school, and I love Floyd too, even Mom, even if she makes me act like a lady!" She put her arms around me and dropped her head on my shoulder. A dog barked.

"I'm glad you don't hate me, Fletcher."

"I know," I whispered. I waited for a while.

She loves you, Fletcher, she loves you a lot, my mother whispered from outside of the window.

"I know," I said again to myself without realizing it. Livvy kissed my cheek and sniffed.

I put my hand inside her pajamas and tried to touch her tiny breast again and kissed her. She pushed my hand away, but held it.

"Fletcher!" she still sounded like she needed cheering up, so I moved my hand to the other one and touched it just a bit too. She held my hand tight against her, and she didn't flinch or pull away, not a bit.

"I won't hurt you, Livvy, I'll never hurt you. I won't let anyone hurt you, never, not ever!" I whispered to her. *"I'll kill everybody that hurts you!"*

"I know that, too! I know you could never hurt me, Fletcher, I know that!" She got up again and looked out the window. *"They must have gone to bed, maybe they made love, too"* she whispered, still looking out the window. *"I wish we were older, I wish I was grown up so we could make love like Jack and Tina!"* She lifted her hair high in the moonlight and let it drop like fine strings of golden moonlit rain.

"I...promise I'll do it with you when you want to—if you want to, Fletcher," she whispered. "No matter what anyone says, when you love someone...I would, I'll kiss you and I'll...I'll do *everything* if you want me to, I want that, too, like Jack and Tina, if you want me to. No, I can't, not right now, but I would do anything you want me to, — only with you, only if you love me and want me to, I love you, you know that. But I promised Mom I wouldn't do anything like that *ever* until I get married."

I want to do that, I want you to do that, why can't we do that right now, — no you can't you're not a slut like Tina, — you're not a slut like Tina. I want her on me, I feel hot, I want her to do it again, I want her to get me again. Not you, it can't be you, Livvy, you're the girl I'm going to marry, you're not a slut. She's a real slut, she can't do it now because she's Jack's, but you can't do it, it can't be you now. It wouldn't matter if she does it, she's already made herself a slut, I want her again, but I can't do it with her anymore, now that damned Jack's got her. He gets her every night, he gets on and makes her scream and laugh, why can't she be here for me, damn him, damn him, I hate him. Don't say that Fletcher, I want you now; you'll like it, come closer, Fletcher. Oh, Tina. Please, Fletcher, you'll like me, Fletcher, you'll like me, Fletcher...

She turned back to me. I jumped and started.

"*Fletcher!*" she stared. She gasped. She didn't have to tell me, but it didn't take me long to see what she was looking at. It stuck out all by itself, I didn't do it. It's not my fault. I grabbed the blanket and put it in front so Livvy couldn't see.

Livvy came closer in the moonlight and looked at me. She was breathing funny, just like Tina.

"You're going to be a beautiful man, Fletcher, I want to touch you, just once," she whispered.

She giggled and quick as a flash she leaned toward me and tried to touch me right on the bump. I backed away. "No!" I said, and right out loud too. "Shshsh!" she said.

You're not a slut, you can't be a slut like Tina. Not now, she can do that but you can't, not now, if you do it now you'll be a slut too.

That is how I know that Livvy wants to touch me and do everything if I want her to, because she tried, but I can't let her. Livvy is a proper lady like Mrs. McAllister, and she shouldn't be a slut and look at it and touch things until we get married or something. I made up my mind and turned away quickly so she couldn't see it anymore and get ideas that she's not supposed to get in her mind just yet.

I didn't say anything after that. I went to my own room across the hall. I knew it was best even though I didn't want to. I heard the clock down in the hallway chime twelve. I sat down on the bed and tried to tuck myself in and thought there was something wrong. I'm going to ask Floyd about it, and he can get me to see Doctor Simpson or something, maybe there's something wrong, I can't be grown up yet, but maybe it's too late, I'm almost fourteen.

Floyd told me the other day, "You're not a *boy* anymore." He winked when he said it.

I changed my mind about talking to Floyd any more about that subject partly because the same thing happened to me quite a bit after that whenever I thought about girls and other things and mostly because Archie McKinley said it wasn't a big deal, it happened all the time.

"Fletcher, you goof, it's just like the hair you're getting on top of your pecker, or ain't you got any yet? -ha ha, I got a lot already, wanna see it? Under my armpits, too. I'm getting to be a real man, how about you, Fletcher?"

"Me too!" I said. "I know all that stuff!" I added for good measure, but I don't think Archie believed me, and I'm not going to tell him. I changed the subject.

"I bet you haven't done anything with girls!" I said, challenging him directly. I wished I didn't do that, but I did.

"I have too, and I ain't telling you about it, either!"

"Sure, sure, I just bet!"

"I have too, more than you," he said, "and I bet I seen something you ain't seen, yet. I saw Sarah and Freddie McClintock screwing in our hay loft, and I whacked off. I bet you don't even know what that means, Fetchie, but I did it while I was watching them. They did it twice that time, and I made a noise, and Freddie said he'd kill me right there and now but Sarah said don't kill him and said two bits will keep 'im quiet. So, he gave me two bits and Sarah promised Freddie I wouldn't tell anyone, not my brother, not him, the little pea brain, chicken shit, he won't tell on us, or I'll tell Pop that he stole a red Swiss army jackknife and some other stuff from the hardware store and he'll get the whipping of his life. So I said, yeah, Freddie, don't kill me, I won't tell a living soul, I won't tell anybody, not me, I promise. So, I didn't, and I didn't tell anybody else that yet, Fletcher, so you're the only one that knows."

"Nice story, I bet!" I baited Archie a bit. "Sounds like a horse-muffin story to me! *Prove it!*"

Archie scuffed his sneaker in the sand.

"Okay" he finally said. "Meet me at the back fence on Saturday, after you see the cows get out and the old man walking up to the house, about seven o'clock. We'll go in the barn, —you'll see! I dare you!" Archie offered.

That Saturday, just a few days after that, Archie came and got me at the back fence just like he said, and before I knew it I was up in the hay with Archie in the barn hiding and waiting to see Sarah and Freddie screwing. That's not what it's really called, I know that, but that's what Archie calls it all the time.

"It's not making love, Fletcher, it's always been called screwing, and that's what it is, screwing" and I said "No, it's supposed to be what you do when you are in love and grown up and got a job."

"Where did you hear that crap?" Archie asked, "It's just good old fashioned screwing just like dogs and bitches and cows and bulls, and I said "That's not what I heard."

"So figure it out for yourself, plum-head!" he whispered. The door squeaked, and Archie shushed me.

Sarah and Freddie came in just like cats, sneaking, nice and quiet, looking around for burglars or something, but we didn't even breathe, we were so quiet. They climbed the ladder.

"Watch them," Archie whispered, "watch this, how they do it," he said, and I did, and before I knew it Freddie had his clothes off and he sucked her tits. She took off all of her clothes and went on her hands and knees and to look at his pepper-shaker, but Freddie escaped from her and got behind her like a boy doggie, leaning over her and she said *"Do it, do it, why can't you do it? Push harder Freddie, can't you get it in? Do it, what's wrong, Freddie, why isn't it hard, Freddie? Freddie, c'mon, Freddie!"*

She looked back at him. His face was red. She said Freddie, you stupid boy, do it now, get it harder, you stupid boy. My dog does it better than you any day of the week, *goddam you*," and Freddie suddenly grunted and fell over and was red and sweaty, and Sarah turned over on her back and tried to do something with her fingers and said "I hate you, Freddie McClintock. You don't know how to satisfy a real woman at all, and don't ever come 'round here again. And if you can't do that, the least you could do is eat me because *that thing* is sure as hell no good, and I hate you, "again and again, and she kept pushing her fingers between her legs.

"*I hate you!*" she screamed again after a minute, and her face got red, and I looked over and saw Archie working his wiener like a water pump and I wanted to do that too, but I didn't know if I wanted to be doing that where anybody could see me. I didn't think Sarah knew much about boys or did those things, because she wore thick glasses and got the best marks in school, especially in science. And she was weird, at least that's what Archie said, but I found out right away that I was wrong. Maybe she's a slut too, but I got stopped pretty fast thinking hard about stuff like that because she heard us when Archie groaned and hooted like a rusty water-pump.

"Oh!" he groaned. His face was red like Freddie's.

We ducked down when she saw us, but it was too late, and she screamed. "Who's there!—what are you doing up there you little bastards. I'm going to kill you right now—I told you not to tell anybody, Archie McKinley, you moron! I gave you two bits too. Now I'm gonna kill you, just like I said!" and she grabbed a pitchfork and came after us, and we tried to check out of there pretty fast, or at least as fast as we could go while Archie was trying to tuck in and zip up without getting pinched by his zipper, but we had to get down the ladder. She got down the ladder on the other side first and we weren't fast enough so she trapped us good while we were still up the ladder, and she poked up at us with the long pitch-fork. We didn't waste any time climbing back up into the hayloft, but she followed us right back up there and came at us with the fork.

Archie yelled, "Don't kill us, Sarah—don't *kill* us, Sarah!" He got behind me and pushed me toward her.

"*You little bastards!*" she screamed at us. I backed up as far as I could go, but Archie got in the way behind me. I thought I was going to be dead right away but Archie saved the day by quick thinking.

"*I brought Fletcher here for you!*" he yelled.

"*Fletcher wants to do it.* He'll do it for free, too, that's why I brought him to see you, —to see if you want to try him out. He wants to have a screw and try you out, and since you hate Freddie real bad now, why don't you give him a chance before you kill us. Just give him *one* chance, and then you can kill us all if you want!"

She stopped screaming right there and lowered the pitchfork, and she didn't kill us *just yet*. She smiled at me and then glared at Freddie who was standing right across from us with his pants off and his mouth wide open. She yelled at him like an army captain. "Freddie McClintock, you get the hell out of here right now and don't you *ever* come back, you useless eunuch bastard. You're just a useless little boy, you only got a little jelly-bean pecker that's good-for-nothing anyway and you don't know how to satisfy a woman *at all*. I told you that already —and if you ever tell anyone a whisper, even a *whisper* about what we done, I mean, what we were *trying* to do," she said sarcastically and then giggled and got fierce as a mad pirate again, "I'll skewer you with this pitchfork and nail your balls to that wall over there right beside those lucky horseshoes, *understand?*"

Freddie turned white and nodded and collected his shorts and pants and moved away to dress himself quick.

I don't know why, but I felt safe now. She looked at me and smiled nice as blueberry pie. She didn't even wave the pitchfork at me again, just at Archie. "Fletcher, you get yourself over here right beside me," so I did what she said.

Archie's face was white. She pointed the pitchfork right at Archie's throat and said, "Archie, you little five-dollar cheating shithead, you get lost right now, and you give me my two bits back or I'll kill you good with this pitchfork right now!"

Then Archie bolted for the ladder, swinging his weight out into space and almost falling all the way down. Sarah stood right there with no clothes on and watched us. Freddie was pulling his pants on and did up his belt buckle and stuffed his useless jellybean behind his zipper and frantically jammed his shirt in. Then he almost fell down the ladder just like Archie had, and limped his way on out of the barn, but even if he broke his leg he clammed up and got lost without any complaints. I noticed that he closed the barn door behind him when he left which is always the polite thing to do.

Before Archie scrambled through the outside door, he smirked up at me and he said, "*You get to it, Fletcher*, you know what to do. You seen Freddie *trying to*—but now *you* gotta do it. You do it *real hard* for my sister or she'll kill you — yes, she'll kill y*ou, too,* duff head, instead of just killing Freddie!"

"Get lost, and don't you forget, you little shithead, you gotta gimme my two bits back, Archie!" she yelled after him. I don't know if Archie heard her or not because he was gone through the door like a flash.

Sarah made me get back up into the hay, and she followed me right away. She shook the old horse blanket and spread it out on the hay, smoothing it out. She got down on the blanket and turned over and showed me her tits, pulling my hands up onto them. They were soft and hot.

"You can suck on them all you want, but don't bite them, either, or I'll kill you, too," she whispered, and I looked at them and they had red marks on them from the hay or maybe from the itchy horse blanket she was laying on, and they were nice as they get, just as big as Tina's except that they had bigger bumps in the middle and they were all red. She saw what I was looking at right away and touched both of them with her fingers. "They're called *nipples* Fetchie-boy, and they're all yours, so you get to it, right now, they're waiting just for you!"

I touched one again. It was hot.

"Are you a slut like Tina McQueeny?" I asked Sarah.

"A — *what?*" She laughed out loud. "What do *you* know about that? You're not supposed to know anything about things like that just yet, Fletcher, but why did you bring up that *old* bitch?" She laughed, so I pretended not to know anything about Tina McQueeny and shrugged my shoulders. I stopped what I was doing and got up and walked around. *"Fletcher Williams,"* she warned. I sat down again.

"I feel like one sometimes, *a slut* I mean, and I guess I act like one too, like now, but I'm not really a slut, Fetchie, honey — I'm just a *nymph,* know what *that* means, Fletcher? Do you know what a *nymph* is?"

"No," I said. She laughed.

"I'm a *nymphomaniac;* that means I gotta have sex. I gotta get a man, *I gotta have it.* I'm horny for *anything* inside me, I can't get

301

enough of it when I want it, which is all the time and right now," she laughed. "No matter who it is, what shape it is, or what it is, *I want it, no matter what I have to do to get it. I have to have lots. I never get enough,* so it's a good thing you're here or I'd have to find *something* to play with, I'd have to experiment with something!" She giggled as she spoke and fiddled with the smooth handle of the pitchfork. I watched her carefully. I didn't want to get jabbed.

"You're *new,* so baby, I'll go easy on you, you'll do just fine, a handsome boy like you, don't worry. I'll teach you everything you'll *ever* need to know about satisfying a *real* woman. You're a little virgin, aren't you? But I can see I won't have to teach you much because you're sticking out like a man already, I can see that!" She licked her lips and kissed me. She tasted like raspberry drops. She ran her hands down my leg and then reached down in front of me and squeezed me hard right on the water-pump handle. I stood there and didn't move much. I tried not to look at her.

"Look at me, Fetchie, honey, since I got my clothes off already, you can take yours off too. Anyway, do you like me — *do you like what you see?*" I don't know why she asked me that because I did. *"Do you like me, Fetchie?"* she asked me again, and she breathed hard and kissed me with her tongue out and stuck it into my mouth. I never did that before.

She undid my belt buckle and laughed. "You're ready to fly, Fetch, it's flying already!" She said and giggled. "You're supposed to say *stick'em up* when you're hard like that. That's what *cowboys* do!" she panted hard and laughed out loud. "All the cowboys in Texas are horny all the time watchin' them bulls and cows," she said. "I'd like to be a cowgirl some day and go to Texas!"

"Me too," I said.

She pulled my pants right down, and she was right, it was right there. She got on her knees and looked at it. She squeezed the water-pump at the same time. "You got a good one, this is good. Good for a man *your age,* Fetchie, she panted. This is good, and you're not soft like Freddie, that useless little *boy!*"

She stopped for a minute and stood up and made me suck on her boobies. They were smoother and a lot smaller than Tina's, and I noticed again that they were both hot. We got down on the blanket and I closed my eyes, and I didn't have to think about Tina, not a bit. We wrestled and played *doggie,* and I can't help it if she pulled me down into her and I said she was slippery. And we rolled over and she got on top of me and laughed and she closed her eyes and giggled and screamed and laughed some more. Then, when we got tired we flopped on our backs and watched the swallows flying in and out of the barn.

"You won, Fetchie! You're it from now on! You come back every Saturday night—after you see the milking cows going out into the field, *got it?* That means the old man's gone up to the house for the night—make sure it's *after* the old man's gone up to the house, *that's an order,* Fetchie honey! You make me feel good. I like that, so I'll even pay you a quarter for helping out if you want, and I could give you fresh eggs for Mrs. McAllister. So you'll have an excuse to come over here, you could say it's for helping with barn chores, feeding the calves and cleaning the duff out of the calf pens and such."

I said, "Maybe, if I ever have time."

"You be here, Fetchie!" she ordered. She grabbed the pitchfork. *"You'll make* time," she said, tapping the handle of the fork on the wooden floor. "Besides, you like it! *You be here!"* I don't know why, but it was more like a warning than an invitation.

I followed her orders every Saturday, just like she said, and the old man went up to the house after the cows got out into the field. When she said it was time to follow orders I did, and got a quarter for duff-slinging, and fresh eggs for Mrs. McAllister, too.

Most Saturdays we saw Archie hiding and watching, but he was smart enough to keep quiet after, but I noticed that we always spotted him anyway. One time Sarah stood up quick and said, *"You must be desperate, you little wiener!"* because he was making fun of us and helpfully groaning behind some hay and when Sarah ordered him to stand up quick he did, and we could see that he was using his hands again.

"Archie, get lost! I'm gonna kill you! Go whack off somewhere else!" she yelled at him.

"Maybe he's a nymphomaniac too!" I said, and Sarah laughed.

"Go find Morrie and jump Freda, Archie!" Sarah called to him.

"Shut up, Sarah!" Archie got red in the face and skedaddled down the other ladder and out the door.

"Who's Freda?" I asked Sarah.

She giggled. "A *cow!* It was gross, Fetch, he and Morrie Tabler were standing on a whiskey-box behind that old cow the other night, they were pretty busy, and it was dark, but I caught them. They had a flashlight shining so they could see what they were doing, and they were taking turns and hard at it, too!" she laughed.

"What were they doing?" I asked. She looked at me like I was dumb or maybe she just swallowed a bug.

"What do you *think* they were doing, Fletch?" she looked at me and started giggling. I thought about it hard and then she didn't have to tell me. I didn't ask any more questions or say anything else because I never even *heard* of that before.

I don't know how many times that happened to Archie, I mean using a flashlight and a whiskey-box behind a cow, because he wouldn't tell me, but I went over to get fresh eggs for Mrs. McAllister quite a few times all summer. Every Saturday night, when I saw the cows heading out into the pasture. Sarah was always waiting in the hay loft, and sometimes she was laying in the evening sunlight and already had her clothes off before I even got there, because she waved at me from up there with everything showing. I climbed up that wooden ladder quite a few times. I only missed a couple of days when I was sick.

"Isn't the hay itchy?" I asked her. She laughed and pulled me down on top of her. I learned a lot about *everything* from Sarah. I guess that was all right, and I needed the quarters too and the eggs for Mrs. McAllister. Now that I think about it, I got fresh eggs home for Mrs. McAllister *a lot of times*, much to Archie's delight.

The Fires of Waterland

"I'm glad you do it, instead of *me*, Fetch," Archie told me after school, "I'm glad you do it *lots*, too. *When you do Sarah, I don't have to,*" he said, he glanced around to see if anybody was listening, but nobody was. I think Archie flipped his lid. I looked at him, and I think my mouth must have been wide open or something.

"What do you mean?" I asked.

"Duff-brain!" When you don't show up, like last Saturday, she makes me, and says *that's what friends are for*, she says, and *'I must be better than that smelly old cow don't you think?'* he mimicked Sarah's husky voice "That's what she says, she always makes me fill in when you don't show up like you're supposed to!"

"Nobody has to do anything if they don't want to, that's a fact, isn't it? And anybody that says else-wise is weak-minded and suffering from senility or something, that's what I heard!" I said, and I remembered who told me that, it was Floyd. It wasn't the same subject, but it was the same *idea*. "That's what Floyd said, and Floyd's always right!"

"I bet Floyd never had no nymphomaniac for a sister either!" Archie said. "Well *did he?*" I shrugged. I never asked Floyd about it, and Floyd never told me if he had a sister or not.

Before I said anything back to Archie, he got on his bike and wheeled around in a big circle and came back and looked at me funny, then he said "I have to jump that witch if you're not there right on time, and according to Sarah that's *every* Saturday night after the cows are put out, and the old man goes up to the house for the night! Sarah, the ugly old *nympho* witch says if I don't go along with her and get along up there to do it right on time for her, she's gonna tell the old man and Mr. Tabler about me and Morrie and what we done to the cows, and they'd send us off to reform school or just kill us quick. Probably just kill us quick, too, I bet, and I'll bet they'll act like *prune-faced goody-goods,* like as if they never done anything like that before and got themselves purified going off to church every Sunday or something like getting blessed with church-biscuits." He tried to spin his bike tires on the gravel. " — And by all the angels in the world or something!" I just looked at him.

305

We rode along and watched the cars speeding past and were almost home when Archie skidded in the dirt and stopped. I thought he had a flat tire on his bike or something but he didn't. I didn't like what he had to say. "Why don't you bring Livvy on Saturday? You can do it with Sarah, and I'll try out Livvy!" he finally said. "Tell her I'll give her a quarter if she lets me."

I said *no* right away. "*Livvy doesn't do things like that!*"

"She's not your sister, duff brain, it don't matter to you if I try her, does it, stupid?"

I got mad. "I said Livvy doesn't do that, didn't you hear what I said?" I leaned close and pushed his bike over. "You stay away from Livvy, I mean it!" I said.

He got up and brushed himself off. "Keeping her for yourself too?" he asked. "I'll get you for that! I'll tell Livvy that you've been doing Sarah!"

"She knows already, duff-head!" I lied, and hinted that if he declared war, other secrets were up for trades. Then, I threatened him. I never did that before, but that's what happens when you get mad. "Nobody's seen me on a whiskey-box, up behind any old cow!" I warned him. "I bet your old man doesn't even know what you and Morrie do with the cows!" He stopped breathing and looked at me. His face got red. "Especially *Freda*," I added. "Sarah told me she's your *favorite* cow."

Archie suddenly swallowed hard and started to look agreeable again. He looked like I got the best of him that time and clammed right up. He picked up his bike and got on it.

"You leave Livvy alone" I warned.

"You're stupid." he said, wheeling around in circles. "Sarah's no better than a stupid cow; *you* don't seem to mind her a bit, seems to me."

"I saved your life. She's a *girl* and I don't get behind real cows, so who's stupid? I don't care what else you do, just leave Livvy alone," I warned him again.

Archie shrugged. "Okay," he pedaled his bike around in circles and screeched to a halt beside me. "So maybe you should try her out yourself then you'll see, Fetch, you might even like it!" he said back at me, and smiled at me *funny*, and then pushed off down the road again.

For some reason, I didn't think that was something to smile about, so I didn't laugh. I got on my bike and raced home. For some reason I don't remember — or maybe it was just because I wanted to get even with Archie, I didn't get to McKinley's barn that Saturday, or for quite a few Saturdays after that.

Floyd didn't notice me *not* going over there, but Mrs. McAllister did as soon as she looked in the egg box. I didn't get fresh eggs, that's the mistake I made. She was whipping up a chocolate cake, and there wasn't an egg in the cooler egg box, not even one. "We're out of eggs, my goodness, Fletcher, you're getting forgetful! You haven't gone for eggs lately."

I headed out the door. "McKinley's chickens died, or maybe they got eaten by a fox or something. I think the eggs dried up — I think," I said back through the screen.

"Would you run over to the store for me then?" she called after me. I did, and I had to pay fifty cents, too, if Floyd and I were going to get any chocolate cake.

I found out that I could not tell Livvy anything about that kind of stuff, not about why there were no fresh eggs, Archie McKinley wanting to give her a quarter for a kiss and try her out in the hay mow, and *certainly not* about whiskey-box cows, or me helping Sarah along with her nymphomaniackery.

We didn't talk about anything related to that for a long time. I didn't go into Livvy's bedroom to look out the window for Tina either. At least not when Livvy was there. Instead, we waited until it was dark and sneaked out of the house, and hid in the old Pontiac in the raspberry canes, and pretended that we were married. The only trouble with that was, the windows steamed up, and I couldn't see to drive anywhere. I took my shirt off. It was hot.

"Doesn't matter, we don't have to go anyplace," I told Livvy and turned to her. I slipped my hand into her blouse and touched her breast. She moved against me and put her face close to mine.

"You shouldn't be touching them, even if I like you doing it, you *know* that. You know I like it but we can't do it, you know *that* too, *you bad boy!*" she whispered.

"I just want to touch your tits a *bit*," I said quietly and matter-of-factly, and laughed nearly like a giggle. Then, I realized that I made a mistake because I know I shouldn't say 'tits' when I'm with *Livvy*. Her eyes opened wide.

"Don't you call them tits, Fletcher Williams! They're called *breasts!"* Livvy scolded seriously. She watched me for a minute with an angry look on her face. It felt like forever, but it didn't really last long, because she finally giggled as she rubbed a tiny hole in the fog on the car window. She peered into the darkness to see nothing, then nested her heated face against my bare chest.

Tina McQueeny had tits, I thought to myself. Big ones. Only mothers have breasts. Tina McQueeny was a slut.

"I'm sorry, that's what I *said*, isn't it? I meant *breasts*," I mumbled, but suddenly I wasn't thinking about the beautiful girl sitting next to me. I was thinking about Sarah, and how I would have to patch things up and get to be friends with Archie again, if I was going to start getting fresh eggs for Mrs. McAllister every Saturday night. I even had to say *they got some new chickens* or something like that, which is lying, *I know that*.

That happened quite a few times after that, both things, I mean, me getting fresh eggs for Mrs. McAllister from Sarah, and sitting in the old Pontiac with Livvy, kissing and pretending that we were married, and being *a man of the world* and driving a yellow convertible, and going for a honeymoon to Egansville, or maybe even Regina.

There were only two things that made themselves get in the way and changed things all over the place for me. One wasn't long after I started getting eggs and other things from Sarah's again. In fact, it was the next time I got hungry waiting for the bus after school. I waited for Livvy, but she wasn't outside because her English literature class was studying *Macbeth* and they weren't finished, so I went to Camson's Drugstore for a hamburger.

When I got there, Sharon Smithson saw me and decided for once and for all to *get me.*

Thirty-Four

I knew that I had made a mistake first thing when I walked in the door. I sat at the first booth right by the window, so that Livvy could see me right away from across the street if she came looking for me. She always looked for me in the same place, and I did the same thing if I was looking for her too. Maybe it was easier to see when the bus came to the stop, too, because we didn't want to make Mrs. McAllister drive twenty miles to haul us home if we missed the bus.

I was putting a nickel in the jukebox and got *B23* playing Gene Autrey just fine on the third try, when Sharon showed up at the table to mop up the chocolate mess left by the McGraw twins and their mother that were just leaving when I came in. I held the door open for Mrs. McGraw, and she said, "Thank you, Fletcher, you're so polite," and "say hello to your mother for me now, won't you, Fletcher?" Mrs. McGraw smiled nicely as she left, hauling the two redheaded four-year-old kids out the door, one on each arm.

Sharon still had short curly dark hair that didn't seem to grow, not even an inch, since I saw her the first time. She smiled sweetly at me as she scrubbed the sticky chocolate off the red tablecloth and reached to the far side to collect all of the dishes. I tried not to see anything, but it was hard to ignore her.

"And how's my favorite customer today — I mean, how's my favorite *man* today?" she asked, blushing just a little. "You *are* my favorite man, Fletcher."

The Fires of Waterland

"I'm doing fine—I'm waiting for Livvy," I said quickly, and I tried not to notice that Sharon smelled nice when she leaned close to me, and she smelled like *Heaven*, extra nice, but I made a point of avoiding looking any more at her by flipping the jukebox selections, and tried to pretend that I didn't notice it at all.

I knew that Sharon's perfume is called *Heaven*. I know that because Livvy told me, and I smelled it right away and it smelled good to me; but it reminded me of getting eggs at McKinley's for some reason, even if I didn't *want* it to. I didn't let on, but the beautiful girl smiling at me knew right away when I sniffed right out loud.

"I think you like my perfume, Fletcher. You do *like* it, don't you?" she smiled and gazed into my eyes, still pretending to wipe the far side of the table. She stopped wiping the table and looked at me like I should know what she's talking about but I didn't, so I really didn't hear her when she said, "*I thought you might like it on me*, so I borrowed some—from *Sarah*." That didn't even register on me. *Sometimes, I feel so stupid. That explains why I liked it.* She was still in front of my face so I tried not to like it right away.

I don't like anybody telling me what I think or what I like. Neither does Floyd, so I laughed to change the subject before anybody could see what I was thinking. I think my face was red. I thought about escaping again. I thought about my brown tweed hat and made myself concentrate on wondering where it was. I smelled hamburgers frying, so I changed to that subject instead. *You should always change the subject to "c" politely if you don't want to talk about "a" or "b" that's what Floyd says.*

Sharon was still looking at me, smiling. She was polishing the shiny sugar dispenser and the salt and pepper shakers.

"*That's what Floyd says*," I blurted right out loud, right at her, and then I realized that it must have sounded stupid.

"You said *that's what Floyd says*—you *did*, Fletcher—so what *does* Floyd say?" I didn't know what to say because I was too embarrassed. My ears were starting to feel hot and she was watching me carefully. "*You must be in love*" she teased. "*I hope it's with me.*" She asked, "*Is it me?*"

"What makes you think that?" I was going to say, but didn't. I looked out the window and thought fast, but nothing happened. The doorbell tinkled, and Mr. and Mrs. Dillon walked in and plunked themselves down in the booth in front of me. Mrs. Dillon carefully piled an armload of packages from shopping onto the seat beside her.

"Mr. and Mrs. Dillon are hungry. Shopping makes you hungry," I said to her quick as a wink. "Good, healthy food, that's what we need — a hamburger," I said to Sharon. Her forehead crinkled up like she was confused.

"What makes you think that?" I asked her without thinking before I spoke. It just came out. I covered up. "Floyd says hamburgers are good for you, make you healthy," I stammered. "I was smelling the hamburgers, that's what I was smelling, and that's what I'll have, ma'am, *no onions*, can you get me one, please?"

Mrs. Dillon turned around and watched us for a minute and smiled at us.

"Oh, Sharon, could we get coffee to start please?"

Sharon nodded. "Fine, Mrs. Dillon, right away," she said to Mrs. Dillon, and "No *onions, right, and right away, sir!*" Sharon said out loud to me, grinning. I think she thought the boss was watching her because she leaned over and pretended to take another swipe at the edge of the table with the dishcloth, but she whispered to me when she saw him looking out the order window at her. No kidding, I was surprised at what she said.

"Is it me, you're in love with, is it me — isn't it, Fletcher?"

I almost fell over.

She came back to the table and arranged my hamburger neatly in front of me. She leaned over and whispered to me. *"I promised myself that I'm going to marry you someday, Fletcher Williams. I've made up my mind, and don't you forget it!"*

"Table nine!" the boss yelled from the kitchen. Plates of French fries appeared on the shelf under the lights.

"Gotta go, *my love!*" She giggled, and the bell rang again. She went to the window to run the orders of French fries and chocolate milkshakes all the way to table nine at the back. "Don't you *ever* forget that!" she reminded me again on another trip by my table. The hamburger tasted like sawdust for some reason, and I didn't want to talk to her again because she got busy. Just as well, *so busy* she didn't even give me the bill for the hamburger. I saw the bus pulling in so I had to leave the fifty cents on the table and got up to run for the bus. Then — I saw Sharon waving at me from table nine.

The girl with her back to me turned around and waved at me too. *Sarah.* I hadn't noticed her, but then I realized that Sharon was standing right beside Sarah McKinley and three other whispering, giggling, smiling girls, and they were all looking at *me*, giggling. Sarah waved at me too. Suddenly I knew why I felt like bait. *I was bait.*

I found that out for sure a few days later. I got proof of that *without a doubt* because it happened the next time I went for eggs to McKinley's on Saturday night. It was quite a while after the old man slammed the barn door and headed up to the house with the old dog. That was the usual routine, and it was strange that Archie was nowhere to be seen, pretending to be doing chores. Normally, that's what he would be doing: *pretending* to do what he really was *supposed* to be doing instead just fiddling about in the yard performing forced lookout labor for Sarah on the threat of getting pitchforked if her plans in the hay happened to get interrupted by the old man due to Archie's negligence.

I heard the screen door to McKinley's house slam, and saw the old man balancing in the screened porch, taking off his rubber boots. He disappeared into the house and I waited a minute, then I walked to the back of the barn. Archie was still nowhere in sight.

The barn door creaked as I opened it and it took a minute for my eyes to adjust to the darkness of the hay loft. I thought I heard more noise than just Sarah giggling, but decided it was the pigeons up in the rafters gurgling for corn. Sarah told me she fed them. The old man preferred to eat them after they fattened up. *Pigeon pie.* I don't know why anyone wants to eat beautiful birds.

The barn door closed itself and squeaked shut behind me just about the time I got to the bottom of the ladder, and then it was quiet.

I put my foot on the ladder and reached up for the first wooden rung. I looked up.

"Hi, Fetchie honey, I've been waiting for you." She suddenly poked her head out and looked down the ladder at me. I could see that she already had all of her clothes off. I started up the ladder. She smiled at me as if she was expecting some nice ladies with white gloves for an afternoon of Earl Gray tea and cookies or something.

"Get yourself up here, honey; I want to show you something. I've got a nice surprise for you, Fetchie, my loving man. Get up here and *close your eyes.*"

I got the rest of the way up the ladder just like she said to, and closed my eyes. She put her arms around me and spun me around while she kissed me. Then she got behind me quick and put her hands over my eyes. I heard giggling. I was dizzy, so I got stopped and she pushed me blindly around the hay pile. I leaned back because I didn't want to fall down the ladder or something like that.

"Well *girls,* which one of you is going to be *first?*" she said, giggling. She pulled her hands off of my eyes and spun me around.

"*What?*" I said, looking at her. Then, my eyes adjusted to the shadows. "*What?*" Then I didn't know what to say. I think my mouth was wide open.

They were sitting on the blanket, *all of them.* The first one I saw was Sharon. She giggled. Like Sarah, she was completely naked. The beautiful white skin glowed in the shadows. Her breasts were small and white. I looked at them and at her. She licked her lips.

"...Hello, Fletcher!" she giggled nervously. "I want to ...to try it too —I do, I *want to.* Sarah says it's fine with her, and you did it with her, so why not me too?" I stared.

Sarah giggled behind me and pushed me towards Sharon again. I almost fell over. I felt my face getting red as I stared at Sharon and tried *hard* not to look at the same time.

You can't do that. *You always look even if you don't want to.* I tried to look away.

"This man wants his hamburger *raw,*" one of the girls giggled.

314

The Fires of Waterland

"We want to try, too. Sarah says borrow you and find out for ourselves," someone said. I couldn't believe my ears. They were red hot. I didn't really know who said that.

"What do you think, Fetchie?" another voice asked. I didn't know who said that, either. *"Can we try too?"*

It was only then that I really paid any attention to the others. They were all sitting cross-legged on a blanket, completely naked, and holding beer bottles. There were three of them, besides Sharon and Sarah, sitting, innocent, giggly-eyed and smiling, just like in a booth with a red tablecloth at the restaurant. They looked up at me.

I tried hard not to—but I stared at Sarah, and Sharon, and the three others, not to be *impolite*, but because all of their clothes were neatly piled in the middle of the blanket like an altar in church. Their shoes were all lined up too, neat as a row of birch desks at school. I notice those things.

I looked again and tried not to know or remember who they are, but I did. I told you about Sharon by *accident,* but it wasn't polite so I'm not going to tell who the others were. Those girls were just like Sharon, I could see that without even trying to. They giggled like cackling nervous high school chickens and everywhere I looked I could see *everything* but I tried hard not to. I think my mouth was wide open. I knew that I had to escape right away so I scooted around the hay pile before they grabbed me for good.

"Fletcher Williams, *you get back here!"* I heard Sarah shout.

"He's mad at us now!"

"No, Sarah, *he's mad at me,"* Sharon said quietly. *She was right.*

I bolted for the ladder and almost fell to the ground, but I didn't look back up at them, not even for a peek. I heard Archie and Freddie laughing as I opened the door. *The door. I had to escape.*

"There's more tits up there than Fetchie's seen in his whole life!" Freddie yelled laughing.

"Fetchie's a chicken! Fetchie's a *chicken!"*

315

"Archie, are you in here spying on us *again?*" Sarah shouted angrily. "*I'm going to kill you!*" The girls were laughing.

"Please, *I'm sorry,* Fletcher!" Sharon called down at me. "*Please!*"

"*Don't forget your fresh eggs for Mommy!*" Archie shouted.

They laughed, but I didn't know where they were, and I didn't care because I grabbed for the dozen eggs from the shelf, but dropped them. I bolted out the door into the evening sunlight.

"*You're dead, Archie!*" I heard Sarah shriek as I ran across the field.

Thirty-Five

Floyd and Mom were sitting on the porch drinking lemonade. He looked up. "Finished duff-slinging for tonight, Fetch?" Floyd asked. He was reading. Mom was knitting.

"Did you forget the eggs Fletch, honey?"

"We got cut off last time — the chickens are too old and don't get many eggs, and they got a hired hand now, Stanley Ergmeyer. He eats 'em all for breakfast," I lied and escaped inside to get a soda-pop. A few minutes later I wandered out on the porch again to act and look as normal as possible. I wondered if Floyd noticed anything. I sat on the steps, and we watched the cars go by. I thought about the eggs.

"Some of Mr. McKinley's chickens got killed again, too," I lied a few minutes later. "Foxes," I added.

"*Oh?*" Floyd raised an eyebrow and puffed on his pipe. He looked at me strangely. "*Really?*" he said. I swatted at a mosquito.

"My, goodness, not again, I'll have to get eggs at the store then, won't I?" Mom said, looking up from her knitting.

"Foxes," Floyd said, offhandedly. He puffed.

"Must have been, Archie didn't say for sure, but it might have been." I lied again.

"Foxes, eh? Foxes love chickens. They get 'em every time, don't they, Fetch?" Floyd said, puffing on his pipe.

"Well, it could be foxes, there's quite a few foxes around here," I offered, and pretended to swat a mosquito.

"Lots of foxes around here, more than enough." He looked at me and winked. "Saw a half dozen tonight, over in McKinley's field right up behind the barn there, too, playful as you please! Maybe I should call old McKinley and warn him about that, he'll be losing his geese too." Floyd looked at me. He raised up *both* of his eyebrows at once. I never saw him do that before. I almost got soda up my nose that time. *Floyd knew.* I don't know *how* Floyd knew, but he did. Floyd always knows when there are foxes in the field. Floyd knows everything.

Even though Floyd didn't say anything about it over the next few weeks it did seem like a good idea to stay away from McKinley's so that was the second-last time I *ever* went there, especially on Saturday nights. I sat around on the back porch with Floyd and read instead. *"Reading's good for the soul. Keeps your mind active,"* Floyd said.

I got Floyd's binoculars out when he wasn't looking, and a few weeks later, it dawned on me how Floyd knew. It was easy to see Morrie, Richard, and Freddie all sneaking their way into the barn after the old man closed up shop for the night, and then there were the girls, Sarah and the others, all in turn and sometimes together. I even saw a real red fox once, but it wasn't heading in the door and up the ladder to get itchy hayseeds all over him like the others. It just had one of McKinley's chickens. The chicken was still flapping.

I said that was the second-last time I ever went to McKinley's barn, and it was. The last time I was in a hurry to get there, and it wasn't to collect eggs, either. It was to punch Archie McKinley in the nose and bring Livvy back home. I saw her walking along the fence, and she met Archie and I dropped the binoculars and got there running, just as he was showing her the ladder.

"I told you to leave Livvy alone, didn't I?" I panted right out of breath and charged him like an angry bull.

I saw the whites of his eyes and swung. I got his teeth and nose in the first bash, and it hurt my fist. My hand got cut. He told me that *nothing happened*, but only after I pounded him until he yelped like a switched dog. Standing over him, I could see that I made his nose bleed. The blood spurted all over the place like it was coming from a murdered chicken.

"*Nothing happened!*" he yelled at me, holding his nose and burbling blood through his fingers.

"*I got here just in time, didn't I?*" I shouted at Livvy, accusingly.

"*What are you talking about, Fletcher?*" she screamed back at me.

"*What were you going to do with Livvy, Archie?*" I demanded. I knew, but I made him answer anyway. Livvy stared at me.

"*Leave him alone, Fletcher Williams!*" she screamed again.

"Well?" I'm waiting!" I ordered. "*Get up!*" I threatened him.

"*What* are you talking about?" Livvy demanded.

"*It's none of your goddam business, you stupid bitch!*" Archie whimpered, pinching his nose. Then, he got up, so I wound up and punched him again in the stomach hard as I could and popped him on the top of the head once more for good measure too. He flew against the wall and sagged down again.

"*Archie McKinley, you're a nasty boy!*" Livvy shouted at him.

"*Don't call Livvy bad names, McKinley!*" I warned. "I'll give you another one, *you want another one?*" Archie shook his head. I punched him again for good measure. "*You sure about that? You going to call Livvy names any more or try to get her?*" I grabbed him by the shirt collar and lifted him up.

"What are you *doing?*" Livvy demanded. "*Stop it!*" She pushed me away from Archie.

"You get on home with me right now!" I warned Livvy. "This duff head wants to get your clothes off and try you out *like he has Sarah and some other whores up there in the hay!*" I yelled at her.

"Even his *sister?*" Livvy gasped. "*Sarah?*" she asked. "*Even his sister?*"

"*Even his own sister.* Sarah's a nymphomaniac slut too, and he thinks *you* should be just like *her* too! Him and Freddie, they're —"

"—Look who's talking!" Archie said, but not too loud. Before he knew what happened, I punched him twice for *that one*, and for the record I was quite happy a couple days later to see that it had blackened both of his eyes good. He looked like a raccoon. He told the teacher he fell off of the hay wagon onto an old wood pop box. Morrie and Freddie laughed right out loud that time. Out in the yard after that I heard Freddie tell Morrie that it was more likely Archie got kicked off of the pop box by the old cow. I told Freddie to shut up unless he wanted to be a raccoon too.

"He was just showing me the rabbits; that's *all* we were doing. We were getting straw for them, *that's* what we were doing!"

"Ain't no damned rabbits up there in the hay loft!" I pointed that out to her and threatened Archie again. *"Ain't no straw up there, either, is there, Archie, you sonofabitch?"*

"Straw's outside in the shed, Livvy," I told her. I ought to know because I got some for the horses every week. Archie got red in the face and looked down at the ground and pinched his bleeding nose some more.

"He told me that he wanted to get you in the hay and *try you out,* —*like he made me get Sarah like that,* and nearly got us pitchforked to death. She was getting stupid Freddie up there with no clothes on, and we were watching, and Freddie couldn't *do it,* and stupid Archie hooted so loud she saw us, and got us against the wall with a pitchfork! *It's the truth."* I said. She shook her head. "She *made me get her, and I got eggs and a quarter for duff-slinging, too."* I scuffed the straw with my foot and then looked at Livvy again. She did not blink. "And that's the *truth,* Livvy."

"Liar!" she said, but she said it to *Archie* for some reason.

"Fetchie's been getting eggs for more than a few weeks, hasn't he, Livvy? What do you *think* he's been doing over here all this time?" Archie said. He made a face at me. *"Shoveling shit?"* he leered at Livvy and then laughed.

Livvy gasped. "Archie McKinley, you dirty boy!" She slapped him and turned to me. She stared, and then slapped *me* too. That was the *only time in my whole life that Livvy slapped me.*

"*Shame on you two! You're a dirty boy too,*" she whispered fiercely, putting her face close to mine. Her breath was hot. "*How could you — do that? You know better!*" She stormed out of the barn. She crashed her way back in like a mad cow and slammed the door shut.

"And *you* know I don't do that anything like that either. You know I wouldn't do that, you should know better than that, Fletcher Carnival Williams! *I promised you, didn't I?* I thought about it, but I told you, remember? We talked about it. *I promised* you that I would never do that!"

Archie took advantage of the disruption and stood up, so I gave him another push against the wall, but I didn't hit him that time. I got his throat up against the wall with my elbow instead, and pushed it hard and shoved my other fist up against his nose and twisted it hard. He yelped, and I got more blood on my hand.

"*Punk sonofabitch!*" I whispered at him. "Go wash your dirty face in the pig trough, *cow-man!*" I ordered him.

He started to move away carefully and slowly, like he was in pain and scared to death, or like he was crotchety, like an old man getting out of my reach. I turned back to Livvy.

"And don't you ever come here again!" I took her hand and opened the creaky door for her instead of hitting Archie some more, even if I wanted to hit him a lot more than I already did. Livvy shook my hand off of hers.

"*You too!* We better get home, *Fletcher Carnival Williams!*" she ordered. "And *don't* think I'm not mad at you." We walked out into the sunlight.

I know I should have trusted Livvy. I knew that when she said *going to see the rabbits* was Archie's idea, so I guess I don't trust him anymore. I helped Livvy through the fence by holding the wire apart while she got through it. She looked up at me and smiled. I nodded. I know she likes me again. We started walking home, and after a minute everything was all right, because she took my hand. She stopped and looked at it. It had blood all over the knuckles. We stopped at the creek and washed it off, then walked around the field through the tall wildflowers, and sat on a big, warm, flat rock in a rock pile under a birch tree, and talked mostly about other things.

Then she said, "I'm sorry, Fletcher." I looked at her and got up and picked her a daisy. She studied the flower.

"No, *I'm* sorry. I should have trusted you, so I'm sorry too." She pecked me on the cheek.

"I know," she said, and then she touched my face and smiled. I knew it was fine, and we walked in the tall grass until it was too dark to see anything interesting.

She picked up my hand and looked at it. It was still bleeding, but just a bit. "I'm sorry, Fletcher," she sighed. "It was my fault."

"There's nothing to be sorry about, Livvy," I said. We got up and walked home.

That was the last time I ever went to McKinley's barn for eggs or anything else.

I didn't go back to Camson's Drugstore for hamburgers and French fries for quite a long time either. I told Floyd that I wasn't hungry and didn't like the smell of cooking hamburgers. It makes me think of duff-slinging and cows and fighting with Archie, and I couldn't tell Floyd about the whiskey crate and Morrie. I was going to, because Floyd and I talk about everything, but I changed my mind and told him that I had a lot of school work; and if he wanted me to do extra yard work and oil the wheels of his chair today, he better not make me go to Camson's.

I know that wasn't exactly honest and God doesn't like that either, but I did not want to see Sharon, or Sarah, or any of the others that I saw getting itchy in the hay. I didn't like to talk about Archie and Freddie, and I hid Floyd's binoculars so he couldn't watch them. It was the end of summer and something changed. Things were *different*.

"Seen those old binoculars, Fletcher?" he asked. He squinted at me and struck a match. I shrugged and pretended that I didn't know. "I like to watch the foxes over in the field; can't do that without *binoculars,*" he puffed. The wheel on his chair squealed as he turned. I went for the oil can.

Even Livvy noticed that things were different. It must have been because I didn't go to her room very much; not to see Tina and Jack out the window, or even to talk, after Mom and Floyd got themselves to bed.

We didn't even sneak out to sit in the old Pontiac. Once I even told Livvy that I have to think a lot. Maybe it is because going to Livvy's room and driving all over the world in the old Pontiac with the mouse nest in the back seat doesn't *let* me think, *it makes me.*

There is a difference, isn't there, and I don't want to. Not right now.

Thirty-Six

"Hello, boy" the voice said from behind me, and I didn't know who said that. I jumped a bit. "Who said that?" I said, right out loud, too, but there *was* no one behind me.

I was kneeling on the ground, leveling the dirt and talking to my mother at the graveyard. She wasn't whispering back to me like she did before. Maybe she was busy with God, or maybe she was over talking to William Yakafluic. His spear-headed fence was rusty. *That's it,* maybe he was complaining to her about his rusty fence, and she was complaining to him that the mound of dirt over her was settled into a hole about six inches deep and got a big water puddle in it when it rained hard. That's why I was there, to fill in the hole.

Floyd told me he thought it might be a fine project since there wasn't any more duff-slinging to do over at McKinley's barn since they got a hired hand that ate all of the eggs, so that's what I did. I came to check it out and see where to get dirt from, and then I was going to go home and bring Floyd's red wheelbarrow and a shovel, but it didn't work out that way.

I already got a shovel. It was borrowed, and I was getting sandy red dirt from the pile by the fence. First thing in the morning, Mr. Johnson was there with his red pickup truck, and he said I could have as much sand as I needed to fill in the hole after telling me that's what the pile of dirt by the fence was used for.

"That dirt there, boy, it's hauled there just for that purpose, boy, to fill in the settled beds of the *sleepers*. The graves, they always sink, you know? So we gotta do what's right; people don't like seeing puddles of water on top of them. Folks come, and want them filled in, and make flower beds for 'em an' such if folks want to do that, make things decent and respectful. So you can help yourself, but you need a shovel. See what we can do, then you fill 'er right up, boy. Your Momma would be real proud of you, wanting to take care of her like that," he said.

He called over to a black man that was working like a slave.

"*Jay Tee!*" he shouted. The man didn't look up.

"You go over and say hello to Jake. He's a good hardworking man, might be able to give you some pointers on doing a proper job. Most of the time *he* does that job, but he won't mind a little help I'm sure. *Jay Tee!*" Mr. Johnson yelled. He winked at me. "Maybe he even got a shovel you can borrow; you go see him."

I did. I walked right over there, and he wasn't paying any attention to me at all because he was painting so carefully. He finally noticed me and squinted up at me. He stood up and wiped his face. He wiped his hands off quickly and jammed the red cloth in the back pocket of his striped engineer's pants. He shook my hand.

"Hello, boy," he said in a soft voice. "I'm Jake, Jake Burnsides, but you can call me Jake, or *boy* even though I ain't a slave. My great-granddaddy was a slave, but not me. I just get working like one, and you can call me Jake, or you call me *Jay Tee* if you like," he said quietly. "My friends call me Jay Tee, so you—maybe you better, too." His eyes were black as coal and bright as night. He smiled and squeezed my hand softly, but his hands were as hard and calloused as black rocks covered with speckles of white paint.

"I'm Fletcher Williams," I said to him. "My mother is Angelina Williams. She got buried over there." I pointed.

"I know, boy. I know who you are and I know about your poor momma gettin' herself killed by the train, and I know your pop too. I knowed 'em for a long time, years back in Morgan County— long 'fore they even moved to Waterland. Ain't that a coincidence, us meeting here like that? " He squinted into the sun. "Nice day ain't it?"

"I guess so" I said and shrugged.

"You know, boy, that's a big job you're taking on, keeping your momma up and all."

"Sleepers don't know the difference," I said to Jake. I felt proud to show that I knew what dead people were called. I looked up at Jake and stood up straight as an arrow.

"Don't be so sure about that, now, boy. Don't you ever think that. I think your momma knows you're here; she knows what you do; she knows what you think; and so does God up there, boy. So don't forget it, hear? And your momma's been walking with God up there, but she's never been a sleeper, boy, not from what I hear." He adjusted the sweat-stained hat on his head. He had some white hair over his ears, but he was pretty bald, like Murvie Klinder that died of cancer. I wondered to myself if Jake had cancer of the balls too because he was sweating a lot just like Murvie did.

"I guess so," I said. I shrugged. "Okay."

Mr. Johnson called over to us. "Jay Tee, you let the boy have all the dirt he needs from the pile. He's a workin' man like you, and he 'tends to level in Angelina Williams' grave. He's gonna build 'er up a little, so the water don't puddle no more over his pretty momma."

The black man smiled wisely at me. "Good boy," he said to me softly, "and you plant some pretty Suzies or some violets over her, too. Pansies is nice too, and don't be forgetting what I said, now," he said. *"Your momma was real special. I knew her a long time before she married your daddy."*

I didn't want to talk about my father.

"Okay," I said.

"I got seeds," I said. *"Suzies."*

"Good boy," he said and looked over at Mr. Johnson. He smiled broadly; his white teeth looked like snow, but his tongue was pink. "My wife's favorite too. My Emma's right over there, been here for fifteen years now." He pointed to a small, old stone cross in the corner of the cemetery by the fence on the far side. He shook his head sadly. "I miss her, boy, but she's up there talkin' to God. *Sometimes I*

326

can hear her. I don't know what they're talking about, but she's there."
He shook his head again and wiped his eyes.

"She was a lot like your momma in some ways, she liked pansies
and sunflowers too, and apple trees and animals and little babies,
most 'specially them tiniest ones got themselves away and born too
soon. She was a nurse, you know? We never got none of our own.
Too bad, she loved kids so much. She even worked over at the boy's
home 'til she got sick. We even 'dopted one of them fine boys, too, he's
all growed up now. It was a long time before that, but I heard it got
burned down. Sad thing, it was, *those boys, and the cook, too,* all killed
like *that.*"

He sort of stopped talking for a minute and rubbed his face hard.
He shook his head.

I didn't get to tell him I lived there, but I suddenly remembered
Mrs. Tickner and Murvie Klinder that died of cancer, and Joe and T.T.
Oinker the pig, and Dickie and Elton and everybody else. I even
remembered Jack that lives next door, and old Tupper and his shiny
tooth; Tupper the old pervert that did things to Jack and me, the dirty
bastard; but then I had to stop thinking right away. I saw Jake looking
at me.

"Boy?"

Jake turned away and answered Mr. Johnson back.

"Hey, Mr. Johnson, sir, this fine boy don't have no shovel. Will he
have to bring one from home, or could...?" Jake mopped his face with
a polka-dot red handkerchief and whispered to me. "Just a minute, I
ain't usin' it. I'm painting, not digging, so you can use mine." He
called back to Mr. Johnson.   "Never mind he ain't got no shovel. You
and me's gonna borrow him my own shovel outta' the truck. He can
leave it under the tree when he's all finished."

Mr. Johnson called back, "Yeah, sure, Jake, suit yourself, that's
real good. We'll pick it up at coffee, 'round three o'clock, just so you
get it back. You don't want to lose it, *your* boy giving it to you for
your birthday, now do you?"

The black man smiled at me again. "You get over there up on the back of that Chevy. There's a real nice, special red-handled shovel sitting there, sharp as a razor. It's got a red handle because it's mine, Mr. Johnson's remembered it right, my boy give it to me special for my birthday, a couple years ago, it's kind of special to me, and I got my initials right there plain as dirt on it, and I painted it the color I like the best, *red*, so you go get it and help yourself to that dirt. And build it up about three, four inches above the grass, that'll be just about right by the time it settles again, and smooth it out real good before you plant any flowers in it, understand? And just remember to leave it under the tree, the shovel—you leave that shovel under the tree against the fence for me when you're all finished, you hear?"

I nodded at him, and he smiled.

"Get to it, you do a nice job, then," he said softly. His teeth were white as the paint he put on the fence, but his tongue was pink like mine. I noticed that right away. I got the shovel and got right to it, and he went back to whistling and painting all around the steel fence. The fence looked like snow white swords and spears standing at attention with the sharp blades up. I liked it better after the black man painted it. After a bit, the men climbed in the truck and drove off in a cloud of dust. Jake waved at me.

I waved back, too; then I was all alone working like a slave by myself. Just like Jake. I like Jake and his red shovel, and I like working like a slave and making my mother feel better and knowing she's not a sleeper. I wonder if William Yakafluic is a sleeper.

I wasn't spilling very much dirt. It was taking a lot of trips back and forth carrying and spreading it carefully to fill in the hole. I dug out the package of flower seeds and admired the picture while I took a rest. *Black-eyed Suzies.* Floyd said it wouldn't hurt a bit to plant some flowers over top of her. *Make sure they're her favorites, and pull all the weeds out, too.*

That's what I was doing when I heard him. I was nearly finished. I just wanted to get finished and stand the shovel under the tree and plant the black-eyed Susan seeds and get it over with. It was hot and the crickets were singing themselves silly. I was tired and wanted to quit, but Floyd said I better get to it and finish anything I started. So I did.

"Up here, boy, *look up here,*" the voice said, and I finally saw who it was. He was up in the tree, watching what I was doing, and sitting over the shiny white steel swords on the fence. It wasn't God. It was my father, and he had black pants on and a red shirt and a brown cowboy leather vest and a dusty brown hat, a derby hat like Jack's. That wasn't a real cowboy hat. He had real cowboy boots on, though, exactly like the big boot on the roof of Shoemaker's factory.

"You know I been watching you, boy," he said like he was asking me a question or something. "You should look up at the trees and the sky more often, Fetchie boy. You never looked up here, not even once. You never looked up here *once*; hell, boy, you never even seen me walking up to the fence and climbing up on this here big branch, now did you boy?"

I kept quiet for a minute. Floyd always says it is better to think first and talk after. I didn't know what to say anyway. I looked around to see if Jake and Mr. Johnson were coming back yet to save me.

"No," I said after I thought about it because I did not know what else to say, and Jake and Mr. Johnson and the pickup truck were nowhere in sight. I was on my own.

"Well, Fletcher Williams!" he said. "Answer me boy, *cat gotcha tongue?*"How you doing Fetchie-boy? Ain't seen me for some time have you?" he said matter-of-factly like it was news of the world or something. "*That* what you thinkin' boy?"

"No," I said. I didn't know what to say. I was a bit scared and feeling like bait again.

He indicated my mother's grave, pointing at it with his finger. His finger had a gold ring on it. "You're doing a real nice job, boy, nice job. Your momma would have liked that, you caring for her... and all —and you don't have to worry none, boy. I ain't here to whip you, Fetchie-boy, you can talk to me." His voice was scratchy.

I looked at him. "I know, but..." I finally said. I fiddled with the shovel. It had initials "J.T." carved into the handle. I studied it and fingered the carved initials for a bit, so that I wouldn't have to look at him. I thought about escaping but decided it was safe to talk because he was up the tree. I looked right at him like I was the boss.

"What are you doing there?" I finally asked. I kept concentrating hard and hauling dirt back and forth with the red shovel, back and forth, and more dirt, and leveled it out and went back and forth, back and forth. He never came around once when I was at Floyd's, and he doesn't have to know what I am doing and I don't really have to look into the sky all the time and at every tree in the world just because he says I should. That's what Floyd would say, I know that.

"I come to see your mother, boy, and I been watching you, too...I know you come here every week to see your momma. I even know you missed two weeks ago when we got the rainstorm. That's what filled up the hole with water. That's why you decided to fill in the hole, ain't it, now?"

I stopped for a minute and stood the shovel up on the ground and put my foot on it, ready to dig a hole. "I guess so," I said. "It was like a *mud hole*, can't leave it like that, can I? *You* don't care about it. You weren't here to see it and fix it up." I think that sounded mad, and I knew I shouldn't have said that because he jumped down off of the branch and landed on the ground with a thud. He was breathing hard and started toward me. I backed up. He stopped and held his hands up like I was robbing him or something.

"It's okay Fletcher, I ain't going to whip you or nothin' like that, I just want to talk. —It's time we talked, there's things I want you to know, that's all." He pointed to the big tree. "Let's just sit down and talk a bit. I got a lot of things to say that you should know about now. You growing up an' all, you're old enough to know things, things I couldn't tell you when I was on the bottle. Hell, I was right in the bottle most of the time, I never had no control over what I was doing. It was like I was right in the bottle all the time, boy; you gotta understand now how evil whiskey can be to a man. It can do him right in, boy. Don't you ever touch the stuff, Fletcher."

That made me think of whiskey boxes; full, new ones and empty old ones, and empty new ones, and dirty upside-down ones, and Archie and Murray standing on one behind Freda in the dark barn with a flashlight; and I didn't want to think about that just now so I got myself over there to get the biggest shovelful of the red, sandy dirt I could lift. I grunted. "I don't drink any whiskey," I said. "I ain't *never going* to drink whiskey. *Not like you!*" I got another shovelful of dirt.

"This shovel belongs to Jake, he worked like a slave painting the fence this morning, he painted it red, that's his favorite color," I informed my father. "He worked hard all his life, *not like you!*" I plopped the big shovel of dirt into the hole and stopped. I stood there like a soldier. I didn't move, not a bit.

"He's letting me use it, and I have to finish so I can leave the shovel right where I promised. So you stay over there, you sit down, and I'll finish what I started. Floyd says I should always finish what I start," I said harshly, sounding just like a boss would talk to a stupid employee that spilled a pail of paint on new concrete or maybe like a man of the world with a yellow convertible would talk to his pet dog if it puked all over the leather upholstery. My father looked at me, almost surprised.

He did what I said. I was surprised. He plunked himself down too hard on the ground under the tree. He looked away shaking his head and took off his hat and smacked the dust off of it, parking it on his knee. He had a bald spot and a shiny belt buckle. I wondered if he had cancer of the balls, too. He was sweating and had a hollow, pained look on his face and lines deeply etched into his forehead.

"Floyd McAllister's a good man," he said quietly. "He took good care of you, boy, better than I ever did. He turned you out real good, I mean him and his Mrs. McAllister, and she's a good woman, too. Not like your mother —but a good, solid woman in her own way, and I think they done good. They done good for you and the girl." I got angry and turned my face away from him; and when I looked again, he was watching me. He shook his head. "I wished I done better for you, boy. I can't take it back; *I can't undo it,* what I done to you, can I, boy?" He raised up his hands like a preacher.

331

"What's the matter, Fetchie-boy, *cat got your tongue*, or you just don't want to talk to me?"

I looked down at the ground for a bit and wished he would go away, but that was wishful dreaming because when I looked back he was still there. He played with his hat, spinning it around on his knee for a bit, then stopped and looked at me some more.

He looked at me for a long time and didn't say anything and neither did I, so he must have gotten tired of waiting. He leaned back and closed his eyes, and then finally pulled out a poke-a-dot handkerchief and mopped off his face. He stuffed it back into his shirt pocket. He closed his eyes, then I saw him opening one and looking at me sideways with it. I don't want him looking at me sideways because that's the way he used to look at me when he was whiskey-drinking and laying on the Chesterfield and ordering more whiskey, *you get that new bottle right away if you know what's good for you, you little bastard.* And I did and he watched me, squinting and looking sideways at me and I don't like that.

> *You get that bottle for me, Fetchie-boy, right now like I told you before I get mad and whip your ass good. Got my belt right here, I ain't kiddin', boy, now, right now, hear me? 'fore I take the belt to you and settle you for once and all. You'll find out who's the boss around here, you little bastard...*

He looked at me more like that; *sideways*, I mean, and still not saying anything, so I started getting back and forth again, back and forth, hauling dirt hard as I could, so I wouldn't have to look at him. The crickets were singing in the heat, and then I noticed he went to sleep with both eyes shut quick as a wink, before he said anything else. I didn't wake him up when I was almost finished and ready to go home, and I was *glad* he didn't wake up.

I examined him for a minute, and he looked sweaty and old and mean, and I was glad again that he didn't open up his mean eyes and talk to me. I finished dirt-leveling and smoothing over my mother nice and smooth. Then I scraped around the edges and cut them nice and straight and made sure I did a good job like Floyd said to. I stood up and stood the shovel up against the fence for Jake just like we agreed.

I closed the gate and forgot to plant the flower seeds, but I saw the deep lines and hollow, sick look on my father's sweating face when I passed him. Then I noticed that his eyes had circles around them like grey-black river mud. I didn't want to look at them. I went home and washed the dirt off of my hands and went to bed without any supper.

"That boy sick?" I heard Floyd ask mom.

"Just tired, I imagine, hauling dirt all afternoon and fixing up that grave site. It was all sunk in from the rain." Then, it thundered outside, and I couldn't hear anything else because I went to sleep.

His eyes looked sideways at me and his mouth was trying to say things, but he didn't move. Then he was lying on his back and his mouth was wide open, and Livvy had to wake me up and stay with me because I screamed in the night. After a while she went back to her own room I went back to sleep with my eyes wide open and saw his sick, sweating face and skinny arms sticking out like a sinner's cross in the garden of white spears pointing up to God. I looked at every one of them. They were all white, even the ones that came through his body, except the one that came up through his heart. It was red.

I woke up screaming. Mom turned the light on. "Go back to sleep, Fletcher, you just had a nightmare...are you all right, son?" My heart stopped pounding, and I nodded and turned over. I heard her close the door. I listened to the rain on the tin roof all night.

Thirty-Seven

I was scared to go back to the cemetery to plant the extra flower seeds over my mother, but Floyd said it's always a better thing to confront your fears, and he bet me a hundred bucks it was just a dream anyhow.

"It was a dream, boy, that's all it was, a dream. Sometimes people harbor bad feelings about other people, or things, and they just want to kill 'em good and choke them to death, or love them or ride them all the way to Regina—*on a rail* or something. Or maybe something completely different; every dream is different, and the imagination can be good or a terrible thing sometimes." He nodded at me. "Don't read too much into it, boy. Some people do, and it makes them get even crazier than they were before they went to sleep the first time."

I didn't argue with Floyd. We were too busy making pancakes and eggs. I thought he didn't know about it but he did, and he told me how he knew. He said I screamed louder than bad brakes on a dusty cement truck, and I thought I only woke up Mrs. McAllister. But maybe I woke up the rest of the neighborhood, too.

"I knew he was going to show up again, sooner or later, and maybe cause you a lot of upset, Fletcher," Mrs. McAllister said as she whipped the pancake batter in the bowl to a froth… "maybe for some other people, too," she added. She rattled the fry pan.

"You kept Livvy awake all night and scared her half to death carrying on with that foolishness about him, your nightmares, and

334

that's just a start, isn't it? Soon your father will be wanting to move back next door here. Where are Jack and Tina going to go? They're not being paid much to run the boy's home now. He should have stayed away from here, and get back out west where he belongs. He doesn't belong here anymore. He hasn't earned the *right*, has he?" she said to me and Floyd at the same time. "I just wish he would get lost, he scares me!"

"Woman, I heard he was back a few weeks ago. If he was here to cause trouble, he would have done it already, wouldn't he?" The pancake batter hit the pan hard and sizzled blue smoke. "Besides, I heard the social services agent transferred the house to Jack and Tina. It belongs to the services department anyway, remember? Angelina and Fletcher here had it, but it was a low-cost, war-time housing county project when it first started. Remember, quick cracker-boxes for the boys coming home?" Floyd looked at me and winked.

"The S. S. Department got them for taxes when nobody wanted them, built too cheap. That's about all. I hear the property wasn't redeemable, the loans weren't paid; that's what happens." He looked at me again but not sideways like my father. "Same as a tax sale," he said.

"Eggs, Fletcher, pass those eggs. I see we're low on eggs again." He winked at me. Floyd always winks when we're low on eggs. We get to pile in the truck and go get some. *It's always fun getting eggs.*

"Don't take no bad meaning at all to what we're talking about here, Fletch," Floyd said, watching the eggs sizzle, "It's time you knew the truth, so you listen good and understand what I'm going to tell you.

"Your momma was a good hardworking woman, and she did good work and paid rent, too. And volunteered at the county hospital too, and she did a lot of dirty work, even emptied bedpans to make up the difference. She was no welfare case, don't you ever think that. She got that so-called *welfare* house because there was nobody in a lineup for it just then —and they didn't want vagrants moving into them, being brand new and all, so they let her and your father have it for fifty a month. That was quite a bit of money even at that, so it was fair enough then, wasn't it, woman?" Mrs. McAllister nodded. She loaded up the plates and put them on the table.

Floyd kept explaining as we ate. Floyd is good at explaining everything. That's why I like living with Floyd and getting eggs, too.

"I have to admit that couldn't happen now because times are getting tough, those projects were built special for so many soldiers coming back with nothing. There were families that were poor and needed a place to live real bad. No matter what, you got nothing to be ashamed about, don't you *ever* be ashamed of your mother, boy. No matter what anyone tells you, you're bound to hear some *nosy-nimble* say something bad, sometime; if *only* because you lived in that house, — and the boy's home, and the publicity from the trial, and so forth." Floyd tasted his coffee.

"You know what I mean, Fletcher? It means *nothing*. People have to talk about somebody, and when you make a difference in the world, people talk about you. I say, if you're going to make a difference in the world, you might as well stand up and make a *real* difference. Attract a little attention to the fact that you care about things, because not too many people are willing to do that. *Do what's right*. Right, Mrs. McAllister, you *wonderful* woman?" he said to Mrs. McAllister, and to me, he said "She's a good cook too, isn't she!" I nodded.

"You're a big tease, Floyd!" Mrs. McAllister poured more coffee and sat down again. "You have nothing to be ashamed of, Fletcher dear, your mother was a good woman; she was a good laundress, the best; a hardworking, solid woman. She earned her way for herself and for you the best way she knew how — and *with no help from your father* most of the time. She was honest, and clean, and she never said a mean word to a soul, so you can be *very* proud of her," Mrs. McAllister added to what Floyd said. "*Understand, Fletcher?*"

I nodded and jabbed at another pancake. Mrs. McAllister knows how to make the best pancakes, too, not just beef stew and biscuits. I made rows across the pancakes for the syrup to cross in.

"Don't play with your food, Fletcher," Mrs. McAllister said. I ate and decided to plant the flower seeds for my mother right after school. Mrs. McAllister bustled around and gave Floyd another batch of pancakes, too. "I certainly hope you're right this time, Floyd," she said and looked at Floyd and not at me.

"Hmmm... good," Floyd said, and winked at me. "Of course I'm right, *darlin'*, these are the best pancakes in the world, right Fletch?"

"Not the pancakes, Floyd, I mean about Fletcher's father showing up and him having first title to the house."

"He never had title to anything. Don't worry about Jack and Tina," Floyd said to her. "The agency isn't going to kick them out on the street with them running the home, now, are they?"

"That's not what I *meant*," she said. She looked at Floyd and I tried not to interfere with their silent talking and looked out the window at McKinley's field. I didn't see any foxes.

The shovel was gone, and the painting was finished when I got there after school. I checked in my pocket to get the seeds ready to plant and counted them. I had thirty-one. That's how old my mother was. *Thirty-one.*

"Hello, boy," My father said. "*Hello, boy!*" he said again to me. He was sitting on the big branch again, right over the spear-fence. I knew where he was right away that time. I pretended to look around again for the shovel, but I knew that Jake came back, because the shovel was gone, and the fence was finished, and all of the grass was cut, too. Jake must have finished up and right on time, too, like he said he would. The fence of spears was white.

I looked up at him. I felt myself getting strangely cold, and the hair on the back of my neck curled.

"Better not fall off of there," I said.

"I've sat up here a hundred times, boy, I ain't fallen off yet," he said seriously, as if he was making an excuse. "I ain't never fallen off of nothin' except the wagon. I fell off of the wagon *a lot*," he said, and laughed. "But you'd know all 'bout that, now wouldn't you, boy? With me you seen it all, no secrets, right Fetch?" His face was still skinny and sweating and pale and sick, like my mother's hands when

337

she did too much laundry washing by hand in the soapy water, and her hands got wrinkled and old and white. I didn't answer that time.

"Regardless, boy, you an' me, we gotta have a talk, I don't want you angry with me your whole life. Don't do a man no good to carry a grudge, does it?"

"I came to plant the black-eyed Suzie seeds; that's *all.*" *I don't really want to talk to you, not a bit*, I said to myself. "I forgot about them last time," I told him, "I was tired," I said. I lied. He shook his head.

"You should of woke me, boy, that was a lot of dirt for a boy to move by hisself. I would've helped you. Anyway ... no matter," he said pleasantly. "You did a nice job, boy. Angelina would be proud of you. I been waiting to see you again. I been here every day this week, waiting for you." He spoke quietly. "I brought you these," he fished in his pocket for something and dropped them to me. "Catch 'em now."

He held up three tiny packages. "Violets, mixed colors, and pansies, she liked them too, remember? In Morgan County, the apple tree, the one you fell out of when you broke the branch and busted your arm, too. Maybe you don't remember that, do you, Fetchie, breakin' your arm? Anyway, those were the flowers around that tree —with the tiny flower garden around the trunk by the porch. The flowers you used 'ta pick for your momma right by the porch, that's what those are for, those seeds. They are violets and pansies. She liked them a lot. I remember the violets were her favorites, she used to eat 'em sometimes." He tossed them down.

"Thanks," I said, and almost caught them. I picked them up and looked at them, studied the pictures for a long time. I looked up at him.

You didn't know her at all, did you, not a damned bit, black-eyed Suzies were her favorite flowers, even I know that I said it to myself. I wanted to say it right out loud, but he knew. He already knew what I was thinking.

"*They* used to be her favorite one time or another," he said.

"Not anymore," I said half out loud.

338

The Fires of Waterland

"It doesn't matter, Fletcher dear, it doesn't matter anymore." I heard my mother whisper. I shook my head.

"It *does* matter, I know she ..." I said out loud. My father was watching me.

"I didn't know her very well at the last, Fetch. I was away most of the time, you gotta understand that. A lot of things changed. Some of them good, some of them not so good, but one thing I know, she always liked all flowers pretty much all the time, no matter what I said and no matter what I did back then. So it doesn't really matter now!" He stopped talking and looked up into the clouds, and the clouds were moving fast. He got off balance and grabbed a branch. A gust of wind caught him off guard again.

"Whoa! This here's something like riding a horse....that's the bottom line ain't it Fletcher, *she liked flowers, that's it!*" He reached over his head and grabbed a branch, steadying himself on the big branch.

"I have to plant the flowers and get back, Floyd's expecting me," I said quietly. He was right. *Whenever you're off balance it's like riding a horse. Life's like that, like riding a horse,* that's what Floyd said. *"Sometimes, it's good, and sometimes it's rough, but you better hang on, Fletcher.*

"Maybe we could plant them *together*," he said. "She'd like that a lot, too."

I looked away from him because I did not want him to see that I didn't know what to say. I stared up at the clouds for a long time until I heard my mother whispering.

"Everything will be all right, Fletcher, dear, he's coming to me now..."

The wind whistled in my ears, and I spun around just as I heard the crack of the weak branch he had grabbed. He fell backwards, his arms flailing like windmills. *"Aaaah!"* he shouted.

I froze.

It was slow motion, and it took forever, and...I saw every bit of it. His feet came down last, and his head jerked hard and his arms stretched out hard when he landed on the white spears of the fence, and they came through him like in the movies. His arms shook, and the legs with the shiny cowboy boots on were jerking and kicking, and he spit blood out with every breath that got faster and faster and gurgled until he choked himself quiet. I knew it wasn't a dream, and his eyes with black circles like river mud were looking at me, wide open, and the spears were in his back and stomach above the shiny buckle and through the side of his throat, and the one through his chest glistened red in the sun. *I could not move.*

His eyes were wide open and stared at me, and his mouth made words; but no sound came out, just red bubbles, begging me to forgive him. *A man's gotta be sorry for what he done wrong... and a man's gotta be sorry for what he did, especially if it's wrong, see? You learn that, boy. If it's the last thing I do, I gotta make you see that I was wrong, and I gotta make you see that I know I was wrong, boy...* His arms suddenly trembled violently and stiffened out straight, straight out like a sinner's cross...

"Fletcher... *I was wrong, boy....*" he gasped, and his throat rattled strangely. His head jerked up and down, his eyes and mouth were wide open, and then he stopped trying to move and stared at me, and I knew he was *right*, every bit, and, I knew he was dying. He was shaking, and I saw my mother coming to get him.

"*Father!*" I screamed, choking. "*Father!*"

"*Shshsh ... Fletcher, it's all right now...*" my mother whispered from up above me in the clouds, and I looked up to see her, but she wasn't there anymore in the white clover with the wet spot on her apron.

He gasped, then he was still. I got myself closer and looked at the spears and found myself reaching out to touch the red one. I got my hands under him and tried to lift him off of the spears but could not. There was blood on my arms and hands and my fingers, and I rubbed my hands together and tried to wipe it off.

It was warm and sticky. I don't know why I said it.

"She likes black-eyed Suzies the best," I told him. His eyes were wide open looking at me. "*She likes black-eyed Suzies the best!*" I screamed at him. "*I hate you for hurting her!*"

340

The Fires of Waterland

The wind howled like death through the big tree.

I turned away from him and kneeled down on my mother's grave. I planted flower seeds. I didn't look at the fence or the cowboy boots or the motionless arms that made a sinner's cross in the sky or the blood that dripped down onto the green grass.

I planted thirty-one seeds. I didn't plant his. I finished my work, smoothing the dirt carefully. I stood up and turned to go.

Suddenly, my legs got weak, and I fell on my knees. After a minute I got up and ran. My eyes were full of tears, and I couldn't see where I was going, but I ran anyway. Then suddenly I stopped, halfway home, and looked at the drying blood on my hands.

I got behind a tree and retched until there was nothing left but sickness in my stomach, and in my heart, too. I got myself home and up on the porch.

"*Oh, my God, Fletcher, what happened?*" Mrs. McAllister stared in horror at the blood on my hands and on my shirt and on my face. "*Floyd!*" she screamed. "*Floyd! The boy!* "

Mrs. McAllister begged for Floyd to make everything all right. After a few days, she said that when I got home I was white as a bleached ghost and covered with blood, and I had collapsed on the front porch with dirt and blood all over my face and fallen like a sack of potatoes backwards down the stairs. Maybe I told her what happened, or maybe I didn't.

I don't even know how I got home. I don't remember.

Thirty-Eight

Everything happens at home when I'm escaping in the old Pontiac or out watching foxes, or helping with accidents. After the inquest I didn't want to talk to anyone, but everybody was gabbling away in the house. I got myself back on the porch to watch the flies on the screen door and listen. That's why I know. I didn't *want* to know, but I do.

Jack and Tina sat across the table from Livvy and Jack had his derby hat perched on his knee. "It's a terrible thing to have happen, no matter what, but I can't imagine seeing something like that happen to your own father," Tina whispered to Livvy. Mrs. McAllister bustled around the kitchen and fussed noisily with the cooking pots on the stove.

"It was an accident, that's all, nothing else. He was probably drinking again and just lost his balance," Tina said hopefully.

"*Nobody can blame ol' Fletcher for what happened,* "Jack whispered. " It could'a happened anytime. A lot a people sat in that tree, *even us,* remember, Tina. We were neckin' an' drinkin'—'" Tina stopped him suddenly. He looked at Mrs. McAllister, but she wasn't paying any attention.

"*Jack,*" Tina whispered, "*that's embarrassing, so shut up*—or I'm going to kill you!"

Livvy shrugged and shook her hair back. She hesitated and shook her head again.

"No, he's right, everyone's sat up in that tree, Fletcher and I have sat up there, too....like everyone else," Livvy said. Mrs. McAllister looked sideways at Livvy, her eyes flashing. "But he hated his father," Livvy added. "Maybe he really didn't, but everyone thinks so, you know that," Livvy said, watching Mrs. McAllister.

"So you know what they could think, you know they probably think he pushed him. They could easily think he killed him, and they must be wrong, they're wrong! I know Fletcher was—they didn't really know each other, and everyone knows his father was a drunk, a no-good, and he was...abusive —but Fletcher wouldn't do that—he just wouldn't do that. Would he, Mom? Will they send Fletcher to trial? I know he couldn't do that, I know he couldn't!" Livvy started to cry.

Mrs. McAllister rushed to the table and put her arms around her. Tina reached across the table and held Livvy's shaking hands tightly. "Now there, there," Mrs. McAllister said to Livvy.

"He's been like this ever since the funeral..." Livvy said. "He didn't do anything wrong—*he just couldn't!*" she wailed.

"I know, child," she said softly, rocking Livvy in her arms, "but you have to expect some reaction, don't you? Him seeing something as terrible as that, and a young man can't lose his father without it affecting him in *some* way." The kettle whistled lightly and then screamed angrily on the stove. Tina rushed over to the stove and poured the boiling water into the teapot.

Jack took over. "Nobody's going to hang Fletch for something he didn't do," Jack said carefully. "Ain't a trial, anyway, it's only an inquest, and even if it was, like a trial like mine, I mean, he can't get found *guilty* 'cause he wouldn't do anything like that, not Fletch. I knowed him ever since we was in the home, an' he ain't ever done nothing like that; he ain't *doin'* nothing like that; he ain't *ever* going to do nothing like that, not Fletch." Jack hauled out his gold-plated lighter and lit a cigarette. He puffed and then set the lighter on the table.

343

"Listen to Jack, Livvy," Tina offered helpfully. "Jack's right, "Fletcher would *never* do anything like *that*." After a pause, she added, "Not at all."

"You shouldn't smoke in here, Jack" Livvy said and took his lighter from him and flicked it, watching the flame flicker. She set it on the table and spun it around and stopped it, examining the initials crudely scratched on it. She fidgeted with it again, flicking it and watching the flickering light.

"I'm so sorry, Mrs. McAllister. I've been forgettin' me *manners*," Jack said quickly, and stubbed his cigarette out on his heel. Mrs. McAllister looked strangely at Tina then busied herself getting teacups.

"*Here they are now*, don't be asking too many questions right away, I'm sure they'll tell us *everything*," Mrs. McAllister said, getting up from the table and hurriedly poured more water into the kettle and placed it back on the stove. There were voices. The wheelchair bounced up the stairs and the screen door opened. Floyd wheeled his way through the door and looked gray and old.

"Tea's on, Floyd," Mrs. McAllister said. Floyd shook his head.

"Got some terrible news, Elizabeth." he said.

"Oh, no, they're going to —" Mrs. McAllister stopped and looked at Livvy and Jack. Livvy had her hands over her mouth, her eyes wide open.

"What did they decide?" Mrs. McAllister asked. She put her hand over her mouth, waiting.

"It's not that," Floyd said, slowly. "Fletcher's fine, the inquest went all right, *death by accidental fall* – just like we thought it would be."

"Yahoo!" Jack shouted. "See, silly, what'd I tell ya, ol' Fletcher's fine. He never killed his old man; I told ya he couldn't do that!" Jack almost yelled and patted Livvy excitedly on the head. Livvy's eyes filled up with tears of happiness.

"*Thank you God*," she whispered.

"Amen to that!" Tina said sincerely but cautiously.

"Oh, yes, dear Lord, we should thank God right now, everyone!" Mrs. McAllister hugged Livvy and Floyd, and Jack and Tina hugged each other.

"Thank you Lord Jesus for keeping our Fletcher safe!" Mrs. McAllister said, and laughed nervously, reaching out and patting Tina on the arm. *Thank God! Where's Fletcher?*" she suddenly asked, realizing that Fletcher was nowhere to be seen.

"But where's Fletcher? Where is he?" Livvy asked.

Floyd spoke kind of quietly. "You leave him alone right now. He's all right, he's out on the porch, getting his head clear, after today. He needs time to himself."

"What's the matter then; get it out, Floyd, *what's going on?*" Jack asked, tapping his lighter nervously on the table.

"It was an accident, *another accident,*" Floyd said, and added quickly "Fletch's all right."

Floyd shook his head and couldn't talk. He raised his hand like he was pointing. "It's...it's..."and sat back fast.

"Well *who* then, Floyd, *for God's sake, spit it out!*" Mrs. McAllister said. "Floyd...*dear?*" she asked, suddenly worried.

Good thing I heard Floyd explain everything through the screen door that time. I did not want to talk much.

"It's Sarah," he looked at Livvy, "not Sarah McKinley, I mean Mrs. Dormally." Floyd finally said, looking around at everyone strangely, and in the most tired voice I had ever heard.

"Oh, no, Floyd, no!" Mrs. McAllister said, asking Floyd what was wrong without asking him. Mrs. McAllister did that all the time. "Is she...?" Floyd says you get used to that.

"She's in the hospital, serious injuries," he said.

"Oh, my God, Floyd, no... Is she...?"

"Well, she's — she's alive, but just barely," Floyd said. "*Just barely.* She's in surgery, and well…it's *not* good…" He wheeled his chair over to the window slowly and studied the gray sky.

"I knew that horse was too high strung, too skittish for her, — her not having much riding experience and all. We —Fletcher and I, we were just out of the courthouse. The inquest finished pretty quick. There was nothing to it, the coroner said it was an accident, no doubt about that, Fletcher's father had an accident, *accidental death caused by falling*, that was all there was to it; but outside, there she was, coming down the street on that black Morgan, what's — his name, *Royal Thraxian? —* And she in her riding outfit, pretty as you please, and Jeremy Kendall drove by just then, that damned old Dodge truck. The power wagon backfired, and up the devil went—jumping around, over to the sidewalk, rearing up and screaming like he was possessed." Floyd's voice got quiet. "And it had to happen; it had to happen sometime, her not being an expert rider. I told her to stay off of the roads. I told her to stay in the fields, it's safer. I told her so many times!

"That devil horse dumped Sarah off, and she… oh, my God! Elizabeth, she landed square on a fire hydrant, right on her back. We got over to her right away, she was unconscious; she must have hit her head on the way down at the same time. We got an ambulance right away. We thought she was dead for sure…"

"Oh, no, Floyd!" Mrs. McAllister gasped, her hands clamped tightly over her mouth.

"Then everyone crowded around her; I knew right away her back was broken, she was shaking, and she was having convulsions… We thought she was dead for sure, at first. She started bleeding real bad in the back, but she came to, shaking, her eyes blinking and fluttering like she was *pole-axed.* Then, she woke up real good, and started screaming she couldn't move her legs, and frightened everyone to death. The ambulance came in a few minutes, and they shot her full of morphine. It took three needles to quiet her a bit, and then they strapped her down, put her on a backboard and hauled her off to the trauma hospital in Egansville. —They're the only people close that can handle something this serious. We stayed there for a couple of hours, but there was nothing, *nothing* to be done, she was up in surgery." He shook his head sadly. "They might even have to ship her in to the city, It's bad, Elizabeth..."

"Oh, Floyd, I'm so sorry about your sister," Mrs. McAllister said. She stood behind him and put her hands on his shoulders.

"Fletcher helped Charlie Bibbs and Jeremy, too. He stopped right away when he saw what happened. They figured out how to catch Thraxian and quiet him down. He was kicking up his heels in a rage, that damned horse, and there's more than one car with dents in it right now... and Charlie, good thing he had just finished hauling a cow in. He was coming back empty right then; he had a bunch of ropes; he was going by and saw what happened. He stopped to help; he had his trailer hooked up. They got him caught and loaded, Jeremy lassoed him, so they took the devil back to McKinley's stable for her." He hung his head.

"Damned horse, I wish now I'd never seen him!" Floyd added. "He was too much horse for her. I never should have allowed her to talk me into getting him for her, that skittish devil. I never should have done that. I knew she couldn't handle him —It's my fault, Elizabeth! Maybe I'll shoot that sonofabitch yet! "Floyd said. He rubbed his face hard. "If she lives, she's going to be a paraplegic, for God's sake, spend the rest of her life in a wheelchair! Like me!"

"*Floyd!*" Mrs. McAllister said loudly. I got myself to the screen door to see what was happening.

"*Now you listen here, Mister,*" Mrs. McAllister said sternly, "we don't know *anything yet... Nobody can know what's going to happen, and moreover, Sarah* having that horse is *not* your fault! I've told you time and time again, that stupid, foolish woman is as hardheaded as you, and she *insisted* that the Morgan was the right horse for her. She would have bought and paid for him no matter what you said about it, and *she told me so.* She's a crazy woman, always has been and don't you dare feel guilty about what's happened to her. *Do I make myself clear?*"

Mrs. McAllister angrily wagged her finger right in front of Floyd's face and then took his face and made him look up at her. I never saw her speak to Floyd like that before. "She wouldn't listen to your advice twenty years ago, either, would she? *She married Charlie Tupper against your best advice too, and look at him,*" she spoke quietly. Floyd looked around quickly at everyone.

"Elizabeth!"

"I'm sorry I called your sister stupid; I did not mean that, but it's not your fault. *Do you understand me, Floyd McAllister? None of it!"* He looked startled and then finally nodded, his eyes not leaving hers.

"Elizabeth..." his voice trailed off to nothing. He shook his head. He looked at me standing outside the screen door.

Jack and Tina looked on with their mouths open. I saw them look at each other in amazement, and then pretend to mind their own business because I was watching them. Livvy came to the door with her mouth wide open and didn't say anything to me because I wasn't looking at her at all. I don't know why. *I finally figured it out.*

That's why Floyd never talked about Mrs. Dormally, but whenever he got a chance he always did things for her and wanted me to do painting and garden weeding and yard work for her...and that's why Floyd didn't like to talk about Tupper, the bastard pervert that whipped Jack and me and did bad things to us and burned the home and killed my friends Marvin Pychinski and Richard Bordon and Joe Coleman and sweet Mrs. Tickner, who was even his own sister, and Ricky Tenberg that got burned and died in the hospital. *Mrs. Dormally was Floyd's sister.*

She was married to Tupper before, and that's why Floyd never told me about her, and that was the first time I knew that Mrs. Dormally was Floyd's *sister.*

"Why couldn't you tell me?" I shouted angrily through the screen door. "Why couldn't *you* tell me, Floyd?"

"Fletcher—" Floyd started to say, but I didn't want to hear what he had to say anyway.

I jumped from the porch and started running.

"Fletcher!" Livvy called me, but I didn't listen to Livvy or anyone else either.

"He's run off!" she told the others quickly. Tina ran to the porch and called.

"Leave him be," Jack said harshly. "He'll be coming back when he's ready." He tapped his lighter.

"Maybe you *should have told him* that she was married to that freak pervert, too," Jack said coldly, spinning the lighter on the table. "It's getting late. Let's go, Tina," Jack got up suddenly. "She will be all right," Jack said, " — your *sister* will be all right," he added, pausing at the screen door. "Fetchie's going to be all right in time, too. You'll see." They hugged Mrs. McAllister quickly, then left silently, walking into the warm night.

"Oh, my God, Floyd, I'm *sorry*. I knew we should have told Fletcher who she was —" Mrs. McAllister said.

"It was my fault, Elizabeth, not trusting Fletcher to be able to handle that one."

"No, Floyd," she said quietly. "Don't blame yourself."

"I made a mistake," Floyd said, picking up Jack's lighter and using it to light his pipe. He put it back on the table. "It's simple as that; I made *another* mistake. I'm getting pretty good at that, am I not, Elizabeth?"

"*Stop blaming yourself, for everything*, my dear Floyd!" She put her hand on his sympathetically and remained silent for a few moments.

"Jack's gone and forgotten his lighter," Mrs. McAllister said.

"So he has," Floyd said.

"*I'll keep it for him,*" Livvy suggested nonchalantly, spinning it on the table.

I didn't stop running until I was at the cemetery to talk to my mother. No matter how hard I listened, I could not hear her. I cried. I wanted to hear her. I didn't know why I was so angry with Floyd that time. It was not his fault: That's what Mrs. McAllister said; that's what Jack and Tina said; that's what Archie said; and Livvy told me so many times that I started to believe her.

349

A few weeks later Livvy told me I was wrong *again*, out in the old Pontiac. She told me I was wrong a lot while we were testing beer that Jack gave us. He's not supposed to give minors any beer, but he does sometimes, because Jack and I are good friends now, and he's still trying to make up for lying to me about the tooth. *That's the truth* and that's what *everyone* said. *I was wrong*, no doubt about it, but I might having trouble admitting it, and, and Livvy told me so.

"*You were wrong, Fletcher.*" I stayed clammed up and watched the clouds drifting across the moon instead. "I hate beer, Fletcher," Livvy said.

"I do too," I said and poured it out the window. It was warm and tasted rotten. I put the empty bottle into the glove box to catch ants.

"Really, Fletcher, why did you hold it against Floyd at all?" Livvy said, poking me with her elbow as we sat in the old Pontiac in the dark. "It was not Floyd's fault."

Maybe it really *wasn't*, but he should have told me anyway," That's what I told her right back.

"I think you're wrong, Fletcher. *You know you're wrong*," she said again, and kissed me on the side of the head.

"*He didn't trust me to know, I was just a kid. He thought I would hate Mrs. Dormally, didn't he?*" I said. "*Just because she was married to him—* he thought I would hate her because she was married to that *pervert.*"

"He told Mom and I that he thought you were hurt enough already," Livvy said, putting her arms around me, tears flooding her eyes. "I remember, he had tears in his eyes when he told us, he cried! He just did not want to bring that man back into your life. I know you were hurt, Fletcher," she said.

"It's a long time ago, Livvy," I said. After I clammed up for a few minutes, I looked at her, and her eyes were full of tears. "Don't cry, Livvy," I said. "Don't cry, the moon's coming out."

"You don't cry *yourself*," she said right back to me, and she moved over on the leather seat, holding onto me tightly. I put my head on her shoulder, and she made us both stop crying after a bit.

350

"I know Floyd loves us," I finally said to Livvy, feeling foolish. "I always knew that."

"Yes, silly," Livvy said. "So do Mom and Jack and Tina, too."

"*You're* the silly one," I said. She jabbed me with her elbow again, then looked at me silently. "*Fletcher...?*" she said suddenly, and reached over to me. "*I'll always love you, Fletcher,*" she whispered. She turned my face to hers and kissed me hard, right on the mouth. I kissed her back and knew I would be loved forever and forgot about Floyd and everything else. I thought she almost started to open up her blouse for me and then looked at me quickly and stopped before I even realized what she was doing.

Livvy went away to university before I realized it too. She agreed to stay with her miserable aunt Barbara while she got herself to school but I didn't like that. I told her I loved her when she left. She held onto my hand and then got on the bus fast, with tears in her eyes. I couldn't tell mom or Floyd not to let her get anywhere near Soggie.

She didn't come back in the summer. I didn't know why.

The next time I saw Livvy, *everything* was different. It was hot in the old Pontiac, and somehow, it smelled old and stale and musty. She leaned across the seat and pecked me on the side of my face. She looked embarrassed and even *smelled* different. I don't know why Livvy smells *different.*

"It's been a long time since we sat in here, Fletcher" Livvy said. "I'm so glad to be back home with you and mom and Floyd. Barbara has been so miserable, she *insists* I stay with her—and that Soggie... just—they're not getting along at all anymore!" she said quickly. Her eyes went dark. She changed the subject. "I'm glad school will be finished next month. *It's almost five years since...*" she fell silent and looked at me. Her eyes were soft.

"I missed you. You're so...*different*" she said. "You grew up—*we both did.*" She leaned over and kissed me quick again. I wanted to kiss her too, but she pulled back. I looked at her breasts. They were a lot bigger.

"You are different too, you've changed a lot" I said. Her hair was tied back with a red ribbon.

"Fletcher..." she finally talked. "Things are...you gotta know—things are different now too."

"I'm the same, Livvy", I said. "That's why we're here, isn't it?"

"We can't...do anything ever again, Fletcher. We're not kids anymore. Remember we agreed that we would never do anything like that, like—*that?*" she talked between kisses. "*Besides, you are kind of spoken for,*" and she pulled away. "We're more like brother and sister now," she looked toward the house. "Floyd and mom...they'll be home from the hospital soon, visiting Mrs. Dormally; mom said *she's doing all right, that's good.*" she whispered.

"She is" I said, watching Livvy carefully. "She's strong enough to wheel herself around now".

"I'm glad" she said. I leaned over and kissed her on her lips before she could say anything else. Her eyes got big.

She shook her head. "We can't do this, Fletcher, we can't—besides—you know Sharon wouldn't like this, would she? She's a wonderful person, I saw her in Camson's on the way back, and she really cares for you." She looked at me like she was studying an ant instead of majoring in Psychology.   I noticed she got *ways* about her. *Lady ways like Barbara. I don't like some lady ways.*

"We'd better go now," she said, checking her buttons again. I don't know why, because she didn't open any. She creaked the car door in the dark and got out. I didn't want to get out of the car just yet but I did, and in a hurry too, when Livvy called.

"*Fletcher, look!*" she said excitedly.

"What?"

"*Look!* Across the field —over there —at McKinley's barn!" She pointed. "There is a light on over there —up in the hay loft...*Listen, I can hear music!*" Livvy whispered. Maybe they're having a party over there!" she said right out loud. I could hear radio music too.

352

The Fires of Waterland

"No, silly, Archie found out at— agricultural college— that cows like music,and that when he leaves the radio on for the cows, they give more milk that way. He told me once."

"But *someone's* up there. There's a light on up there."

"So what?" I said. "Archie's forgotten to shut the light off, he's always doing that. Or maybe Archie's got his girlfriend up there again—or all of his friends are taking advantage of the fact that old man McKinley is away for his heart operation. —I heard he's going to be gone for a couple of months, but probably, Archie just forgot to turn the lights off."

"Or maybe Sarah's back in town too, maybe *she's* at it again," Livvy offered, then giggled. "That nymphomaniac! I wonder who she's got over there now. She's not waiting for *you* is she?" I didn't answer for a moment. "*Fletcher Carnival Williams?*" she asked sternly.

"*Not funny*" I said, huffing a bit.

"She taught you *a lot,* I seem to remember," she giggled again.

"Don't remind me, I was just a *kid,* I didn't—"

"We could go see who's there," Livvy suggested.

"No," I said, "We agreed we would never go back there anymore. I haven't seen Sarah. I promised you I wouldn't, and you said you promised me you wouldn't' go back with Archie and the others, too —remember? We promised!" I said.

"I know we did," she said, "but we're older now... She looked at me with that questioning look she always used when she knew I could be persuaded that she was *right*. The moonlight gleamed in her eyes. "It might be fun," she said. "*For old times' sake,* wouldn't it?"

"No, Livvy—"

"*—But it wouldn't hurt if we went together would it?* Let's get over there!"

I thought I didn't want to see Sarah McKinley or Archie, her brother that I pounded good because he wanted to give Livvy a quarter and try her out up in the hay loft back in those days, but I changed my mind about going over there. *I don't know why.* Maybe it

353

was because I had just kissed Livvy in the old Pontiac, or *remembered too much about Sarah in the hay* for my own good that time.

The music was going on and off again, like a radio station. A set of headlights turned into the yard across the field and parked behind the barn. The lights flicked off.

"Come *on*, Fletcher, let's go sneak up there and see who's up there, that's all —*for old times' sake!*" Livvy whispered excitedly and laughed and grabbed my hand and pulled me to running across the field. We stumbled across the field in the moonlight and hid behind a storage shed just as another car drove into the yard.

"*Don't move,*" I warned Livvy. "They can see that white blouse of yours a mile away in this moonlight!" She was breathing hard. She giggled. "*Shh!*" I said. "*Stay back until they're gone inside!*" I whispered to her. We could hear voices.

"It's about time you got here, honey!" a woman's voice said. "You're never on time, I've been waiting. What happened? Oh, I know, it was Barbara, that *witch*. Didn't she want to let you out to *play* for the night?" The couple embraced and kissed.

"*That is Sarah,*" Livvy whispered excitedly. "*She's back from school too!*"

I looked around the corner. It was Sarah, but the man had his back to me. They finished kissing.

"*Hello baby.*" It was a man's voice. There was a pause, and a flash from a sulphur match as the man lit a cigarette. "It's not easy to get away from Barbara," he whined. "She's a proper bitch. I hate her." Sarah giggled.

"If it wasn't for you I'd be real frustrated with that bitch and have to kill her someday. She's getting on my nerves. *Maybe I'll do that anyway,*" he said. I recognized his voice just as Livvy turned around, almost knocking me over.

"*Fletcher!*" Livvy gasped. "*It's that bastard Soggie, that dirty bastard Soggie!*" She peeked again, and then she turned to me, shaking, her face suddenly whiter than the moonlight. I looked again. Livvy was right. It was Sogman Sweeny looking around suspiciously as he held the barn door open for Sarah. The door closed silently behind them.

"Over there, behind the hay pile, oh, Soggie," Sarah said, from inside the barn. "That *stupid* brother of mine, that stupid Archie, he's still got no imagination at all. He left the light on and the radio too, and what did he leave this pile of hay in the aisle for? C'mere, the ladder's over here, behind the hay pile, over here, baby, you can't see me? Maybe it's a tight squeeze for you."

She laughed. "Let's get up there, they're waiting for us, honey, hurry up, they're waiting up in the loft. Good times tonight, Soggie, and they promised they would bring the beer too. We can see the moon and the whole world better from up there— over here, don't worry. It's only forty feet. I've been up this ladder a million times. *Get up the ladder, here, c'mon!* It won't break, it's safe, Soggie honey. Don't you worry about Archie none, that dough-head, he's sleeping. He has to get up at six to milk, he's gone to bed long ago. Get up here, right now, or we'll have to do it right down there!" Sarah's voice drifted down through the thin board walls. I listened to them for a moment, then turned away.

"They're going up the ladder to the loft," I said to Livvy without looking at her, and turned to tell her again, but Livvy was gone. She was halfway across the field in the moonlight, running, her white blouse glowing in the white moonlight. I had to run faster than Royal Thraxian at a full gallop to catch up with Livvy. I got in front of her and then stopped her and caught her, and made her walk instead of running. She was sobbing.

"Don't cry, Livvy," I said.

"He's, he's..." She sobbed. "He's a *filthy* man, Fletcher! I still hate him!" She said, finally. "That's why Barbara has been away so much, she can't stand him anymore!" she sobbed. *"He's a pig! He beats her!* Last time I saw her she was wearing sunglasses, she had bruises on her face. I finally got her to admit it. He gets drunk all the time, he was drunk and hit her. I hope he burns in hell. *I hope he burns in hell!"* she spoke angrily, right out loud. *"He's going to burn in hell! I'll make sure of it!"*

"Shh! They might hear you!" I looked back at the light high in the open door of the hay barn.

"I don't care if they hear me or not, Fletcher!" she said just as loudly. " — Besides — *listen, they're drunk.*" The music was blaring.

I didn't say anything. We walked the rest of the way home slowly and watched the clouds floating across the moon.

"I hate him," she said, over and over again. "*I hate him!*" Livvy shook my hand off, so I didn't pay much attention to her as we walked home. I just wondered if Sarah would ever be going back to university and if she was studying *nymphomaniackery* again. I wondered if that's part of *Humanities* at University. Like Floyd took.

"I'm going to sit out here for a while" Livvy said, and sat down on the wooden steps, her head resting on her knees. She was *humming.*

I went in the house and finally went to bed. Something made me think of T.T. Oinker and Mrs. Tickner and Marvin Pychinski and Richard Bordon and Ricky Tenberg and Murvie Klinder, and I finally fell asleep. I dreamed about fire right away.

> *I don't know why fire was lighting up the sky. The wooden door closed silently as the tiny flame flicked gently, then licked ferociously at the pile of hay beside the ladder. Voices high up above rose in concern, then fear, and then horror, and finally shrieked in terror. Then in agony, and then they flew, fell to silence and the flames roared, reaching ever higher, to the moon; higher and higher, reddening the sky and turning the moon into blood, and cattle bawled helplessly to silence. Archie McKinley ran from the house and towards the barn, falling to his knees, crying in horror and disbelief. I was afraid and choked, breathing hard in the smoke.*

I woke up. Smoke was drifting into the open window, and the sky was eerily red. I got to the window. Archie's barn was on fire, the flames a hundred feet in the sky. I gasped and shouted for Floyd and Mrs. McAllister.

"*Fire!*" I screamed to God.

The Fires of Waterland

"Fletcher?" Floyd called from his bedroom. *"Fletcher? Fire? Get out of the house, get out of the house!"*

"Fletcher?" Mrs. McAllister screamed frantically. *"Fletcher!"*

"Fire!" I screamed at them. "Archie's barn is on fire! It's McKinley's barn!"

"Get Livvy!" Floyd shouted. I saw the fear on my face in my reflection in the window. I had to do what Floyd said. I ran across the hall to get Livvy. She was gone.

"She's gone!" I screamed at Mrs. McAllister, who came rushing up the stairs, wrapping herself in her housecoat. *"She's gone!"*

"No! Where is she!" she screamed. *"Oh, no. No, no! Livvy!"* she screamed. *"Livvy!"* She turned white in the moonlight, the glow of the fire reddening the side of her face in the window. *"Where is she?"* she screamed frantically. *"Floyd, our Livvy's not here!"* she screamed, rushing down the stairs. *"Livvy!"* she screamed again.

"Oh, God no!" Floyd swore. *"Livvy!"* he shouted.

"Fletcher! We gotta go see if we can help! Get the truck, quick!" Floyd yelled. *"Hurry!"* I ran down the stairs and out the screened door. Floyd was bumming his way down the porch stairs. As he grabbed the wheelchair, the back wheel fell off.

"Goddam!" Floyd said. *"Goddam!"* That was the only time I ever heard Floyd swear. One of the wheels fell off of his chair. It fell off because I didn't look after it properly and oil it. I must have forgotten to tighten it again.

"I'll fix it, Floyd," I said. I grabbed the wheel and tried to stick it back on, but I did not know where the wrench was. *I forgot. It's my fault.* I looked down at Floyd. *Get used to it, Jack* his eyes said.

"I couldn't do anything anyway, Fletch — you know that. What's a man with no legs going to do? Go in and rescue everyone like a hero?" Floyd must have read my mind or something that time. "I wouldn't be able to do anything anyway, Fletcher." He said, looking old and gray like I had never seen him before. "I don't think you'll be able to do much either, it's pretty far along. This chair... It's not your fault, Fletcher, this ain't your fault! There's not likely anything we can do, Fletcher, you do know that," he said quietly. "Maybe save a couple of cows. —Go do what you can to help, and be careful. *Find Livvy!*"

"I'll get you in the truck, Floyd!" I said, trying to lift him.

"No, Fletcher! There's no time, you gotta go, get in the truck yourself, now, boy! See if you can be of any help, an' you'd better find out—oh, my God, you gotta see if Livvy's there. You gotta find our Livvy, maybe she's there. I'd better stay here with your mother, and never mind going by the road, boy. Go across the field, not by the road, it'll take too long. Just bust through the fence! Hurry, go, boy, go now!" I did exactly what Floyd said.

It was a good thing Floyd lets me drive in the fields when nobody is looking. I know how to drive. I got in the old red truck and pumped the gas pedal hard and started it and jammed the stick-shift into first gear and popped the clutch, crashing through the fence just like Floyd said to. I got myself to Archie's barn by driving right through the ditch and crashed the fence at Archie's place, too. It seemed as if it took a very long time to get there, and I had to drive around rock piles and trees, and I know that everything tried to slow me down.

By the time I got there, the yard was already filling up with vehicles and frightened neighbors. The flames reached hundreds of feet in the air and the heat made the truck window hot; the heat was soaking right through. Mr. Wharton and the firemen ordered everyone to stay back.

"Get back, folks, nothing can be done, *she's gone*. The barn is going to collapse this way. *Move back! Get the vehicles back, everyone back!*" he yelled.

I tried to start Floyd's truck to move, but it wouldn't start. A few minutes later the barn timbers fell towards the house in an explosion of flame that sent a column of fire high into the night. Burning hay was flying everywhere, even onto the roof of the house and Floyd's truck. We saved Floyd's truck by pushing it away from the house and stamping out the burning hay in the back.

The Fires of Waterland

The men, their sweating faces glowing in the firelight, were frantically trying to get more water pumped on the farmhouse roof with a pump that was carried to the edge of Archie's pond, but the stubborn motor wouldn't start. The wall of the old house burst into flame, and the flames were on the roof in a minute.

They told Archie they called the fire trucks in from Egansville on the radio. Archie just shook his head. Mr. Bibbs said I had to stay back with Archie and the neighbors, and the fire department and a big crowd of men from Egansville got there in fifteen minutes to help, but the fire chief said the house was a lost cause, too. Watching the house finish burning to the ground, we stood silently, grimly, watching the eerie flames that burned white-hot, with blue and red and green and all of the other terrible colors of hell.

When I drove the truck that time I forgot to put the lights on, and it didn't matter at all, nothing matters now. I asked Floyd why it took me so long to get there to save everybody, but the next day Floyd said there was really nothing at all that I could have done. Nothing that anyone could have done, and that in reality it only took me a couple of minutes to get there because he was watching me and looking for Livvy with his binoculars. There were a hundred men there before me, and there was plenty of light from the fire.

He cried, and Mrs. McAllister did too, when he told us what he was watching with binoculars from the porch. He saw *everything*. He said Mrs. McAllister fainted when they saw the five people jump the forty feet to their deaths, one after the other, as if from hell itself, screaming, twisting in agony, burning, their clothing in flames from the exploding, white-hot fury engulfing the hay loft behind them. Floyd said it was the worst thing he had ever seen. We were sitting out on the porch, watching the fireflies. I had to agree with Floyd that time.

Livvy was not there. I found out. After the barn collapsed in an exploding fireball that forced everyone to jump back to safety, and the house was gone too, the men just stood around whispering until the fire was nearly burned out. Some started coiling up the dirty fire hoses and putting them back on the trucks. I told a fireman I was looking for her and that I had to go and look and see. I had to know, but when I walked over there like a frozen ghost, the firemen said it wasn't a good idea.

"You don't want to see anyone that's burned, boy, *trust me,*" the man said grimly. "It's not a pretty sight. It's gonna stick in your mind forever, you'll *never* be able to get it out of your head." Mr. Wharton and the fire chief looked under the sheets for me and said she was not there. He looked strangely at me.

"*Was* she here?" he asked me.

"*I think so,*" I said. "*She's not at home.*" He shook his head and looked again, covering them up quickly, one after the other.

"Who are they?" I asked.

"You go home now, Fletcher," Mr. Wharton said roughly. "The coroner's office, well—never mind who they are right now, *you go home, boy. They must be worried sick. You go tell Floyd and Elizabeth that, well – just thank God, Livvy's not here,*" he said. "*You better find her.*"

I did exactly what he said. I walked home across the field. I forgot Floyd's truck.

Thirty-Nine

After I told Floyd and Mrs. McAllister that Livvy wasn't there they cried and hugged one another. I don't know if I told them I was going to find Livvy like Mr. Wharton told me to or not, but I got a jacket on. I felt cold.

I closed the door quietly on the way out and walked in the cool moonlight. I looked in the old Pontiac. When I found she wasn't there, I knew right away that I had to go and get Livvy for Mrs. McAllister and Floyd. I had to find Livvy for *myself,* and then I thought about the church. I ran all the way. I don't know why I went there first, but I knew all of the places that Livvy went to, and Livvy went there quite a lot when nobody was having Sunday school or Bible lessons or church. She never told me *why.*

It was still dark, and the heavy wooden door was closed, but I knew it would open because Mr. Drummond, the new preacher, always leaves the church door open so that sinners can talk to God any time they like. Mrs. Drummond said it was a good idea. I opened it carefully. She was there. A strange, small flame flickered on the floor in front of her. I thought it was a candle, but I was wrong.

She was huddled on the floor in a nearly shapeless mass of shadows in front of the first pew, her eyes clear and ice blue, and her face blank and white and colorless in the moonlight. She was sitting with her arms wrapped tightly around her knees, shivering, and whispering inaudibly to herself. She was staring at the flame, then at the moon shining on the wooden cross in the window. The flame flickered, flashing in her eyes.

"Livvy?" I whispered, trying not to scare her. She did not seem to know I was there. She shivered violently. I put my hand on her shoulder. I shivered myself when I touched her because she did not move. Not a bit. The hair stood up on the back of my neck.

"Livvy?" I said louder. I shook her shoulder. *"Livvy!"* I implored her, very loudly. I looked closely at the flickering flame on the floor. The metal glistened. I looked closer. It was Jack's lighter. She turned and looked up at me. Her face was pale and sick and cold like Murvie Klinder. She took my hand and put it on her face. It was ice cold. I looked at her. I didn't' know what to say. I looked again at the flame. It was Jack's lighter. She whispered.

"Fletcher? Will you stay with me?" She shivered violently. "Just —just stay with me *for a while,* Fletcher. I need you to stay with me for a few minutes, *just you and me,"* she said. She reached for the lighter and snapped it shut, putting out the flame. She clicked it open and lit it again. The flame spurted from the wick and flashed in her eyes. It made her face even whiter.

"Jack's lighter, I forgot to give it back to him," she said. She frowned. *"It was so easy to just keep it."* She touched my arm. Her teeth flashed in the moonlight. She flicked the lighter again, watching the flame. *"Just like that, it was so easy,"* she said, and looked at me strangely. *"It was so easy."* She turned and studied the moonlight shining on the cross. The sky was cloudless.

"They are going to take me away, Fletcher. They will take me away. *I don't think you'll ever see me again."*

"Away? No. *Archie's barn burned down,"* I whispered, not realizing what she had said. "Five people burned. They—they jumped out, killed. The house, the barn, Archie's cows, all gone, all burned; I asked—they wouldn't let me look. They checked for me, and Mr. Wharton said it wasn't you under the sheets. He said I better go find you, but *we thought you were in the barn."*

"*I was,*" She looked at me suddenly " *– before,*" she added in a whisper.

"*Before?*" I shook my head. "No, I woke up and saw the fire out the window, and called Floyd and Mom, and you weren't there! I took Floyd's truck, Floyd said to. The wheel came off of his chair. I had to get over there myself to help, I drove myself. Floyd said go help, and go find you, and I crashed through the fences just like he said. I drove across, and I got there—I *know* you weren't at the fire. I didn't see you. I looked all over for you!"

"*My Fletcher,*" she said softly. The moonlight glowed on her pale face. "*My dearest love Fletcher came looking for me,*" she said. "*You've always looked out for me, Fletcher. I love you, Fletcher Carnival Williams.*" She hugged me. She let go of me, and then her gentle smile turned hard and pale and white.

"*I was there, Fletcher!*" She toyed with the lighter. She showed it to me. "*See?*" She looked at me and then put her arms around me again. We stayed quiet for a minute. "I'll always love you, Fletcher, no matter what happens. You know that, don't you?"

"*Livvy?*" I asked. I was mixed up. "*Before? You were there before? We went home, remember?*"

Her voice went cold when she answered me. "Yes." She gasped and shivered violently. "I was there before you got there. *I went back!*" I put my jacket around her shoulders. I did not understand. What she said did not sink in right away. Floyd says that's because my head is hard as a rock, but I finally realized what she had told me. I suddenly knew.

"*You better give me Jack's lighter,*" I said, holding my hand out to her. She looked at me strangely.

"*Maybe you should go home now, Fletcher, my darling love. Leave me alone now.*" Her eyes softened in the light. She closed them and rocked back and forth for a minute, humming a lullaby. She stopped suddenly and looked at me.

"You know I hated him. I hated *them. They gave me babies, and took them, so I started the fire.* I waited until they went up into the loft. They were having a party, so I sent them to hell for what they did to us. It's that simple, isn't it? I told you I was going to send them to hell. *I sent them all to hell where they belong,"* she said quietly.

"Us?" I said. "For what they did to *us? They* gave you babies? What do you mean?"

"Go home, Fletcher," she said, her voice suddenly turned cold.

"No, Livvy, I want to stay with you," I said. "We can talk about nice things like we always do. We can go and sit in the old Pontiac like we used to do."

"There is nothing to talk about now, Fletcher. *It's too late.* Please, *please*, Fletcher, go home now."

"Where are you going?" I asked her. She stood up suddenly. "I'll come with you" I said.

"You can't come with me, Fletcher." She sat back on the pew like she was tired.

"You can't stay with me, *not where I'm going,"* she said quietly.

"Where are you going?" I asked. *I should not have asked. I did not want to know what she could not say, but I did.* The hair on the back of my neck stood up, making me cold.

She flicked the lighter and stared at the flame. Her eyes glistened with hate.

"Go now!" she ordered. I backed away from her. She leaned down and pulled the red kerosene can from under the seat of the pew and stood up.

I froze.

"Go home, Fletcher!" she suddenly screamed at me. *"I love you, I don't want you here!"*

"No, Livvy, don't do that!" I shouted at her.

"They will take me away and put me in a straight jacket!" she screamed. *"They'll say I'm crazy or put me in jail to rot for the rest of my life or hang me first thing. I can't be with you anymore, can I? Don't be so*

364

stupid, Fletcher. No matter what happens, it's all over, isn't it? So go away!" She pushed me away.

"No, Livvy. I'll tell them what they did to you. *I'll tell them,* they'll understand."

"They won't believe *you.* They don't care, they won't believe you; nobody will believe you!"

"*I'll tell them for you, Livvy, I'll tell them. I'll tell everyone what they did to you, I promise!*" I shouted at her, trying to put my arms around her. She was sobbing. "*I'll make them understand!*" I pleaded.

"*Nobody cares, don't you understand? Nobody! I can't stand it anymore. I have to kill myself now, I have nothing to live for, so, go away!*" she screamed and pushed me away like a mad woman. "*I have to go to hell too!*"

"*No, Livvy, don't do that, it'll be all right, you'll see!*" I shouted again.

"*No, I have to do this!*" she screamed. "*I killed five people. It's better this way. I have to die!*" She pushed me away again. I fell backwards but got up and grabbed the lighter and kerosene can from her and ran faster than I had ever run in my whole life.

"*Fletcher!*" Her scream followed me down the street. "*They're going to take me away forever!*"

I kept running and did not look back. She was right. They came and took her away. *Forever.*

Forty

The telephone rang. I just listened. I go and answer it if Sharon doesn't get it by the third ring.

"It's for you, Fletcher," Sharon said out through the screen door. She gave me that look.

"It's *her* again, I don't know why," she sighed and opened the screen door, hauling the telephone out on the long extension to the table. She covered up the phone and whispered. "*I don't know why they let her bother you. It's Livvy again.*" I shook my head.

"Can't possibly be Livvy," I said, as loudly as possible. "She's in Europe! Last time I heard she was wandering around in Italy!" I winked. She smiled and shook her head.

"It's Livvy, *again,*" she insisted. "You know it's Livvy. You know where she is. It makes no difference where she is, does it, why do you pretend?" She shook her head.

"Well maybe she's back in the country, but don't be worrying about it, it's all right," I said loudly again, toward the telephone in Sharon's hand. "You don't have to worry about a thing. Maybe she's back in the country and wants to come visit. Won't it be nice to see Livvy again?" I put my finger to my lips. Sharon has the patience of God. Good thing.

Sharon nodded resignedly. "*I know, honey,*" she said, whispering, frowning. "But do they have to let her call you *all the time?* She thinks you're her only friend," she said, shaking her head, "and I—I know should know better by now. At this stage of the game I should know there's nothing to worry about." Sharon handed me the telephone and closed the screen door on the curly wire. "You *are* her only friend," she reminded me quietly from the other side of the screen. *"Be nice."*

I covered the phone.

"Never mind, dear, cross your fingers, maybe by some miracle, someday she really will be calling from Europe some place, or at least we can hope so, can we not? It's possible she's somewhere else, in a different section; maybe she's been given a job to keep her busy, something like working down at the Puffery," she added, raising her eyebrows and smiling at me through the screen. She shook her head again and turned away to the kitchen.

"Livvy?" I spoke into the telephone cautiously. I don't like talking on the telephone. It makes me nervous.

"*Fletcher?*" The voice was pale and weak. "It's been a long time, Fletcher," she started. "Wasn't that Sharon that answered the phone?"

"Yes, Livvy, that was Sharon," I said, "it has been a long time, what, a week or so? Since we talked, I mean." I added.

"No, Fletcher, it's over thirty years, since we've talked, it's been way too long," she answered after an awkward silence. "You never call me, and it's forever since I sent Soggie to hell," she reminded me. "It doesn't seem like it's that long, does it? And I've been working down at the Puffery all that time too!"

"No," I lied, "it hasn't been that long." It seemed like it was only yesterday or last week or last month to me. I shook my head and watched a car race by. "I remember," I said to her. I remember every detail, because she calls once a week, *every* week; I have to admit in fact that it's been every week for the last 40 years.

"I'm well now Fletcher, the doctors say I am well. They tell me I need more treatment to help me take my medicine, so I have to be here, even if I take my medicine. They gave me some white and yellow pills to take; I take seven of them every day. Sometimes I flush them down the toilet, it makes me laugh." She giggled. "They won't let me smoke either. They can't give me matches; *they keep saying I burn people."*

"I know."

"When I got out—it was ten years, Fletcher. I was a good girl for ten years, remember? Then they talked at me and got me crazy and made me come right back," she said. "I hate it. They lied. They came and got me, just like I told you they would, do you remember, Fletcher, just like they got me in the church? I told you they would come and get me again, just like the first time, and they did, see? I told you so. I hate them. They lied and said I will keep burning people. They took me away again, that's two times, Fletcher. I didn't want them to do that." Her voice was strained. "They get on me and hold me down and give me babies. I don't like them doing *that*, Fletcher."

"I know, Livvy."

"They give me needles, Fletcher. I hate needles, and they said that if I'm a good girl and take my pills I won't have to get needles. I hate needles." She sounded frightened. "I run away, but they keep getting me. Will you come and get me Fletcher, *come and get me now?* I don't want any needles."

"I hate needles too," I said. She was silent. "Needles make me nervous," I added.

"Me too," she said. "My friend Monica gets out *every day.* They let her out, *she gets all dressed up.* You should see her, Fletcher, and she goes to work down at the Puffery, she puts whipped cream into the pufferies. That's what she *says,* says she uses a thing that's just like a big needle. That's how the pufferies are made, Fletcher."

"Isn't that interesting," I said. "Does she ever bring you pastries back from the hospital bakery?"

"She *says* she does, only burned ones, but the nurses take them away from her. That's what she says, she says the nurses are mean and slap her and take away her pufferies."

"I see."

"I want to work at the puffery, too, Fletcher, but they won't let me. Could you tell them to give me a nice white uniform, too? —Like Monica, so I could work at the puffery. They told me you have to have a nice white uniform to go to work at the puffery, and I don't have one yet. Could *you* tell them to give me one?"

"We'll try," I said.

"I don't like being here, Fletcher. I want to go back to Waterland."

"I know, Livvy."

"The nurses tell me to *shut up* too; they slap me and make me take my medicine. I don't like them, not one bit." There was silence. "*Fletcher?*"

"Livvy?" I asked. There was no response momentarily. I could hear her breathing into the telephone. "Livvy?"

"*Fletcher?* When—" She gasped.

"Take your time, Livvy." She hesitated again; then finally spoke.

"When—when I heard that woman's voice—*who was that anyway?* When I heard that voice, *her* voice just now, it made me remember something, Fletcher. I remembered you and that Sharon got married just before I got out the first time, you know, before I went to Italy? Are you divorced yet, Fletcher? I don't want you to be married to Sharon. I want you to be divorced, right now. Go see Soggie. He's a lawyer. He'll cut you free, understand, so we can get married tomorrow."

"Yes, I know, Livvy."

"And we *can* get married tomorrow. *I* shall come tomorrow, Fletcher darling." There was silence again. "Soggie's a dirty bastard Fletcher. Don't do anything he says. *He's not nice.*"

"Soggie's *dead,* Livvy, remember?"

"He's a dirty bastard, Fletcher. I told you what he did to me, didn't I? I think I did. So, I sent him to hell too, and then I waited for you at the church, Fletcher. I *knew* you would come. When I was locked up in there it was all I could think about; it was all that kept me alive, knowing that I loved you," she said strangely. "I loved you

369

so much. I'm *ready* now, Fletcher. I can get married to anybody I want to now. *Everybody* wants to marry me right now, but I want to marry *you*, Fletcher. I have my dress picked out and everything."

"That's wonderful, Livvy," I said.

"Fletcher? There are flowers outside my windows. They are yellow. I like yellow flowers." She spoke slowly.

"So do I, Livvy, they are my favorites. Black-eyed Suzies, remember?"

"Fletcher? *I love you.* I still do—a whole lot!"

"I know, Livvy, I love you too," I said, glancing at Sharon on the other side of the screen door. "I'll always love you, Livvy."

"Why won't you *wait* for me, Fletcher? Why won't you wait for me? *Please?*"

"I've been married for a long time, Livvy. *I'm married to Sharon, remember?*"

"Sharon? You mean Sharon Smithson? You married *her?* She's only a slut waitress, Fletcher."

" — A long time ago, Livvy. It was a long time ago, *remember?*"

"Why couldn't you marry *me,* instead, Fletcher? Why can't you marry *me,* Fletcher?"

"I don't know, Livvy," I said.

"Maybe you're right, Fletcher. Maybe there aren't enough flowers to get married anyway. I keep looking for flowers. I can see some outside my window, but maybe there aren't enough yellow flowers just yet, and I have to get used to things that happened just like you do. I know you don't really want to marry Sharon, I know that—" She suddenly stopped talking. *"No!"* she screamed to someone on the other end of the line. *"Not yet!"* she shrieked. There were sounds of a struggle. *"Okay!"* she screamed, *"give me a minute!"*

"Livvy, *Livvy,* honey," I said. "Maybe someone else needs to use the phone now."

The Fires of Waterland

"It's just *them*, Fletcher, they want to grab the phone from me, but it's my turn, Fletcher, *it's my turn!* ...But Fletcher—maybe Sharon got you because of the fire. Maybe it was just the fire; you know—the fire, —you going away."

"—And our losing Floyd and Mom," I added quickly, "Livvy, we've talked about it so many times, you know? The accident; things happened, Livvy— maybe it was never meant to be that way. It's just the way things happen, I guess."

"How are Floyd and Mrs. McAllister?" she asked. "Are they well, Fletcher?"

I hesitated again. "Livvy..." I started out slowly, "You remember they...they were both killed in accidents, remember? They got hit by that bus when the wheel fell off of the old truck, and Mom, -Mrs. McAllister- was in the ambulance when it was hit by the train on the way to the hospital. It crashed too—*she* was killed too, Livvy, remember?" She fell silent for a moment. It sounded like she was interrupted.

"Someone wants to use the phone, Fletcher. *Just a minute*—yes, that was terrible, Fletcher," she said, her voice rising. "Fletcher? I'm glad you're married and happy, Fletcher," she said. "Who did you marry anyway? It's not too late, Fletcher, we can be married if you still want me. Will you marry me now Fletcher? Today?"

"I'm married to Sharon, remember?"

"Is Sharon good to you?" she asked, "Like I would be? Never mind her, Fletcher, we can get married today. Fletcher, would you like that? We can do anything you want."

"Yes, Livvy."

"Does Sharon do *everything* with you Fletcher? I would do anything with you, Fletcher."

I didn't answer. I knew what she was going to say next.

"*I hate Sharon, she's a liar,*" she said suddenly. "She's just a waitress slut. She told me she'd get you and she did, just like Tina got Jack, remember? But *guess* what I heard... I heard that Sharon's a slut too, like Tina, that's what *your friend Floyd* told me *yesterday*, but he's

371

lying. She's really only a waitress, she *told me* she would get you, and marry you, too. And I remember you telling me the same thing, and she did it, too, but I don't hate her for *that*. I hate her because she got you away from me. Fletcher, I wasn't there at your wedding to kill her. They wouldn't let me come. They should have let me out, but now they'll let me out to get married. I think they'll let me out, won't they? If I *promise* I'm not crazy? I'm not crazy, Fletcher. I wasn't crazy, was I? Doctor Timmy thinks so, that's what he said. He said I had lots of unresolved issues, but I don't believe a word he says."

"It's all right, Livvy, never mind that now. We better hang up now. Someone needs the telephone."

She kept talking. *"Get lost!"* she screamed at someone. "And why should I believe him, I mean that Doctor Timmy, he's a shrink — well he's supposed to be helping me, that's what he says — but him, he's useless too. I told him I had to get out so I could go to your wedding and kill Sharon and marry you, but he's only a doctor. What does he know about anything anyway? Well — you know Dr. Tenberg? Would you believe this? He said he couldn't allow that *just yet*. He's my analyst, isn't that funny? He pretends he's a psychiatrist, and I pretend that I believe him — just to make him happy.

"I don't know why I listen to him, he's so old and crotchety, and get this, *he's* a liar too. I told him I love you. I even told him your name, and that we're picking yellow flowers and getting married tomorrow, but he said the wedding will have to wait for a few days. Then I told him who you are. I told him your name, and he told me he was in a home with you when he was a boy too, but he's lying, I know he's lying because he's too old. He said it was the same one that *you* were in. He told me that last week, again. Do you remember him? He's a liar, you can tell, he's an old man. He's old, Fletcher, he must be crazy. He's way too old, he's at least sixty. He's too old to be in a home for boys, he's got a white mustache. I still go see him once in a while even if he is a liar, I don't want to, but they said I have to go see him.

"He said I shouldn't *hate* her, but I hate Sharon anyway because I wasn't there to save you from her. He wouldn't let me go, and he said he was sorry *once*. He said I was locked up for my own good, that's why I know he's a liar, too. That's what they all said, every one of them, but I still think it wasn't my fault that slut Sharon got you, so don't go blaming me, Fletcher Carnival Williams!"

"It's wasn't your fault, Livvy."

"I couldn't make them believe me, Fletcher."

"I know you don't hate Sharon," I said, "and Livvy, she knows that you and I... she knows we're just good friends."

"So *what?* I hate her anyway, no matter what she says, no matter what you say, and she knows *I'll kill her if I get a chance, wait and see,"* she said. *"I'll chop her to pieces and burn her good too, that little bitch,"* she said, menacingly. *"See if I don't, and it'll serve her right for stealing you from me!"*

"Don't talk like that, Livvy," I said. "It's not nice."

"Why not, Fletcher?"

"It's not nice, Livvy." There was silence on the other end of the line. "It's not nice to talk about good people like that."

"They gossip and talk about me all the time, Fletcher," she finally spoke. "I know they talk about me, everyone talks about me, not that I care. I don't blame them; it was a horrible thing I did, but I can't seem to stop laughing about it when I think of it; it's so funny, it served them right. What's wrong with me, Fletcher, what's wrong with me, — but know what? Those dirty bastards, it served those bastards right, that's what. I tell them every chance I get, that's what I always say. I hate Soggie, he was a *pervert* — you know that, Fletcher. Do you know what he did to me? *Do you know what he did to me?*

"That's why I burned them. I sent them to hell, and I hate every one of them. Did you know that they are all friends of his? They all laughed about it, so it serves every one of them right, that's what I told them. *I had to do it, didn't I, Fletcher?*

"I had to burn them so they couldn't hurt me anymore, but Dr. Timmy says it's all in the past now, what does he know anyway? He says I am well now, that's what he told me. He said the needles fix me, but I didn't really believe him that time. He's not a real doctor, just a *shrink.* What does he know anyway? And he thinks he's been in a boys' home just like you; he should be in a shiny rubber room himself, Fletcher. I think he's a mental case, he's *insane.*

"I told the nurse yesterday again, I warned her. I whispered at her, *he wants to get us babies* too, but she won't give him any needles to quiet him down. He said he used to slide down the hallway on the wood floor polishing it for the janitor. So look who's crazy, Fletcher, isn't that funny? What does he know about *anything?* And besides that, what does anyone know about how I feel, even *you?*

"Sometimes I hate you too, Fletcher; you know, you're not nice either, Fletcher Carnival Williams; I asked you to get my babies back for me, and you didn't get them back for me, and you couldn't even *wait* for me. That's *two* things, and they came and took my babies away from me when I wasn't watching. They took my little babies when I was sleeping, they came and got them. They took them and stole them and put *them* in a home, too. They won't tell me *where.* They just laughed out loud.

"They laughed out loud, Fletcher. They said criminally insane murderers aren't allowed to *get* babies, and they took them last night. And now I miss them, and I don't know where they are. I'm sure Soggie has them hidden in his attic with the others, that's why I called you. Can you go over to his place and get them for me? But if they're not there, look in Archie's barn; he and Archie have them hidden up in the barn. They've got them wrapped up tight in a blanket behind the hay piles so they won't cry. That's what they did with them—or maybe they're out playing in the yard so they don't have to wait for you at the home either.

"I made sure of *that,* and I don't really give a damn what they say to me about it anymore. I don't believe them, not even Doctor Timmy, I'm not crazy—who does he think he is, telling me *I'm* crazy? I'm not, —*they're* crazy, and he's the worst liar of all!" she said angrily. "I hate him! *I'm going to give him all of my needles,*" she whispered, and then "*I miss my babies, Fletcher, do you know where they are, Fletcher? ... No!*" She fell silent.

"Don't be upset, Livvy, you're not crazy. I know where they are," I said. My voice shook. My eyes filled with tears. *I still hate lying.*

Always did. Sharon opened the door and walked out onto the porch. She shook her head gently and put her arms around me.

"Hang up, Fletcher, just hang up," Sharon whispered. *"Hang up."* I shook my head.

"I can't. I can't hang up on her," I said, choking. I cleared my throat. I listened, but there was nothing.

"There they are, Livvy, I can see them. They're playing out in the park across the street. They're playing hide and seek. It's a nice day outside; it's not raining, it's warm out in the park. Don't worry, I'll take care of them for you. They won't ever have to wait for me. It's *all right Livvy, they're fine. They'll always be safe."* I wiped my eyes.

"Yes, Fletcher, my darling, thank you, Fletcher. —Oh, wait, *I can see them too*—right out there in the park. —Oh, no, *that's* not them. Oh, never mind, Fletcher, I guess they're around here somewhere. They're out in the yard. I don't know why I bother you so. I'll tell them you love them when I see them, and you know that I love you, but I must go right now, Fletcher. Nobody has any patience at all in here. They keep banging on the doors and the nurse says Doctor Timmy wants to talk to me again, *right now!"*

"They're fine, Fletcher," my mother whispered. *"The children are right here. They're playing with Floyd and Elizabeth."*

"Livvy?" I swallowed hard. *"I still love you, Livvy. Remember I told you I'll always love you, no matter what?"* I waited for her to answer. *"Livvy?"* There was silence. *"Livvy?"* The line clicked dead.

"Nothing has changed," Sharon whispered and took the phone. I nodded.

"Remember what he told us so long ago? *She's safer there. She'll never get out.* Tim says *she'll always be in — for her own good. She thinks you're her only friend,"* Sharon said gently.

"I am," I said, trying not to look at her, the tears welling up in my eyes. Sharon cradled me in her arms and rocked back and forth. I cried.

Forty-One

The memory of my Livvy could be offered to everyone as an example of a good *comparative* case. After all, it must have occurred to *someone* other than me. No matter *what happened*, no matter *what she did, she deserved respect and peace.* Once lost to the world, the guilty are quickly discarded, rightly or wrongly; are quite often *feared* unreasonably — and *incorrectly* judged. Floyd and I agreed not talk about Livvy. It was too painful.

Some folks scream blasphemy and rage at what they find, especially if it is not to their liking. Those folks, completely ignorant of the necessity of allowing things to rest in genuine eternal peace and privacy, may never recover completely — when truth strikes them smartly in the face.

Floyd and I came to terms with life, and helped each other invent that *concept* in the time after the tragedy; or at least I like to *pretend* that we might have. We concluded that certain things are better left appropriately acknowledged, admired from a safe distance, and carried along further into history — *with warm admiration and respect, but minimal examination and criticism.*

It was easier to ignore the gossips … and our own feelings, and *let God handle it.*

It is true that the patina of time provides a fascinating breastwork of cobwebs that — *conveniently at times, obscures terrible facts, or just as inconveniently, obscures a wonderful – or painful – truth.*

The Fires of Waterland

Cobwebs can be swept aside easily with a good corn broom like the ones we made at the factory; it is *so* simple, but confusing. At times, poking around in the dirt from the past will yield a lost diamond ring, a green penny, a lost spark plug, a correctable travesty of justice, a forgotten gem of knowledge — or even a priceless old bottle of wine.

Sometimes, just *thirsting for the past* and studying it proves to be a valuable and often substantially cherished diversion from real life *and* a worthy lesson; however, *it is not always so.*

Places are like that too. Any village past its prime seems to get its moral fiber tested and provoked and challenged to the core of its very being, soon becoming a *deserted parking lot for old stuff.* Sun-faded old Chesterfields sit in the long grass with fireweeds, where rusty, bared springs pop up through rotted cloth. Rusted, derelict cars head in every direction without drivers or wheels. Poplar trees grow up through missing floorboards. Squirrels store hazelnuts where the engine used to be, and mice build nests — like in the old Pontiac.

Homes end up being *dilapidated houses* without families or windows; roofs always have shingles missing, and empty dog houses hide wild skunks that scratch like chickens for bugs in gardens overgrown with tangles of wild buckwheat or hazelnut brush thickets.

It is a subtle thing; at first nothing changes, but a beautiful village gradually becomes a place without a future, a temporary home for dressed-up lonesome old people with *sometime* Sunday visitors. Their *purpose* in life is mostly forgotten, or merely outlived — if the truth be admitted.

Usefulness slowly turns to doubt; the very existence of the worn-out collection of homes becomes *something that might happen* in the future, for reasons known only to God. Houses neglected are left to fade, eventually disappearing, except for old and gnarled apple trees with huge branches, broken, trailing to the ground to rot. Lilac bushes are gone to suckers, and the odd clump of tiger lilies, turned wild next to tangles of raspberry canes, hide derelict, cracked foundations.

Raymond Alexander Kukkee

I have often contemplated my elderly neighbors going to seed themselves, *like me, truth be known*, blowing away in the wind like dandelion seeds; kind, amicable, *silvered folks*, good people silently passing away, one by one, sadly but decisively, in neat, seemingly preordained order.

They are embalmed, pasted and powdered, dallied up *neat as you please* and looking like grim, silent, painted dolls; *unfinished* Egyptian mummies, as it were, rolled out for display in their best Sunday duds. It seems no matter *how* carefully they are arranged, perhaps you have noticed, they always have their hands folded to keep the devilment out of their hearts — and the little old ladies always hold perfectly-folded blue handkerchiefs. If you are brave enough to look closely, any fool can see they *never* really look like the person they were. *That never fails to amaze me.*

At the viewing, if there is one, their families and friends are graciously allowed, perhaps encouraged — to pretend their *dearly departed*, complete with painted, eternal secrets, are being sent to a glorious meeting complete with *revelations* — rather than simply accepting the admittedly *difficult* idea that all pitifully-deceased souls get scientifically tucked away out of sight for eternity — *at least until God says so.* Getting them painted and jammed into smothering gleaming boxes of polished oak, with six cast brass handles shining like the sun and screwed on in just the *right* spots — is only the *start. Don't forget the lilies.*

On the day of any such occasion, and that's been two or three times a year lately, a predictable frenzy takes place without much notice or concern for the cost, much to the delight of Arbo. That's Arborucci Mechini, the florist in Egansville with a drop-dead gorgeous wife, Maria. She hates the smell of white lilies. *The smell of death* she calls it.

Officially, dignity must prevail and usually does. Arbo's pretty good at making it so; anyone not showing signs of life is pasted thickly with those same choking snow-white lilies. They smother any remaining life out of the deceased, *just in case.*

The Fires of Waterland

Mrs. McDaltie's custom wedding cakes are like that too, says Floyd. Yellowing and drying, they turn as hard as a brand new red granite headstone.

After the ceremony, some celebrants mysteriously disappear into a crematorium long before anyone can raise any objections — or even *hears* about it, and they get reduced in bulk quite a bit so their ashes fit into a green see-through cookie jar, or maybe just a cute little varnished oaken box or pewter vase.

Everyone is sad-faced and touches the cookie jar at the wake, but the crumbles are eventually tossed to the wind, or plunked neatly underneath a little slab of granite somewhere that makes a nice, dry place for black salamanders to hide.

The more *traditionalist,* by nature or belief, are thoroughly buried in a hole dug six feet deep in gummy red clay; the fancy oak casket, six brass handles and all it contains, are left rotting to await the Coming — which might be immediately, just before, or long after the *lifetime* warranty for the gasket runs out.

Being packaged into a cookie jar or an extravagant airtight box with shiny brass handles fails to change the inevitable fact that all of us are going to meet the Lord, genuine rubber gasket on the box lid with a *lifetime warranty* preserving our permanently-powdered faces or *not.* That's what Floyd always said. It's not my personal choice; I prefer *see-through* cookie jars myself. I get claustrophobic. Anyway, like I always told Floyd, '*I want to be able to see God com*ing'.

We discussed the concept of trying to preserve all life further, if not forever, too, while we were at it. Some folks believe they foil the devil a little while longer, and eat multivitamins that sit, pretending to be real food, in a myriad of brown and green bottles stored in the top shelf of the kitchen cabinet. The worst surprise is getting to see their Maker, a God that *may or may not* be glad to see *them.* That's the way it goes.

'*No one can be certain of that,*' Livvy once said to me, '*maybe we're all going to Hell with buttons on,*' she said. She *did,* but before she went away forever, I convinced her to believe Floyd instead; he said I did right getting her to believe in God *no matter what.*

As far as old folks go, it was long theorized by Floyd, and discussed on the back porch, many times, too, that *after the fact, their stories, fears, secrets and memories should be left undisturbed in the glorious mystery of eternity.*

"It's a simple idea," Floyd said, "because people, although admittedly being truly *spiritual* creatures full of curiosity, also perpetuate habit and strange convention, and *most* deserve dignity and privacy."

I had to agree. I *like* Floyd's idea. *Leave well enough alone.*

I say *don't sort it out;* just give everything to the Salvation Army where they play trumpets, and they're *Nearer to God than We.*

Forty-Two

Floyd and I *always* agreed to respect the past, but we also promised *to* prefer and practice the *unaltered, untarnished truth.* We even spit off of the porch and shook hands on it.

Mom said, *'No spitting off of the porch, boys, what would the neighbors think? What are you two reprobates shaking hands on now? I know you're up to something! What would our Livvy say about that?'*

'Oh, nothing,' we said. I don't know who said it *first,* Floyd or me.

"I'll find out sooner or later," she said, flapping a rose-patterned dust cover in the wind, making the dust go west. *"The truth always comes out."*

'Yes dear,' Floyd said that time and winked at me. *'That it does,'* he said to himself. *'That it does,"* he repeated. *'The truth always goes west'.*

"Give them peace, if not freedom." Maybe Floyd was *right.*

"Get used to it, Jack." That's what I said, too, when I tossed his ashes to the west wind.

If she were *here,* Livvy Manlin would agree.

~

381

Raymond Alexander Kukkee

About the Author

Raymond Alexander Kukkee is a published author and independent freelancer living in Northwestern Ontario, Canada.

Being an enthusiastic and dedicated observer of humanity, Raymond prefers to write when inspired. His writing is highly varied, including short stories, poetry, knowledge-based, unique niche articles and screenplays, but his favorite *genre* remains the novel; modern, literary classic writing and experimental fiction which include the study of human nature itself.

Raymond also scribbles a diverse and eclectic blog where he encourages dialogue and questions the *status quo* of society when warranted. *Incoming Bytes* *(Is that Incoming I hear?)* explores the unique and the mundane. Encouraging readers to become proactive in their own lives and think for *themselves*, *Incoming Bytes* includes selected material from his author portfolio, issues of interest, human curiosity, and upon occasion, timely and highly controversial subject matter.

Along with the pursuit of happiness, numerous other hobbies and interests, he continues to create experimental fiction and explore the demands of the human psyche — and the *at-times-elusive and challenging* muse.

Raymond most recently published the **3nd edition** of *Morgidoo's Christmas Carol **(The Bells of Blister)**. This unique, timeless Christmas classic for readers of all ages* is published in print and eBook, and is available at Amazon and fine bookstores everywhere.

~

Raymond Alexander Kukkee

The Fires of Waterland